The dream horse

When he came across her in the early dawn, the chill of a desert night already invading her body, Philip Nolan recognized her at once. The seventeen-year-old had been a student at the exclusive private school where he taught.

In the dust of a dried-up puddle the toe print of a running-show was clearly visible. And nearby the embers of a fire were still warm . . .

The suicide of a troubled girl with nowhere to turn? An accident following a late-night party? Or plain, cold-blooded murder?

Talk of drugs, dealers and death threats fill the pages of the dead girl's journal. *I told him I'd kept my side of it, and now he could keep his. No more smack for B. I'd go to the cops if I had to, wreck myself, wreck B, wreck anything so long as I wrecked him too . . . And he said that for the rest of my life I'd never forget what I'd done, and he wouldn't forget it either. It would be our secret. Always . . .*

As Nolan teams up with Police Lieutenant Jacobsen to pursue an intricate trail of avarice and duplicity, they discover a man who fights fire with *more* than fire, a ruthless killer of snake-like charm with a poisoned mind, a murderer with a deadly secret and a chilling motive.

The dream horse is a spine-chilling story of relentless suspense – and bloody justice.

THE DREAM HORSE

John Griffiths

Constable · London

First published in Great Britain 1990
by Constable & Company Ltd
10 Orange Street, London WC2H 7EG
Copyright © 1989 by John Griffiths
ISBN 0 09 470110 5
Printed in Great Britain by
St Edmundsbury Press Ltd
Bury St Edmunds, Suffolk

A CIP catalogue record for this book
is available from the British Library

Prologue

When the man came in with the rats the snake was waiting, reared up to the glass, hood spread, mouth gaping. It watched him balefully, swaying a little and hissing – a fierce, throaty sound like a burner blowing back or a sailcloth ripping. Its eyes were black and glittering, beads of polished jet.

He put down the cage and stood for a moment admiring, approving the ominous grace of the thing, its malevolence and dark beauty. He took a step towards it. Instantly, on the snap of a hair-trigger reflex, it struck, head thudding against the glass. It reared to strike again, but by then the man had retreated.

'Always dying to get me, aren't you?' He spoke softly, with a sort of satisfaction. 'You never learn, and you never will.'

He reached down and took a rat from the cage. It squirmed a little in his grasp. For a moment he gentled it, smoothing the fur between its ears with the tip of his forefinger. The snake, watching, made short stabbing movements with its head. The man crossed over to the case. Ignoring the lashing attacks on the glass, he opened a trapdoor at the top and dropped the rat through.

At first nothing happened. The rat, oblivious to danger, explored the front of the case; the snake, uneasy, kept its eyes on the man. The man stepped back. He wore a strained, expectant look – part hunger, part horror – like a witness to a hanging. Reassured, the snake turned its attention to the rat. At last the rat understood. Frantic to escape, it scuttled back and forth across the front of the case, taking refuge finally in one of the corners. There, wedged into the angle, it turned with bright terrified eyes to watch the approach of its death.

The attack was deliberate, almost leisurely. The head advanced to within a foot of its target and paused there, inspecting. Satisfied, it advanced a few more inches. The rat watched, frozen. When the strike came it was like the springing of a trap. One moment, in a tableau of motion suspended, snake and rat were separate; the next, just the flicker of an eyelash later, they were joined, jaws clamped to the small, shuddering body and chewing at it with vicious, stabbing bites. The whole thing lasted perhaps three or four seconds. Once, as if tired of waiting for the venom to act, the snake lifted its victim and smashed it, in a sudden spasm of violence, against the glass. Then the fangs released and the lethal head drew back.

The rat lay on its side, bleeding from punctures at the shoulder and abdomen. For a second or two it kicked feebly, clawing the air, then it twitched once, convulsively, and stiffened, quivering. The snake inspected it briefly, retired to the opposite corner of the case, and went back to watching the man.

The man picked up the cage and headed for the door. In the doorway he turned and once more spoke to the snake.

'Nicely done . . . Now eat.'

When the man returned later the snake had eaten; the rat was a bulge in the sinuous curve of its body. At the man's approach, the snake threatened as before, but its movements were lethargic, lacking in conviction. The man had armed himself this time with a thirty-gallon trash barrel and a pole the size of a broom handle, with a blunt metal hook at one end. Placing the barrel underneath the case, he stepped to one side and opened the glass front.

At once the snake attacked. The man fended it off with the hook. Recoiling, it made for the grotto of rocks at the back of the case, but found itself encircled and dragged back by the hook. Struggling, it slid out of the case and flopped heavily into the barrel.

With the snake neutralized, the man went to work on the case. He dismantled the grotto of rocks, exposing a small patch of sand in the centre, and scooped out a shallow trough six inches long and half as wide. From his pocket he took a small, wallet-shaped package, plastic wrapped, and placed it in the

6

trough. He covered it with sand and rebuilt the grotto around it.

Returning the snake was more of a problem than taking it out. It had been angry to start with, and its stay in the barrel had not improved its mood. But gorged with rat and correspondingly sluggish, it couldn't summon its normal spirit. On the first few attempts it slithered off the hook, once almost making it out of the barrel. But soon, tiring, it allowed itself to be lifted and returned to its home in the case.

Before the man left, he stood for a few seconds watching. The snake had taken refuge in the grotto. From there it peered out, hostility undiminished, its hiss of thwarted fury still tearing the silence.

The man smiled.

'OK,' he said. 'Now that you've got it, guard it.'

Part 1

1

Philip Nolan stuck a sheet of paper in the carriage of his typewriter. He glanced at the letters in front of him, then gazed up at the ceiling, hoping that inspiration would strike. It did. The letters that so peremptorily demanded his attention had been sighed by a Mr Miera. It occurred to him that a simple, one-letter addition to this name might give its owner a good deal of offence. The idea pleased him. It was economical, and economy was always desirable, especially when giving offence.

'Dear Mr Mierda . . .' he typed.

No one had ever accused Nolan of being sweet-natured. His detractors, of whom there were several, were apt to describe him as a smartass. His students, who were usually not among his detractors, had nonetheless nicknamed him 'Captain Grief'. He accepted the nickname, having no choice in the matter, but rejected the implications. He preferred to think of himself as a kind of gadfly, giving the world hassle because hassle was what it deserved. No one, he felt, deserved it more richly than the Internal Revenue Service.

'I've got letters from you,' he continued, 'postmarked Albuquerque and Sante Fe, both dated April 24. They invite me to meet you in those cities on July 19 at 10 AM, for an audit of my 1975 federal income tax return. Inability to be in two places at once – I so envy you for having mastered that trick – prevents my attending one of those meetings; a prior commitment to go climbing in Nepal, alas, scratches the other. Should you wish to reschedule, please let me know. I'll be back in the US by August 30. Santa Fe, being closer, would suit me better than Albuquerque. Taos, if you have an office there, would be more convenient still.

11

'In the meantime, since one copy of any letter from the IRS is already more than enough, I'd be grateful if you'd stop corresponding in duplicate. The amount of federal income tax I paid in 1975 struck me at the time as excessive. It dismays me to think that some of it has been used to finance this kind of waste.'

He toyed for a while with the idea of adding some insulting valediction, but decided, in the end, on 'Yours sincerely'. Keep it short and dignified, he told himself. Economical. In insult, as in architecture, less was more.

But at the same time he wondered why he bothered. The letters had clearly been written by computer and signed by rubber stamp. The duplication had been caused by an innocent snafu, not some sinister plot to harass him. His response would almost certainly be read, not by Mr Miera, but by some unoffending clerk. In due course he would no doubt receive a polite reply, changing the date of his audit and switching the location to Taos. So his protest, if it merited that title, was unnecessary, and his scatological slur would miss its mark . . . Gadfly? he thought wryly; he was no such creature, in this instance, at least, he was a smartass, pure and simple.

That was no reason, on the other hand, not to send the letter.

He looked out of the window. To the east the grey of the early sky was giving place to silver; the silhouettes of the mesas were edged with the halo of dawn. Northwest, beyond the creek, the escarpment of Buckskin Canyon was taking on warmth and colour. Soon sunshine would strike the cliffs behind the Fremont School. It was time to get going.

Time to get going. He tried to trick his body by standing up briskly, with a show of enthusiasm, but it wasn't fooled. His legs felt wooden, his gut empty, and his shoulders drooped, anticipating their burden. His spirit sagged in sympathy. Perhaps he could let up a bit today, pack a shade less weight, cut a mile or two from the distance. But he silenced these whispers by reminding himself that in less than six weeks he'd be in Nepal, where weakness would meet the contempt it deserved. He wasn't, as yet, even halfway fit. Now was not the time to think about slacking.

He forced himself into the hallway where his backpack stood from the day before, against the wall next to his boots and a jumble of climbing equipment. The pack was loaded with forty pounds of rock. Each week he would add five pounds or so, increasing the load until it was time for Nepal. By then it would be up to sixty-five pounds, or seventy, and he'd be fit enough, or so he planned, to keep up with the young lions who'd be his companions – and competitors – on the climb. He turned the pack so that the straps were facing him. Then, lifting it on to one partially raised knee, he slid his right arm into its strap and swung the weight onto his shoulders. It was a practised movement that cost him as little effort as shrugging on an overcoat. The weight was not so bad, he thought; the jogging was what killed him.

Fifty minutes later he was slumped, utterly exhausted, on the ledge surrounding the great sandstone butte that rose up, like a fortress, behind his house. To atone for earlier temptations he'd decided, on impulse, to do *more* today, to round off his job through the valley with a scramble up the slope to the ledge. It was an impulse that, as always, he'd regretted. For though the distance was barely a hundred yards, the slope was a killer and the footing shale and loose sand. Just walking up it was good exercise, even for someone in his condition; running up it with a forty pound backpack was mortification of the flesh, just torture. No matter how often he faced it, the ordeal of two steps forward one step back left him gasping and retching, his legs jelly, the blood at his temples roaring like the surf. For a while he just sat there, catatonic, too tired to move or even think, but now as the symptoms of physical distress receded and his thoughts were released from the immediate claims of his body, it struck him that it was not yet seven and this part of the ledge was still in shadow; instead of letting the chill from the rock invade and stiffen his muscles, he would be better off on the far side of the butte, keeping warm in the sun.

Forcing himself to his feet, he started out, leaving the backpack where he had sloughed it. Twenty yards or so brought him to the northernmost end of the butte, where the ledge, curving round towards the south, broadened out into a platform some twenty feet in diameter. There was sun here, room to stretch out, and a view down the valley to Buckskin Creek. It was one of his favourite resting places, but someone – probably students – had used it for a party. There was now a fire pit surrounded by blackened boulders, and the area was littered with cigarette butts and empty beer cans. He gathered the cans into a pile, to be removed on his way back down. Then, having no wish for the company of anyone's garbage, he moved on a little, following the ledge as it circled back south.

On this side the topography was different. The ground fell away in a sheer drop of almost eighty feet to a dry wash strewn with boulders. And the ledge itself was narrower, barely a yard across in places. People uneasy about heights tended to step carefully here, keeping close in to the rock, but Nolan, who had *slept* comfortably in tighter spots, sauntered along the very edge, neither hesitating nor looking down, trusting to instinct to guide his feet.

Halfway along he stopped and turned outwards, cast his gaze to the horizon and let it wander over the landscape, lingering on the dark line of cottonwoods that bordered the creek, then meandering back across the flinty red earth whose harshness was softened by the dusty greens of juniper and yucca and orange-yellow patches where mesquite was coming into bloom. He loved this time of morning, when nobody else was about, the desert empty, as desert was meant to be. One could imagine oneself in earlier, more innocent times, the land untouched yet by the fear and greed that seemed the constant companions of people.

He stood, absorbing the silence, the sun warm on his skin, the air pure and cold in his lungs, then something below caught his attention. A jackrabbit, ears at the alert, loped off into the bushes. But though this movement attracted his glance, it was something else, something *not* moving, that held it. A woman's foot – for some reason he was instantly sure it was a woman's – was sticking out from behind a boulder in the wash. It was bare and pale, twisted into an awkward looking position, toes down, heel outwards. Its stillness was absolute, as if it had been carved out of bone.

All he could see was the foot. The rest was hidden by the boulder and a bulge of overhang below the edge. He moved to his right, leaned out and peered down. A second foot came into view, this one wearing a sandal. Then legs, pale as marble. Then the whole body.

She lay face down among the boulders, one arm flung out behind, the other crushed underneath her body. Her head was half twisted beneath her shoulder, the long hair spread out around it, like a fan. She wasn't, as he had at first feared, naked; her skirt had somehow ridden up around her waist. But his relief at this was lost almost at once in the shock of a discovery.

He knew her. She was Lisa Bronowski. A student.

2

She was obviously dead. On the ledge it had been possible to nurse a feeble optimism; down here it was not. Her head was twisted at an unnatural angle, sideways and half underneath her. Flies were already swarming on the crust of blood around her mouth and nostrils. There were ants in her hair and crawling all over her body. They looked like an army of occupation.

He knelt down and placed an ear against her back. No heartbeat. He put his fingertips on her upper arm. It was cool, much cooler than it should have been. For a moment he crouched over her, indecisive, unwilling to accept what sense so plainly told him and tormented by the thought that there was still – if he could only figure out what – something he could do. The imperatives of his emergency first aid training kept coming back to him, like echoes from space . . . *Ensure an open airway. Place the heel of the right hand on the lower sternum. Alternate chest compressions and lung ventilations in a ratio of fifteen to two at a rate of eighty per minute. Maintain till the arrival of properly trained and authorized personnel* . . . But these were soon silenced by another recollection: a body stored at room temperature loses heat after death at a rate of roughly one degree centigrade per hour. She hadn't been at room temperature, of course – the desert in the small hours of a spring morning was closer to freezing – but the loss of heat had been considerable. CPR wouldn't help. Nor would the arrival of properly trained and authorized personnel. Nothing would help now. She was gone.

He reached over to pull down her skirt over her thighs. Then he hesitated. Perhaps he shouldn't. The police might want her left exactly as he'd found her. But she seemed too naked that way, too vulnerable. Though common sense told him nothing could harm her now, instinct forbade him to treat her like a corpse. She was still a person; the requirements of her dignity outweighed, even now, the wishes of the police.

He covered her and sat down to wait for Sinclair.

Sinclair arrived within minutes. He'd been running but still looked somewhat dazed, as if in spite of the shock and the exercise he wasn't yet fully awake. When he saw the body, however, all traces of sleep left him. He shut his eyes for an instant, but when he opened them he was all business, ready, as ever, to take charge.

'I've called the police and an ambulance. They should be here shortly. She is dead, I take it?'

Nolan nodded.

'Shit . . .' Sinclair said.

Silence.

'Any indication of what happened?'

'She must have fallen. Her neck's broken, I think. She was climbing around up there, by the looks of it.' Nolan pointed to the ledge. 'I imagine she slipped in the dark and fell.'

'In the dark?' Sinclair gave him a sharp look. 'You think she's been here that long?'

'Several hours, at a guess. The body's starting to get cold.'

Sinclair walked over to the foot of the cliff. He looked up to the ledge and back again to the body, his head moving out and down in a kind of arc, as if tracing the path her fall had taken.

'That must be it, then. She slipped and fell . . . But what was she doing up there in the middle of the night?'

'They were partying up there recently,' Nolan said. 'There's garbage that wasn't there the last time I was. It could be several days old, however.'

Sinclair frowned and pursed his lips.

16

'Let's hope so.' His tone conveyed rather the opposite conviction. For a while he said nothing, pondering implications, then he brightened.

'But *she* couldn't have been partying, could she? . . . If there'd been others with her, someone would have come to get help.'

'I guess . . .' It struck Nolan that there was an element of wishful thinking in Sinclair's speculations, but this didn't seem the time to mention it. This was police business, in any case, and they'd be here soon enough to take care of it.

'I don't think we need share our suspicions, though.' It seemed the police were on Sinclair's mind, too. 'If she was drinking, it'll show in the autopsy, presumably. If not, I'd rather not slander her memory by suggesting it.'

Nolan said nothing. Clearly Sinclair's concern was not entirely for Lisa. It was natural that, as headmaster, he should also be anxious for the Fremont's reputation, but this was early, Nolan thought, to be showing it.

Something of this may have shown in his look. Sinclair, at any rate, seemed suddenly to recall that he hadn't paid the debt owed by propriety to grief.

'Dear God, how self-centred we are . . .' He shook his head, as if in disbelief at his own flawed humanity. 'Here's this child scarcely cold, and me already worrying about public relations.'

He seemed genuinely abashed. But the effects of this insight into human character barely outlived its utterance, for at the mention of public relations he was instantly reminded of the two people he would above all have to worry about.

'Oh Jesus . . .' This time the distress was unquestionably real. 'What the hell will I say to her parents?'

Nolan didn't reply. Indeed he had stopped listening. He was trying to remember Lisa, trying to recapture her as she had been, only a few hours before . . . A tall slender girl, rather pale, with a shy beauty she had seemed almost unconscious of, and a slow smile, not often seen, that seemed to betoken some inner amusement. She had reminded him slightly of Alice in Wonderland in the Tenniel illustrations, in part because of her paleness and the way her shoulder-length hair, straight and perfectly blond, was swept back from her forehead and kept in place by a band, and in part because, like Alice, she had always

17

seemed somewhat aloof from the world around her – a spectator, so to speak, at some Mad Hatter's Tea Party, a little bit puzzled, a little bit lost. But the comparison was probably inaccurate, he thought, because he hadn't taught her and hadn't, therefore, got to know her very well. Now he never would.

He was suddenly swept by a wave of regret.

The police arrived shortly thereafter, their patrol car followed by an ambulance. Turning off the dirt road that led to the school from the creek, the vehicles lurched across country to the butte and halted at the edge of the wash.

Two men emerged from the patrol car. One of them Nolan recognized as Lieutenant Jacobsen of the Buckskin Police Department. The other, also in uniform, was shortish and heavyset, his features partly hidden under a pale beige Stetson and further obscured by Polaroid sunglasses. A plastic tab on his breast pocket informed the world that he was the county sheriff. He moved with a massive deliberation that reminded Nolan of the shorthorn cattle sometimes found wandering on the campus at night. Like them, he seemed watchful and slightly uncertain in temper.

Sinclair stepped forward. Jacobsen nodded a greeting. The sheriff, ignoring Sinclair, marched directly to the body. For some seconds he stood over it, inspecting. Then he took off his sunglasses, squatted down, and placed his right hand on Lisa's arm.

The others went over to join him. Hearing them, he stood up and glanced back over his shoulder. The removal of the sunglasses revealed a brick-red, fleshy face that might have seemed belligerent but for the eyes. These, Nolan saw, were grey and steady; noticing eyes, not hard exactly, but used to sights they didn't relish.

'What happened?'

The question was addressed to Sinclair. The tone implied he owed explanations. Perhaps for this reason, he chose not to offer any.

'Ewing Sinclair.' He'd evidently been about to offer his hand but had the sense, just in time, not to. Instead he gestured to Nolan. 'And this is Doctor Nolan.'

'Sam Plunkett . . .' The sheriff nodded to Sinclair then turned to Nolan. 'Doctor? . . . You mean medical doctor?'

'PhD . . .' Nolan shrugged apologetically. He felt foolish and irritated with Sinclair. Public relations were all very well, but this was hardly the right moment.

Plunkett turned back to Sinclair. 'Are you the one that called?'

Sinclair nodded. 'I'm the headmaster.'

'Are you?' Plunkett seemed unimpressed. 'Then tell me what happened.'

'I don't know much more than you. We found her like this. She slipped and fell, presumably.' Sinclair pointed to the ledge. 'Beyond that, I can't help you, I'm afraid.'

Plunkett looked up at the ledge. Visibly, as Sinclair had done, he estimated how far the momentum of a falling body might carry it out from the cliff.

'Who was she?'

'Lisa Bronowski,' Sinclair said. 'One of our juniors.'

'Boarder?'

Sinclair nodded. 'Most of our students are.'

'Who saw her last?'

'I don't know. Someone from her dormitory, I imagine. I assume she was there for the room check at 10:30 last night, but I can't say for certain; there hasn't been time to check.'

Plunkett thought for a moment.

'Was there any reason she might have taken her own life?'

'Not that I know of.' Sinclair was clearly startled. 'Is there any reason to believe she did?'

'I'm not believing,' Plunkett said. 'I'm asking. There've been three suicides in five years at the public high school. I figure it can happen here too.'

He paused, inviting comment. Sinclair said nothing.

'What do you think she was doing up there?'

Sinclair shrugged. 'I can't imagine . . . meditating . . . looking at the stars . . . I really have no idea.'

This answer, or the manner, struck Nolan as unconvincing, but the sheriff didn't seem to notice. In fact, he seemed not to be listening. He stepped over the body and gingerly, as if he were handling something fragile and slippery, lifted the out-stretched arm.

He turned it over. Nolan saw that he noticed Lisa was

19

wearing a watch. A man's watch, one of the elegant dress models often worn by women, its movement about the size and thickness of a silver dollar. The crystal was broken.

Plunkett took the watch from her wrist. He examined the face, shook the movement gently, held it up to his ear. He wound it once or twice then repeated the previous procedure.

'Busted . . .' He looked pleased. 'If we don't know *what* happened, we have a good fix on *when*.'

He put the watch in his pocket. Whatever information it had given him he clearly had no plans to share. This irritated Nolan; it struck him as vaguely accusing.

'What time did it stop?'

'Early hours.' Plunkett looked deliberately cagey, a low-stakes poker player calling a moderate raise. 'Who found her?'

'I did,' Nolan said.

'When?'

'Early hours.'

'When exactly?' Plunkett's tone took on an edge.

'I don't know *exactly*. I wasn't wearing a watch . . .' Nolan paused rather longer than necessary before adding, 'Six-thirty at a guess. I was on the ledge when I spotted her.'

Pause. Plunkett's gaze had become chilly.

'And what were *you* doing up there . . . meditating?'

Nolan was tempted to retaliate to this needling but refrained. In the circumstances one smartass was already too many. He explained how he had come to be up there.

'When you saw her what did you do?'

'Ran down to my house and called Sinclair, grabbed a first aid kit and a blanket and ran back. I had to pass my house to get here anyway, so I thought I should get some help. I figured the extra time that I took wasn't going to make any difference.' Nolan was annoyed to find himself explaining – it sounded too much like justifying – but there was something about Plunkett that put him on the defensive.

'You found her exactly like this?'

Nolan hesitated. 'More or less.'

'More or less – What does that mean?'

'I had to make sure she was dead, for one thing . . . and her skirt was up around her waist. I rearranged it.'

'Rearranged it? Why?'

Nolan shrugged. 'It seemed the right thing to do.'

'Did it?' Plunkett raised an eyebrow. He gazed at Nolan a moment then turned to Jacobsen. 'We're assuming she fell. She may not have . . . You'd better go up and take a look. Chances are you won't find a whole lot, but we need to check.'

Jacobsen nodded and set off. He was slim and wiry, not much above medium height, with pale blue eyes, short blond hair, and little expression on his face. The kind of man, Nolan guessed, who listened, watched, and kept his thoughts to himself, the kind of man who was easy to underrate. He didn't hurry, just picked his way through the brush, yet in spite of the rough terrain and the shale underfoot, he covered ground fast and never hesitated nor stumbled. He moved like an Indian, Nolan found himself thinking, or like a hunter.

Sinclair turned to Plunkett. 'What now?'

Plunkett shrugged. 'We take pictures. We wait for the Lieutenant. Then we load her into the ambulance and take her to the morgue. And if the autopsy comes up clean, that's it . . . We give her back to her parents and they put her in the ground.'

He looked up again at the ledge. 'You *let* your students play around up there?'

It was more an accusation than a question. Sinclair ignored it.

'Autopsy?' He looked unhappy. 'Is that standard procedure?'

Plunket nodded. 'Unexplained death. It looks like she fell and broke her neck, but we have to be sure. Plus there are some unusual circumstances here.'

'Unusual?' Nolan queried.

'They strike me as unusual,' Plunkett said. 'Why was she up there in the middle of the night? . . . Doesn't that strike you as a little bit strange?'

'Not necessarily,' Nolan said. 'Kids like to go out at night.'

The look he got in return was one he'd got used to since coming to Fremont. He got it just about every time he took students into town. It was the kind of look, he'd decided, which crew cuts and polyester pantsuits were apt to give Afros, patched Levi's, and tie-dyed T-shirts with peace signs front and back. Just what kind of kids *are* these? it asked. What kind of a place are you guys running out there?

'My daughter took off at night like that, I'd warm her backside.'

Nolan shrugged. 'I can imagine.'

Plunkett gazed at him for a moment. 'What you can't imagine,' he said, 'is how much I hate it when kids die in stupid accidents like this.'

Replacing his sunglasses, he turned and walked back to his car.

3

Jacobsen squatted down by the remains of the fire and, using one of the beer cans, scraped off the top layer of ash revealing the cinders underneath. They were warm, too warm to risk touching. Next to the fire pit were one or two small sticks, all that was left of what had once been a woodpile. The sticks were mesquite, a wood that burned hot and fairly slowly. Three to four hours, he guessed, judging by the depth of ash and the heat still left in the cinders. Five at the most. There'd been three people up here originally, assuming the fourth set of footprints belonged to the teacher, Nolan, and if they'd been careless enough to let their fire burn out unattended, at least they had the sense not to build it too big in the first place. That was something, he thought; not enough to atone for the beer cans, but something.

And they had an excuse for not killing the fire. There was nothing up here to kill it with. Not enough sand. And no water, of course, unless they'd brought it with them, which they hadn't. They should've used some of the beer, he thought. They sure as hell had drunk plenty.

Then he remembered the rain.

There'd been a downpour in town last night. Around 10:00, he recalled. One of the brisk, thirty-minute thundershowers common at this time of year. It had hit here too, by the look of things. Therefore all the footprints had been made after 10:30. In turn, that meant most of what had happened – at least, who had gone where on this chunk of rock last night – should be as easy to read as a child's picture book.

Of course, as Plunkett had said, the odds were it wouldn't matter much. Most likely the girl had just slipped – zonked on the beer – and broken her neck. But if his guess about the fire was right, a disturbing possibility emerged: that while she had been sprawled in the wash, with the chill of a desert night invading her body, a party had been going on up here, just two hundred feet from where she lay.

He stepped away from the fire pit into bare rock, taking care, as he had since reaching the ledge, to keep his own footprints separate from the others. Not counting his, there were four sets of prints: running shoes with waffle soles, cleated hiking boots, sneakers, and the kind of Mexican sandals whose soles were made from the treads of old automobile tyres. The waffle prints presumably belonged to Nolan who was wearing running shoes. The other tracks, therefore, were the ones to focus on, especially those made by the sandals. The girl, he recalled, had been wearing some kind of sandal.

For the first dozen yards the ledge was bare rock. He found nothing, not even scuff marks. Then, in a small declivity where dust had gathered, he spotted a heel print. It belonged to the running shoe and was headed back to the fire. In the next few yards there were three more prints, all made by the running shoes – one coming, two going. The tracks, he observed, were all close to the outside edge, where a slight depression had trapped patches of sand and dried mud. Closer to the cliff, where caution guided his own footsteps, the rock was mostly bare. Someone nervous about heights, especially someone walking this ledge in the dark, would tend to stay close to the cliff and therefore might leave no tracks. Alternatively, since this ledge seemed to circle the butte entirely, the girl could have come from the other direction. It was possible, too, that he was wrong about the sandals, that none of the prints around the fire were hers. There was also a chance that the prints around the fire had been made at different times, though all, of course, after 10:30 last night. He liked any of these possibilities, which allowed that the girl had not known about the beer drinkers nor they about her, better than the one that had first occurred to him.

A little farther on, about thirty yards from the fire pit, he came to the place where Nolan must have spotted the body. In the dust of a dried up puddle was the toe print of a running shoe, facing the edge. Beyond that point there were no more waffle prints. Instead, in a long patch of sand that spanned almost the width of the ledge, were the tracks he had been expecting, the ones made by the sandals. They went in one direction only.

She hadn't gone much farther. A short stretch of bare rock was followed by another patch of sand. Here she had halted. Six inches from the edge there were two complete footprints, side by side and facing outwards, as detailed and as sharp as if they'd been cast in plaster. Beyond them was nothing.

He knelt down and examined them more closely. The right one was perfect, a clear impression in the sand showing every detail of the tyre pattern. The left print, on the other hand, had slid laterally about a quarter of an inch, and in its final position was clearer at the outside edge, smudged and faint towards the inside. He thought about this for a moment, then examined the prints again to confirm his first findings.

It didn't make any sense.

4

Institutions deal with the outrageous by clinging to the ordinary. And the Fremont School, though its members liked to think otherwise, was at heart an institution. Apart from the assembly called by Sinclair to announce Lisa's death, there was no departure that day from the schedule; the routine of a normal Monday was carefully preserved.

Nolan expected to find his classes subdued and his students prone to distraction. Instead they struck him as more attentive than usual; their questions were more pertinent, their note-taking more assiduous. It was as if they were trying, in ordered and focused activity, to forget the glimpse of chaos the morning had brought them.

By mid-morning, however, the mood began to lighten. Sinclair, too, was more cheerful. He'd been able to confirm that Lisa was present for the room check the night before, and a preliminary search of her room and belongings had not turned up a suicide note. It seemed clear she had broken the curfew, and while doing so, had met with an accident. This was tragic, certainly, but there was consolation in the fact that no blame seemed likely to fall on Fremont.

This, at least, was the assumption that prevailed until a senior named Robert Anderson asked Nolan if he could talk with him privately.

'Drugs . . .' Sinclair gave a long disgusted sigh. 'I might have guessed. As if tragedy weren't enough, we have to have scandal.'

Nolan said nothing. If the tragedy dismayed Sinclair visibly less than the scandal, it was hard to blame him. A student might be dead, but Fremont and its problems remained, and Sinclair was still the headmaster. While others might enjoy the luxury of unalloyed regret, his feelings were bound to be mixed with a certain regard for the practical. It was he, after all, who had to endure the sheriff's abrasions, who had made the announcement in the assembly, and broken the news to the parents. Sinclair already had a very rough day, and the news that Lisa had been high as a kite on LSD at the time of her death did not bode well for the future. He must feel, Nolan thought, like a man who had survived a coronary only to learn that he has terminal cancer.

'Let's get this straight.' Sinclair spoke resentfully, as if Nolan were heading a conspiracy to disturb his peace of mind. 'There was a party on that ledge, you say, involving Robert Anderson and others?'

'One other,' Nolan corrected. 'Not counting Lisa, of course.'

'Who?'

'Robert didn't say.' This was prevaricating slightly. Robert had *refused* to say. He didn't see the need to give names, and wasn't going to. Nolan hadn't pressed him; it wouldn't have done any good.

'They climbed all the way up there – at that hour – merely to drink and take drugs?'

Sinclair's puritan instincts were clearly outraged. Yet it wasn't exactly an unheard of occurrence. Parties were usually what they went up there for. And the beer, probably, had been the least of it. Freedom and privacy, Nolan guessed, were what they wanted – an escape from the too many rules and oppressive togetherness of boarding-school life. The beer had been for mood, mostly, to give things that necessary touch of the illicit. The drugs, it seemed, had been an afterthought.

'Lisa wasn't there at first,' he said. 'It was just the two others, according to Robert, having a few beers around the fire. She showed up later, "uninvited," Robert said. But of course they asked her to stay.'

'When was this?'

'One-thirty. At least, that's when they started. She showed up about an hour later.'

Sinclair pondered.

'But if they didn't invite her,' he objected, 'what was she doing up there?'

Nolan shrugged. 'Robert didn't know. He said she stayed only about twenty minutes. But when she left, he noticed, she went out along the ledge, not back in the direction of campus. He said he figured she had plans of her own.'

'Then where do the drugs fit into this? I thought you said she was on acid.'

'She was. She was high when she arrived. At least, that's what she told them. And before she left, she gave them a couple of hits . . . as a thank you, I guess, for the beer.'

'And you mean to say they just let her go?' Sinclair sounded stunned. 'She was drunk and maybe hallucinating, and they let her wander off along that ledge? . . . Alone? . . . In the pitch dark?'

'She wasn't drunk.' Nolan had asked the same question, and in roughly the same tone of voice. 'She had only one beer, it seems. And as for the acid, she was used to it, Robert said; they thought she could handle it. It never occurred to them to worry.'

'Never occurred to them . . .' Sinclair's tone was withering. 'It never does occur to them. Nothing *ever* occurs to them, I sometimes think, beyond the gratification of the moment.' He leaned forward, elbows on the desk, and rested his forehead on the heels of his hands. 'So she didn't necessarily just slip. She may easily have thought she was . . .' He shrank, almost superstitiously, it seemed to Nolan, from uttering what both of them feared. 'Who knows what she thought she was doing, with that stuff poisoning her mind.'

That was only too true, Nolan thought. It was all very well for Robert to say she'd been used to it, but the mental wards were full of kids who had thought they were used to it. The mortuaries, too.

'What I still don't understand' – Sinclair shook his head in weary bewilderment – 'is how they heard nothing . . . Surely she must have cried out?'

'Robert said not. He said they never heard a sound. We can't assume they would have, of course, because we don't know exactly when it happened. Perhaps she fell later, after they'd left.'

But he knew she hadn't. Intuitively he was sure she'd been lying in the wash while the others had still been sitting around their campfire, less than a hundred yards away. And their hearing nothing, in that case, struck him now as ominous. Had she slipped, he thought, she'd have screamed. And had she screamed, they'd have heard her. Instead, it seemed, she had calmly sailed into space, launched herself, perhaps, lured on by the promise of some gaudy illusion.

'I suppose,' Sinclair said, 'we can rely on Robert's story?'

'I don't see why not.' On Robert's behalf, Nolan found himself somewhat offended. 'He didn't have to come forward. In any case, let's not jump to conclusions about the acid. She may have slipped . . . or jumped . . . anyway. The acid may have been irrelevant.'

'Irrelevant?' Sinclair stared. 'You can't be serious. I'm tempted to think it's the only thing that *is* relevant. If *we* don't jump to conclusions, we'll be the only ones who don't. No matter what really happened, people will blame the acid. And they'll blame the acid on us. At least,' he amended, 'they will if they *hear* about it.'

It seemed to Nolan that the tone of this was just faintly interrogative.

27

'No question of if,' he said. 'They will hear about it. There's the autopsy, for a start. It'll be in the coroner's report.'

'But will it, necessarily?' Sinclair's voice was thoughtful. 'Would something like that show up in an autopsy? . . . Unless one were looking for it, I mean.'

Silence.

'We can't do that.' Nolan shook his head. 'That's concealing evidence. We have an obligation to tell them. Besides, if you think this'll look bad, think how it will look if we don't tell them and they find out anyway.'

'True . . .' Sinclair smiled faintly. 'So I'd better get on to the sheriff.' He paused, and catching Nolan's gaze, held it for a moment. 'You think I'm unfeelling, don't you? Machiavellian?'

Nolan shrugged. 'I'll put it this way: I think you have a healthy regard for the practical.'

'Perhaps too healthy a regard?'

'Perhaps.'

'I have to,' Sinclair said. 'We're a small private school. A good one, I think. But for small private schools life is always precarious. We can't afford much scandal. So I'll be doing my damnedest to head this one off. Even at the cost of appearing' – he paused and gave Nolan a small, rueful smile – 'too ruthlessly practical.'

5

'Problems?' Plunkett sounded wary. He gazed at Jacobsen over the tops of his sunglasses. His expression, owlish and sceptical, conveyed that he felt somehow put upon. 'What kind of problems?'

Jacobsen considered. Where to begin? 'It's kind of complicated . . .'

'No complications.' Plunkett cut him off. 'Not now. Just give me the bottom line.'

'OK.' Jacobsen shrugged. 'I don't think she slipped and I don't think she jumped.'

28

Silence, pregnant and protracted. Plunkett pushed the sunglasses back on the bridge of his nose, got up and walked over to the window. He stood for a moment looking out, then he took off the sunglasses, turned, and treated Jacobsen to his bleakest stare.

'Shit . . .' Plunkett said.

Jacobsen said nothing. *Shit* was right, he thought. If Plunkett was dismayed by the bottom line, he'd despair when he heard the details.

Plunkett sighed. 'OK. Let's hear it from the beginning. Why don't you think she slipped?'

'You're not going to like this,' Jacobsen warned. 'It has to do with tracks.'

'Tracks? . . .' Plunkett rolled his eyes. 'Fogarty will just love that.'

Jacobsen said nothing. Fogarty, the county medical examiner, had no time for expertise other than his own. Screw Fogarty, Jacobsen thought: Fogarty was a pain in the ass.

'Make your case,' Plunkett said. 'How do you know she didn't slip?'

'She knew where she was, for one thing. When she was moving she kept close to the cliff. She took care, in other words, not to slip. And that ledge, at its narrowest, is more than two feet wide. Where she fell from it's closer to four. You just don't slip in those circumstances.'

Plunkett considered. 'Reasonable, but not conclusive. You need more.'

'I've got more. When she got to where she fell from, she was standing still. Her feet were together, facing outwards, six inches from the edge. You don't slip when you're standing still. Even Fogarty should be able to grasp that.'

'So she jumped,' Plunkett said. 'Don't tell me you can't *jump* when you're standing still.'

'You can.' Jacobsen shrugged. 'But you don't usually jump sideways.'

'The tracks can tell you which way she jumped?' Plunkett, clearly, had problems swallowing this. 'How?'

'Actually, what they tell me is she didn't jump. The right footprint was almost perfect, see, no indication of slippage whatsoever. But the left print slipped laterally a bit and showed

29

more weight on the outside edge, suggesting she went forward and sideways. Now of course,' Jacobsen went on, 'there's no law that says when you jump off a ledge like that you have to jump straight ahead. But if you do decide to go sideways to the left, then the main thrust has to come from the right foot. In which case you'd expect to find slippage in that print, with more weight towards the inside edge. The exact opposite, in other words, of what we got. What we've got is more consistent with sideways movement when the thrust . . .' He paused and gave the next words deliberate emphasis, making sure he had Plunkett's full attention. '. . . is applied externally.'

'Applied externally . . .' Plunkett frowned. 'Pushed, you mean.'

Jacobsen nodded.

'Oh great,' Plunkett said. 'Terrific. You're saying we've got a murder on our hands, and the only evidence is two lousy footprints and an analysis so goddamned complicated you need an engineering degree to follow it.'

'Actually,' Jacobsen said, 'the mechanics are fairly simple. Try it yourself. Try jumping to your left from a standing position and pushing off with your left foot. It's impossible. Or very unnatural. There's nothing complicated about it,' he insisted. 'There's no mystery to tracking. It's just a question of using your eyes.'

'Oh sure,' Plunkett grunted. 'Try telling that to a jury. Try keeping it simple with some smartass lawyer on your case. He'll have you modifying and qualifying and contradicting yourself till you'll wish you never opened your mouth. Ever see what they do with medical witnesses? They can make them look like a bunch of fucking clowns. And those guys are doctors. Medicine is a science.'

Medicine is a science. And that, of course, was the problem: tracking wasn't. Juries wouldn't buy it. Where a forensic pathologist, even some jackass like Fogarty, would be believed without being understood, he, with his talk of tracking, would be dismissed without even being listened to. Yet the skill he had learned from the old Navajo was not essentially different in method from pathology. Both used experience and observation to reconstruct events. And the Navajo tracker who could glance at a patch of ground and pronounce that three riders had recently passed by, one of them a woman whose horse was going lame, was no more guessing than a pathologist who examined a head wound and declared it caused by a blow from a blunt instrument, probably a hammer, delivered from behind by a left-handed male of medium height. Science, Jacobsen thought bitterly, was simply the title conferred by respectability on superstition. The history of science, after all, was most of the time a history of error.

'Plus there's something you haven't touched on yet,' Plunkett said. 'If she was pushed, there had to be someone up there doing the pushing. What do the tracks have to say about that?'

Jacobsen made a face. 'Here's where it gets complicated. Since ten-thirty last night when that rainstorm hit, a total of six people have been up on that ledge. Nolan and me, and the girl herself, of course. And then there were three others. It seems there was some kind of party going on up there. I found the embers of a fire, still warm, and a bunch of empty beer cans.'

'A party?' Plunkett was stunned. 'You mean going on when she fell?'

'I can't say for certain. I figure the fire was lit not much before two. So if the time she fell was when her watch broke – about five after three – then the odds are there were people around that fire when it happened. That's to say barely two hundred feet away.'

'So someone from the party could have pushed her, *if* we accept your theory about pushing.' From Plunkett's tone it was clear that he, for one, didn't.

Jacobsen shook his head. 'There were three people at the fire. One of them was the girl herself. Hers were the only tracks – I'm not counting Nolan's of course – that left the fire and went south along the ledge on the east side of that butte. Whoever pushed her came from the other direction.'

Plunkett thought about this. 'There are tracks to back that up?'

Jacobsen hesitated. 'Up to a point. The problem is I can't prove they ever got to where she fell from. Just south of there, it's bare rock for about fifteen yards. There are tracks as far as that stretch of bare rock, but none on it of course . . .' He paused. 'I warned you it was complicated.'

'No . . . shit,' Plunkett said.

31

Jacobsen shrugged.

'Now let me be sure I have this right,' Plunkett said. 'You say she was at this party at the north end of the ledge. She left, leaving the others there, went down the east side of the butte and ran into her killer coming up. He pushed her off and left the way he came, at the same time managing not to be heard by the others. Do I have it more or less straight?'

'More or less,' Jacobsen nodded. Put that baldly, he thought, it sounded far from convincing.

Plunkett thought so, too. 'Christ, Olin, that's the flakiest thing I ever heard in my life.'

'I know,' Jacobsen admitted. 'And I can't be certain about the timing either. I could be wrong about when the fire was lit. Maybe her watch stopped before it broke, so maybe the party was over by the time she went up. I'm pretty certain about the tracks, though. She sure as hell didn't slip, and I'd be willing to bet she didn't jump.'

'Yeah. Well what you'd be willing to bet and what you can prove in court are two totally different things,' Plunkett said. 'And I have to be more concerned with what you can prove in court. I'm not saying you're wrong, mind. I'm saying you don't have enough. And unless and until you do, we'd be fools to go public with this . . . You do see that, don't you?'

Jacobsen said nothing. He did see it, of course. It would be worse than foolish, it would be irresponsible. But what bothered him was the knowledge that Plunkett was unconvinced. He hadn't said so straight out, but the fact remained that tracking wasn't, and never would be, included in his notion of what constituted evidence. To him it was mumbo jumbo, part of a culture for which he had little sympathy or understanding, a ritual that for reliability was roughly on a par with a rain dance.

'What I don't want to do is upset people,' Plunkett said. 'Not without cause. And talk about murder will do exactly that. So what I think we'd better do here is play this close to the chest: wait for the autopsy and until then act as if everything's fairly straightforward.' He shrugged. 'Who knows? Those guys at that school may turn up a suicide note.'

32

6

The autopsy was completed by mid afternoon. It showed that Lisa had died of a spine fracture at a time estimated, on the basis of medical evidence, at between one and four that morning. The cause of death and her other fractures and contusions were 'generally consistent' – Fogarty's phrase – with her having fallen from the ledge. Traces of alcohol were found in her stomach and blood. Otherwise nothing unusual was discovered.

Since no suicide note had turned up, the autopsy findings did nothing to clarify the confusion resulting from Jacobsen's discoveries on the ledge and Robert Anderson's disclosure, communicated to the police by Sinclair soon after his conversation with Nolan, that Lisa had been on LSD at the time of her death. Plunkett, though still unimpressed by Jacobsen's deductions, was sufficiently disturbed by the acid to postpone his report to the coroner until Jacobsen had been able to interview Robert. On the morning following Nolan's discovery of the body, therefore, Jacobsen drove out to Fremont.

In his four years with the Buckskin Police Department, he had never previously had reason to visit the school. He was conscious, nonetheless, of having formed a somewhat unfavourable impression of it and its students. When he thought of them, which admittedly was seldom, what came to mind were visions of punks with purple hair and a murmur of dismissive phrases . . . 'Baby-sitting for poor little rich kids' . . . 'That place where the weirdoes examine their navels.'

Jacobsen was an intelligent and fair-minded man. He knew where those phrases came from. He knew that age has no real love for youth, that those who were born into money are mostly resented by those who were not. He knew also that purple hair, though not conclusive evidence of moral depravity, can, to those raised in an ethic of cold showers and crew cuts, tend to seem so. But though he understood that the good citizens of Buckskin, given their average age and economic status, were bound to feel prejudice towards a school like Fremont, this didn't stop him from being somewhat infected by that prejudice himself. He had not been a rich kid. He'd never had the time to examine his navel. He had gone to public school, worked a paper route in the mornings and another after classes, and paid his own way through college. He believed the experience had been good for him, that what you hadn't worked for you tended not to value. He didn't, in short, believe in free rides. And Fremont, with its air of affluence and reputation for permissiveness, sounded to him like a very plush free ride. He'd expected to find it a combination of dude ranch and hippy commune, and he hadn't in the least expected to like it.

But he did like it. At least, he liked the look of it. He was struck at once by the charm of the place, its air of spaciousness and calm beauty. The whole property, to judge from the distance between the driveway entrance and the campus proper, was three or four hundred acres, but the campus used very little of it. The remainder, a landscape of coarse grasses and reddish, flinty soil, scored with innumerable ravines and washes and dotted with mesquite, juniper and cactus, had been left wild, a sort of insulation between the school and the world, and a natural playground for the students. As land, it wasn't much different from any other in the region; what gave it distinction were the cliffs and buttes that surrounded it: a chain of sandstone fortresses whose shapes altered subtly with every shift in perspective and whose colours, in the mid-morning sun, exhausted the varieties of red, ochre, copper, gold, and grey. The place had a glowing tranquillity that made it easy to understand why the local guidebook described it as 'very possibly the loveliest small valley in the region', and why realtors tended to sigh when Fremont came up in conversation. Since the campus occupied not only the loveliest but also the last undeveloped valley around Buckskin, the Fremont School, Jacobsen reflected, was sprawled casually on a gold mine.

The suggestion of graceful affluence in the cavalier use, or nonuse, of so much valuable real estate, was underlined by the buildings themselves. They were adobe, shaded by cotton-woods and willows, and surrounded in most cases by flower beds and lawns. They looked like private houses, and though some of them obviously contained classrooms, it was hard, on

34

casual inspection, to tell which. And the offices, where Jacobsen found himself, ten minutes early for his appointment with Sinclair, sprawled in an armchair and leafing through the school's prospectus, seemed, with their Calder lithographs, Scandinavian furniture, and conspicuous absence of typewriters and filing cabinets, to be more like the lobby of an exclusive resort than a place of serious business.

Exclusive it certainly was. It excluded, he figured, anyone who couldn't come up with about ten thousand a year for tuition and the numerous extras. But to judge from the earnest prose and glossy photography of the prospectus, life there was anything but a vacation. The pictures were of students all very busy at something – studying, climbing rocks, chasing footballs, raking leaves, and mucking stables. The text proclaimed work as the school's central value and went on to describe a curriculum which, strictly followed, could hardly leave anyone with very much free time. Jacobsen approved of all this; it embodied the principle by which he raised his own children. But theory and practice, he knew, were very apt to diverge. He recalled, to help him resist the seduction of the prospectus, that two nights previously three of the members of this educational Eden had been up a mountain drinking beer and popping acid, and that one of them had afterwards turned up dead in a wash, with the flies crawling over her body.

This, he decided, was an appropriate thought to take to his interview with the headmaster.

But his interview with the headmaster was brief. Sinclair spared him just enough time to assure himself that in this instance the school's encounter with the law could be safely handled by a subordinate. Within five minutes of being ushered into Sinclair's office, Jacobsen found himself ushered out and walking across campus with Nolan.

'You've never been here before?'

'Never got around to it.' Jacobsen shook his head. 'But I've heard a lot about it.'

'I can imagine.' Nolan's voice was dry.

Jacobsen let that one go. In the matter of prejudice, no doubt, the school was as guilty as the town.

'We're not all that weird,' Nolan pursued.

'I hope not.' Jacobsen grinned. 'It'd be hard.'

He was glad that Sinclair had handed him over to Nolan. He felt much more on Nolan's wavelength. And this way he would get a closer look at the school. If it weren't as weird as they claimed in town, it was still, he thought, pretty weird.

The students engaged in weeding the flower beds that bordered the pathway from the quad, for instance, looked as if they'd acquired their costumes – there was really no other word for them – from army surplus and the local five-and-dime. One very pretty girl was doing her best to disguise her good looks in an outfit that consisted of hiking boots and knee-length socks, a once white cocktail dress with 'Help' spray-painted in purple across the chest, and a Marine Corps tunic, unbuttoned; the ensemble rounded off by a little cloche hat trimmed with a wisp of black net. Next to her was a girl in military fatigues, flip-flops, and a black derby. Farther along, a boy with orange hair and an earring was wearing what looked to Jacobsen suspiciously like a skirt.

Nolan, observing his companion's startled inspection of this trio, caught his eyes.

'Punks,' he explained, sotto voce.

'But not all *that* weird.' Jacobsen grinned and rolled his eyes.

A sudden blast from the flower bed pre-empted the conversation. From a portable tape deck beside the girl in the Marine Corps tunic there issued the strains of a currently popular anthem. 'We don't want no gang boss. We wanna equali . . . i . . . ize.' The students put down their tools and took up the chant, assuming attitudes that might have looked menacing had their grinning not spoiled the effect.

Nolan stopped and held up his hand for quiet. The music stopped.

'Alan Nicholson.'

'Yes sir, Captain Grief, sir.' The boy with the orange hair stepped forward and saluted. The smile he gave Nolan was frank and easy, Jacobsen noticed. The nickname, clearly ironic, was used affectionately.

'I need a favour.' Nolan returned the smile. 'Find Robert Anderson, will you? Ask him to come to my house. Tell him it's important.'

'With pleasure, Captain.' The boy saluted again and turned to go.

'Oh, and Alan . . .' Nolan stopped him, inspected him gravely. 'I approve of the hair. *Much* more radical than green.'

'Sorry about the mess.' Nolan surveyed the chaos of his living room, the stacks of papers on every available surface. 'I seem to be in a temporary grading crisis.' He paused and inspected Jacobsen for signs of disapproval. Finding none, he continued, 'Actually, let's be honest about this, it's a permanent grading crisis. One oughtn't to get behind, but I always do. I like to teach, you understand, but God how I hate the way they write.'

Jacobsen smiled and shrugged. He looked round the room, searching from habit for clues to the character of its owner. It was large and airy, with a stone fireplace and a picture window that looked out over an expanse of lawn to the most spectacular part of the valley. Bookshelves, the volumes crammed into them with no regard for order, took up most of the available wall space. Elsewhere, there were reading lamps, a stereo, a shelf of LPs, mostly jazz, but no pictures apart from a framed snapshot of a woman on one of the tables and two large framed photographs above the fireplace, portraits of nineteenth-century soldiers in what looked to Jacobsen like Confederate uniform.

'You're a southerner?' He cocked his head at the portraits. 'I don't detect an accent.'

Nolan shook his head. 'Civil War buff . . . Actually, I'm not even a southern sympathizer. Politically, I'm for the North. I just find the southern soldiers more personally sympathetic.'

Jacobsen thought about this. He found it odd to hear the Civil War referred to as an ongoing issue, in which sympathies could be enlisted and personalities liked or disliked. To him it was just history, part of the vanished past. He inspected the nearest bookshelf. Most of the volumes dealt with history, but there was also a smattering of fiction, mostly thrillers. One of the titles caught his eye: *The Economics of Slavery*. The author, he saw, was a Philip Nolan.

He took the book from the shelf and showed it to Nolan. 'This you?'

Nolan nodded. Jacobsen inspected the title page. Nolan, he

learned, had been schooled at Exeter and Yale. He was described as a professor of history at Harvard.

'You taught at Harvard?'

'Still do.' Nolan smiled. 'Technically, I'm on a sabbatical. A friend of mine is a trustee here. I'd just been through a divorce and needed a change of scene, so he arranged for me to come here for a year and teach a few classes. They give me room and board, not much money, but an awful lot of free time.'

'Which you use to write?'

'Actually not.' Nolan grinned. 'Mostly I use it to climb.'

'Climb? You mean mountains?'

'Rocks more than mountains.' Nolan nodded. 'I'm into technical problems more than blood and guts. Ever done any?'

'Rock climbing? A little . . . when I was younger.'

'Did you like it?'

Jacobsen nodded. Actually, he'd liked it a lot and had often wondered why he no longer did it. It wasn't, he thought, something he'd ever made a conscious decision about. It had simply fallen by the wayside, edged out of his life by family and job. 'Matter of fact, I did . . . I'm always telling myself I'd like to start again sometime, but I never seem to get around to it.'

'You should,' Nolan said.

'One of these days.' It seemed to Jacobsen he'd been in the spotlight long enough. 'Who are those guys in the portraits? Ancestors?'

'Personal heroes.' Nolan smiled. 'The one with the white beard is Robert E. Lee . . . my voice of conscience. Whenever I'm faced with a question of honour, I ask myself what General Lee would do. I find him almost infallible.'

A question of honour. It was an odd, old-fashioned phrase. You didn't hear much about honour these days, Jacobsen thought; it wouldn't hurt to hear more. He found himself warming to Nolan.

'You decide what he'd do, and do the same?'

Nolan grinned. 'Mostly I do. Sometimes the General sets rather exacting standards.'

Jacobsen smiled. He used a roughly similar system, but with his grandfather, who also set exacting standards.

'So who's the other one? The one in the big boots and plumed hat?'

38

'That's Jeb Stuart. Lee's cavalry commander. Brilliant but unreliable. Had a habit of being where he wasn't meant to be. I have sort of a soft spot for Jeb.'

Jacobsen studied the portrait. In spite of the graininess of the print and the fuzziness caused by enlargement, the face that looked back at him across the intervening century or so seemed still very much alive. There was something about it, moreover, that reminded him strongly of Nolan. It wasn't the features, which in the portrait were largely obscured by a full beard and a magnificent set of whiskers, but something about the eyes. Their mild, direct, unsettling gaze suggested that their owner was perhaps not subject to the ordinary constraints on behaviour, or at least not to those of commonsense and caution. And that was the point of likeness, Jacobsen decided: Jeb Stuart and Nolan both had these don't-give-a-damn eyes.

He turned to Nolan. 'Tell me about this Anderson kid.'

'Robert? . . . I like him. He's smart. Brilliant, in fact. A bit snotty, perhaps. He's not at all one to suffer fools gladly. But then I,' Nolan said, 'am not about to fault him for that.' He paused. 'I hope you don't mind seeing him here, but the alternative is the admin office. When they're called in there it usually means trouble. Master Anderson, in my opinion, has enough of that already.'

'Understood.' Jacobsen nodded. 'But you don't have to worry. We gave up the thumbscrew a few years back.'

'Oh I didn't mean that exactly.' Nolan's grin acknowledged that it more or less was what he'd meant. 'Only right now he's inclined to hold himself about ninety-eight per cent responsible for what happened. "If we hadn't been partying, she'd still be alive." That sort of nonsense. I'd just as soon keep the guilt to a minimum.'

'I'm not planning to interrogate him,' Jacobsen said. 'Just ask a couple of questions. To satisfy my curiosity, mostly. Nothing more.'

This was intended to reassure, but the effect, Jacobsen saw, was the opposite. Nolan's eyes narrowed; his smile vanished.

'Perhaps you would explain that when he gets here,' Jacobsen added. 'He'll be more likely to accept it, coming from you.'

'Possibly . . .' Nolan shrugged. He left the sentence unfinished, but the meaning was plain from his manner: he wasn't about to lend his credit where he himself was unconvinced.

39

'Something bothering you?' Jacobsen asked. 'You don't like us questioning your students. Is that it?'

'Not exactly.'

Jacobsen waited for more, but Nolan didn't clarify.

'What is it then?'

'Robert's a minor,' Nolan said. 'And while I want him to help you in any way he can, I'd like to be sure his rights are protected. So when I hear you being . . . less than candid about your reasons for questioning him, it makes me uneasy. Do you see what I mean?'

'I'm not sure. Which of his rights are we talking about?'

'Self-incrimination,' Nolan said. 'In an effort to be helpful, he came to me and admitted breaking the law. In an effort to be helpful, I passed that information on. I assumed – and still do – that your interest was in Lisa. If I find you asking questions on other subjects, the acid, for instance, I shall tell him not to answer. And if you attempt to use any of my statements on the subject, I shall deny I ever made them.' He paused and looked Jacobsen straight in the eye. 'If necessary, I shall perjure myself blind.'

'It won't be necessary.' Jacobsen returned the gaze steadily. 'I don't give a damn about the acid. That's your problem and, frankly, you're welcome to it. All I care about is the girl's death. I need to clarify some things about the time and circumstances. Robert Anderson may be able to help. Is that candid enough for you?'

For a moment Nolan didn't speak. His reaction to the hostility in Jacobsen's voice was not an answering antagonism but instead a kind of intentness. It was as if now for the first time he were bringing his full attention, all his resources of intuition and intellect, to bear on the problem of Jacobsen's character. Again Jacobsen was reminded of the eyes in the portrait. Mild, inscrutable, uncomfortably direct, Nolan's stare weighed and assessed him. It made him feel painfully transparent.

'I guess that's candid enough,' Nolan said. 'I think it'll have to be, since it's clearly as candid as you're planning to get.'

7

Robert Anderson was a surprise. Jacobsen's encounter with the students in the quad had led him to expect, at the least, sartorial eccentricity, but the young man who presented himself in response to Nolan's summons looked almost normal. His dress – alligator shirt, corduroy shorts, and loafers – was respectable, if not conservative, and his haircut would have passed muster in any police department in the country. He had a hatchet face, very tanned, the beaked nose a shade prominent, the eyebrows arched in a way that made him look permanently quizzical, an effect enhanced by the satirical twist of his mouth. His air was aloof and self-possessed, but his eyes were quick and restless, never settling anywhere for long. He evidently had been warned about Jacobsen, for he showed no surprise at meeting a policeman in Nolan's drawing room. But his greeting, when Nolan made the introductions, was more polite than friendly, his look guarded and appraising.

'The lieutenant is investigating Lisa's death,' Nolan told him. 'I thought he ought to know about your party, so I told him what you told me.' He paused. 'All of it.'

Robert looked startled, but the glance he flicked at Nolan showed no resentment. He made no answer to what Nolan had said, but a muscle in his cheek worked involuntarily.

'So now he wants to ask you some questions. But it's my understanding he's not interested in the acid, except insofar as it bears on Lisa's death.' Nolan turned to Jacobsen. 'Am I right?'

Jacobsen nodded.

'And your answers are off the record.' Again Nolan turned to Jacobsen. 'Correct?'

'Correct.'

'All of which, however, doesn't mean you *have* to talk to him.' Nolan's voice was relaxed and friendly. 'I think you should. But if you'd rather not, you don't have to. Not now, anyway.'

Robert thought for a moment. He turned to Jacobsen.

'What did you want to know?'

This was a matter to which Jacobsen, prior to setting out, had devoted considerable thought. In fact there were just two questions he wanted Robert to answer, but simply asking them point-blank would reveal to anyone with any powers of deduction the trend of his thinking. Since this was something Plunkett had more or less forbidden him to reveal, and since Nolan's powers of deduction were clearly well-developed, he would need to dress things up a little. He therefore began by confirming with Robert the facts he'd already obtained from Nolan: that Robert and friend had gone up to the ledge at about 1:30 and stayed till about 4:00; that Lisa had joined them, uninvited, at around 2:30 and left half an hour later; that she'd claimed to be tripping on acid but was not, visibly, out of control; and that she'd departed not in the direction of campus but out along the ledge. Jacobsen attempted, in these preliminaries, to come across as conscientious but plodding, the rural flatfoot, gamely trying, but somewhat out of his depth. He felt he succeeded admirably – a success, he suspected, not altogether due to his talent as an actor.

'You've said that when she left you, she went out along the ledge.' His cover established, and his purposes, he hoped, sufficiently disguised, he started to edge towards his target. 'Didn't that strike you as odd?'

Robert shrugged. 'I didn't think about it much. I figured maybe she wanted to look at the stars. Or maybe she wasn't going back to campus. Not directly, that is.'

'Not going back? Where else might she have been going?'

'I don't know . . . maybe to meet someone.'

'To meet someone.' Jacobsen worked hard to keep the interest out of his voice. 'What makes you say that?'

Robert hesitated. For just a moment, Jacobsen thought, he looked uncomfortable. 'She looked at her watch. Then said she had to split . . . as if she were late for an appointment or something.'

'An appointment? Did she normally meet people off campus at 3:00 in the morning?'

'I really couldn't say. I didn't keep track of what she *normally* did.' A note of impatience entered Robert's voice. Jacobsen recalled what Nolan had said about his not suffering fools

42

gladly. His impression, though, was that Robert's present edginess was not entirely caused by the question's ineptitude.

'But you did raise the possibility. Can you think of anyone she might have been meeting?'

Robert shook his head. He held Jacobsen's gaze steadily, more steadily, Jacobsen noted, than he had so far held it.

'No one? You can't even hazard a guess?'

'No . . . look.' Robert gave him a cold stare. 'I don't know that she was meeting anyone, and I don't know where she was going. I didn't ask. She didn't say.' He brought out the last words one by one, articulating very clearly, as if speaking to someone who was hard of hearing.

'What *did* she say?'

'She said . . .' Robert faltered, self-possession crumbling. He became, Jacobsen thought, what his earlier manner had made it easy to forget he really was – a teenager beset by guilt and grief.

'What did she say?' Jacobsen repeated gently.

'She said . . .' Robert closed his eyes, as if he wanted to shut out the memory. 'She said we should remember rule number one.'

'Rule number one?'

'It was a joke we had, about tripping. Rule number one: you cannot fly.' Robert's voice was bleak with misery. 'I shouldn't have let her go. I didn't think at the time, but I should have. And now, because I didn't, she's dead.'

'That's nonsense, Robert.' Nolan shot an admonitory glance at Jacobsen. 'You thought she was OK, and she probably was. It's not at all clear that the acid was even a factor. You couldn't possibly have predicted what would happen. It makes no sense to hold yourself responsible.'

'It makes no sense logically.' Robert shrugged. 'But that doesn't change how I feel.' He turned to Jacobsen. 'Was there anything else?'

Jacobsen felt a twinge of compunction. Let's try to keep the guilt to a minimum, Nolan had said, and now here was this kid, thanks to him, awash in it. He didn't let himself feel too sorry, however. This kid might feel bad, but another kid had died, and he, Jacobsen, had a job to do.

'Yes,' he said. 'Just a couple more questions. After she left, you and the other person heard nothing?'

43

Robert shook his head.

'But then I guess you were making a bit of noise yourselves?'

Robert thought. 'Not really. We were talking, but not being rowdy.'

'Then you'd have heard, you think, if she'd cried out?'

Robert nodded. 'That's what puzzles me. We could hear coyotes down in the valley. Why didn't we hear her?'

Good question, Jacobsen thought. What Robert had told him, taken together with the broken wristwatch, put the time of her death, almost certainly, at a few minutes after three. This meant she had fallen without making a sound. And this was odd, because whether she had slipped or been pushed he'd have expected her to utter some kind of involuntary cry . . . But she might not have, he thought, if she'd been hit on the head when she was pushed. The autopsy, of course, had turned up no evidence of blows to the head; it had simply found injuries 'generally consistent' with her having fallen. This phrase, especially now, aroused Jacobsen's suspicions. It was typically Fogarty, characteristically vague. What it probably meant was that Fogarty, assuming the obvious, hadn't bothered to look any farther. He could be asked to, Jacobsen supposed, but he'd probably refuse unless the request came from Plunkett. And Jacobsen couldn't see Plunkett making that request. At any rate, not just on the strength of the tracks.

'Now suppose she hadn't fallen,' he resumed. 'Suppose, for the sake of argument, she'd circled the butte and gone back down the way she came. She'd have passed quite close to you in that case. Would you have heard her, d'you think?'

'I don't know.' Robert, Jacobsen was pleased to note, looked mystified by the question. 'Depends on how much noise she was making. But unless she'd knocked down some rocks or something, I don't think we'd have heard her.' He paused. 'But of course that's all hypothetical. I don't really know what we would have heard. All I know is what we did hear.'

'And what was that?'

'Nothing.' Robert's face was expressionless. 'Nothing like that at all.'

Jacobsen received this without comment. He sighed and leaned back in his chair, his manner suggesting he had learned nothing useful, that the interview, in fact, had been a chore he was glad to have out of the way.

'Then I guess that's it,' he said. 'I appreciate your help. It took guts to come forward the way you did – more guts than your buddy seems to have had.'

Robert stared at him.

'My buddy' – there were ironic quotation marks round the phrase – 'would have come forward. I just happened to call it wrong.'

'Call it wrong?' Nolan looked totally incredulous. 'You mean you *flipped* for who would come forward?'

Robert nodded. 'We knew somebody would have to. But there seemed no point in both of us taking the grief. So we flipped.' He smiled faintly. 'And here I am . . . Was there anything else?'

Nolan glanced at Jacobsen. Jacobsen thought for a moment. Ordinarily he might have insisted that Robert's friend be identified and asked for his version of events. It was not that he thought Robert had lied or concealed anything – or at least not anything much – just that two recollections were usually better than one. But in this case insisting would involve him in explanations. And explanations were what Plunkett had told him to avoid. He shook his head.

'Nothing else,' Nolan told Robert. 'Unless you need reminding you owe me a term paper outline.'

'I'm working on it.' Robert smiled. When dealing with Nolan, Jacobsen observed, Robert became a different person, relaxed and far less prickly. 'I'm thinking of chronicling the founding of Fremont, using interviews and original documents. Make an interesting case study, don't you think? A miniature US of A.'

'A miniature US of A?' Nolan raised an eyebrow. 'OK, Robert, I'll bite. Why like the US of A?'

'Such high ideals setting out . . .' Robert paused, gave a lopsided grin. 'And now look at it.'

On that note he left.

'Smart kid,' Jacobsen said.

'Nice, too.' Nolan nodded. 'You didn't see him at his best. He was scared and trying not to show it. It made him come across a bit hard.' He gazed at Jacobsen with undisguised speculation. Since Robert had left his manner had noticeably changed; it was serious, even grim.

I didn't fool him, Jacobsen thought. Robert, maybe, but not him.

'I'm not convinced he told everything, however.'

'About whom she might have been meeting? . . . I noticed that, too. I sensed he could have hazarded a guess, but didn't want to.' Nolan paused. 'I guess he was protecting someone.'

'Who?'

Nolan thought for a moment. Not about what to answer – at least this was Jacobsen's impression – but whether.

'I don't know . . . a boyfriend, perhaps. Maybe someone from town.'

'Why from town?'

'Had it been someone from here, I doubt they'd have bothered to go off campus to meet.' Nolan paused. 'May I ask you something?'

'What?' Jacobsen was wary.

'What was all that with Robert about?'

'That?' Even to Jacobsen's ears, it sounded lame.

'Yes,' Nolan said. 'That. It was either the most inept piece of questioning I ever heard, or it was some kind of smoke screen. Now, I don't know you very well, but at a guess I'd say the one thing you aren't is inept. That leaves me with the smoke screen.'

'Smoke screen . . .' Jacobsen pretended to ponder the notion. 'What would I be concealing, according to you?'

Nolan looked at him for a moment, then he smiled. It was not an altogether friendly smile, more the smile of someone about to trip you up. There was, it struck Jacobsen, more than a touch of the smartass about Nolan.

'"Suppose she hadn't fallen . . ."' Nolan was quoting. Jacobsen recognized the words as his own. '"Suppose, for the sake of argument, that she'd circled the butte and gone back down the way she came." But she didn't, did she?' Nolan paused. 'So why, I ask myself, would you want to suppose it?'

'And what's your answer?' Jacobsen kept his face blank. 'It's a thing I've noticed about teachers. They always have the answers to their own questions.'

'Haven't they, though?' Nolan agreed. He paused. 'What you

46

were really asking was would they have heard something had *anyone* circled the butte. You think there was someone else up there.'

Silence.

'At this point I'd rather not speculate.' Lacking anything better, Jacobsen took refuge in his official manner.

'You don't have to,' Nolan said. 'It's obvious to me she didn't jump. And obvious you don't believe she slipped. That leaves us one alternative. Murder.'

Silence.

'We have to consider all possibilities,' Jacobsen said, heavily. 'We'd be irresponsible not to. But we'd also be irresponsible to air premature speculations.'

'I see that.' Nolan paused. 'But then you need to know about the truck.'

'The truck?'

'The strange truck seen on campus night before last. It was the early hours of the morning, actually, about the time Robert and his friend were having their party. A faculty member coming back late from town saw the truck in one of the washes. He didn't think much about it at the time, but later, when he heard about Lisa, he remembered and told Sinclair.'

'What kind of truck?'

'Grey pickup. Fairly ancient. A Ford, he thinks, but he's not sure.'

'Licence plate number?'

Nolan shook his head. 'He didn't think of getting it. It could just be coincidence, of course, that it was parked where it was on that particular night. Only the thing is if you follow that wash to its origin, you end up very close to the northern end of the butte from which she fell.'

Silence.

'Which is another reason why I thought that if she had been meeting someone, it might have been someone from off campus,' Nolan continued. 'When I realized where your questions were heading, I immediately thought of that truck.'

Silence.

'Which wash was that?' Jacobsen asked.

'It crosses the driveway just after the cattle guard as you come here from town,' Nolan said. 'I could have someone show you, if you like.'

His helpfulness struck Jacobsen as slightly intrusive. Why the probing? he wondered. Why the concern about what the police were thinking? It was a little baffling. Such answers as suggested themselves suggested also that it might be wise here to play his cards close to the chest. Though the truck interested him very much and the wash would obviously have to be checked for tracks, he declined Nolan's offer. He would check this out in his own time and his own way, not under the curious eye of some emissary of Dr Philip Nolan.

He just hoped to hell it wouldn't rain.

8

The conversation with Jacobsen left Nolan in a moral dilemma: whether or not to tell Sinclair? On the one hand he'd given Jacobsen a tacit promise to be discreet – a promise Jacobsen, almost certainly, would take as an absolute vow of silence. On the other hand it was clear that, if Lisa had been murdered, the involvement of a person, or persons, connected with Fremont was not only possible but likely; Sinclair, therefore, had a clear right to be told. But had Lisa been murdered? Jacobsen, evidently, was a long way from being sure; suspicions could turn out to be unfounded. This being so, it seemed to Nolan, to tell Sinclair now might merely be to add, quite gratuitously, to a cup of sorrows already overflowing. And even if Jacobsen proved in the end to be right, it was not at all clear what purpose would have been served by involving Sinclair. After some internal debate Nolan decided, for the time being, not to involve him.

About his own involvement there was never any question. Character, as someone once said, is destiny, and curiosity – the historian's consuming need to know what happened and why – was the keynote of Nolan's character. Lisa's death and the suggestion that someone had deliberately caused it shocked and saddened him, but more than anything they confronted him with a mystery. Who could have wanted Lisa dead? What possible motive for her murder could take root and flourish in a setting as sheltered as Fremont's? The answers, he decided, must lie in the circumstances of her life. Perhaps the setting was less sheltered than it looked. If so, he was better placed to investigate than anyone, including the police. He had the run of the place, a lot of local knowledge, and the trust, more or less, of the students. He would need to start, he decided, by finding out more about Lisa.

The person to help him with that was Diana Pritchett.

'Don't look so bummed.' Diana opened Lisa's door, peering into the gloom beyond. 'It won't be that bad. This is less of a pigsty than some I could show you.'

Diana was Lisa's dorm head and therefore responsible for cleaning out Lisa's room and packing up her belongings. If Nolan's offer of help had struck her as out of character, she had nevertheless accepted with alacrity. They'd become friends almost from the moment of his arrival at Fremont, and she had intimated, on occasion, a willingness to be more. At another time he might have been tempted. She was attractive – tall, athletic, with very blue eyes and very dark hair – and more important, he liked her. He suspected, however, since her temperament was volatile, that an affair with her would be stormy and ultimately destructive of their friendship. Having recently escaped from a stormy marriage – ten years of unremitting psychological warfare that had produced no winners, only casualties – he was ready, he felt, for something calmer.

He looked around. Presumably Diana had been speaking from memory, for he couldn't actually see very much – not enough, certainly, to judge how much of a mess they would have to deal with. Both windows were covered with some heavy fabric that excluded the daylight entirely. Illumination was provided only by a reading lamp on the bedside table, and it was obscured by tapestries suspended from the ceiling, one screening the doorway, others the bed. The room was thus sunk in a subterranean gloom. His impression, due in part to the darkness and in part to the spooky, cobweb effect of the hangings, was not of a pigsty but of the den of some nocturnal animal.

With the removal of the window screens, however, the place lost some of its mystery, revealing itself as the room of a moderately tidy but not otherwise unrepresentative Fremont student. Against one wall was an unmade bed, queen-sized, with matching sheets and pillow cases. Above it, an early poster of Jim Morrison, beardless and stripped to the waist, his face sullen and anguished, like a fallen angel's. Along the far wall stood a medium-sized refrigerator and a pair of enormous speakers. But this was all standard, minimum equipment for life as an average upper-middle-class American teenager. What was lacking, it struck Nolan, was anything *un*standard, any signs of taste distinctively Lisa's. Some Levi's and a shirt, sloughed off and abandoned where they lay, were sad reminders that the room had been lived in and very recently, but they offered no clue to the character of the tenant. Even the screens and hangings, he suspected, had served mostly to cover a withdrawal – school rules prohibited the locking of doors from the inside, so Lisa had simply made the room dark enough to protect her from any but the most determined intrusions. It was a common solution to the privacy problem – the soft furnishings store in Buckskin did a roaring trade in cotton tapestries – but Lisa was unusual in the lengths to which she had gone, and the fact that *her* innermost sanctum wasn't the bed but instead the writing desk tucked beyond it in the darkest corner of the room.

It was her own desk, he noticed, not the standard steel and Formica model issued by the school, but something less stark and functional, in oak, with a set of drawers on the left and an architect's lamp clamped to the work surface. Flanking it, screening the desk from the rest of the room and forming with the walls a kind of open-ended cubicle, was a book case made from planks and concrete building blocks. On the upper shelves were a turntable and amplifier, a sizable collection of records, and a few books, mostly textbooks. The lower shelves were bare.

The arrangement created a sanctum within a sanctum, a hideaway both private and decidedly businesslike. And businesslike, Nolan thought, was not at all what he'd have expected from Lisa. She'd been a perfunctory student, capable enough, but doing no more than she had to and not wavering much in her belief that schoolwork was an arbitrary and tedious exercise, devised by the old for the torment of the young. It was all the more curious, therefore, to find her work space so carefully protected and located, almost literally, at the centre of her life. He was reminded, once more, of how little he had known her. But then no one, he suspected, had known her well.

And that in itself was a challenge.

'I'd rather not deal with underwear,' he told Diana. 'You pack the clothes. I'll do the rest of the stuff – the books and papers.'

He started with the records and, against his expectations, found something almost at once – a loose sheet of paper sandwiched between albums, on which was a drawing of a naked woman, full-frontal view, with handwritten comments connected by arrows to various parts of the body. At a glance it seemed to belong with the graffiti normally to be found on the walls of public restrooms, but a closer look revealed that the intention here had not been pornographic. The arrows didn't point to the woman's sexual parts, and the drawing was titled, intriguingly, 'A Map of My Scars.' It bore, as a kind of epigraph, a couplet:

These, the scars that mark my hide,
Are not as deep as those inside.

The handwritten notes, he found, were each a description of some physical injury or other. The tone was jaunty, as if the bearer of these scars had been proud, both of them and the life that had led to their acquisition. An arrow pointing to the right upper arm, for instance, bore the comment: *'Flesh wound 1974. Clark practising his knife throwing. He needed to. Twelve stitches.'* Another, going to a shaded area on the left calf, read: *Second degree burns. 1976. Otis – who else? – wiped out at Greaves Corner on the Honda, me on the pillion. Hurt like a bitch.'* Most of the notes were like that: good-humoured commentary on the physical mementos of a life that had been active, sociable, and not, by the sound of it, notably law-abiding. Only once was a bitter note sounded, in a gloss on some unspecified injury to the right

51

ankle: *'This one I owe to dear old Dad. Some day I'm going to murder the son of a bitch.'*

The whole thing, Nolan was quick to note, was at odds with his previous 'Alice in Wonderland' image of Lisa. Despite the epigraph's allusion to inner scars, the personality that emerged from the comments was humorous and tough-minded, fully able, it seemed, to cope with whatever came along. Then why the obsession with privacy? he wondered.

'Look at this – ' He held up the drawing for Diana.

She was sorting clothes as a preliminary to packing, and doing it, he noted, with her habitual thoroughness. She had removed the drawers from the bureau and was picking through the jumble left by Lisa, separating clean clothes from dirty and placing the former in neat piles on the bed. She'd probably launder the dirty clothes, he thought. He would have left them for the parents.

She glanced at the drawing, smiled, nodded, and went back to sorting.

'Take a look,' he insisted. 'Read the notes. It's not what you think. Not porn. It's a kind of pictorial autobiography, a "Map of Scars," she calls it. Each one has a history. Just reading this gives a good idea of what she was like.'

'I know,' Diana said. 'I've read it.'

'You?' He was stunned. 'When?'

'She drew that for me. As an assignment, actually, in one of my classes.'

'You have them draw in your classes? Graphics instead of grammar? No wonder the test scores are plummeting.'

She rolled her eyes. 'You are a pain when you want to be, Philip. I sometimes wonder why I like you.'

'I keep you on your toes.' He grinned. 'I improve you. But seriously, why have them draw in an English class?'

'Are you interested? Or just setting me up for some smartass remark?'

'Interested.' He really was. Though interest, he felt, didn't preclude the other.

'OK then . . . They draw to help them remember.'

'Remember? Remember what?'

'It's like this. What scares them about writing is they think they have nothing to say. If you get them remembering, recalling their lives – where they got their scars, for instance – and in a way that doesn't seem like writing, then they find they have plenty to say. Pretty soon they want to say it, and you're off and running. They've a reason to learn grammar and the rest of that good stuff. At least,' she smiled, 'that's the theory.'

'But does it work?' he asked. 'I mean, how do you get them from the drawing stage to papers and stories? The moment they have to actually write something, doesn't the old block return?'

'They don't make the jump that abruptly. They need a bridge. That's where the journals come in.'

Later, Nolan would sometimes think that had he known then where the conversation might lead him, he'd have dropped the whole thing, left Diana to her task, and put all the distance he could between himself and everything connected with Lisa. At the time, however, he felt only a sudden quickening of interest.

'Journals? You had them keep journals?'

'Yes. Someplace they can write and not worry about grammar because, unless they choose otherwise, no one but them will read what they've written. It's to encourage them to delve into their lives, to get them comfortable with the notion of writing and give them things to write about when the time comes for a more formal assignment.'

'Was it mandatory? Did they all keep journals?'

'Oh sure. I'm not completely permissive. I didn't read them unless they wanted me to, but I checked regularly to make sure they were actually writing.'

'So Lisa would have kept one?'

Diana nodded. 'Not that she needed to. She wrote well without it. But she took to it like a duck to water. Never shared it, of course, but wrote reams . . . I've often wondered what about.'

Nolan wondered too. Lisa's journal might shed light on her life, and that in turn might shed light on her death. And that, after all, was what he was there for.

The place to start looking, obviously, was the desk.

The desk drawers were locked. It was Diana who thought to look under the desk. And the key was there, taped to the underside of the work surface. Next to it, and held in place the same way, was a thick envelope of money, bills of various denominations, and a handful of loose change. The amount was more than two hundred dollars. Even by Fremont's standards this was a lot of money for a student to have, and the hiding place, though in keeping perhaps with Lisa's secretive nature, struck Nolan and Diana as odd if not suspicious. The discovery made Nolan more determined than ever to find the journal.

It was in one of the drawers, an ordinary exercise book, spiral bound, its covers decorated in black ballpoint with borders of highly stylized rambler roses. The front cover bore no name, but inside, in large black capitals, was a message:

THIS IS A PRIVATE JOURNAL. WHEN YOU READ IT, CONSIDER WHAT THAT SAYS ABOUT YOU.

For a moment he felt like a grave robber, disturbing the peace of the dead. The message, like a curse inscribed on the entrance of a tomb, forced him to confront his own motives, to acknowledge how much – his claims to serious purpose notwithstanding – it was simply nosiness that drove him. But there was a serious purpose, he told himself, and the fact that his motives were far from pure did not make it any less serious. Lisa had died mysteriously; the diary might clear up the mystery; and so whether or not he enjoyed the reading, it clearly ought to be read. And he was not going to waste time, he told himself, feeling guilty for not feeling guilty.

The text was separated by cardboard dividers into sections entitled: 'Thoughts', 'Feelings', and 'Transactions'. The plan suggested by this division, however, seemed not to have been consistently followed. The entries in all the sections consisted of more or less unconnected jottings, some no more than a line or two, others filling pages, whose organization, if any, was chronological. On a page taken at random he found, for instance, the following:

54

There is infinite hope, but not for us. (Kafka)

CD 750 × 350 = 1050

Creeked it pm with the Bronc. A there, wouldn't skinnydip, seemed bummed by display of female f, got an eyeful. At last said, 'Bronco, tell your slut to get dressed.' Gay or sexless? I wonder. Either way gives me the creeps. I hate it that B seems to treat him like some sort of guru.

Mannequin – mannikin – miniman? Check.

A perfect egg what the old geek said about foxes.

Told B most beautiful man in world was Bowie because not hung up about manhood. B said, 'Hung up? Of course not. Bet he's not even hung.' Typical. Mamas don't let yr babies grow up to be cowboys . . .

Other pages contained a similar mix of anecdote, quotation, and narrative. There were also several poems and fragments of poems, apparently written by Lisa. Apart from the quotations, which were generally given in full and attributed, the entries were cryptic, sparsely punctuated, and full of contractions and abbreviations. The spelling, however, was mostly correct, and if one understood the allusions – there were many that Nolan, at first glance, didn't – the writing was seldom incoherent. It was almost as if Lisa, not trusting to the warning on the front cover, had devised a shorthand to baffle the obstinately curious, but hadn't always bothered to use it. Nolan felt sure that in time he would be able to decipher most of it. The only parts he felt doubtful about were the odd pieces of arithmetic that cropped up on every page – odd because the calculations seemed invariably to make errors too gross to be merely careless – and three pages or so towards the end of the notebook. These pages, in particular, fascinated Nolan. They were covered entirely by groups of numbers, irregular in length and separated by spaces, a format that reminded Nolan irresistibly of cipher. If this was cipher, he thought, the encrypting must have taken Lisa hours. This argued, surely, that here at least was one secret she'd been truly determined to keep. And that was exactly the kind of secret he was looking for.

'I'm borrowing this,' he told Diana. 'I bet I can learn more about her from this than anyone learned the whole time she was here.'

'Very likely.' she stared. 'But does that mean you should?'

He shrugged. 'It can't hurt her now. And who knows? It may even shed light on her death.'

'Light?' She looked startled. 'I thought her death was an accident.'

'Maybe not. It seems they haven't ruled out suicide.'

'Then give it to the police. If there's light to be shed, shouldn't they do the shedding?'

'Well, theoretically, I suppose. Only this could shed light on more than it should. About the school, I mean. I'd like to know what I was giving the police before I went ahead and gave it.'

Silence.

'You sound reasonable.' Diana eyed him sceptically. 'But then you always sound reasonable. But since when, Dr Nolan-on-sabbatical-from-Harvard-and-gracing-us-so-briefly-with-your-presence, have you been so concerned with the interests of Fremont? I don't believe you give a hoot about Fremont. I think what you mostly are is nosey.'

He shrugged. Nosey was right too, of course. But at least it had the merit, as an explanation of his interest in the journal, that it covered convincingly for the real interest.

'Philip . . .'

Nolan looked up from the desk where he'd been poring over the journal. Diana had finished with the clothes and had started cleaning out the refrigerator. She sounded worried.

'Come here a moment. There's something I want you to see.'

He went over. She held out for his inspection a sheet of coarse brown paper. It was perforated into tiny squares, each about a quarter of the size of a postage stamp.

Acid.

'It was under the ice tray,' she said. 'In an envelope wrapped in a sandwich baggie. To keep it fresh, I guess.' She unfolded the sheet and counted the lines of perforation along each edge. 'Eighty-four.' Her voice rose in incredulity. 'Eighty-four hits of LSD. That explains where that money came from.'

Nolan thought. Something he had noticed in the journal now started to make sense to him.

'You're probably right.' He nodded. 'She was dealing, I

56

wouldn't mind betting. And if she was dealing acid, I wonder what else she was dealing.'

'What else?' She stared.

He went back to the desk and got the journal. 'There's a poem in here. It's dedicated to someone called Bronco who seems to have been her boyfriend. At least, he figures prominently in the rest of the journal. It's called "The Dream Horse." Listen.

'You need more space
than this straitjacket, Here-and-Now, will give you;
to ride the high country
and camp out nights
in the pines on the rim;
to listen at your campfire
to the orchestra of silence
and hear in your heart
the song of the wind.
It isn't easy;
the undertakers and mortgage people
have cut down the trees and made them into boxes
of one kind or another;
the forest has signs saying "keep off the grass";
the cities are full of dead people,
lined up to buy postcards of tomorrow.
(They don't want to know about now.
Can you blame them?)

There's still a place where your pickup won't take you,
where your footprint in the snow
can be the first and only.
But to get there you need
The Dream Horse.
But look out, Lone Ranger,
this horse is headstrong.
His stride is stronger than silver stallion's.
The ride will take your breath away.
And one of these days when he takes you dream riding
he won't bring you back.'

He looked up at her. 'What do you make of it?'

'It's hers,' Diana said. 'She read her poems in class, sometimes. I recognize the style. When you read that just now I could almost hear her voice.'

She turned away for a while to gaze out of the window. When she turned back her eyes were full of tears.

'It's so hard to believe she's dead. To accept such . . . waste. I don't want her to just vanish and leave so little behind.' Her gaze wandered over the room. 'A couple of suitcases and a handful of poems.'

'But this poem,' Nolan said, 'what's it about, exactly?'

'Drugs.' She said sadly, 'Isn't that what they always write about? Sometimes I wonder if they think about anything else. There's this cowboy friend of hers, obviously, who takes drugs and she's scared for him . . . That's what it's saying.'

'She's scared because of this drug,' he agreed. 'But what drug exactly?'

'Who knows? . . . Some mind-blower. Acid maybe.'

'I don't think so. She took acid herself; to her it was no big deal. This was different, though. This scared her.'

She looked blank.

'Horse,' he prompted. 'The Dream Horse. What drug did they use to call horse?'

She thought a moment.

'Oh Christ . . .' Her eyes widened in dismay. 'Heroin.'

9

One of the hazards of a life spent dealing with adolescents, Nolan had often thought, was that it could leave you unfit for dealing with anyone else. The danger, greatest in boarding schools like Fremont where there was little relief from the company of students, was not so much one of reverting to childhood, though he had seen that happen to a couple of his colleagues, as of going too far in the other direction – regarding the world as a bunch of untrustworthy children with oneself as the sole, beleaguered adult. This was a tendency that surfaced occasionally in Sinclair. It was surfacing, Nolan observed, this afternoon.

'Heroin?' Sinclair's tone suggested that somebody, probably Nolan, had exceeded the bounds of good taste. 'You're telling me there's heroin on campus?'

'It seems so,' Nolan said. 'At least it's a reasonable inference from the facts.'

'Then perhaps you'd better give me the facts.' Sinclair's tone remained starchy. If there were any inferring to be done, he implied, it was his job, not Nolan's, to do it. Not that you could blame him, Nolan thought. In the last thirty-six hours the man had received a lifetime's supply of bad news; you could hardly blame him for bucking the latest delivery.

'I think Lisa was dealing drugs. We found more than two hundred dollars hidden in her room, and more acid than she can possibly have wanted for herself. We also found . . .' Nolan fished in his pocket to extract two letter-sized envelopes, each folded several times to form a small packet, 'these.'

'What are they?' Sinclair made no move to pick them up. From his expression you might have thought they were toads.

'Cocaine and heroin, I think. Though, to be honest, that's an inference too. What I know is they contain white powder, and they were both taped to the underside of the toilet tank lid in Lisa's bathroom.'

'Under the toilet tank lid?' Sinclair permitted himself, for a moment, the distraction of idle curiosity. 'Whatever made you think of looking there?'

'It was Diana's idea,' Nolan said. 'When we stumbled across the acid, we figured a thorough search was called for, to find out what else she'd been hiding. The tank lid was just someplace Diana knew to look. Those packets contain drugs, of course. No reason for hiding them, otherwise.'

'Drugs of some description.' Sinclair nodded. 'But why heroin and cocaine? Surely there are other drugs that come in the form of white powder?'

'Lots, I imagine. But those are the most common. And if you'll open those packets, you'll see that on the back of one there's a drawing. It was put there for identification, I think, to indicate what kind of drug it contains.'

Sinclair examined the envelopes.

'A horse? What's the significance of that?'

Nolan told him about the journal and Lisa's poem. When he'd finished, Sinclair sat for a moment not speaking, head tilted back, eyes cast upwards, fingertips pressed together and supporting his chin. He looked as if he were praying.

At last he sighed. 'You're probably right. It probably is heroin. In fact' – bleak smile – 'the way our luck's been running recently, how could it be anything else? . . . You haven't mentioned this to anybody, have you?'

'No.'

'And Diana knows to be discreet?'

'I'm sure she does.'

'Good . . .' Sinclair relaxed a little. 'The question now is what do we do about this?'

'Do? You mean do we tell the police?'

Sinclair nodded. 'What do you think?'

Nolan considered. 'I don't see that we have to.'

'That's interesting.' Sinclair tilted his head to one side. 'In the case of acid you leaned strongly the other way. Why the change of heart?'

'Not a change of heart, it's a change of circumstance. She was on acid at the time of her death; there seemed a good chance that the acid was a factor. We've no reason to believe, though, that the heroin and her dealing – if she was dealing – are in any way connected with her death.' At least, Nolan thought, *you* have no reason to believe it. 'I don't see why we have to tell the police every bit of dirt we happen to dig up about her, just on the off chance that it may be relevant.'

Sinclair gazed at him for a moment. 'What is it you teach at Harvard . . . moral philosphy?'

'History . . . Why?'

'You sound like a Jesuit.'

Nolan smiled. 'I was trying to sound like a headmaster.'

Sinclair ignored this. 'What you're saying, then, is you don't think we need tell them about the heroin until we find out whether it's relevant.'

'We?' Nolan didn't like the sound of this. 'You mean you're planning to investigate?'

'Obviously. From what you've told me, there are lethal drugs on this campus. I have to investigate. I'd be culpably negligent

60

not to.' Sinclair paused. 'I'd like to think I could count on your help.'

'Mine?' Nolan shrugged. 'I guess I can probably decipher most of the journal fairly quickly. That will probably tell us something.'

'That would be very helpful, of course.' Sinclair sounded dubious. 'But I think we may need to look further.'

Nolan could sense what was coming. He said nothing.

'It's not only a question of Lisa's death,' Sinclair said, 'but of whether and how much she was dealing. To what extent, in other words, there's a problem with hard drugs on this campus. For the health of Fremont, I need to find out. If possible,' he paused and let his gaze rest on Nolan, 'without having to go to the police.'

'Sounds like a job for the dean of students.'

Sinclair shook his head. 'Peterson has admirable qualities, but he's too much identified in students' minds with discipline and punishment. We need someone who isn't . . . I was thinking of you.'

Nolan was silent. The journal was something he wanted to do, the kind of puzzle that intrigued him. But this? . . . He'd come to Fremont to teach history, to climb, to goof off mostly, if the truth were known. He hadn't come to play secret policeman.

'I'll be candid with you,' Sinclair went on. 'I know you don't owe us anything. The deal was you'd teach history, and you've done it admirably. But you realize your position here is special. The students don't see you as a "schoolteacher", so they talk to you more freely. That puts you in a much better position than the rest of us to find out what's been going on. And something definitely has been going on.' He paused. 'I can't expect you to do this for us, but I can ask. And that's what I'm doing – asking.'

Crafty bastard, Nolan thought. Aloud he said: 'My father always told me, when someone said he was going to be candid, to hang on to my wallet.'

Sinclair smiled faintly. 'I'd like us to be clear about one other thing. I'm not looking for names; I'm not interested in punishing people. What I want to know is how much of a problem we

61

have with hard drugs.' He paused. 'The students like you. It's obvious you like them. So I'm asking. Will you do this for us?'

Moral blackmail, Nolan thought; and in its most elementary form. So crass that even his mother would have scorned it. But then, in spite of his disingenuous assertions to the contrary, he believed the drugs and the death of Lisa probably were connected. So what Sinclair was asking was little more than he himself had already decided to do. Sinclair, actually, was giving him a mandate.

'Put it that way,' he said, 'how can I refuse?'

10

About once a day since his arrival at Fremont, Nolan had found himself envying the English, whose homes were their castles. The same claim, he felt, could hardly be made by the average boarding-school teacher, whose home, depending on the current requirements of his charges, could be social club, soup kitchen, counselling centre, or call box. On a bad day it could be all four together. Which made today only a moderately bad day, he supposed, since to judge from the situation that greeted him on his return from school after lunch, his home was serving only two of the possible functions.

He smelled coffee brewing as soon as he opened the front door. Almost at the same moment he registered the familiar female voice, evidently solo, in the study. 'This is a collect call, operator. Person to person to Mrs Delafield from her daughter.'

Christie.

She was perched in an easy chair next to his desk, her legs tucked under her, the receiver wedged between shoulder and chin. In one hand she held a cigarette, with the other she flipped through a magazine – *Vogue*, by the look of it. She was dressed, for her, conservatively: Levi's, cowboy boots, a man's white shirt, and a man's suit jacket, ancient and funereal, which she wore with the collar turned up. Matching the jacket was an equally funereal tie, knotted loosely so that the collar and top buttons of the shirt could be left undone. The total effect was at the same time scruffy and oddly elegant. The masculine and cast-off character of the garments emphasized, by contrast, the femininity and freshness of the wearer, drew attention to the energy and humour in her greenish blue eyes, the cat's grace of her small, slender body.

She looked up as he entered, smiled dazzlingly, and blew him a kiss.

'Christie – What the hell are *you* doing here?'

She waved him to silence. 'Mother? Look, I have this minor emergency. I need three hundred dollars.'

Pause.

'What kind of emergency? Well, let me put it this way. How do you feel about becoming a granny?'

Pause.

Nolan, conscious that a certain sardonic emphasis had been laid on the word granny, tried to visualize the reaction of Abigail Delafield, reluctant parent and fading society beauty, to this latest act of guerilla warfare by her daughter. Christie was not pregnant; of that he was sure. Had she been, she would never have gone for help to her mother. The real purpose of the call, he guessed, was simply to jolt. For after three marriages, dozens of lovers, and thousands of dry martinis – after eighteen years, in fact, of absentee parenthood – the bond between Abby Delafield and her daughter, though stronger than cables, was more like that which linked members of a chain gang than anything contemplated by Dr Spock. And Christie, reacting with wit and spirit to a situation that normally provoked only sullen delinquency, was conducting the relationship as a series of hit-and-run raids to remind her mother, uncomfortably, of her existence. The success of this latest one, Nolan expected, would depend on whether and to what extent Abby Delafield was drunk.

'What do I need the money for? Jesus, mother, what do you think I need it for? Baby clothes? . . . Look, I know you have moral objections to abortion, but what am I supposed to do? Have the little bastard and put it up for adoption?'

Protracted pause. Strong emotion, evidently, was receiving expression at the other end of the line. Christie held the receiver away from her ear and took the opportunity to blow another kiss at Nolan.

'You don't believe me? You think I want it for drugs? OK, mother, have it your way. Only don't blame me when you're canned from the Junior League because your illegitimate grandchild is a darkie.'

She hung up and turned to Nolan.

'Good try, no points. Must be one of her days for making sense. Just my luck to catch her sober.'

'Tough . . .' He couldn't summon much sympathy. Whatever Christie lacked, it wasn't money. 'At least she paid for the call. And at least you got to make it in comfort . . . courtesy of the house. Think nothing of it.'

'You mind?' Her face fell. In her voice, beneath the wail of almost theatrical embarrassment, there were undertones of genuine dismay. 'I was sure you wouldn't. I was going to ask, really I was, but you didn't come back soon enough and I needed to catch her before she took off for Southampton. The phones at the dorms are just so *public*.'

He wondered why he had even mentioned it. The truth was he didn't mind but felt that maybe he should. Or at least that, in deference to conventional wisdom regarding teacher-student relationships, he should fake it. Yet if he were honest, he had to admit that being her teacher had little to do with the matter. She didn't in general presume, and certainly not in a way that could cause him embarrassment in the classroom. In public, indeed, she was a model of tact, neither trading upon, nor even alluding to, a relationship that had started, in some sense, before she was born and which made them virtually family. It was not much a matter of blood, though his being her father's cousin made him, he supposed, some kind of distant uncle, but of long and comfortable familiarity. He had been an usher at her parents' marriage, sent flowers to the maternity wing of New York Hospital and been named in due course a godfather. In time Abigail, who'd believed in delegating as many as possible of the duties of motherhood and would have delegated them all, no doubt, had nature so permitted, had delegated Nolan to become, in the house on Eighty-third Street, the official teller of bedtime stories and the organizer of skating expeditions to the rink at Rockefeller Plaza and trips to feed the sea lions at the Central Park Zoo. Later there'd been movies and visits to Lincoln Center, matinées preceded by lunch at the

64

Harvard Club. He'd been, among other things, Christie's first ski instructor, her backgammon teacher, her initiator into the mysteries of five card stud. All of which, he felt, entitled her to a fair amount of presumption, and that certainly included the occasional use of his phone. Besides, he enjoyed her invasions of his house, her cheerfully disruptive presence in his life. In a way she was like a surrogate daughter. And since, to help fill the emptiness that had entered his life since the breakup of his marriage, some kind of family was what he obviously needed, it puzzled him that his instinct, these days, was to keep his distance.

'I'm sorry, Philip.'

'No biggie.' Whatever his instinct, he could never resist her contrition. 'God forbid your efforts to get money by false pretences should have to be made in public. Those were false pretences, I take it?'

Silence. Her eyes rested on him speculatively.

'Worried you, did I? Thought I'd been whoring? Well, it's OK, old turtleman, you can relax. My heart's still pure, and it still belongs to Nolan.'

It was her usual flirting. Yet the words cost him a sudden pang – a whisper of jealousy, instantly stifled, and an answering whisper of guilt. For there would be, sooner or later, some boy or other. And he, her almost-but-not-quite uncle, who could almost but not quite have been her father, had no business at all feeling jealous. But then such a feeling was natural – wasn't it? – akin to what fathers felt when their daughters turned into women. It was only natural, and only proper to ignore it.

'Turtleman?' She seemed to have some new nickname for him every time she saw him. 'Why Turtleman?'

'In view of your vast age.' Her smile was dazzling. 'And your generally scaly behaviour.'

'Scaly?' He protested. 'Look who's talking. Aren't you the notorious juvenile extortionist? Faker of pregnancies to upset your poor mother?'

She rolled her eyes.

'Poor my ass. Three hundred wouldn't cover a week of mother's cab fares. As for being upset, you know what I think would upset her most?'

He shook his head.

'Being a grandmother . . . I'm serious. The social disgrace wouldn't faze her; she's been there . . . and my feelings, naturally, would hardly register. What would really get her is not being able to lie about her age, at least not so radically as she does right now. She wouldn't be able to claim thirty-five any more.'

It was unkind, of course, and not wholly accurate either. Abigail did care. She'd simply lost, through lack of use, the talent for expressing it. Yet there was more than a grain of truth in Christie's judgement, and because of it there was, beneath her shell of heartlessness, a core of hurt. He changed the subject.

'What did you want the three hundred for?'

'Operating expenses.' She shrugged. 'Tell me, Turtle, would you care?'

'Care?'

'If someone knocked me up.'

'Well of course I'd care. I'd hate to see you in that kind of fix.'

She made a face. 'Well of course. You'd hate to see anyone in that kind of fix. But that wasn't what I meant, now was it?'

She got up and came over to him, placed her hands on his shoulders. Her face, with its mane of silky hair, was tilted up at him. Her eyes were alive with mischief.

'What did I mean, Turtleman?'

For a moment he gazed at her, deadpan. Then, reaching up, he took her hands and disengaged them. 'Coffee,' he said. 'We need to go deal with the coffee. We wouldn't want it to boil, now would we?'

'Operating expenses . . .' Nolan mused. 'With barely six weeks left of the semester? None of my business, of course, but three hundred seems a hell of a lot for six weeks' operating expenses.'

They had moved to the kitchen. The coffee had brewed and they were drinking it, he at the table and she on a stool by the counter. With the change of scene, the subject of their earlier conversation had been dropped. Christie had made no effort to retrieve it.

'Expensive tastes.' She grinned.

'Expensive tastes in what? Drugs? Your mother seemed to think so.'

'Mother' – her tone was withering – 'blows thousands a year on booze, but hits the ceiling if she sees me with a joint. It's fine for her to be permanently looped, but I'm expected to get high on life.'

There seemed no point in responding to this. Instead he went over to the phone and scribbled a note on the pad beside it. He tore off the page and handed it to her.

'CD 750×350 = 1050,' she read aloud. 'What is this? Some kind of puzzle?'

'Does it mean anything to you?'

'Should it?' She examined the note again. 'Someone needs a review of multiplication. Otherwise not.'

'How about CD?'

She thought.

'Certificate of deposit, maybe? And me, of course.'

'I got this from Lisa Bronowski's notebook,' Nolan said. 'Does that help, at all?'

Clearly it did. Her manner became guarded.

'What are you doing with Lisa's notebook? And what's with all the questions?'

He ignored this.

'Where I found this,' he said, 'there were other equations like it, each preceded by two or three letters, and in every case with mistakes in the multiplication. I couldn't make any sense of them, but the CD reminded me of your initials. On a hunch I got a list of students from the office and checked the letters preceding the equations against students' initials. And you know what? In every case I came up with a match.'

Pause. A smile began to gather at the corners of her mouth.

'Sherlock Nolan,' she said.

He waited for her to continue, but she didn't. He returned to the attack.

'So I wondered about the meaning of all this screwy arithmetic, and since your initials cropped up with fair regularity, it occurred to me that you might be able to enlighten me.'

He gave her a long, interrogative stare.

She met it without blinking, her gaze clear and candid. 'Look, Philip, she's dead. Why not let it go?'

He thought about this.

'*De mortuis nil nisi bonum*, you mean? Nothing but good to be spoken of the dead.'

She nodded.

'And nothing but good of the living either, perhaps?'

'That, too.' She frowned. 'I'm not about to help you make a bunch of busts.'

'I'm not out to make a bunch of busts.'

'I didn't think so.' She eyed him steadily. 'What are you out for?'

It was a reasonable question. To answer, however, he'd have to go back on his undertaking to Jacobsen, and burden her unfairly with what, at this stage, were no more than suspicions.

'I can't tell you right now,' he said. 'I'm not out to bust, but I'm not just indulging my curiosity either. Could we leave it like this: that until we agree otherwise, this conversation is confidential, on both sides?'

She thought for a moment then nodded. 'What did you want to know?'

'Lisa was dealing, wasn't she?'

She hesitated, then nodded.

'Big time?'

'Yes – At least by Fremont's standards.'

'And those equations were records of drug transactions?'

'I think so. What I bought from her was acid mostly. Two or three hits at a time. The going rate was three-fifty a hit. When I recognized my initials in front of those numbers and you told me about the notebooks and how the letters all matched up with students' initials, it jumped out at me that's what it had to be. The acid she sold was in hits of two-hundred-and-fifty micrograms, so seven-hundred-and-fifty mikes would be three hits. And three hits at three-fifty comes to ten-fifty.'

'Then that note is a record of her selling you three hits of acid?'

She nodded. 'What beats me is why she wanted to keep a record. It's so risky. I guess she thought that by measuring in micrograms and using people's initials she'd created some kind of uncrackable code.' Christie shrugged. 'But she reckoned without the suspicious nature and superior sleuthing abilities of Mr Sherlock Nolan, didn't she?'

'I think what she mostly didn't reckon on was dying,' Nolan said. 'I doubt she thought anyone would poke through her stuff and find her notebook.'

'I guess you're right.' Visibly, Christie's imagination grappled with this irony. Her face clouded. 'It's so hard to think of her as dead, of not seeing her again, not ever . . . I wasn't exactly close to her, but we sat up late and talked sometimes. I liked her a lot. And now she's dead.' Christie paused and turned earnestly to Nolan. 'That's why I didn't want to talk about her dealing. I didn't want you to think of her as . . . some scumbag drug dealer, because she wasn't like that at all. To tell the truth, I don't even know why she did it. It wasn't for the money . . . at least she never seemed to spend any. And it wasn't to win friends, because she didn't need to.' Christie shrugged and shook her head. 'It just didn't make any sense.'

'Maybe she did it for kicks,' Nolan said. 'Because rules are made to be broken . . . that kind of thing.'

She shook her head. 'She wasn't that stupid. Besides, she dealt a lot. If you're in it for kicks, you don't turn it into a business.'

This made sense, he thought. The journal recorded more than a hundred transactions. If the sale to Christie had been about average, that argued a take in the thousands. Even in a school of rich kids, like Fremont, this wasn't pocket money. So Lisa's motive probably had been financial. But if she wasn't spending the money, who was?

'What else did she deal, apart from acid?'

'The usual.' Christie shrugged. 'Pot, of course. Mushrooms, in season. A little coke once in a while.'

'And a little smack once in a while?'

There was no mistaking this for a casual inquiry. Christie stared at him; her manner again become guarded.

'Smack? Not that I ever heard of . . . What makes you think she did?'

Nolan hesitated. To go on, he would have to reveal that his knowledge of Lisa's activities extended further than he'd admitted so far. But then his question itself implied that he already had, at the least, grounds for suspicion. He told Christie about finding the acid and the packages taped to the toilet tank, but not about his conversations with Lieutenant Jacobsen.

She listened without interruption.

'She wasn't dealing it.' She spoke with conviction. 'Using, maybe, but not dealing. If there'd been smack in circulation, I would have heard.'

He nodded. If there'd been smack in circulation, she would have more than heard. It was the one thing about her – her openness to neurochemical adventure – that sometimes worried him. But if she said she hadn't heard, she hadn't.

'I need to ask one more question.' He caught her gaze and held it. 'Only now we're not in confidence any more. This one is for the record. Where was she getting it from?'

'The drugs?'

He nodded.

Silence. Her face clouded again. He had become authority, alien not only for what he was asking her to do but in consequence also of her generation's instinct to mistrust its elders. She was caught in a web of conflicting loyalties; extricating her would take patience and tact.

'I'm not out to bust students,' he reminded her. 'I think someone off campus was selling smack to Lisa, and that's who I want to bust. Pot is one thing, and so are mushrooms and maybe acid, but smack is a whole different story. Smack can kill you. People who sell it are unscrupulous and vicious.'

She didn't speak. She was swayed but not convinced. He could almost hear the objections rehearsing themselves in her mind. 'What people put into their bodies is their business' . . . 'Squealing is still squealing.'

He tried again.

'Think about Lisa. You say you liked her, really liked her. And now, age seventeen, she's dead . . . slipped and fell, so we're told, from a ledge she must have known blindfolded.'

It jolted her. She stared at him, colour draining from her face.

'What are you saying? That you don't think she slipped?'

'I don't know what I think.' The suggestion planted, he retreated from it. 'What I do know is she was using heroin and now she's dead. And what I'd like you to think about is this: If you know something and won't tell me, what kind of scum are you protecting?'

'I'm not protecting anyone. I just don't know what you're

70

asking. I have no idea . . .' She broke off, hearing herself, registering suddenly the exact significance of her words.

'No idea?'

'Look . . .' Her eyes begged him to stop, not to force her into what was still, to some part of her, treason. 'It's no more than a guess. Coincidence, most likely. There could be no connection.'

'Tell me anyway.'

'She didn't always deal . . .' She looked away, her voice barely audible, as if she wanted to disown what she was saying. 'Last quarter was when she really started. About the same time she got a new boyfriend, someone from town. I figured she was getting it from him.'

'The boyfriend, does he have a name?'

She shook her head. 'I don't know it.'

'What was he like?'

'I don't know. I never met him.'

'Well, didn't she ever talk about him? Mention anything about him? I mean, you knew she had a new boyfriend; she must have said something about him.'

She hesitated. 'He had a nickname. I heard her mention it once or twice, but I can't remember it. Something western, I think. Something cowboy.'

'Bronco?' he asked.

'Bronco?' She looked surprised and relieved. 'Yes, that was it.'

11

When he got to the wash, Jacobsen pulled to the side of the road, parked the car and got out. He yawned and stretched, flinging back his arms and arching his spine to drive the last traces of sleep from his system. A bluejay, startled, rose from the branches of a nearby juniper. Quail, foraging somewhere in the bushes, called out softly to each other. Otherwise the valley was still, the tall buttes looming like sentinels in the silvery grey of the dawn. He looked at his watch. 6:30. In ten minutes or so the sun would rise over the cliffs to his left and there would be enough light.

Jacobsen didn't normally start work at this hour. He'd done so this morning to avoid being spotted by anyone from Fremont. He'd left home at 6:00 wearing Levi's and a faded T-shirt and driving his own '69 Ford Falcon which, because he'd been careful to service it properly, still ran like a sewing machine in spite of the 160,000 miles he'd put on the odometer. Though it was early, he might still get unlucky and be spotted – the kids at Fremont, apparently, kept pretty odd hours. But without his patrol car and uniform, he doubted he'd be recognized. And he was anxious not to be recognized because at least one member of the Fremont community had shown a disturbing ability to put two and two together. Philip Nolan, Jacobsen was sure, would know exactly what the police were after, poking about in this wash.

The wash intersected the road about half a mile from the school. At that point it was some twenty feet wide: a shallow gully, edged with mesquite and yucca, its floor of bare rock strewn with boulders and streaked with patches of sand and dried mud. From the road Jacobsen could trace its course almost all the way back to its origin, three quarters of the way up a large mesa to the southwest of the campus. It was clearly an artery of the system that drained the mesa, and as Nolan had told him, one of its tributaries led down from the saddle that joined the mesa to the tomb-shaped slab of sandstone from which the girl had fallen.

Where it crossed the wash the road showed signs of repeated patching. Jacobsen wondered why the school didn't put in culverts. Perhaps the people who ran it belonged to some lunatic environmentalist fringe and would rather see their roads devastated by floods than countenance anything as unnatural as a culvert. Or perhaps, since culverts were in the short run much more expensive than patching, it was simply a question of dollars and cents. But for whatever reason there were no culverts, so a vehicle, clearance and suspension permitting, could simply turn off the blacktop and drive up the wash.

The truck, evidently, hadn't driven very far. Its tyre marks stopped barely twenty feet from the road. Beyond, in a broad

72

patch of sand, were footprints leading away from the road and another set returning. The prints in both cases were identical.

Because there had been no rain since the night of Lisa's death, it was clear that both tyre tracks and footprints had been made in the last two days. It was therefore a good bet that the tracks had been made by the grey truck Nolan had mentioned and the footprints by its owner. Unfortunately, the footprints were partly eroded by wind. They were easy enough to follow, but he couldn't be absolutely sure they were the same ones he'd seen in his earlier investigation, looping around the south side of the ledge. The outline, in each case, suggested a sneaker, size six or seven, he guessed – but the soles had been worn almost smooth. And their pattern, faint enough on the ledge, had here been more or less obliterated. To make sure they were the same he would have to trace these tracks to their destination, and even that might not do it, he realized, because dollars to doughnuts the ledge would be pretty thoroughly trampled by now. The original tracks were probably lost. In any case, there wasn't enough time. Even jogging, he would need fifteen minutes to get up to the ledge and another hour or so to track the prints. If he were still poking around up there at 8:00 or 8:30, he might just as well announce his intentions with a bullhorn. Sam Plunkett, for one, would not appreciate that. He decided, therefore, to settle for reasonable inference. It was reasonable to infer that the tyre marks belonged to the grey truck and the footprints to its owner. If he could establish that the footprints led to the ledge, it would also be reasonable to infer that they were the same ones he'd found going around the south side of the ledge. But even as he made the decision, he found himself wishing that he'd been less reticent yesterday with Nolan, when the prints had been more than eighteen hours fresher. Inference, reasonable or not, was never as convincing as fact.

It took him roughly twenty-five minutes to satisfy himself that the prints did indeed lead to the ledge. At a quarter past seven he was standing at the junction of the wash and the tributary that led down from the saddle. The footprints headed up the tributary. He followed them another fifty or sixty yards, almost to the top of the saddle, and was rewarded for his efforts by seeing them turn right, out of the gully, and head up the slope towards the ledge. There was no need, he felt, to follow any farther. It was time to get back and share his inferences with Plunkett.

Ten minutes later he was back at the car and wishing himself someplace else altogether. For waiting there, leaning against the car with the patient air of someone prepared if necessary to wait all morning, was Nolan.

'Dr Livingstone . . .' Nolan let him come all the way to the car before speaking. He was wearing a faint smile, quizzical but not unfriendly. His voice had an edge of mockery. 'Did you find it?'

'Did I find what?'

'The source of the Nile.' Nolan shrugged. His smile became broader. 'Whatever it was you were looking for up there.'

Jacobsen let that go. Nolan, he saw, was dressed for running – cutoffs, T-shirt, sneakers, and a coloured bandanna around his head. That he had in fact been running was evident from his face, almost purple from exertion, and from his hair and clothes, which were drenched with sweat. Next to him, on the ground, was a large backpack.

'Hiking?' Jacobsen cocked an eyebrow and nodded to the pack.

'Jogging,' Nolan corrected.

'Jogging!' Jacobsen stared. 'With a backpack?'

Nolan nodded. Apparently he was used to this kind of reaction. 'I'm going climbing in the summer. The other members of the party' – his grin was wry and self-deprecating – 'are all much younger men.'

Jacobsen went over and tested the weight of the backpack. It was seriously heavy. He tried to imagine running with it, but he cringed at the thought. He could, however, being about the same age as Nolan, understand the motivation.

'Jesus . . .' He laid the pack down with a pantomime of exaggerated effort. 'What the hell do you have in there? Rocks?'

'Yes,' Nolan said. 'This week forty-five pounds, next week fifty. I'm not looking forward to next week.' He paused. 'So did you find it? Or should I say "them"?'

Jacobsen considered. On the one hand, Nolan clearly knew what he'd been looking for and, denied an answer, could go and look for himself. On the other hand, he himself had no business airing his theories until he had talked to Plunkett. If Plunkett and the medical examiner decided, say, on a verdict of accident, it wouldn't do for Nolan to have learned from the horse's mouth just how strongly Lieutenant Jacobsen disagreed.

'I'd prefer not to comment at present.'

He expected the reply to be cutting, that Nolan would make this tired formula seem even more pompous and foolish than he himself felt it to be. Instead Nolan just nodded.

'Have you had breakfast yet?'

'Breakfast?' Jacobsen was startled. 'Not exactly. I've had coffee. Tell the truth,' he said with a grin, 'I didn't feel much like eating at half past five.'

'Well then,' Nolan said briskly, 'if you'll give me and my backpack a ride to the school, I can offer you eggs and bacon, orange juice, toast, and all the coffee you can drink. There's no charge,' he added, seeming to sense the other's hesitation. 'I'm not planning to pump you. In fact, just the reverse. I'm looking to give information, not get it.'

'And that's why you were waiting?'

'Partly.' Nolan nodded.

'But I'm not using a department vehicle. How could you know it was me?'

Nolan shrugged. 'I couldn't. But when I saw the car parked, this early and in this particular wash, I knew it had to be one of you. Either way, I was curious, so I waited.'

'One of us?' Even to Jacobsen's ears, the evasion sounded lame.

'You or the other guy.' Nolan's grin was mocking. 'The one whose tracks you were following back there.'

12

Jacobsen took a final swallow of his coffee, declined the offer of a refill, and stacked his dishes in the sink. Nolan's breakfast had been exactly as advertised but Jacobsen was glad to bring it to an end. The conversation, though not exactly awkward, had been constrained, oppressed by the sense of issues unresolved. It was time, he thought, to resolve them.

'You say the journal proves she didn't jump,' he began. 'How exactly?'

In response, Nolan got the journal and handed it to him, open at a point about two thirds through, and showed him a note at the top of the left hand page. It was the final entry, Jacobsen noticed, beyond it the pages were blank.

'*Town today pm,*' he read, '*No B. Sadness. Note Ac. Same time, same place. Lots to talk about. Think B maybe finally off the hook. Nunc dimittis . . .*

'Can't say I get much from this.' He felt a sense of letdown. After Nolan's build-up, he'd expected something more significant, something at least comprehensible. 'This "*Nunc dimmittis*", for instance, is it supposed to mean something? It sounds Greek to me.'

'Latin, actually,' Nolan said, smiling. 'It's the opening of one of the psalms. "*Nunc dimittis, Domine.*" Odd, nowadays, to find a kid who knows her Bible. Most of them have barely heard of it.'

Jacobsen didn't respond. In fact, he had hardly been listening. Instead he'd been reminded, by some sideways skip of memory, of the birth of his son. His wife's labour had been long and difficult. The doctor, fearing that the child would get exhausted, had hooked her up to a machine that monitored contractions and the child's heartbeat, recording them on a strip of graph paper that issued from the machine. He remembered how moved he'd been by that first visible evidence of his son's struggle to be born, how fragile the wavering ink line had seemed, with the heartbeat going frantic at the onset of each contraction. Even now, ten years later, seeing that strip of paper was like reliving the experience; it could still bring tears to his eyes. Lisa's journal was like that, he thought, but instead of a beginning it recorded an end, the half-finished quotation suggesting that moment when her young voice, almost in mid-utterance, had fallen silent.

He was conscious, suddenly, that Nolan had stopped talking and was looking at him strangely. '*Nunc dimittis . . .*' he murmured, embarrassed by his lapse of attention and the emotion that unexpectedly filled him. 'What does it mean?'

'Lord, now lettest thou thy servant depart in peace,' Nolan said. 'At least that's the King James version.'

'And it shows she didn't jump? Strikes me as just the opposite.'

Nolan shook his head. 'Not if you take it in context. And especially not if you know the rest of the quote.'

Jacobsen felt a twinge of irritation. He'd been promised more, he felt, than this display of erudition.

'What is the rest of the quote?'

'"For mine eyes have seen Thy salavation, which Thou hast prepared before the face of all people." Relief or perhaps even joy, not a sad farewell. Now, put that in context – Same time, same place – suggests she'd set up a meeting with someone, probably her boyfriend, Bronco. They had things to talk about because she thought he was off the hook, out from under some problem or other. I don't know exactly what she's talking about, but I get the drift. And there's no mistaking the tone. It's optimistic. She feels good about the future. These were her last words in a diary to which she apparently confided the important things in her life, but she didn't know they were going to be her last words . . .' Nolan paused. 'However she came to fall off that ledge, she sure as hell didn't jump.'

He looked at Jacobsen for comment. Jacobsen hesitated. It wasn't that he disagreed, but rather that his policeman's instincts distrusted information freely volunteered. Why had Nolan volunteered it? Furthermore, and this was the question that bothered Jacobsen most, what was it that he hadn't volunteered?

So instead of answering at once, he stalled. 'Note Ac?' he queried. 'What's that mean?'

'I don't know,' Nolan shrugged. 'Maybe she left a note someplace. There's an awful lot of this I haven't yet figured out. It's because it's so obscure, in fact, that I hesitated to bother you with it.'

Hesitated to bother you with it . . . That, Jacobsen thought, was obvious bullshit. Whatever else Nolan might be, he sure as hell wasn't diffident.

'Then what made you change your mind?'

'You did,' Nolan said.

'I did? How?'

'By really investigating. By making it clear you weren't just interested in closing the file. I heard you question Robert, and I saw you investigating that wash this morning. It's clear you're not happy with the obvious – suicide or accident – so I thought you'd be interested in contrary evidence.'

'Contrary?' Jacobsen frowned. 'I'm not sure I follow that. The journal argues against suicide, possibly, but not accident.'

'Not directly,' Nolan said. 'But just for the sake of argument, let's assume you were working on the theory that she'd arranged to meet someone on the ledge that night. Then that last entry could be taken as support for your theory, couldn't it?'

'Not really,' Jacobsen said. 'At best it wouldn't help much. We don't know who she might have been meeting. We don't know where. And, most important, we don't know when. The entry is not dated, right? It could have been written days before she died. Maybe even weeks.'

'I don't think so.' Nolan shook his head.

'Why not?'

'"Town today pm." She wrote that on a day she went into town. She died in the early hours of Sunday morning. And it just so happens that Fremont runs one trip a week into town – on Saturday afternoon.'

'So . . .' Jacobsen shrugged. 'She either wrote it on the day before she died, or she wrote it some other Saturday. She could also have gone into town, but not on the school trip.'

Nolan smiled. 'You'd be an ornament to any logic class. But we can eliminate some of those alternatives. She did go into town the day before she died, and she didn't go the previous two Saturdays. We keep records for billing, and that's what they show. So either she wrote the entry when I think she did, or she got into town by some unusual means, or she failed to write in her diary for the three weeks before her death. But she wrote in that journal practically every day. I can't date the entries exactly, but the continuity is obvious. Nowhere else is there a gap of anything like three weeks.'

'Then perhaps she got someone to give her a ride into town.'

'It's possible,' Nolan conceded, 'but she had school engagements after class every afternoon except Saturday and Sunday. If she went into town she'd have to have cut something. And if she cut, there'd be some record of the fact. So I checked. It seems she didn't cut.'

'Then you think – '

'I think she wrote that entry the day before she died.' Nolan nodded. 'I think it records, among other things, her arranging to meet her boyfriend Bronco to discuss something important affecting him. And if you think it's possible she planned to meet someone on the ledge, then I think Bronco is the logical candidate.'

Jacobsen considered this.

'You're suggesting, in other words, that I should have a talk with this Bronco?'

'Yes . . .' Nolan gave an innocent looking smile. 'If you think there might be something useful to talk to him about.' He paused. 'Problem is, though, I don't have a clue who Bronco is.'

Silence. Jacobsen experienced a powerful urge to give vent to the irritation that had been mounting steadily through this conversation.

'I have the sensation,' he managed to keep his voice level, 'of being slightly jerked around. On the one hand, you offer information and seem to want to be helpful. On the other hand, the information you actually come up with is excerpts from a journal that only you can decipher, and advice to talk to someone whose identity you don't know. I'm afraid I don't find that very helpful.' He paused. 'Something else bothers me. Where do *you* stand in all this?'

Silence. It was Jacobsen's impression that his reaction wasn't entirely unexpected. Nolan seemed neither surprised nor offended; he seemed to be considering his options.

'Where do *I* stand?'

'Yes . . . I'm wondering why you're so interested, so eager to help.'

Nolan thought for a moment. 'Natural desire of concerned citizen to assist the police.' The reply was followed instantly by a grin.

'Bullshit,' Jacobsen said.

'So you tell me.' Nolan was unfazed by this. 'What sinister motive do you think I have?'

'Unnatural desire of concerned citizen to manipulate the

79

police. I get the feeling you're pushing me to a certain conclusion.'

'No,' Nolan said. 'It's not that.'

'What is it then?'

'A combination of things. The natural desire of a concerned citizen to assist the police, plus the natural desire of a vulnerable institution to keep its name out of the papers.' Nolan paused. 'Look. When I started reading that journal, two things jumped out at me: first, that if there was any chance that Lisa's death wasn't an accident, you guys needed to know about the journal; second, that when you looked at it, you were going to learn things about the Fremont School that the Fremont School wouldn't want publicized. What it boils down to is I didn't want to show it to you unless there was a need.'

It was on the tip of Jacobsen's tongue to point out that the police liked to decide what the police needed to see, but he restrained himself. The situation here wasn't all that unusual. In almost every major investigation closets were opened at random and skeletons found. For that reason witnesses often held things back.

'Things you wouldn't want publicized?' he queried. 'You mean things you want us to ignore?'

'To be frank, yes.'

'Drugs, in other words?'

Nolan nodded. 'If we must put it into other words, yes.'

Jacobsen shrugged. 'I've said it once. I'm not interested in drugs.'

'I'm not talking about acid this time,' Nolan said. 'Now we've moved into the major leagues.'

'Still not interested.' Jacobsen regarded him steadily. 'What you guys will tolerate is your affair. Just so you keep it away from town.'

Nolan frowned. 'I don't think it's fair to say we're tolerating it; we just found out about it. As for keeping it away from town, it's actually the other way round.'

'Keeping the town away from the school?'

'Yes. We've discovered that Lisa was a big dealer on campus. I've been studying the journal partly to try and find out who supplied her. What I've gathered so far is that she was involved with what sound like some fairly shady characters – from town. One was her boyfriend Bronco, who apparently was a heroin addict. The other was someone she says very little about. In the journal she refers to him only as A, but who I'd guess was the real connection.' Nolan paused. 'Perhaps you can see now why I wasn't that keen to give you this until I was sure it had some bearing on the case?'

Jacobsen nodded.

'And does it?' Nolan asked.

'Does it what?'

'Have some bearing on the case? If it does, I imagine you'll want to study the journal. If so,' Nolan shrugged, 'you're probably going to need me.'

'To decipher it? Is it that hard to figure out?'

Nolan nodded. 'Unless you know the jargon and a lot about the school, it is. And even then it's not always straighforward. The bit I showed you was one of the easier ones. Some of it is flat-out baffling, even for me. So far, I've barely scratched the surface. I'm just getting things in sequence and trying to establish a rough chronology. The question is: now that you know about it, are you interested?'

Jacobsen thought. The journal was hearsay, of course, and therefore unusable as evidence. On the other hand, it might shed a good deal of light on an event which his own research to date had succeeded only in obscuring. But then again there was Plunkett. Jacobsen tried to imagine the sheriff's reaction to this collection of juvenile confessions written in some teenage dialect that only Nolan, apparently, could understand. He also tried to see himself explaining to Plunkett how Nolan had come to figure as a kind of consultant in the case, a development he himself didn't entirely understand. Neither prospect was inviting.

'I don't know,' he said. 'I'm going to have to think.'

13

'Tracks again.' Plunkett shook his head sadly. 'I swear to God, there are times when I wonder about this department. I mean, take the other day. I go to the pisser to take a leak, and what do I see? Cliff Parsons, waving his pistol around, admiring himself in the mirror. And when I ask him what in the hell he thinks he's doing, he says he's practising quick on the draw. Quick on the draw, for Chrissakes! . . . On top of everything the damn thing was loaded. It's a marvel he didn't shoot himself in the foot.'

He gave Jacobsen a triumphant stare, as if he'd just drawn a telling point. Experience told Jacobsen not to be drawn. Plunkett's non sequiturs were usually setups for some kind of zinger; the best response was none at all. Curiosity overcame him, however.

'Beats me how Cliff fits into this.'

Plunkett's look was pitying. 'First Cliff plays cowboy, now you play Indian. But at least he's young, and at least he's not doing it in public. What's your excuse?'

'I'm trying to do my job.' Jacobsen was never offended by Plunkett's zingers. His relationship with the sheriff was like an old and comfortable marriage; the bickering hid mutual respect and affection. Plunkett would bitch because it amused him, and Jacobsen would put up with it because that was easier and because Plunkett's bitching amused him, too.

'Doing your job? . . . How do you figure that?'

Jacobsen shrugged. 'I think a crime's been committed. I think whoever did it should have to pay.'

Silence. Plunkett reached for the penknife he kept on his desk for opening letters and started to tap, bouncing the point of the blade off the desk top in a rhythm that always bothered Jacobsen because it was almost regular but not quite and thus impossible to ignore.

'OK,' Plunkett said. 'Make your case.'

'It's mostly based on elimination. As I said before, her tracks

82

on the ledge show she didn't slip. They also suggest she didn't jump. Her journal appears to confirm that.' Jacobsen paused. 'We're left with pushed. On the ledge there's a set of tracks that could belong to her killer. There's the reported sighting of a truck near the scene at around the proper time, and another set of tracks leads to the scene from the wash where the truck was sighted. On top of that, there's the suggestion in her journal that on the afternoon proir to her death she made arrangments to meet someone, and her behaviour just before her death, as described by Robert Anderson, suggests that when she showed up at his campfire she may have been on her way to this meeting. All in all, I'd say there's a fair presumption she was murdered.'

'A fair presumption,' Plunkett echoed sardonically. 'Christ, you sound like a training manual. Let's start thinking like real-life cops. Let's take a look at what you can actually prove.'

'Fine.' Jacobsen shrugged. 'For one thing I can prove she didn't slip.'

'Can you?' Plunkett challenged. 'Can you really? Proof is mostly a matter of who you're talking to, isn't it? I mean, maybe you could sell that tracking stuff to a jury of Navajos. But what about your average suburban housewife, with an attention span of fifteen seconds and a tendency to go blank at the mention of anything even slightly complicated? How do you think you'd make out with her, when the defence is doing its best to make you look like an asshole?'

It was a good point. Jacobsen said nothing.

'It gets worse,' Plunkett went on. 'These new tracks you found, you can't prove they were made the night she died. You can't even prove they're the same ones you saw on the south side of the ledge. And as for the diary,' he shrugged, 'it's hearsay, Olin, statements made out of court by someone not available for questioning, and therefore – as I'm sure you'll remember from that training manual of yours – not admissible as evidence. To tell you the truth, I don't think you can prove a single, goddamn thing.'

'But what I can prove isn't really the point,' Jacobsen objected. 'Not now, at any rate. All I want right now is authority to investigate. Proof is what I'll turn up.'

'But will you?' Plunkett demanded. 'I mean, where will you even start? With tracks that are now more than two days old and mostly obliterated? With a grey pickup, make undetermined, licence plate number unknown? Or maybe with a young girl's diary, which seems to be written in some kind of code and could easily turn out to be romantic fiction?' He paused. 'Did I leave anything out?'

Jacobsen ignored the sarcasm. He leaned forward, urgent now because he was losing, because once Plunkett made a decision there was almost no budging him from it. 'Look, Sam, she didn't slip. You can sneer all you want, but I know tracks and I know she didn't slip. I'll admit I'm not quite as certain that she didn't jump, but the evidence points away from it. I don't even think we'd seriously consider it except for what we're left with otherwise. Murder, Sam, the murder of a seventeen-year-old schoolgirl, a kid. I don't like it either, but that won't make it go away.'

Plunkett gazed at him thoughtfully for a moment, then reached for the penknife. Before he could start tapping, he caught Jacobsen's frown. Shrugging, he put down the penknife.

'What are you asking for?'

'Time to investigate,' Jacobsen said. 'Ask the medical examiner to leave things open, and let me nose around. Maybe I can find this boyfriend, Bronco, and get him to shed a little light.'

This time, whether Jacobsen liked it or not, Plunkett was going to tap. Jacobsen let his eyes drift round the room. Plunkett had been sheriff for fifteen years, and the comfortable wood-panelled office offered ample testimony to the oddly soothing effect his grumpy personality and abrasive manner had always had on his constituency. On the walls, along with the mounted head of an elk he'd shot down south and the glass case containing the five-and-a-half pound brown trout he'd pulled out of a creek in the Sangre de Cristos, was a pictorial record of Sam Plunkett, keeping his people happy – chatting with the senior US senator for New Mexico, addressing a meeting of the Buckskin Lions Club, inaugurating Road Safety Week, proposing a toast at a dinner of the Antelope Creek Volunteer Fire Brigade, distributing prizes at the local public school. These photographs, the sporting trophies, the framed certificate that testified that Samuel Hanson Plunkett was a member in good standing of the NRA, even the poster bearing the message, 'Eat American Lamb; Ten Million Coyotes Can't Be Wrong', all bore witness to one central fact: Sam Plunkett was good people. And in a community whose average age was considerably more than fifty, this solid virtue stood him in very good stead – far better stead than energy or intelligence, qualities he also possessed in abundance but preferred, for the most part, not to put on display.

The tapping stopped.

'No leaving things open,' Plunkett said.

Jacobsen said nothing.

'Leave things open, you invite publicity,' Plunkett said. 'Unless you rule out foul play you practically admit you suspect it. And you don't even have the beginnings of a case, Olin. No suspect. No motive. No certainty even that she was murdered. You could easily end up with egg on your face. I just don't believe in programming for failure, not in public.'

'I guess that makes a certain kind of sense.' Jacobsen's voice was dry. 'Political sense, at any rate. No crime, no inquiry, and therefore no chance of a screw-up. Everybody's happy, especially the killer.'

Silence. Plunkett stared at Jacobsen; Jacobsen stared back.

'You could see it that way.' Plunkett's face was expressionless, his voice even. 'Sam Plunkett worrying about his future, the election two years down the road where, if history is a guide, he'll probably be the only candidate.' He paused. 'Or you could quit acting like a goddamn schoolboy, and think for a moment about what a murder investigation is likely to do to the other people involved . . . her parents, for instance. Think how you'd feel if the cops told you your kid had been murdered but, sorry about that, they didn't know who did it. Think of their anguish, the effect on Lisa's friends, the turmoil it would cause in that school out there . . .' He paused again, shrugged. 'Think what you must, Olin, but understand this. I'm not putting anyone throught the trauma of all that, just on the basis of your hunch about a footprint.'

'On the basis of my hunch about a footprint.' Jacobsen stared. 'I'd say it rests on slightly more than that.'

Plunkett shook his head. 'It rests on that footprint. The other stuff – the truck, the journal, the drug dealing, the fact that she *may* have been on her way to meet someone – none of that would impress you if you weren't already convinced she didn't

85

slip. And the only evidence she didn't is the footprint. And that, of course – '

'And that, of course, is not real evidence,' Jacobsen said bitterly. 'You think tracking is bullshit, don't you?'

'Not bullshit.' Plunkett gazed at him steadily. 'I'll put it this way, Olin. There's a chance you could be mistaken.'

'And because of that you're going to let this thing slide?'

'No, I'm not.' Plunkett paused. 'I'm not convinced that she was pushed, and even if she was, I don't see much chance of you making your case. But you're a good cop, with good instincts, and I wouldn't feel easy just ignoring them. So I'm going to let you run with this one a bit. Only the thing is, Olin, you'll have to be quiet.'

'Quiet?' Jacobsen queried. 'How quiet?'

'Very quiet,' Plunkett said. 'No open verdict. No involvement of other department personnel. And especially no reporters crawling all over the place. No public admission, in other words, that there even is an inquiry. Just you, Olin, poking about on your lonesome, until either you find something concrete or you get fed up and pack it in.'

'I see,' Jacobsen said. 'And I expect you'd like me to do this in my spare time, so it won't interfere with the work of the department.'

Plunkett grinned. 'That'd be nice.'

Jacobsen said nothing. Perhaps he should be grateful. He'd been granted this limited hunting licence mostly as a sop to his feelings. But the hunting licence was awfully damn limited, wasn't it? No publicity and no department help meant the chances of turning up concrete evidence were, realistically, slim. There was Nolan and the journal, of course, and the possibility of a lead to the mysterious Bronco, but apart from that the horizon was empty. It was almost enough to make him quit right now . . . except she had been murdered – he was positive of that – and if he quit, the killer would go unpunished. So he was not going to quit.

'Another thing . . .' Plunkett said. 'This Nolan . . . I don't want him involved.'

'Not involved?' Jacobsen stared. 'He already is. Apart from anything else, I need him to decipher the journal.'

Plunkett frowned. 'It's occurred to you, of course, that if

you're right about the murder, he has to be considered a suspect?'

'Sure it has.' Jacobsen shrugged. 'And it's also occurred to me that doesn't make much sense. If he were the killer, he wouldn't have come forward with evidence.'

'If it *is* evidence.' Plunkett obviously had doubts. 'What I'm saying is don't take him into your confidence. Use him to help with the journal, if you must, but none of the old amateur-assists-cops routine. If any of this does get out, I don't want us looking like assholes. At least,' he amended, 'not any more than we absolutely have to.'

'I'll bear it in mind.' Jacobsen shrugged.

'You do that. And remember,' Plunkett put a finger to his lips, 'make like a mouse.'

14

Nolan could never take a trip into Buckskin without being reminded of the classic *New Yorker* cartoon, which, because it seemed to express an abiding truth about his country, he had taken the trouble to frame and hang on the wall of his class-room. Two pilgrim fathers were talking on the deck of the *Mayflower*. 'My short term goal,' one was saying, 'is freedom of worship. But in the long run I plan to make a killing in real estate.'

Buckskin reflected the same easy compromise between God and Mammon. It had attracted a bewildering variety of churches, Christian and otherwise, but without ever swerving from its devotion to the dollar. Nolan had once had a class research the matter and had discovered, with astonishment verging on disbelief, that the town contained thirty-six registered churches and no less than forty-one licensed real estate offices. Which would have been OK, he'd often thought, had the two industries not contrived, between them, to make the place so ugly. But Buckskin was one of those cases, unfortunately common in the West, where the design of nature had been thoroughly worked over by the hand of man. And to

Nolan, whose religious feelings were seldom aroused except by mountains, the foisting – on a landscape of wind-sculpted monoliths and massive sandstone cliffs – of one of the nastier instances of urban sprawl (McDonald's next to Tastee Freez and cheek by jowl with Kentucky Fried Chicken) was like scrawling graffiti on the walls of the Sistine Chapel.

It was in Buckskin, however, that a memorial service for Lisa was being held. Sinclair had suggested a service at Fremont, but her parents, feeling, perhaps, the awkwardness of accepting favours from an institution against which they were contemplating a lawsuit, had preferred a service in town. So Sinclair had brought in a bus load of Lisa's friends from the school. Nolan, driving his own car, had brought Christie.

The chapel chosen for the service made no compromise in its commitment to bad taste. The stained glass window showed a simpering Christ with a tangerine halo, earnestly preaching to an audience of sheep. A life-sized crucifix dominated an over-elaborate altar. The walls were painted purple, cream and gilt. This colour scheme, however, had not succeeded in making the place cheerful. Indeed, with its dismal lighting and faint but persistent smell of disinfectant, it had a sullen, mean-spirited air, redolent of pain and damnation.

Nolan and Christie, arriving after Sinclair and the others, sat towards the back. They were thus well situated to observe the rest of the congregation. Apart from Lisa's parents and the Fremont contingent, it seemed to consist mostly of members of the regular flock – a couple of elderly men, and half a dozen sombrely dressed women of the type whose idea of a good time was attending a church service, preferably a funeral. The only person whose presence couldn't immediately be accounted for was seated close to the exit. He was young – mid-twenties, Nolan guessed – and had arrived late, to the accompaniment of venomous stares from the women. He didn't look as if he spent much time in church.

He looked, in fact, like a cowboy. His brown corduroy jacket was of western cut, and his dark pants fitted snugly over high-heeled western boots. His bootlace tie, tipped at both ends with silver, was held in place by a chunk of Navajo jewellery. This outfit was worn with an awkwardness that suggested its wearer felt excessively dressed up.

He was an anomaly, unconnected with Fremont or Lisa's family or, to judge from the looks cast in his direction by members of the regular flock, with the church. His clothes and his manner, on the other hand, argued against his being some casual dropper-in. His gaze was remote. He went through the motions of following the service as if he were in a trance, as if the last thing he cared about were the forms of religious observance. He was there, Nolan guessed, only for Lisa.

He was Bronco. The inference was impossible to resist. Yet somewhat to his surprise, Nolan found himself wanting to resist it. His image of Bronco – derived, admittedly, more from prejudice than anything concrete in the journal – was of some scumbag needle addict, the kind of scruffy anti-hero whose sheer raunchiness was a standing affront to middle-class America and thus irresistible to a young girl rejecting, as so many of them were, the values of her parents. But the young man was nothing like that. He was clean-cut; a trifle haggard, but hardly an affront to anyone's values. In fact there was something about him, not just the cowboy clothes and the Wyatt Earp moustache, but the way he held himself, upright with a hint of stubbornness in the tilt of the head and thrust of the jaw, that suggested a commitment to frontier virtues. And studying him, inspecting him covertly while the rest of the congregation laboured through a hymn, Nolan found himself reminded of Lisa's poem and the Dream Horseman, striving to recapture space and freedom in a land that no longer had them to offer.

But whatever his character, this cowboy would bear looking into. When the service was over, Nolan thought, he must find some excuse to get into conversation. But the service, unfortunately, was far from over. When the hymn ended the congregation sat, the regulars assuming a resigned, glassy-eyed expression that reminded Nolan of a Monday morning class. The minister rose, glanced around, waited for the shuffling to subside. He had the air, Nolan saw with dismay, of a man who intended to share his thoughts.

'On my way here today . . .' The minister was pink and shining, with a singsong delivery pitched towards the upper end of the tenor register. 'On my way here today from my home in Antelope Canyon, I was struck, as I always am, by the beauty with which we, who have the good fortune to live here, are surrounded. I looked out over the glowing desert, so glorious that it invites the poet in all of us to describe it, so subtle it defeats anyone bold enough to try, and I wondered how a Creator so generous as to give us all this beauty could at the same time require of us, so prematurely, the life of this young child. And as I pondered this mystery, the central one of our faith, I was reminded of the sonnet in which Milton, complaining of his blindness, receives the answer: "They also serve who only stand and wait." And I was rebuked for my presumption, as Milton was for his, in questioning a design which, by our very natures, we cannot begin to imagine, let alone to understand.

'So I shan't offer you today, like a quack doctor peddling patent medicines, the easy balm of explanation. We can't know what God meant in taking Lisa from us so abruptly, and I'm not sure that if we did it would make us feel any better. All I do know is that there was a purpose, that, as the Bible tells us, without God's knowledge and consent, not even a sparrow falls to the ground, and that we must *all* of us,' he cast, here, a warmly sympathetic look at Lisa's parents, 'find the patience to stand and wait until he is ready to reveal to us what that purpose is . . .'

There was more in this vein – a digression revealing that the Latin root of patience meant suffering, some musing on the role of innocence in a world peopled largely by the guilty, meanderings that the street-smart Lisa of the journal would surely have found hilarious had she been around to share them; but in the end the sermon reminded Nolan, not of Milton, but of a speech in which Elizabeth I, faced with some meddling query about foreign policy, had obfuscated the issue for half an hour and concluded by requiring her questioners, graciously but firmly, to 'take their answer, answerless.' Given that the minister's subject had baffled better minds than the minister's, this was, Nolan thought, as good an answer as any.

Absorbed in the pedagogical habit of grading oral presentations for clarity and content – he gave the sermon a B for clarity and rather less for content – Nolan almost lost track of the cowboy. At some point early in the final hymn he noticed that the young man's seat was empty. Turning to the exit, he saw someone leaving.

Almost without thinking, he followed. In part of his mind he

90

recognized that his exit would raise eyebrows, and that an early confrontation with Bronco, if this was Bronco, might well be counterproductive. But instinct told him to seize the chance. So he followed, ignoring the stares of the women, and emerged from the gloom of the vestry into the blinding glare of the parking lot just as the cowboy was climbing into his pickup.

Afterwards Nolan would blame himself for the way he handled the situation. He had almost no time to think, however, and so called out the first thing that came into his head.

'Bronco – '

The cowboy was halfway into the pickup. He stopped dead. Slowly and with evident reluctance, he turned. When he saw Nolan, his look became unfriendly.

'Who the hell are you?'

Again, with more time to think, Nolan might have retrieved the situation by coming up with something plausible and unthreatening . . . Lisa had mentioned Bronco to him, perhaps; he wanted to introduce himself, offer his sympathy, thank him for attending the service. Something pompous and schoolmasterish like that, he later thought, might have let Bronco dismiss him with a shrug. But instead he compounded his error by trying to back away from it.

'I'm sorry, I mistook you for somebody else.'

Bronco was still halfway into the truck. For a moment he didn't reply. When he did it was almost deadpan, but with a faint, sardonic emphasis on the second word. 'The *hell* you did.'

And that was it. Bronco climbed in, started the motor, threw the truck into gear and roared off.

What made it worse was that this clumsy overture was not needed. While he waited in the parking lot for Christie, Nolan found himself spoken to, peremptorily and with obvious disapproval, by one of the stern-faced women from the chapel.

'Well? Did he say what he wanted?'

'He?' The snappish tone caught Nolan off balance.

'Billy.' She inspected Nolan grumpily, as if to make sure he wasn't a mental defective. 'He ain't set foot here in more than five years. When he does come, it's when he's got no business. And he comes late, of course, and leaves in the middle.'

'You know him then?'

'Of course I do.' From her tone it was clear the experience was one she wished she'd been spared. 'He's Billy Dabbs, isn't he? Poor Eugene Dabbs's boy.'

'What was all that about?' Christie asked.

'That?' Nolan looked blank.

'The abrupt departure of Nolan from the service.' Christie cocked her head on one side and eyed him speculatively. 'Hot in pursuit of a cowboy in Sunday best whose presence in church was a puzzle to most. But not to clever Nolan . . .' She paused. 'You thought he was Lisa's boyfriend, didn't you?'

Nolan considered his options. He could deny it, of course, come up with some story she could at least pretend to believe, which would solve the immediate problem. But after their last conversation about Lisa, evasiveness would in the long run only increase her curiosity, encourage her to the kind of speculations that were better not encouraged.

'Yes . . .' he said. 'It occurred to me that he might be.'

'And were you right?'

'I'm not sure. I didn't get to ask.'

'Shined you, did he?' The thought seemed not to displease her. 'What did you get to ask? . . . If he'd ever sold her smack?'

He was going to protest that he deserved more credit for his subtlety than that, when it occurred to him that he really didn't. For all the progress he'd made, he might as well had asked exactly that.

'I didn't get to ask anything, actually.'

She digested this in silence. 'Well, at least they can't accuse you of letting the grass grow under your feet. No sentimental time-wasting for Sherlock Nolan. Even in moments of mourning, business is business, right?'

Her tone startled him. Beneath the irony there was anger and hurt.

'What's bugging you?'

'I don't know.' She shrugged. 'It just seemed a little callous, that's all. I mean, couldn't it have waited?'

'Waited? He was leaving, Christie. It may have been my only chance.'

'And that was vital, of course . . . busting drug dealers is priority number one. Far more important than some kid's memorial service.'

'Not busting them,' Nolan said. 'Stopping them. There's a difference. And yes, I think it is more important. Maybe if I'd known her better, if I thought a service would do her any good, I'd feel different. But I didn't know her. I think the dead are beyond our reach. I'd rather spend my time on the living.'

For a moment they exchanged angry stares. Christie shrugged.

'I'm sorry . . .' Her expression softened. 'That service depressed me, I guess. It seemed so . . . matter of fact. A quick prayer, a hymn or two, a brief outpouring of bullshit from the minister – maybe fifteen minutes of official bumming out – and then we all go about our business, glad to have that over with.' She paused. 'I wanted there to be more. I wanted to get up and scream at that unctuous clown that she *wasn't* a goddamn sparrow; she was a person, seventeen years old, just starting her life, and that all his crap about God's inscrutable will just didn't begin to cut it. And then you got up and went chasing after that cowboy, and I guess I started wondering if there was anyone at all at that dismal charade who was grieving, I mean really grieving, for Lisa.'

'Not that I was, myself . . .' she went on, 'grieving, I mean. I tried to, but instead I kept remembering something Robert once told me. When his brother died, for some reason there had to be an autopsy, only they couldn't do it until morning and insisted on keeping the body in the morgue. Robert told me his father sat up there all night, with blankets and coffee, and sat until morning keeping watch. To keep his son company, he said. No child of his was staying alone in a place like that; if his son had to stay, then so would he. There had been no one to do that for Lisa, I thought, and it made me sad. But that really wasn't what was bothering me most. What was bothering me was would there be anyone to do it for me? . . . I mean, Jesus, just how self-centred can you get?'

Her look was awkward and slightly anxious, a plea for absolution and reassurance. How very vulnerable she was, he thought. For all the surface cynicism she was too young still, too self-demanding, to forgive herself even for being human.

'Not that I want to encourage your morbid speculations' – it was clearly time to lighten the mood a little – 'but what conclusion did you come to?' Nolan asked.

'About who'd sit up with me if I died?' She hesitated, looked at him sideways. 'It seemed to me my best chance was you.'

'Despite my great heartlessness in the matter of memorial services?'

She gazed at him steadily. 'Yes. We're talking about caring, aren't we? If I needed you to do that for me, you would . . . wouldn't you?'

He pursed his lips, waggled his head judiciously from side to side. 'I s'pose I might. I'd take cognac rather than coffee, though. And a good book, of course. And a portable tape deck in case it got gloomy and I needed some tunes . . . But yes, if you twisted my arm, I guess I might.'

'Bastard.' She was laughing now. 'You're always such a bastard. Such a cynical coldhearted bastard.' She paused. 'It beats me what I find to love in you.'

15

The service for Lisa had other consequences, some rather damaging for the school. A reporter from Albuquerque had driven up having read about Lisa in the *Buckskin Gazette* and scenting scandal, and had afterwards spoken to Lisa's parents. From them he had learned about the acid, also that they'd consulted an attorney with a view to suing Fremont. Afterwards he'd talked with some of the students.

The resulting story was everything Sinclair might have conceived in a nightmare. Though the individual statements were more or less accurate, they combined to paint a wholly inaccurate picture. It made Fremont a kind of asylum for rich problem children, with little adult supervision and a moral tone like that of the later Roman empire. The piece also implied, though it stopped carefully short of saying so, that the constant exposure to drugs had been too much for Lisa so she had taken her own life. The concluding paragraph was a small masterpiece of innuendo. It consisted of quotes presented without comment: a statement from Lisa's father that he'd sacrificed to send Lisa to Fremont precisely to get her away from unhealthy influences in her local public school, and another from an anonymous student that of course most kids at Fremont used drugs of one kind or another, but there was nothing remarkable about that because most of the faculty probably did, too.

The service was held on the Wednesday following Lisa's death. The story appeared two days later. Just in time, as Sinclair observed bitterly, to be read and discussed by the school's board of trustees at their meeting at Fremont on Saturday. The tone of that discussion, Sinclair and Nolan were given to understand, had not been happy.

'The bad news is they cancelled the phonathon,' Martin Delafield said. 'The good news is nobody quit yet.'

He leaned back and regarded them calmly, hands clasped behind his head, his cigarette held between his teeth like a gangster's stogy. A slim, well-cared-for man, with a year-round suntan and restless, intelligent eyes that were normally, but not on this occasion, concealed behind Ray-Bans. He was Fremont's chairman of the board as well as Christie's father and Nolan's cousin. Though his recent movies had not done especially well, he projected the image of the successful movie producer, contriving to look as if his time was more or less evenly divided between the South of France and the Polo Lounge at the Beverly Hills Hotel. But then Martin had always projected the popular image of something. At Exeter, three years ahead of Nolan, he'd been impeccably preppy. At Harvard he'd been impeccably radical, all denim, dark glasses, and existential despair. Now he was impeccably Malibu, designer jeans faded but freshly laundered, soft, newly shined Italian loafers, cream silk shirt with the enormous collar looking as if it had just come out of the box.

In most people, Nolan thought, this preoccupation with image would probably have struck one of as tiresome; in Martin it was largely redeemed by the sense he conveyed of not taking himself, any of his selves, entirely seriously. His personae were offered with a hint of caricature, the suggestion that while he

95

found them amusing and hoped you might, you were both too intelligent to take them at face value.

The image for today, Nolan gathered, was Machiavellian Martin, the campus politician.

'The operative word, of course, is yet,' Delafield went on. 'And the bottom line on that one is easy. If you want them to stay, there'll have to be changes.'

'Changes?' Sinclair asked.

'Changes.' Delafield nodded. 'I mean apart from gutter journalism, it's clear to the board things are out of hand. Those of us with kids here have been hearing horror stories. Pot sold under the counter at the tuck shop; entire dorms out of their minds on acid; kids experimenting with coke, and worse. Parents are getting nervous. Karen Hopgood, for instance, is threatening to withdraw Matthew, with less than six weeks left to graduation.'

'Threatening to withdraw him?' Sinclair frowned anxiously. 'Why?'

'She thinks this isn't a healthy environment. And I'll be frank with you. It's hard to disagree.'

Nolan felt bound to intervene. The board, of course, was entitled to its concern, but this was surely going a little far.

'Karen Hopgood?' he asked innocently. 'Wasn't she the one who gave that fund raiser? The one in Laurel Canyon where the hash pipe circulated all evening and those not smoking were mostly doing lines. You were there, Martin, I seem to recall.'

'Sure I was.' Delafield grinned. 'And so were you. But the point, Philip, and you know it, is there were no kids there.'

Pause.

'Not that night, at any rate,' Nolan said.

'All this is neither here nor there.' Sinclair frowned quickly at Nolan. 'What parents do at fund raisers is not the issue. The issue is what they expect of us. There won't be any fund raisers if people can write this kind of garbage about us. I must say,' he turned to Delafield, 'cancelling the phonathon won't be seen as a vote of confidence either.'

'True.' Delafield nodded. 'But let's face it, this is hardly the time to be asking people for money. You guys can make noises like Plato's academy, but the kids carry on like some X-rated movie . . . No one gives for something like that, and no one wants to look like an asshole for asking. And things aren't going to change until they think someone is dealing with the problem . . . The question is, how are you guys going to deal with the problem?'

'What are we doing?' Sinclair hesitated, glanced at Nolan. 'Well, our first step, obviously, is to try and assess the problem.'

'Assess?' Delafield was withering. 'Who needs it? I can tell you the problem right here and now. It isn't drugs, it's PR. It's a dead kid, a negligence suit, and some very smelly publicity. What's needed here isn't some bumbling inquiry that drags ass forever and ends up nowhere. What's needed here, and the board's behind me on this, is action, fast.'

'I see,' Sinclair said coldly. 'Can anyone on the Board suggest what action, exactly?'

'All the board knows is something had better be done. I guess it won't matter what, so long as you make lots of noise and act tough. After all, you guys are the experts. At least, at ninety-two hundred a year plus extras, you'd damn well better be.'

'Activity, in other words.' Nolan raised an eyebrow. 'Anything to raise a little dust. Doesn't that strike you as just a shade cynical?'

Delafield shrugged. 'Maybe. But look at the realities. Take a look at Karen Hopgood, since she's the reality we're dealing with here. She can't handle Matthew at home, so what does she do? She goes out and hires you guys. And of course she feels guilty about it. What consoles her is the thought that she's doing what's best for Matthew, that you guys are tough and you know what you're doing. So the last thing she wants to hear is you don't know what you're doing. She doesn't want to hear talk about the drug problem nationwide, the erosion of moral values and the decline in parental authority. She knows about the decline in parental authority; she's been there. What she wants is to see something being done. So my message is this: if you don't have it, fake it. Because otherwise you're going to lose Karen. And when you lose Karen, believe me, the rest will be hard on her heels.'

He paused, looked from Sinclair to Nolan and back again.

'I've got to say, it's hard to figure why that other kid is still here.'

'That other kid?' Nolan felt a prickle of uneasiness. 'Robert Anderson, you mean?'

Delafield nodded. 'The one that was with her that night. Drinking and doing acid.'

'You think we should expel him?'

'Of course, I do. I mean, Jesus, Philip. Look at the message you're sending the parents. The students too, for that matter. Two kids go out at the dead of night to slam beers and pop acid, and one of them doesn't come back. So the school slaps the other kid on the wrist and sends him off for a session with the shrink. Big fucking deal. As a parent let me tell you, I'm less than impressed.'

As a parent? The temptation to comment on Martin's performance in that role was almost overwhelming, but Nolan refrained. It wouldn't help Robert. And Robert, it was starting to seem, might need some help.

'What would impress you? Making a scapegoat of Robert?'

Delafield made a face. 'Scapegoat my ass. The kid broke half a dozen rules. I'm talking example. A message to the students: "Cool it with the drugs."'

'You think that's how they'd read it?' Nolan shook his head. 'They'd read it as a message about turning yourself in. "Don't tell the truth" is how they'd read it. "Don't talk, and above all don't ever try to be helpful, because if you do they'll nail you to the wall." Is *that* the message you had in mind, Martin?'

Silence. Delafield, at a loss for an answer, shrugged. Campus realpolitik, Nolan thought; Martin must have been reading Machiavelli. But it was grade school realpolitik, wasn't it? The kind of cunning that defied its own logic, and therefore uncharacteristic of Martin. Surely, as an unwavering advocate of good PR, Martin must realize that expelling Robert would achieve exactly the reverse: just more smelly publicity for Fremont.

'This is, if you'll forgive me, academic.' Sinclair's voice was quiet but firm. 'Decisions about discipline, while I'm the headmaster, are mine. In this case the decision has been made, and I've no intention of changing it. To expel Robert when we don't normally expel first time drug offenders would be to invite another lawsuit, and one lawsuit at a time, it seems to me, is plenty. But that's not my main concern. What's more important to me entirely' – he looked Delafield straight in the eye – 'is that it wouldn't be fair.'

Silence. Nolan resisted an impulse to cheer. For a moment it seemed Martin might go on arguing, but he was too intelligent to fight for lost causes.

'Fine.' He shrugged. 'You're the experts. Sit tight and play it cool and hope I can keep Karen Hopgood and the rest of them in line. But I'll tell you one thing: you'd better pray for no more accidents. Another little scandal like this and the trustees will be scrambling for the lifeboats. And I' – he fixed Sinclair with a very cold stare – 'will be right there with them.'

Again there was silence. Now that the danger to Robert was over, Nolan felt a little guilty. Without meaning to, he had pushed Sinclair into a confrontation with Martin. Martin wasn't normally vindictive, but he wasn't used to losing either; he might hold the loss against Sinclair. It was up to Nolan to mend fences, if he could.

'I think we're going about this wrong,' he said.

'Wrong?' Delafield's look was unfriendly. 'How?'

'We're going after the wrong people. We're debating what messages to send to the kids and parents and forgetting the people we really should be sending messages to. I'm talking about the dealers, the guys who create the problem in the first place. I'd like to send those bastards a really powerful message: "Stay the hell away from our kids." And at the same time, of course, we'd be addressing the concerns of the board and the parents.'

'Send a message to the dealers?' Delafield looked sceptical. 'And how, exactly, do you plan to do that?'

'Bust a couple. That ought to get their attention, don't you think?'

'Bust a couple?' It was clear the suggestion had got Delafield's attention, at least. 'What makes you think you can do that?'

'Because I know who dealt drugs to Lisa,' Nolan said.

He thought afterwards that his mistake had been to ignore the psychology. Martin had suffered a defeat and Sinclair had been forced into an unwanted victory. So Martin had been looking to repair his self-esteem and Sinclair to mend his fences with

99

Martin. They'd combined, therefore, to attack Nolan's suggestion with a vehemence that had seemed, at the time, inexplic-
able, though a rationale for their views had not, of course, been
lacking. They had agreed that an attempt to prosecute Bronco
and/or the mysterious A of Lisa's journal would involve the
school in publicity more likely to hurt it than help it. Even
though the journal couldn't be used as evidence in court, once
its existence was made public, Sinclair had also argued, her
parents would no doubt demand its return and use the contents
to bolster their suit against the school. Martin had agreed. The
best thing to do with the journal, he'd suggested, was to 'give
it the deep six.'

Nolan hadn't heard from Jacobsen since their mutually
guarded discussion over breakfast. This suggested that Jacobsen
had either thought better of his suspicions or, more likely, of
the wisdom of confiding them to Nolan. But so far as he knew,
the journal was still of interest to the police. In any case, he had
suspicions of his own. They might not extend, yet, as far as
murder, but his instinct said that Lisa, and therefore the school,
had been mixed up in something distinctly ugly – something,
moreover, that might still be going on. There was no way,
Martin and Sinclair's objections notwithstanding, that he could
leave this mystery unexplored. He therefore nodded and made
noises of obedience while privately resolving to explore the
mystery to the limit of his powers. If what he discovered
threatened to cause scandal, there'd be time enough, then, to
consider his options. In the meantime, let Sinclair and Martin
worry about PR. He, Nolan, planned to ferret out the truth.

Step one, obviously, was somehow to get Jacobsen to level.

16

Until the overhang, Jacobsen had enjoyed himself. Though he
had accepted Nolan's invitation with misgiving, he'd found
Nolan interested in climbing, and not, as he'd at first suspected,
in fishing for information. And the climbing, once they were
into it, had proved exhilarating. Granted, a four-hundred-foot

pillar of almost vertical sandstone hadn't conformed to his notion of what Nolan, on the telephone, had described as 'a staircase', but close to and under Nolan's expert guidance, he'd found it less formidable than it had seemed at first sight. Nolan, indeed, was an excellent teacher, offering little by way of instruction but instead communicating wordlessly such cheerful confidence in Jacobsen's abilities that Jacobsen had been quickly induced to share it and had found himself, as if by instinct, doing the right thing, climbing, in fact, better than he'd ever done before. He had negotiated, with minimal help from Nolan, two fairly tricky traverses and he'd pulled off a number of difficult moves. He had been feeling, in consequence, not just confident but positively cocky. He had been, that is, until he inspected the overhang.

From the ledge where they had paused for a breather it looked, he thought, next to impossible. To their right the ledge sloped up sharply, narrowing to nothing where it met the overhang. The overhang itself jutted out some eight or ten feet at forty-five degrees past the vertical and also sloped up to the right, though less acutely than the ledge, terminating in what looked like the point of an anvil. Unless you were willing to hammer in pitons and just muscle yourself up and over – and Nolan clearly wasn't the kind of climber to countenance *that* – the only way to tackle it, Jacobsen guessed, was to worm up the ledge till you got to the overhang, then, defying gravity for three or four feet, somehow wriggle over the point. The worming up, he saw, would be made easier by the crack that ran parallel to and slightly below the overhang; but how the wriggling over was to be managed was not immediately apparent. Presumably there were handholds on the far side of the point that would have to be groped for, but in the meantime you would be leaning out at a forty-five-degree angle, hanging on desperately with your other hand, and nothing between you and the murdering earth but a slender rope and 350 feet of empty space.

He glanced down. Below, more than a hundred feet, he guessed, the crows looked like small obsidian arrowheads, slicing the wind or tumbling, in sudden dizzy spirals, towards earth. The desert floor seemed flat and featureless, the junipers just smudges of dusty green on a background of washed-out ochre, and the pillar, rising from it like a mast, seemed slender and fragile, less a pillar than some immensely elongated cone, inverted and balanced precariously on its point. Indeed, it was hard to convince himself that the whole thing, earth and rock together, was not, under the pressure of the wind, ponderously swaying, like a tall ship on a barely breathing ocean, miles of interval between the swells. He pressed back, closer to the wall, and his stomach gave a small, admonitory lurch, like the first intimation of sea sickness.

He nudged Nolan.

'Should we get going?'

Until then the decisions had been made by Nolan, but if he found anything odd in Jacobsen's sudden initiative, he didn't show it. He just nodded and prepared to move out towards the point. It was noticeable, however, that his preparations for this pitch were more careful than before, as if he were conceding, though he'd at no time been casual about protection, that here, for the first time, there was danger.

'Not too much slack,' he told Jacobsen. 'No tension, of course, but if I do come off, I'd rather not fall very far. No point in giving the rope too much to do.'

'Got you.' Jacobsen nodded. 'No excess slack. No tension.'

He settled the rope around his back and across his left shoulder, so he could pay out with his left hand yet grasp it firmly with his right. He himself was anchored to the rock; if Nolan fell, he'd clamp the rope across his chest, turning himself into a kind of capstan, using friction to withstand the shock. His competence at belaying, he now recalled, was the one thing Nolan had bothered to check before starting.

Later, when Jacobsen recalled the details of that pitch, it seemed as if Nolan had done it in slow motion. There'd been calmness, a marvellous unfaltering precision to his movements, as if he'd wished each of them imprinted on Jacobsen's memory so that when his turn came he would know what to do. For the crucial move, however, since the hands and feet were not always in Jacobsen's sight, a commentary was added.

'I've reached the end of the crack. My hands are together now, the left holding the lip, the other wedged in, palm up, in

102

a fist. I'm bringing my feet up, one at a time, to a small lip just below the crack . . . Now, give me a tad more slack and I'll be set.'

Jacobsen paid out just enough to let Nolan clear the point freely, the rope neither holding him back nor getting in his way. Even so, it was clear that if he came off he'd fall more than twelve feet, a big jolt for him and a strain on the rope. The rope, of course, was tested to several times that distance and many times Nolan's weight, but testing was one thing, betting your life on the outcome was another. A good many climbers, Jacobsen knew, had made that bet and lost.

Nolan was just below the point. Arms between his knees, feet almost level with his hands, he looked like a backstroke swimmer set for the start of a race, a coil of compressed energy and tension. The lip his feet were on, Jacobsen noticed, was almost nonexistent, hardly more than a ripple on the surface of the rock.

'Now . . .' Nolan's voice was still conversational, but a fraction higher, as if physical tension had raised its pitch. 'My right hand's palm up because I'll be reaching up and over with my left. This way I've got more stretch. When I've found the hold, which should be directly above where my hands are now, I'll slide my right laterally out of the crack and bring it up to join my left.'

He sounded like a PE instructor describing some simple exercise. And the move, when he made it, seemed effortless, like standing up and reaching for the rung of a ladder. But it was a curve of motion, not a series of separate steps; there was rhythm to it, timing, and, Jacobsen guessed, considerable strength. The left hand slid out of the crack and reached up at exactly the moment the legs straightened. As the left was grasping the hold, the right was already slipping out of the crack to join it, the timing so precise that for a split second Jacobsen could have sworn that neither hand was anchored and only willpower and momentum kept Nolan from falling. Then, when both hands were solid, the feet swung sideways, found a small vertical crevice, and shuffle-stepped up a foot or two.

'Now . . . I move my right hand up and to the right . . . about eighteen inches . . . and I find, to my *enormous* relief' – Nolan's grin was just about audible – 'that no one has taken away the handhold that was here last time. And now . . . I'm up.'

His legs disappeared from Jacobsen's view.

Now, Jacobsen thought, my turn.

Although he'd felt fine as a spectator, absorbed in the mechanics and admiring Nolan's mastery, when his turn came he was not fine. The confidence he'd achieved earlier had left him, taking with it his sense of physical well-being. His limbs were heavy, gut hollow. He seemed out of energy. Worse, for the first time all day Nolan was out of sight. An irrational loneliness came over him, aggravating the sense of exposure. He felt isolated, unequal to the test ahead, scared.

He had difficulty just getting set. When he tried to bring his feet up to the lip, they kept slipping off. He spent anxious seconds scrabbling at the rock, so by the time he was set he was already half exhausted, his legs trembling, shoulder muscles burning with fatigue.

'All set?' Nolan's cheerful call came from just above.

'All set.' He could hardly make himself say it.

'Come on, then. You don't want to let yourself get tired.'

What happened next he could never really recall except as a debris of fractured impression, a scene reflected in a shattered mirror, his gathering himself for a despairing, half-hearted lunge at the handhold; his left hand clawing at the rock, getting the top joint of a finger over the lip of a crevice, then slipping; his hearing himself call out a warning to Nolan and noting with relief – things seemed to happen so slowly – that his voice was properly matter of fact, not the outraged scream that instinct demanded; above all, his terror when he knew he had fallen, when he was off the rock and toppling backwards, a mindless panic so intense it seemed that he must be dying. Beyond these he retained nothing until what felt like a lifetime later, when the rope brought him up with a gut-wrenching jerk and he opened his eyes to find himself not dead but dangling over a 350-foot drop and feeling both very relieved and more than a little bit silly.

It was then that he heard Nolan's voice, calmer than ever, a languid drawl tinged with wicked amusement.

'I think there's something on my line.'

For some reason – the unexpectedness, the inanity, his relief

104

at finding himself alive, or a combination of the three – the remark struck him as extraordinarily funny. For the next minute or so he dangled at the end of a rope, unable to get back on to the ledge because he was shaking with helpless laughter.

And with that there was no problem. Nolan could have solved it for him, of course, but dignity prohibited that. It had to be done right; he would make it up there by his own effort, not be hauled like a sack of potatoes. So he got back to the ledge, and on the second try, breezed over the point as if he'd been doing it forever.

So the climb was to blame, he told himself afterwards. Or rather the euphoria that followed. You sat on a platform far above the world, the breeze ruffling your hair, the sun still warm on your skin, the landscape below turning gold in the afternoon light, and you felt special. You felt, just by virtue of having made it up there, that you had placed yourself for a moment above the common run; that because you had risked and sweated you had earned a satisfaction denied to most. And you felt too, of course, a kinship with anyone who shared that satisfaction, as if you both belonged to one of those select clubs where membership, in itself, was a guarantee of character. He had sprawled on the warm rock, sipping at a beer Nolan had produced from his daypack, and when Nolan had asked whether the Lisa investigation was now closed, he'd responded by describing his most recent conversation with the sheriff, in rather more detail than was strictly proper and in a tone that indicated how much he disagreed with the outcome.

'So it's you, solo, and more or less in your spare time? . . . I wouldn't want you to think I underrate you, of course,' Nolan's face gave nothing away, 'but that sounds a bit like a vote of no confidence.'

Jacobsen nodded. 'That's what it is. Sam's keeping the file unofficially open, letting me poke around some more, but mostly as a sop to my pride. He says he doesn't think I can prove anything, but he really thinks there's nothing to prove. Those tracks on the ledge don't mean what I think. I've been reading too many detective stories. His own theory is it was probably the acid. She was out of her mind and decided she could fly. Who knows?' He shrugged. 'Maybe he's right.'

'Bullshit,' Nolan said.

Jacobsen stared.

'You don't think he's right,' Nolan said. 'You know you are. You know in your gut she wasn't trying to fly, but you hope that if you keep telling yourself she was, you'll end up feeling better. But it's not working, is it? If it were, you wouldn't be telling me about it.'

Why was he telling him? Jacobsen wondered. He was more or less under orders not to.

'What am I supposed to do?' he demanded. 'Sam's the one they elected sheriff. It's his job to call the shots. My job – '

'Your job is to follow orders?' Obligingly, Nolan finished the sentence for him. 'You're convinced a kid was brutally murdered, but when Uncle Sam Plunkett tells you to lose this one in the files, it's "yes, sir" and the quick salute.'

It surprised Jacobsen that he wasn't more offended. Here was Nolan, pissing on him, so to speak, from a great height, yet somehow he didn't resent it very much. Perhaps, he thought, it was because what Nolan had just told him wasn't much different from what he'd already, repeatedly, told himself.

'What would you do?' he retorted. 'Tell Plunkett to go screw himself?'

Nolan shook his head. 'If you're going to be insubordinate, you need to be very polite.'

Jacobsen stared. 'Who's going to be insubordinate? What are you suggesting, exactly?'

'Partnership,' Nolan said.

Partnership? Fat chance, Jacobsen thought. He didn't know what happened to insubordinate history professors, but insubordinate cops got fired.

'You need the journal,' Nolan pursued. 'If this was murder, someone had a motive. The most promising place to start looking for one is the journal. So you need me to interpret. But to do that effectively I have to know what I'm looking for. If I don't know what the puzzle looks like, I shan't be much help in finding the pieces.'

106

Jacobsen thought about this. It sounded plausible. But then Nolan, he guessed, made a habit of sounding plausible.

'And you're a teacher.' He smiled faintly. 'My teacher told me to watch out for people who argue from analogy.'

Nolan didn't answer. He took a pull at his beer and sat silent, frowning and gazing into the distance. It was a while before he spoke again.

'What haunts me is how she must have felt.'

'Felt?'

'When she was falling, I mean. It always terrifies me. But then it's not the same, is it? For us there's always the comfort of having the rope and someone reliable at the other end. There's that split second of panic, then you know you're OK, you'll be getting back on the rock. But how must she have felt, knowing her life had run out, that now it was lights out, forever?'

It was impossible for Jacobsen not to be reminded of his own recent experience. He could still feel the sickening lurch in his gut, the outraged protest from the whole of his being, those moments of absolute terror. Impossible, too, for this vivid recollection not to be followed by a nasty suspicion. He stared at Nolan.

'You planned this, didn't you?'

'This?' Nolan looked utterly innocent. Far too goddamned innocent, Jacobsen thought.

'You bastard.' He was caught between outrage and laughter. 'You sneaky manipulative bastard. You did plan it. You knew damn well I was going to fall and you let me. You scared the shit out of me, not to mention endangered my life, just to make some kind of point?'

Silence. Nolan struggled to maintain a poker face. A grin started at the corners of his mouth.

'But I did,' he said, 'check the rope very thoroughly.'

Check the rope? Jacobsen's outrage got the better of his laughter. 'You've got some goddamn nerve, don't you? I could have been killed – '

'She was killed.' Nolan cut him short. 'Murdered. Deliberately and coldly. For some small selfish purpose. And if you don't do something, nobody will. Whoever killed her will get away with it . . . Is that what you want?'

Of course he didn't. All his instincts rebelled at the thought. But couldn't Nolan see that in practical terms Sam Plunkett was right? There was no proof, no reasonable prospect of getting it, no clear suggestion even of where to start looking. But before he could put any of this into words, Nolan spoke again.

'I've found out who Bronco is.'

And that was the trouble with speculation, Jacobsen thought. It took you too far from the ground. You started with reasonable assumptions, proceeded with reasonable inferences, but you ended in Cloud Cuckooland.

'Billy Dabbs?' He shook his head. 'I can see him messing with one of your girls. I can see him dealing, maybe, on a nickel and dime sort of scale. I can even see him shooting himself full of smack. But murder? No way.'

'You know him, then?'

'Better than I want.' Jacobsen made a face. 'Must have booked him half a dozen times in the last few years. Drunk and disorderly, mostly.'

'And in your opinion he's not the type to commit murder?'

'Not premeditated murder,' Jacobsen qualified. 'He might brain you with a bottle if you got him pissed off enough. But sneak up behind and shove you off a cliff?' He shook his head. 'Last time we booked him he was trying to punch out an entire gang of bikers. Seems one of them had the infernal gall to buy Billy's girl a drink. He was about dead when we came and pulled them off him. That's how much he premeditates.'

Nolan thought about this.

'I knew a killer once. Nicest man you could hope to meet. Mild mannered, amusing, great with kids. We must have had him to dinner half a dozen times in the year we knew him, and each time we liked him better. One day we saw his picture in the paper. Wanted in six states for rape and murder. He was eventually convicted on nine separate counts of killing and mutilating teenage girls. *Nine counts*.' Nolan paused. 'Whenever I'm tempted to make judgements about types, I think of him.'

Jacobsen shrugged. 'Nut cases are different.'

'Maybe.' Nolan looked dubious. 'Only how do you know when you're dealing with one? In any case, it doesn't make any difference. At least now you've got a suspect. Two actually, since there's the other one.'

'Another suspect? What makes you think there's another one?'

'Logic,' Nolan said. 'If she was murdered, it had to be by someone who was waiting on the ledge, someone who knew she'd be there at three o'clock that morning. Someone she'd arranged to meet there, that is, or someone who knew she'd made that arrangement. Now the someone she'd arranged to meet was almost certainly Billy. So if Billy didn't kill her, then it had to be someone who knew about that meeting.'

'Some*one*?' Jacobsen queried. 'Why just one? Couldn't there have been several people who knew about the meeting?'

'Sure. But the one we're looking for had to know she'd be there alone. I mean, if you were planning to shove someone off a cliff, you'd pick a time when she wasn't with her boyfriend, wouldn't you?'

Jacobsen nodded. 'What you're saying, then, is that if Billy didn't kill her, whoever did would have to know that she'd be there and Billy wouldn't because – '

'Because he knew Billy never heard about the meeting.' Nolan completed the thought. 'Because, let's say, he'd been asked to give Billy a message and deliberately hadn't.'

Jacobsen thought about this. He frowned.

'I'm not very happy with this. It's sounding like Sherlock Holmes, long on speculation, very short on fact. We start with a murder, and before you can blink, we're assuming meetings, messages not delivered, and God knows what else.'

Nolan shrugged. 'The tracks prove, you say, that someone lay in wait and pushed her. I'm merely pointing out what's entailed by that belief. Besides, it's not as bad as you say. There is some corroboration.'

'There is? You mean in that journal, I suppose.' Jacobsen looked unenthusiastic.

'"Note Ac."' Nolan quoted. '"Same time and place." Look, I know the journal technically isn't evidence, but it's not fiction either. It's a record of her life. Not very complete or systematic, perhaps, but most of the entries deal with what she'd done or planned to do. And the more I think about that "Note Ac", the clearer it is that that's what she meant. She left a note with someone called Ac, asking Billy to meet her on the ledge. So either it was Billy waiting for her up there, or it was Ac.'

Silence.

'Or it was someone *from* Ac,' Jacobsen said. 'Ac could be a place.'

'True.' Nolan nodded.

'And that's only if you're right about what the journal meant.'

Nolan nodded. 'Surely it's worth checking.'

You mean it's worth me checking, Jacobsen thought sourly. The professor will supply the bright ideas; the dumb cop gets to do the legwork.

'I suppose you don't know who this Ac is, by any chance?'

'Not yet. But Billy must.'

Billy . . . Jacobsen kind of liked Billy, but the feeling was anything but mutual. At the best of times Billy was a confirmed cop hater. He would talk to Jacobsen only in the presence of a lawyer, and what he'd say would be monosyllabic and almost certainly obscene.

'Well here's where we have a problem. Billy would never talk to me. We go too far back. The only way he'd let me in the door is with a warrant. But to get a warrant I have to go through the sheriff. And I'm not,' Jacobsen said flatly, 'about to do that.'

'You want me to talk to Billy?' Nolan looked doubtful.

'Who else is there?' Jacobsen shrugged. 'You seem to get on well with people like that.'

'People like what?' Nolan demanded.

'Juvenile delinquents.'

Nolan said nothing. A grin began to steal across his face. 'You want me to stick my neck out, lay my job on the line, you'll have to contribute more than bright ideas. Get me something to work with is what I'm saying, facts I can go to the sheriff with. Maybe then he'll authorize a real investigation, something to get this mess down from the clouds and on to solid ground . . .' He paused. 'You don't look like the type to lead from behind.'

His look was a challenge.

'You've got yourself a partner,' Nolan said.

110

17

It was not until mid-afternoon on the next day that Nolan was free to tackle the problem of Billy. Since two rather somnolent classes of juniors had put him, by then, in the mood for exercise, he decided to start by making a reconnaissance on foot.

The distance was greater than he'd been led to believe, but otherwise Jacobsen's directions were accurate. At the end of a dirt road that forked off the short cut between Fremont and Buckskin, on a small rise overlooking the creek, was a kind of compound formed by three cottages built around a square. Two of them were run down and clearly unoccupied, but the third, presumably Billy's, was in good repair, securely roofed and glazed. At one time the creek had evidently run right below Billy's doorstep, but the channel had since shifted; thirty yards or so of boulders and sand now separated cottage and creek. Around the compound, giving shade and privacy, were cotton-woods and sycamores through whose branches a soft breeze sighed and twisted. From one of the branches someone had suspended a swing. The trees gave the place an air of lazy tranquillity, a peace somehow deepened by the murmur of insect voices and the soft, distant splashing of the creek.

All in all, Nolan thought, not a bad spot to live, if you could ignore the human additions. The cottages themselves were all right – unobtrusive, one-storey structures, built with rock from the creek – but their vicinity had been used, apparently, as a kind of graveyard for ruined machinery. To one side of Billy's cottage, for instance, in what had once been a garden, was an old air-conditioning unit and a pile of worn out auto tyres, their rubber cracked and stinking. Next to them lay an engine block, stripped and abandoned, an ancient boiler and the chassis of a jeep, half-buried by tumbleweed and invaded by vegetation, doing its best, it seemed, to sink back into earth.

All this was depressingly familiar, an unnecessary reminder of what Nolan's countrymen, given half a chance, were apt to do to their wide open spaces. But in this instance the presence of so many broken-down vehicles was atoned for by the absence of any in running order. The grey pickup, specifically, was nowhere to be seen.

This was what Nolan had hoped for. Though uneasy about snooping, and disliking even more the hazards of what could technically, he supposed, be called 'breaking and entering', he could see no alternative. It was easy for Jacobsen to talk airily of 'paying a visit', but barging in on a perfect stranger required at least a halfway convincing pretext, and in the twenty-four hours he had to reflect on the matter, a halfway convincing pretext was what Nolan had failed to find. His previous encounter with Billy, moreover, had clearly aroused Billy's suspicions; it was rather unlikely, with or without a convincing pretext, that Nolan would even be let in the house. But Nolan wanted to get in the house. He wanted it more than talking to Billy. Billy, most likely, would tell him very little; the house, on the other hand, might tell him quite a bit. So what he'd decided on was breaking and entering, though of course this was not how he liked to think of it. He preferred to think of it as 'looking around'.

He didn't expect much trouble getting in. Locks, he had discovered as a boy, were mostly for show; they were generally no match for a strip of celluloid or a piece of bent piano wire. Their resistance, in any case, was usually proportionate to the value of what they protected, and Billy seemed unlikely to own much worth protecting. Besides, this was the West, easygoing and openhanded; most likely there wouldn't be a lock at all.

More worrisome to Nolan was the chance that Billy kept a dog. But Nolan's preliminary and deliberately noisy approach had failed to provoke any barking from within. It was possible that a Doberman, or something equally ferocious, lurked silently inside, but in that case there would be evidence, somewhere, of its existence – a dog door or a food dish.

He marched up to the front door and knocked loudly.

This was elementary. Before you did any breaking and entering, before you so much as loitered with intent, you made damn sure there was no one inside. The best way to do this was knock. If anyone answered, you explained you were looking for a friend's house and must have lost your way. You might not be believed – in this case he almost certainly wouldn't be – but at least misleading householders was not a criminal offence. Breaking and entering, on the other hand, was.

No one answered.

Time to reconnoitre. He toured the outside of the house, pausing at each window to peer in. There was no dog door and, though the gloom inside made it hard to be sure, no sign of any lurking Doberman. There was, however, a back door, and for this he was grateful since it gave him an escape route; if any one came in at the front, he could exit quietly from the rear. With any luck he would not be detected, and if not he would make a dash for it. With all his recent training, he was sure he could outrun Billy. He just prayed there wouldn't be a dog.

He tried the back door. No lock.

He eased the door open a crack. No dog.

As a final precaution he called out, 'Anyone home?' No answer. He stepped inside, leaving the door ajar.

The small kitchen, very low and dark, seemed to belong to an earlier, simpler era. There was a light switch by the door, but the only light socket, on the wall above the sink, was empty. An oil lantern, which Nolan just missed hitting his head on, hung from one of the rafters, and in the corner, where one might have expected a refrigerator, there stood instead an old-fashioned ice chest. The stove was wood burning, and the square procelain sink, very chipped and stained, was served by a single brass tap. Under the sink was a bowl of water and, next to it, a dog dish.

Ignoring the feelings aroused by this discovery, Nolan moved into the room beyond the kitchen. Like the kitchen, it suggested a life deliberately simplified and Spartan. A single armchair of indeterminate colour and almost threadbare faced an open stone fireplace, next to which was a small wood bookcase, stocked with tattered paperbacks, mostly Westerns. Against the far wall was an oak table, unpainted, and two straight-backed oak chairs. Next to the table was a dresser with a stack of dinner plates on one of its shelves. And that was all. Apart from the sparseness of the furniture, the most striking thing about this room was its lack of decoration. Excluding the Winchester that rested on pegs above the mantel and whose purpose, Nolan suspected, was not decorative, the only relief from bare practicality was the row of carved wood figures on the lower shelf of the bookcase.

Even here, it seemed, the intent had not been decoration. At least the arrangement, or lack of it, suggested otherwise. They looked, these five or six carvings, as if they'd been just shoved there, for neatness perhaps, but with little thought of display. Next to them were some blocks of raw wood and a penholder cutting tool of the kind used by model builders. Nolan examined one of the carvings. It was a bear, competently done in pine, about six inches in height. On the base was a pencilled number, '8.50', which he took to be the price. The other figures, he noticed, were unfinished. One of them, only the torso roughly completed, was of a naked woman with waist-length hair.

His attention was caught by a stack of papers on the table. Most of them were bills. An exception was what appeared to be an estimate from a firm of local scrap dealers 'For the removal of listed items: one jeep (no salvage value), one truck chassis (ditto). $150.' Across it was scrawled in heavy black pencil the word 'THIEVES'.

Having apparently exhausted the information offered by the living room, he moved on. Simplicity prevailed in the bedroom also. Narrow box bed. Horsehair mattress. Sleeping bag on top of the mattress. Chest of drawers. Wardrobe. Along one wall a row of wooden pegs, from which hung a yellow slicker and a wool jacket with leather patches on the shoulders. Below these, boots – hiking boots, work boots, cowboy boots – lined up by height, like soldiers on parade. Again he was struck by the almost monastic austerity with which Billy had deliberately surrounded himself.

But information about the man's character, however odd and intriguing, was not what Nolan had come for. He needed to confirm beyond question that Billy was the Bronco of Lisa's journal. So far he'd found nothing to suggest that the monkish streak he discerned in Billy had been mitigated by his having any love life at all, let alone one with Lisa.

Daunted but not defeated, Nolan investigated the wardrobe. He found a suit and two jackets, nothing in any of the pockets. He tried the chest of drawers. The first drawer was empty. The next contained some pairs of socks and a pile of shirts, each neatly folded. The next yielded Levi's, underpants, and a couple of sweaters. In the fourth drawer, however, just as he was starting to contemplate defeat, he found his confirmation.

114

It was a jumble of old papers – letters, photos, newspaper clippings, odd sheets torn from a yellow pad and covered with jottings in pencil. The photos were of Lisa: Lisa in profile, a posed studio portrait inscribed, 'To Bronco with kisses.' Lisa on horseback, smiling rather nervously. Lisa skinny-dipping, waist-deep in the creek, covering her breasts with her arms, laughing. Lisa, aged about five, dressed up in a party frock and contriving to look at the same time angelic and slightly mutinous.

The letters were mostly disappointing. They were all from 'Your Loving Mother', but the first sentence that caught Nolan's eye was such an ugly mix of priggishness and disapproval he was reluctant to read any more. It was unlikely, he thought, that Billy had confided much in someone who could write: 'The way you've been going, dragging our name in the mud, me and your Dad don't care to see you, and we won't till you make it up to us.' He hoped Billy hadn't bothered to reply.

The yellow sheets suggested he probably hadn't. They were mostly notes from Billy to himself and revealed a variety of preoccupations, none of which had anything to do with his mother. Most of them, in fact, concerned Lisa. The longest was a letter to her that Billy had started but for some reason never finished.

Faced with it, Nolan was assailed, surprisingly, by scruples. He'd been brought up, of course, to believe that gentlemen refrained from reading each other's correspondence. But it was strange to find himself choosing this to worry about when the entire code of gentlemanly behaviour was at odds with his presence in the house. Gentlemen didn't suspect each other of murder, either. They didn't break into each other's houses and pick through each other's belongings. And to balk at the one while doing the other seemed like swallowing a camel while straining at a gnat. But he was inclined to balk, and on looking at the reasons, he was further surprised to discover that they had to do mostly with the impression which somehow, in spite of the journal, he'd formed of Billy. Billy, though probably a drug addict and possibly worse, in some sense was a gentleman and ought to be exempt from this snooping. But Nolan was here now, committed. He'd come to snoop, and he did.

115

You told me once, how it could make you feel better to write a letter you didn't plan on sending. I don't think anything can make me feel better right now, but I will try anyway. I will write though there's no place to send this and you couldn't read it if there was. Maybe if I concentrate real hard, a thought or something will get through to you where you are and at least you will know I love you and think about you always.

But thinking won't bring you back. Concentrating won't either. I think about you, but nothing comes back. There's only me here, thinking. Nobody's listening. I won't be seeing you, or hearing you, or touching you any more. Not ever. When I remember that, I can't stand it.

What makes it worse is how close it seems, like I just looked away for a moment and when I looked back you were gone. When I missed you Saturday, I called your dorm Sunday and they couldn't find you. I figured I'd see you Monday then, but on Monday you were dead. I have to get it into my head that you aren't coming back, but all I can think is if I could only go back and have Saturday over, I could somehow change things, reach out and grab you and stop you from falling. But I can't. You get farther and farther away, and all I can do is write this dumb letter.

I don't think this writing was such a great idea. I don't feel better, I feel worse. Maybe this only works when you know you could send the letter if you wanted. I figure only one thing's going to make me feel better right now. I know you wanted me to quit, and maybe I would have. But that was when you were around and I had something to quit for. Now I can't think of a reason.

There the letter broke off. Whether it was finished was not clear, nor, Nolan thought, did it matter. What mattered was that it completely exonerated Billy. Unless you believed he'd expected it to be read and had set out deliberately to mislead – a suspicion impossibly far fetched and belied, in Nolan's view, by the obvious sincerity of the writing – then you had to conclude that Billy hadn't known about the death until sometime after it had happened.

This was a big step forward. Eliminating Billy as a suspect

freed him up to be a witness. Though he hadn't gone to meet Lisa on the ledge that night, he might very well – once the existence of 'Note Ac' had been brought to his attention – know who had. Once he was convinced that Lisa had been murdered, he'd surely be willing to sink his dislike of the police in order to help them nail the killer. In the meantime Nolan had got what he had come for. It was time to leave.

Almost exactly as that thought occurred to him, he heard the truck.

Later, he would again blame himself for what happened. In all his dealings with Billy, it seemed, snap decisions led to mistakes. But again there was not enough time to think. Reflexes took over. He was through the living room and into the kitchen before the footsteps reached the front door.

With a little less haste he might have made it, might have remembered the lantern that was hanging from the rafters at the level of his head. As it was, however, he hit it squarely, hurling it to the ground with an explosive crash, like a grenade going off in a greenhouse.

For one startled moment there was silence. Then a furious voice, Billy's, called out, 'Who the hell is that?'

Then a dog started to bark.

The dog was in the truck. Billy had to let him out, and it was this, ironically, that let Nolan escape. It gave him, at least, a head start across the creek before the pursuit was properly organized. The creek was waist-deep. Nolan cleared it, boulder hopping, in two adrenalin-powered leaps. The current was swift enough to slow-down Billy's half-grown German shepherd. It dashed back and forth at the brink, barking but without real conviction. So Nolan was spared the embarrassment of a citizen's arrest and being handed over to Jacobsen for housebreaking.

This was not quite the stroke of luck he took it for.

117

Part 2

18

Jacobsen wished he had a warrant. He didn't like unofficial inquiries, and he didn't like bluffing. They put him at a disadvantage and he didn't like that either. Especially when dealing with someone like Billy, he liked to be backed by the authority of the law.

But the authority of the law, in this case, meant a warrant. He had the patrol car and his uniform, but the record showed that Billy had never been much impressed by patrol cars and uniforms. And the nature of Jacobsen's present business with him, not to mention resentment accumulated from past encounters, made it unlikely that this attitude would change. It was more likely, Jacobsen thought, that on seeing him Billy would ask to see his warrant and, when none was forthcoming, would show him the door.

He wished he had a warrant. But to get one you had to show probable cause. For that he would have to explain how he'd come to know about Billy's connection with Lisa. And that presented a problem. Apart from his natural reluctance to go to Plunkett and admit he had ignored a direct order and involved himself, albeit unwittingly, in the illegal search of Billy's house, there was also a small matter of the Fourth Amendment: evidence unlawfully obtained couldn't be used as the basis for issuing a warrant. Far from being backed by the authority of law, he was operating dangerously outside it. To be precise, he was compounding a felony.

It could cost him his job. But this bothered him less than the breach of trust he'd committed. He took his job seriously. He respected the law. He believed that those entrusted with authority owed it the very strictest obedience. And though, like most policemen, he'd found that the law, especially the Fourth Amendment, could occasionally obstruct what he conceived to be justice, he'd never before deliberately flouted it. So what he was doing here made him profoundly uneasy. Billy might be a drunk and an occasionally tiresome rowdy, but it was his rights, as much as anyone's, the Fourth Amendment existed to protect. He had the right not to have his house broken into, even in the pursuit of justice, and also the right, if it were broken into, to expect the police to pursue and prosecute the culprit, not conspire to profit from the results.

There was a lesson here somewhere. You started by bending the rules a little, and before you knew it you were breaking them right and left. And now there was no way back. He couldn't got to the sheriff, for he had nothing at this point but insubordination to show him. Billy might be a useful witness, useful, that was, if he could ever be persuaded to tell what he knew. But equally he might not. On the other hand he was a very promising lead – far too promising to pass up – and Nolan, who would have been the natural choice to follow it up, had disqualified himself with his stupid and botched break-in. There was no help for it, Jacobsen thought. If he wanted to get to the bottom of this, he must stick his neck out. Again.

He hoped he wouldn't get it chopped off.

It was almost a relief to find Billy not home. Or not in the house. His pickup was in the yard and the dog was inside, barking hysterically when Jacobsen knocked. But Billy evidently wasn't, for though Jacobsen called repeatedly and the dog made a racket to raise the dead, no one came to the door.

Perhaps he'd gone for a walk. Or maybe fishing. It was a fine evening for it, one of those lovely spring evenings, filled with the promise of summer, when you didn't care what you caught and fishing became meditation. It was a feeling, in spite of his mission, that Jacobsen could have brought himself to share. He almost wished he'd brought his rod. To the east, up the valley, the red sandstone cliffs seemed to glow from within, their colours so rich that it was hard to believe they were real, and above them, wisps of cirrus, catching the last of the sun, burned in the sky with plumes of fire. The wind in the leaves overhead and the distant rushing of the creek served only to deepen the sense of peace. Police work, and the aberrations that gave rise to it, seemed in these circumstances almost irrelevant, chatter that fell silent before the hushed magnificence of the landscape. It was perfect, Jacobsen thought. Or would have been, but for the yapping of that goddamned dog.

But the dog meant Billy was around here somewhere. Had he planned to be absent long, he wouldn't have left his dog in the house. Jacobsen decided to wait. He'd sit on the tree stump next to the truck, smoke a cigarette and enjoy the evening. In time, no doubt, the dog would quit.

But it didn't quit. It kept on insistently, pausing at intervals to scrabble at the door. And afer some minutes of trying to ignore it, Jacobsen found himself bothered, not only by the noise itself, but by the note of something other than aggression in it. This, he began to suspect, was not a dog warding off an intruder, it was a dog in distress. A dog, in fact, close to panic.

Jacobsen searched the yard until he found something to defend himself with, a piece of lumber about the size of a baseball bat. It was one thing to guess that the dog was scared out of its wits, but another to risk his safety on that judgement. It was best to be prepared.

He approached the porch. The barking redoubled.

He tried the door. It was unlocked. Placing a foot against it as a stopper, he eased it open a crack. A black snout thrust itself into the crack and worked this way and that, as if hoping to worm its way through. Stepping back and to one side and holding his club at the ready, he pulled the door open.

He didn't have to defend himself. The dog bolted for the pickup and disappeared, tail between its legs. From beneath the pickup it peered out, ears laid back against its head, whining.

The body was slumped in an armchair, head back, mouth open. One arm dangled limply over the side of the chair; the other, clasped across the chest, was holding something. The eyes were open and staring. Later, when he'd had time to take in the details, saw what it was that was grasped in that hand and what was wrapped around the arm, Jacobsen would understand

123

perfectly what had happened. In that first moment, however, all he could focus on was the face. And one glance at the gaping agony of the mouth, the eyes wide with sudden surprise and terror, told him that Billy wouldn't be helping him with the inquiry. Not now, not ever.

19

'Cardiac arrest,' Fogarty said. 'Respiratory failure. According to the lab, that kid shot up with fifteen per cent heroin. That's six times as strong as the stuff they sell on the street. His whole system closed down. He must have died immediately.' Fogarty shook his head. 'Happens to most of them in the end. They build up a tolerance, so they have to keep upping the dose. Then they're always pushing the limits. Sooner or later they push too far . . .' He jerked a thumb towards the chilly, evil-smelling room they had just left, where the remains of Billy Dabbs lay quietly under a sheet. '. . . Like that one.'

That one? Jacobsen, as often before, was offended by Fogarty's tone. He tried to put out of his mind the image of Billy, mutilated, on the slab. Another of Fogarty's unpleasant characteristics, Jacobsen thought, was his delight in showing off his handiwork. Plus he was always labelling people – taking pleasure in regarding what had once been a human as just a piece of defunct machinery, an assemblage of muscle and cartilage, bone and sinew, formerly inhabited by a bundle of more or less psychotic impulses, and now, mercifully, reduced to meat . . . That was wrong, Jacobsen thought. Wrong morally and wrong in fact. And wrong especially in this case. For even on Fogarty's own terms, even accepting his sweeping exclusion of all the qualities that had made Billy essentially Billy, the classification was inaccurate. Billy was not just a dead heroin addict. Jacobsen was willing to bet he hadn't been an addict at all.

'Can you tell us about the state of his health?'

'The state of his health?' Fogarty echoed the phrase condescendingly. 'I think you could say the state of his health is critical . . . Of course, it often is when you're dying.'

124

Jacobsen repressed a sigh. 'I meant the state of his health before he OD'd. He didn't strike me as all that sick or emaciated. But then I guess I'm not qualified to judge.'

'No.' Fogarty smiled faintly. 'I'd have to say not.'

'Which is why I'm asking.' Jacobsen prayed, inwardly, for patience. 'Was he, in fact, sick or emaciated?'

'Not particularly.' Fogarty shrugged.

'Was there much needle scarring?'

'There was some scarring at the left elbow. Not a lot.'

'But no collapsed veins, or anything like that?'

Fogarty shook his head. 'What are you driving at?'

'What I'm driving at is whether it was accidental. As I hear it, ODs generally occur either to beginners or to those in the very late stages of addiction. With people who don't know what they're doing, in other words, or those who're too far gone to care. Billy doesn't fit in either category. He sounds to me like someone who was developing a habit, who wasn't very far gone but knew enough not to OD by mistake. So I'm wondering perhaps if it wasn't accidental.' Jacobsen paused for a moment to stare at Fogarty. 'See I may not be much at forensic pathology, but I am quite good at premises and conclusions.'

'Now hold on there, Olin,' Plunkett jumped in to head off hostilities. 'Because Dabbs doesn't fit the categories doesn't mean he didn't OD by accident.'

Jacobsen nodded. 'Of course it doesn't. I'm talking possibilities here. But as the ME himself says, Billy died of a massive overdose. Now surely he couldn't have shot himself up, by accident, with six times the normal dose?'

Silence.

'Maybe he did it on purpose.' Plunkett shrugged. 'I don't see it making a hell of a lot of difference, anyway. Heroin is just a slow process of suicide anyway. Perhaps he decided to step on the gas.'

Bullshit, Jacobsen thought, but said nothing.

'You seem unhappy,' Plunkett pursued. 'You have other ideas, perhaps?'

Jacobsen did. Unfortunately, thanks to Nolan's methods of investigation, he was not able to explain these ideas to Plunkett. It was clear, moreover, that without far more evidence than Jacobsen could presently muster Plunkett wouldn't listen to any more talk of murder. Murder, however, was what Jacobsen suspected. That Billy should have chosen this precise moment to OD struck him, to say the least, as suspiciously untimely. And there was more than timing to fuel his suspicions. There was also 'Note Ac'.

At least he was almost certain that was what it was. Once he'd made sure Billy was past help, he'd taken a thorough look around and had found the note in the same drawer of papers that Nolan had poked through. It was from Lisa to Billy – the handwriting, at any rate, was the same as the handwriting in the journal. Seemed to confirm, in detail, the theory that Nolan suggested.

Missed you here. Bummer. Need to talk, urgently, but no chance till tomorrow. It'll have to be late (rumours of a late night check). So let's say the usual place, at three, when the fuzz will be copping its z's. Be there, cowboy of my heart. I miss you.

It was odd that Nolan had missed it. Or not odd, Jacobsen thought, because he'd lay odds Nolan hadn't missed it. Nolan had operated, admittedly, under the stress of not knowing when Billy might come home, so his search of the drawer had no doubt been hurried; it was at least conceivable that he'd missed it. What made Jacobsen doubt this, however, was the fact that Billy's letter to Lisa, the one Nolan said exonerated Billy, had vanished.

There was no trace of it. Not in the drawer, nor among the papers on the living room table, nor in the trash. Nor, so far as he'd been able to discover in half an hour of very careful searching, was it anywhere else in the house. And that meant, since it was inconceivable that Nolan had been mistaken about it and hardly less so that he had lied, either that Billy himself had removed it, or that someone else had.

So Jacobsen was profoundly unhappy. The simultaneous appearance of one piece of evidence and disappearance of another greatly disturbed him, as did certain aspects of Billy's death. So did his continued deception of Plunkett. He was very much tempted to come clean, in fact, to admit that he'd ignored Plunkett's order and to lay out, in justification, what he and

Nolan had so far discovered. But that was the problem. What had they discovered? A romantic connection between Lisa and Billy. A note from Lisa inviting someone, presumably Billy, to meet her, possibly at around the time she'd been killed and perhaps on the ledge. And a letter from Billy, now inconveniently lost, suggesting that he'd not received her note and had therefore not made it to the meeting. A combination of circumstances, in other words, on which it was possible to place a sinister construction if – and the 'if' here was crucial – you were willing to accept in the first place that Lisa had been murdered. But Plunkett was far from willing. He believed she had slipped or jumped, and, as he'd be very quick to point out, there was nothing at all in what Jacobsen and Nolan had discovered to make him change his mind. In short, the consequences of coming clean now were likely to be a sharp deterioration in Jacobsen's relations with Plunkett and a revocation of the limited hunting licence that Plunkett had reluctantly granted him.

The deterioration in relations Jacobsen could handle. He would regret it, because he was genuinely fond of Plunkett and knew the feeling was mutual. But the revocation of his hunting licence would be more serious. He was convinced, now, that both Lisa and Billy had been murdered. The illicit partnership he had formed with Nolan was now the only thing operating to bring their killer to justice. This partnership must not be jeopardized by premature confessions. So when Plunkett, a little sharply, repeated the question about other ideas, Jacobsen shrugged and said no; it wasn't that he disagreed, exactly, just that the whole thing struck him as odd. As he said so, however, he promised himself, soon, a talk with Nolan.

20

'It wasn't there,' Nolan said. 'I didn't read everything, but I looked at everything. This note wasn't there.'

'You're sure of that?' Jacobsen asked.

'Positive.'

'And this is her handwriting?'

'No question.'

Jacobsen sighed. 'Then this opens a whole new can of worms. I mean, if Billy never got this – '

'Wait,' Nolan held up a hand. 'If we're going to be thinking, we'll be needing more beer. And a pen and paper.'

He got up and went over the counter where he got two Heinekens, a blank sheet of paper, and a very fetching smile from the barmaid. Jacobsen, observing him, grinned to himself. There was something about Nolan that seemed to make people smile.

Returning to the table, Nolan pulled out a ballpoint. 'What we've got here,' he told Jacobsen, 'is a five-step sorites. And those can be bastards, so it's best to write them down.'

'Sorites?' Jacobsen queried.

'A chain of syllogisms in which the conclusion of the first is tacitly assumed as a premise in the second, and so on.' Nolan started writing. 'Lewis Carroll loved them.'

'Lewis Carroll? . . . The guy who wrote *Alice in Wonderland*?'

'Also a noticed logician,' Nolan added. 'Queen Victoria read *Alice* and liked it so much she asked for everything written by the author. She got a stack of tomes on mathematical logic. I'll be bet she was bummed.' Nolan grinned and kept writing. He handed the results to Jacobsen.

1. Either Billy put the note to meet Lisa in the drawer, or someone else did.

2. If Billy's letter to Lisa is taken at face value, Billy didn't put the note in the drawer.

3. If someone else put it there, the motive was probably to persuade anyone who looked that Billy did receive the note.

4. In that case, whoever put the note in the drawer:
   a) probably removed Billy's letter to Lisa.
   b) expected that the drawer would be searched.

5. If someone expected the drawer would be searched, he must have had reason. (He anticipated Billy's death from an overdose, possibly?)

'Impressive . . .' Jacobsen made a face, handed the sheet back to Nolan. 'I'm sure Lewis Carroll would've been proud of you.

Trouble is, this is all so hypothetical. Nothing but if, if, if. What I'd like to see is just one piece of solid fact.'

'You want a fact?' Nolan scribbled a final sentence on the sheet of paper, and handed it to Jacobsen. 'How's this for a fact?'

6. There's no earthly reason, even for a nasty-minded, super-sceptical cop, not to take Billy's letter to Lisa at face value.

Jacobsen took a long pull at his beer. He gazed at Nolan. Nolan held his gaze.

'That's always assuming you trust me,' Nolan said.

'I don't,' Jacobsen said, 'drink with people I don't trust.'

'A sound moral principle,' Nolan smiled. 'Then there's your fact. And there's a real knockdown argument for you. Hypothetical syllogism, followed by a disjunctive syllogism, followed by three more hypotheticals. Bam . . . Bam . . . Bam . . . What more could you ask for?'

'Facts,' Jacobsen said.

Nolan rolled his eyes. 'Facts? You've got Billy's fingerprints on file somewhere, don't you? Have someone fingerprint this note. If Billy's prints are on it, my theory is shaken. If they're not, on the other hand . . .' He paused. 'I'd be willing to bet money they're not.'

'Money?' Jacobsen queried. 'How much?'

'A hundred bucks. Am I on?'

For a moment Jacobsen considered it, then he shook his head. 'You're probably right,' he said. 'Plus I don't like to bet against myself. I want this thing to start making sense. I want you to be right.'

'I am right,' Nolan said. 'But get it fingerprinted anyway. In the meantime, let's think about what we've got. Someone expected that drawer to be searched because someone knew Billy was going to die. And the only person who could possibly know that is the person who arranged for it. Correct?'

'Another murder.' Jacobsen nodded gloomily. 'But why? And why now?'

'To shut Billy up, of course. Because once Billy knew we suspected . . .' Nolan, launching once more into confident explication, faltered and broke off. He looked sick, almost stricken, as if, in his jaunty ascent of the staircase of his logic, he'd rounded a corner and come face to face with a ghost. 'Oh Christ,' he muttered. 'It was me, wasn't it? I must have left that drawer open. If I hadn't gone blundering in, he might not have been harmed. He wasn't before, because he wasn't perceived as a threat. But when someone started poking around in his papers . . .'

'Wait a minute,' Jacobsen interrupted, 'this is way too fast for me. You're saying, if I've got your right, that Billy was killed to stop him from leading us to Lisa's killer. That assumes Lisa's killer knew we were after him. But how could he? The coroner's verdict was accidental death. And no one knows there's even a question about it, except you, me, and the sheriff. And I haven't told anyone, and I'm sure Sam Plunkett hasn't. Have you?'

Nolan shook his head.

'Then he can't know, can he?'

'I guess, strictly speaking, he can't *know*,' Nolan said. 'But I wouldn't mind betting he worries. He's safe so long as everyone thinks Lisa was an accident or suicide. But the moment someone starts thinking murder, he's at risk. Or he is, at least, while Billy's around, because Billy can connect him with Lisa.'

'But is he at risk?' Jacobsen objected. 'At least, why should he think he is? . . . I mean, we've got this theory about meetings and notes because we've got Lisa's journal. But the killer most likely doesn't know it exists. Why should he think we can connect him to Lisa?'

'Logic,' Nolan said.

Jacobsen sighed. 'I was afraid you were going to say that.'

'It's like one of those puzzles,' Nolan said. Now that he was back into problem solving, Jacobsen noticed, his dismay at his assumed involvement in Billy's death was forgotten. 'Those ones where, if you assume someone else can reason, you can infer the solution from his behaviour.'

'Oh, those puzzles,' Jacobsen feigned enlightenment. 'I just love them. Do one every night at bedtime. Helps me sleep.'

'Just think about it,' Nolan insisted. 'We became interested in notes because logic demanded, if we assumed a murder, that we assume a meeting as well. And that in turn meant the killer was either the person whom Lisa had arranged to meet, or

130

someone who knew about the meeting and also knew that the person she'd arranged to meet wouldn't show. All that was just logic. Now my point is this. We don't have a monopoly on logic. If we can work that out, so can the killer. And if he can, he'll assume we can. He'll know, in other words, that once we start thinking about murder, we'll be thinking about meetings. And once that happens, we'll most likely be wanting to talk to Billy.'

'Objection . . .' Jacobsen held up a hand to stop the flow. 'Why Billy, specifically?'

'Because the killer knew that Lisa had, in fact, tried to arrange a meeting with Billy. We have the note to prove that. So the killer would have to figure there was at least a chance she'd have told *someone* about it. One of her school buddies, for instance. So, if we started asking around, as indeed you did, Billy's was the name that was likely to come up.'

'OK.' Grudgingly, Jacobsen gave ground. 'Let's say I buy that. There's still a problem. Why would the killer worry about us talking to Billy? I mean, Billy can't tell us the killer knew about the meeting, because Billy himself didn't know about it. So what can Billy tell us?'

'Maybe not much,' Nolan shrugged. 'But then again, who knows? Let's say, for instance, that Lisa was in the habit, as the journal suggests she was, of leaving messges for Billy with this Ac character. And let's also say, because it's at least possible, that Billy learns that she tried to fix a meeting with him for the night she died. Might not he put two and two together?'

Jacobsen pondered.

'He might. But if so, this Ac simply denies it. He burns the note, denies all knowledge, and leaves us sucking our thumb.'

'It's an option, I suppose,' Nolan conceded. 'But not one I'd expect him to find appealing. It brings him to our notice, doesn't it? Shoves him under the microscope. For a killer, I'd imagine, not a comfortable place to be. But if he eliminates Billy, on the other hand, kills him in a way that looks like suicide or accident, and at the same time plants the note so the suspicion, if any, for Lisa's murder falls on Billy, then the killer is in the clear. His name simply never comes up.'

'OK,' Jacobsen sighed. 'We'll grant that too. You still haven't covered my original point: how does the killer know we think Lisa was murdered?'

'He doesn't,' Nolan said. 'But he worries. He realizes Billy is his Achilles' heel, so anyone taking unusual interest in Billy is going to alarm him. Now, look at what he sees. First, I accost Billy at the service with some half-baked story about mistaking him for someone else, a story he doesn't even begin to believe. Then, on top of that, someone breaks into his house, not to rob him, but to poke around in his correspondence with Lisa. Someone is showing marked interest, in other words, in Billy's connection with Lisa. Put that together with the paranoia natural in the circumstances, and it seems to me you have a surefire formula for panic. Bells start going off in the killer's head. "Get rid of Billy," they say. "Get rid of him now, before people start talking to him."'

'So we have to assume, too, that Billy told the killer about your break-in? Otherwise, how would the killer ever know about the break-in?'

'Right,' Nolan said. 'If A and Ac are the same person, Billy spent a lot of time with him. It bothered Lisa, in fact, that Billy was so close with him. So it doesn't seem unlikely that Billy would have told him.'

It doesn't seem unlikely? It was a phrase Jacobsen had heard too often. It ran, in fact, like a fraying thread through the whole complex web that Nolan, so plausibly, had woven. Jacobsen found himself thinking of Sam Plunkett. It was not hard to imagine his reaction to all this. Webs were all fine and dandy, Jacobsen could hear him saying, but like all webs, this one was mostly holes.

'I don't know,' Jacobsen said. 'It all sounds very neat, but there's an awful lot of "let's assume this" and "let's say that". Far too much guesswork for my taste, and still not nearly enough facts.'

'True,' Nolan conceded. 'It's a complicated hypothesis and it makes a lot of assumptions. But it does cover the facts . . . And that's what hypotheses are meant to do, isn't it? They explain the known facts by postulating others. If the other facts start turning up that tends to confirm the hypothesis, doesn't it?' He paused. 'And the other facts *are* turning up. Your original theory, for instance, entailed a meeting, and my hypothesis as

132

to how that meeting was arranged postulated a note. And Bingo! We discover a note. One would think,' Nolan grinned, 'that instead of giving me all this grief, you'd be putting me up for sheriff. I mean, the thing is almost solved, isn't it? We more or less know who did it.'

'This mysterious Mr Ac.' Jacobsen made a face.

'Of course. Now all we have to do is find out who he is.'

'All?' Jacobsen stared. 'You think that's all?'

'What more is there?'

'I'll tell you what,' Jacobsen said. 'We identify Ac, let's say. And let's say we satisfy ourselves he did indeed do it. We've still just hardly begun. Because then, Mr Logicman, we have to *prove* it.'

21

In the days following his conversation with Jacobsen, Nolan was unable to give much thought to the identity of Ac. His time was all taken up with the annual production known at Fremont as 'The Open House'. This two-day junket, Sinclair invariably declared in his speech to open the proceedings, was the means whereby the school expressed its gratitude to its principal supporters and benefactors, the parents. That it did so by drawing them into the bosom of the family, inviting them to join, more or less, in the daily life of the school, was carefully premeditated. It was vital, as Sinclair also remarked, though not to the same audience, that the parents receive a thoroughly satisfying account of just what they were shelling out $9,200 a year, plus extras, for. And it was always a good idea, when expressing gratitude, to do it in circumstances likely to encourage more generosity. As Nolan readily conceded, there was much hard sense in this. But the occasion wasn't one he looked forward to. He anticipated two days of misleading parents about the talents of their children and seeing his classroom turned into a circus where he, undoubtedly, would be the performing seal. Experience, moreover, suggested no one would have a good time. When you brought together the parties

133

involved in a teenager's education, you created, on all sides, a sense of strain.

'Poetry.' Mrs Carmichael awoke with a gasp of rapture. 'But I adore poetry.'

Though slurring her words a little, she managed to convey, with the rapture, a certain indulgent amusement. Now that she'd napped, she intimated, she was perfectly willing to play school, but only so long as she wasn't expected to take it too seriously. She yawned and sat up, assuming a look of earnest attentiveness and perching on the very edge of her seat, so her legs, turned sideways, were clear of the desk and directly in Nolan's line of sight. Her skirt, he noticed, was hitched rather higher than comfort alone demanded. Mrs Carmichael's legs were her best feature; she was clearly in the habit of making the most of them.

'But why poetry?' Her tone grew puzzled. 'I thought this was a history class.'

Nolan's heart sank. When Mrs Carmichael, arriving ten minutes late, had seated herself and fallen promptly asleep, he'd been somewhat offended. Now he viewed it as a temporary blessing. Sinclair had blundered, he felt, in serving wine with lunch.

'It is history,' he tried not to sound too weary. 'We were inquiring, if you recall, into contemporary attitudes to the Great War. We've been looking at war poems: one from the trenches by Wilfred Owen, and one from the home front by Edgar Guest.'

'Ah . . .' she sighed. 'Edgar. He was one of my favourites at school. Such depth, don't you think? Such exquisite rhythm.'

Edgar's verse, Nolan thought, had neither sense nor music, but a literary argument with Mrs Carmichael was not what the moment called for.

'The class tended to prefer the other, actually.'

'Really? How interesting.' The tone was polite but puzzled. 'But what about Poe, in that case? Are you familiar with his work at all? . . . "Annabel Lee", for instance.'

An unnatural stillness, evidence of their glee at these exchanges, had descended on the students. It was an unwritten

134

rule with them not to hassle a teacher when there were strangers in the classroom, but good nature had its limits. There was no rule against their enjoying themselves if one of the parents hassled the teacher. And it only added spice to the situation that Nolan, an expert hassler himself, should this time be on the receiving end.

'Let me see now . . . How does it go?' Mrs Carmichael threw back her head and shut her eyes. Her lips were slightly parted. She seemed to await possession by the muse.

It was many and many a year ago,
In a kingdom by the sea,
That a maiden lived whom you may know,
By the name of Annabel Lee.
And . . .

Her voice trailed away. She made a sort of imperious beckoning gesture, like an actress demanding a prompt. It seemed the muse, at this critical juncture, had withdrawn.

Nolan considered his options. This was getting awkward. In other circumstances he might have shut her up, but there were other parents present. There was also Evan Carmichael to think of. Evan had taken refuge in dignity, sitting bolt upright and staring straight ahead, his neck about an inch longer than normal and his cheeks somewhat flushed. His look said that anyone daring to laugh would have him to reckon with later. God rot parents like Mrs Carmichael, Nolan thought, and preserve their children from them.

'Interesting man, Poe,' he said gently. 'To return to the subject at hand, however – '

He was interrupted. The muse had returned to Mrs Carmichael.

She was a child, and I was a child
In this kingdom by the sea,
But we loved with a love that was more than love,
I and my Annabel Lee . . .

How long this might have gone on Nolan was never to know. There were forty odd lines of 'Annabel Lee', and Mrs Carmichael, clearly, was bent on reciting them all, or as many as she could remember. Before she could get any farther, however, she was interrupted. Not by Nolan, but by the sudden wail of a siren and an earsplitting crash from the back of the class where three members of the school's fire crew, rushing to answer the summons, obeyed, in doing so, another unwritten rule – one that forbade fire crew members to respond to the siren without in the process upsetting their desks. A practice drill, Nolan thought. Another move in Sinclair's campaign to show the parents value for their money. Quite an astute move, really, and, in the circumstances, a blessing.

It was not, however, a practice. The students were all accounted for quickly, and nobody was hurt, but that was the best that could be said. Otherwise Sinclair's sour verdict on the incident seemed wholly fitting. Had the thing been carefully rehearsed, he said later, had months been devoted to the planning, a more damning display of incompetence could hardly have been contrived.

A dormitory was gutted, for one thing, a dozen rooms and their contents totally destroyed. It was not immediately clear how the fire had started, but it had spread quickly. By the time the school's fire crew showed up the flames had taken hold, and the crew, with its less than professional equipment, had achieved little more than a kind of impotent sprinkling, a procedure described by one onlooker as 'a bit like peeing on the fires of hell.' Had the blaze been caught sooner, as the town's firemen pointed out when they arrived, the school's crew could probably have handled it. It was all the more embarrassing, therefore, that the school's crew had taken so long to respond.

You couldn't blame their lack of zeal. The students had all answered the siren with the enthusiasm displayed in Nolan's classroom. The problem had been the fire truck, which refused to start. After some minutes it was found to be out of gas. From that point, events had moved with the inevitability of Greek tragedy or, as Sinclair preferred to believe, of French farce.

The gas pump had been locked. It shouldn't have been at that time of day, but it was. The lock was self-latching, and perhaps the last person at the pump had inadvertently clicked it shut. In any case, the fire marshal's key was at home, on the far side of the campus, and the only other key was kept by Sinclair, who had rushed to the scene of the fire. All kinds of sprint records had been broken retrieving the key from the fire marshal's house, but it still took several more minutes to get gas to the truck. Even then the firemen's problems were not over.

The carburettor was dry. To prime it they'd had to remove the air filter. This was not hard, but even a racing mechanic could scarcely have done it in less than a couple of minutes, and the firemen had no one of that calibre. In any case, they were flustered. It was much to their credit, indeed, that the entire performance – from the discovery that the truck wouldn't start to the moment it did – took less than ten minutes. But this was at least five minutes too long. When the firemen did finally get themselves to the fire, they were last by a wide margin. By that time the dorm was blazing like a torch and the audience included just about everyone on campus: the students, the faculty, and fifty or sixty stunned and angry parents.

22

'Zero . . .' Martin Delafield said. He seemed to derive satisfaction from the statement. Not exactly pleasure from another's misfortune, perhaps, but rather the gratification of having been proved right. 'Zero contributions and zero pledges. Last year we got $35,000, every cent unsolicited. This year a big fat zero.'

'Can you wonder?' Sinclair inquired nastily. 'Last year we avoided the public display of incompetence. We omitted to set fire to a dormitory before an invited audience of parents, having first forgotten to put gas in the fire truck.' He made a point of not looking at Andy Redfern.

Silence. Sinclair examined his fingernails. Martin looked out of the window. Andy Redfern flushed. He seemed angry and despondent, determined to stick to his story, but without much hope of being believed. He didn't deserve this, Nolan thought. Andy was fresh out of college, new to the faculty this year. What he was guilty of was mostly inexperience. At the time, no doubt, volunteering for fire marshal had seemed a good idea, a way for a newcomer to show concern; it hadn't occurred to him

137

to wonder why there was no competition for the job. But being fire marshal, as he'd quickly discovered, was time-consuming and thankless; you spent hours practising and responding to false alarms, but you never got noticed unless something went wrong. It was little of Andy Redfern's fault that one of the dormitories was now a pile of ash, but that wouldn't stop him from catching most of the blame.

'Aren't we making a bit much of this?' It was time, Nolan thought, to mount a rescue. 'Do we really need an extended postmortem? The message is obvious, I should have thought. In the future we need to check the fire truck.'

'We check it now.' Andy would have none of this charity. He wanted justice. A mistake, Nolan thought; he'd do better with charity.

'We do?' Sinclair raised an eyebrow. 'Who checks it? You?'

Andy hesitated. 'Not personally. Lewis does it, actually.'

'Lewis Fairchild?'

'Yes.'

'In other words,' Sinclair said, 'you entrusted the job to a student.'

Silence.

'But Lewis is reliable,' Andy protested. 'He checked only two days ago. Took the truck out and checked everything, the gas specifically. He swears there was half a tankful.'

'He swears . . .' Sinclair's tone was pitying. 'We've got students living in tents and more than a quarter of a million in fire damage because someone let the fire truck run out of gas, and the student you left in charge swears black and blue it wasn't him. Now, from your vast experience of dealing with students, exactly what would you expect him to swear?'

Andy flushed. 'I'd expect him to say what I'd say in the circumstances. If it was his fault, I'd expect him to say so.'

'Would you?' This seemed to strike Sinclair as a novel idea. He examined Andy with a kind of intrigued sympathy, like a doctor faced with the symptoms of some rare and fatal disease. 'Would you indeed?'

'So would I,' Nolan said. 'I've always found Lewis pretty straight. If he says he checked and there was gas in the truck, I think you can take it that there was.'

'Then what happened to it?' Sinclair demanded. 'Did it

138

evaporate? Half a tankful overnight? Or are you saying perhaps that someone sneaked into the compound and siphoned off the gas? I hadn't thought the shortage was that acute.' He glanced at Delafield, inviting acknowledgement of the hit.

Delafield didn't smile. 'Actually,' he said, 'if you'll think for a moment, you'll see that's pretty much what must have happened.'

Sinclair reddened. Nolan and Andy turned to stare.

'Someone siphoned the tank,' Delafield said. 'That has to be it. There's too much coincidence otherwise.'

'Coincidence?' Sinclair looked puzzled.

'The truck wouldn't start.' Delafield sounded patient but bored, like a parent adjudicating a nursery squabble. 'It wouldn't even fire. Yet it was last driven only two days ago. If you want to believe it just ran out of gas, you have to assume that the last time it was out there was just enough gas to get it back to the garage, but not a drop more. Not even enough to make it cough two days later. I wonder what odds I could get against that?'

Silence.

'Maybe there was a leak,' Nolan offered.

'Maybe.' Martin nodded. 'Though that in itself would be quite a coincidence. I imagine it can be checked, however.'

'Certainly it can.' Sinclair nodded briskly and turned to Andy Redfern. 'In fact it can be checked right away.'

Redfern ignored him. 'But that means it was arson, then.' He addressed Delafield. 'If someone drained the tank, that would have to be the reason. To stop us from getting to the fire.'

'Of course,' Sinclair said. 'It's obvious, isn't it? If someone drained the tank, someone deliberately set fire to the dorm. And that makes it all the more vital, I should have thought, that we find out whether the tank was in fact drained.'

'But that makes it better for us, doesn't it?' Andy continued to puzzle the thing through. 'If it was arson, no one can blame the firemen. Or the school, of course.'

Sinclair sighed. 'You're missing the point. Arson acquits us of incompetence, certainly, but it leaves us worse off. Would you want your child in a school where someone was going around burning down the buildings?' He glanced at Delafield, this time anxiously.

'Actually you're both missing the point,' Delafield said. 'If it was arson, PR is the least of your problems. The real headache is insurance.'

'Insurance?' Sinclair queried.

'Insurance,' Delafield nodded. 'More specifically, the quarter of a million you won't be getting to rebuild that dormitory with. They don't pay if they can prove arson. No insurance does. No matter who did it.'

He turned to Andy Redfern.

'So let's hope you find a leak in the gas tank. Or better yet, let's make sure you do. Otherwise those kids are in tents for the duration.'

Once again Andy was confronted by implications. Before he could respond, however, Sinclair's secretary stuck her head round the door.

'It's Lewis Fairchild,' she announced. 'I told him you were busy, but he insists on seeing you. He says it's about the fire.'

'It was sabotage,' Lewis said. 'I didn't forget to check. That truck was deliberately put out of action.'

Martin Delafield cocked an eyebrow. 'Oh? What makes you think that?'

'It's not a question of thinking.' Lewis regarded him bleakly. 'What I'm talking about is proof.'

He stood facing them in the centre of the room, a short, plumpish figure with the curly hair and apple cheeks of a cherub. Lewis was not notably clean or well cared-for – his pants were torn at the knee, buttons were missing from the front of his shirt, his thick-lensed glasses were held together with Band-Aids – but he achieved, nonetheless, a remarkable self-assurance. A large part of it, Nolan knew, stemmed from his perfectly justified conviction of being the intellectual equal of anyone in the room; the rest seemed to centre round the brown paper grocery bag, folded over at the top, which stood on the carpet a pace or so in front of him. He had placed it there on entering but had not so much as glanced at it since. In consequence, like a conjuror's top hat, it radiated promise. Sooner or later, presumably, it would give birth to some kind of rabbit, but in the meantime Lewis was content to let it sit and

140

gather scrutiny. He planned to be a trial lawyer, Nolan knew; he'd be a good one.

'Proof,' Lewis repeated. 'You see, I *know* I checked the truck, but I don't expect you to take my word for it.'

'Actually,' Delafield said, smiling, 'we do.'

'You do?' Some of the wind left Lewis's sails.

'Certainly.' From Sinclair's tone, Nolan observed, you'd have thought him incapable of distrust. 'We're satisfied there's no negligence involved. Least of all on your part.'

'So what do you think happened to the truck?'

'Clearly there was some kind of leak,' Delafield said. He and Sinclair, Nolan noticed were like a kind of chorus, alternating responses as smoothly as if they'd rehearsed.

Lewis disturbed the harmony. 'Unfortunately not.'

Sinclair raised an eyebrow. 'How do you know?'

'I checked,' Lewis said. 'There's no leak now, and there never was. Unless it miraculously mended itself.'

This turning of his own polemical methods against himself left Sinclair temporarily silenced. Delafield, however, came to the rescue.

'So no leak,' he smiled pleasantly. 'Since you checked personally, I think we can take that as fact. And that certainly suggests someone drained the tank. The carburettor, too, probably. But suggestion is one thing. As I recall you said something about proof?'

In response Lewis reached for the grocery bag. From it he withdrew something long, tube-like, and dusty black, which he held at arm's length between forefinger and thumb. It hung like a dead snake, heavy and black.

'People's exhibit A,' he announced. 'Discovered by yours truly in the compound trash. Four feet of perfectly serviceable garden hose, obviously cut to order. And in answer to your next question, yes,' he paused, 'it smells of gas.'

23

'Someone out there doesn't like you guys,' Jacobsen said.

Nolan nodded. 'Only I'm not so sure about the "out there",' he said. 'It was someone who knows the school well. Or well enough to have known about the fire truck.'

They were in Nolan's office, a former storeroom in the administration building, assigned to him for the duration of his stay. By tacit agreement with Sinclair, he'd assumed responsibility for liaison with the police and had just got through giving Jacobsen the details of the fire. On his desk, amid a jumble of books and papers, stood the grocery bag from which Lewis had produced the length of hose.

'The tank was drained beforehand, obviously.' Jacobsen gestured to the grocery bag. 'What puzzles me is the fire itself. Someone put a match to that building in broad daylight. That's taking a man-sized risk. He could have been caught in the act, for one thing. Or someone could have spotted that the truck had been tampered with. Me, I'd have done it in one fell swoop; drained the tank then torched the dorm. And at night, when there was less chance of being caught.'

Nolan smiled. 'I must remember to consult you next time I'm planning an arson. But in this case, broad daylight was probably safer. There are always people around the dorms at night, some of those kids stay up to all hours, but that afternoon almost all the kids were in class.'

'So our firebug knew about the schedule, most likely. That helps, I suppose.' Jacobsen didn't sound notably encouraged. 'The hose won't, that's for damn sure. That kind of ribbed surface doesn't take prints, plus the guy wore gloves, more than likely. We're thrown back on motive and opportunity. Someone with access and a grudge against the school.'

'I suppose so.' Nolan nodded.

'I know so,' Jacobsen insisted. 'I mean, ask yourself, why do people set fire to buildings? Not counting screwballs who just like the pretty colours, there are only two motives that make any kind of sense. There's profit, then there's malice. And while I don't automatically rule out that you guys would fire your own dorm to collect on the insurance, I do tend to doubt that you'd screw it up so badly, leaving damn great chunks of hose in the trash for any claims adjuster or teenage Sherlock Holmes to trip over.' He grinned sardonically. 'And you guys all so highly educated. I have to figure you for smarter than that.'

'We're not that smart.' Nolan returned the grin. 'Otherwise we wouldn't be teachers, right? But at least we can add and subtract. The most we could collect is the cost of rebuilding. I don't see much profit in that.'

'So it boils down to malice. And that way the hose makes more sense. When you take all that trouble to shaft someone, you at least want him to know he's been shafted, don't you?'

'And that way he gets to shaft us again,' Nolan agreed. 'He lets us know the fire was no accident, and at the same time makes sure we can't collect on the insurance.'

There was an interval of meditative silence.

'Mr Nice Guy,' Nolan said.

Jacobsen nodded. 'And Mr Psychopath.' He paused. 'You wouldn't happen to know anyone like that?'

Nolan thought.

'Sinclair could answer that better than I. But a couple of possibles do spring to mind. There was a kid they kicked out earlier in the year. Now *he* was a psychopath. Went after his roommate with a hammer, I recall, and couldn't understand why people objected. Very pissed off when they canned him. Left uttering all kinds of bloodcurdling threats. Last I heard, though, he was in military school back east somewhere. Virginia, I think.'

'So we check if he was there yesterday. Anyone else?'

'There was the maintenance man they let go last month for supplying the students with booze, as I understand it. He's local, which means he had access, I suppose. Only the thing is . . .' Nolan hesitated, 'he doesn't really strike me as the type.'

'Type?' Jacobsen raised an eyebrow. 'I seem to recall you don't believe in types.'

Nolan grinned. 'Sometimes I do. I find my own judgement of character almost impeccable. It's other people's I don't trust.'

'That's how I feel,' Jacobsen said. 'So maybe we'd better

143

check this guy, too. He'd know how to drain a tank, I'd imagine. And he'd know when the kids are in class.'

Nolan thought.

'Actually, he wouldn't. There was a special schedule, you see. For the open house. And it was finalized only last Friday, at least two weeks after he was fired.'

'Special schedule?' Jacobsen stared. 'Are you saying that normally there would have been kids around the dorm that afternoon?'

'Could have been . . . You see, normally not all kids are in classes all the time. But that day there were classes for everyone all day long. A show of industry,' Nolan smiled, 'for the parents.'

Jacobsen rolled his eyes. 'Now he tells me. First useful evidence in the whole case, and I have to drag it out of him with forceps.'

'Didn't think of it before.' Nolan was unrepentant. 'Besides, I doubt it's as useful as you think. It doesn't narrow the field of suspects much. You're still looking at the faculty, the staff, the students, the parents, and anyone they may have happened to tell. Three or four hundred people, at a guess.'

'Oh well,' Jacobsen said with a shrug. 'Good try, no points.' Nolan nodded. But absently, Jacobsen saw, as if he'd left the conversation to pursue some other train of thought. He stared out of the window, frowning.

'Did you find Billy's prints on that note?'

It took Jacobsen a moment to catch up. 'That note? You mean the one I found in his house?' He shook his head. 'It seems you were right about that. They found only one set of prints and they weren't Billy's. Must have been hers, I guess. I assume the killer was smart enough not to leave his.' He paused. 'So at least we're making progress in one direction.'

Nolan nodded. 'Maybe even in both. I have this funny feeling there's a connection.'

'Between the murders and the fire?'

'Yes.'

Jacobsen thought.

'I don't see it. Both things happened at the school, of course, and within two weeks of each other.' He shrugged. 'Could simply be bad luck.'

144

'It's too much bad luck. More than they've had in twenty years. Suddenly they're the target of a minor crime wave. I can't help seeing a pattern.'

'That's only natural,' Jacobsen said with a smile. 'When you get hit twice in a row, you start asking, "Why me?" But bad luck can run in streaks. The best answer to "Why me?" is, "Why not you?" There's no need to get paranoid about it.'

'Perhaps not.' Nolan shrugged. 'But even paranoia has its logic.'

'Logic? . . .' Around Nolan, Jacobsen had learned to be chary of the word. 'What logic?'

'Just because you're paranoid,' Nolan quoted, smiling, 'doesn't mean they're not out to get you.'

24

Back at the office, Jacobsen wrote up a report on the fire then turned the case over to somebody else. He didn't believe, paranoid logic notwithstanding, that the fire and the deaths were in any way connected. He felt guilty, besides, that the affairs of Fremont had taken up so much of his time and left him with so little to show for it. It was almost with relief that he turned back to the routine of his work, resolving to devote the next few hours, at least, to matters unmysterious and totally unconnected with the school.

But the relief hardly outlived the resolution. The school and its concerns refused to be pushed aside. In the third item he removed from his in-tray that afternoon – a computer printout of traffic citations issued in Buckskin and its environs in the past thirty days – he confronted once again the name of Billy Dabbs.

It did not, initially, stir him to more than mild irritation. Billy's name, to his recollection, had appeared on many such lists. The difference this time was that Billy, having placed himself permanently out of reach of traffic courts, might just as well be taken off the list. He was just about to scribble a note to this effect next to Billy's name in the print-out when he happened to notice the date of the citation. April 14.

And the citation had been issued at 11:30 PM on State Road 61A, about one mile west of Buckskin Creek.

Which meant, as Jacobsen verified by consulting his wall map, that Billy had been very close to the Fremont School property just a very short time before Lisa's death.

'But he used to be a buddy,' Cliff Parsons said defensively. 'Hell, I've know Billy since the seventh grade. We sat in the back and flicked spit wads at the girls. I couldn't book him for DWI. They'd have jerked his licence.'

They should jerk your head, Jacobsen thought. Jerk and then twist. Not that it would harm you at all.

'I was using discretion,' Cliff said. 'You're always saying I should use my discretion, so I did.'

Jacobsen uttered an inward prayer for patience. Cliff was twenty-three years old, and the proud owner of a mentality that, to outward appearance, had not yet graduated from junior high. Asking him to use discretion had not, as he'd evidently assumed, been anything in the nature of a vote of confidence; it was rather the expression of a very forlorn hope.

'Exactly how drunk was he?'

The citation had said nothing about drinking; all it had talked about was dangerous driving. But that, Jacobsen knew, could cover a multitude of sins. And that Billy, at 11:30 on any given night, had been anything other than thoroughly plastered was an improbability of very high order. Besides, when questioned about the citation, Cliff had looked more than a little uneasy. So Jacobsen had probed. Billy's dangerous driving, it transpired, had consisted of taking a blind corner on the wrong side at roughly double the posted speed limit, narrowly missing Cliff's patrol car in the process. It had not been hard to read between the lines.

'How drunk, Cliff?'

'I've seen him drunker.' Cliff's expression was wooden. 'I've seen him a whole lot drunker than that.'

Jacobsen sighed. 'I'm sure you have. But that wasn't what I

146

asked, now was it? Was he swaying drunk? Staggering drunk? Falling down drunk? . . . Or what?'

Cliff hesitated. You could almost, Jacobsen thought, hear the wheels turning. Would he catch more grief for dereliction of duty or for lying to his superior? An intriguing conflict of self-interest.

'Shee-yit . . .' Cliff plumped for honesty. 'Truth is he was a basket case. Beats me how he could drive at all. The state he was in, he could hardly stand.'

'But because he was a buddy, you didn't book him for DWI. Just gave him a ticket for dangerous driving and sent him off to run somebody over.'

'Hell if I did.' Cliff seemed genuinely offended. 'I'm not that much of a jerk. I had him give me the keys and I drove his car on to the shoulder. Then I poured him into the patrol car and drove him home.'

'Chauffeur service. Very considerate.' There was something about Cliff's story that struck Jacobsen as not quite right though. It was not that Cliff was lying or leaving something out, but rather that his present reconstruction of the incident differed, in some obscure and troubling way, from Jacobsen's own imagining of it.

'Seemed the least I could do.' The sarcasm, of course, went right by Cliff. 'He didn't live but a couple of miles from there, and no way he was going to be able to walk it. So I took him home, left him in an armchair, and put the car keys and the citation on the mantel along with a note explaining what had happened. When I left he was out for the count. He wasn't going anywhere else that night. Or if he was, he wasn't going to be driving.'

Drove the car on to the shoulder. Left the car keys on the mantel. Car keys. Suddenly Jacobsen recognized what seemed wrong. Billy didn't drive a car; he drove a truck. A grey Ford pickup similar, if not identical, to the one someone had spotted only a few hours later in the wash. But Cliff was definitely right in saying 'car'. It was there in the citation. A Toyota Celica hatchback, licence plate number AGH 7046.

'What about his truck?' He kept bullying Cliff to conceal his interest in Billy. Besides, Cliff deserved it. 'He owned a truck too, you know. He could have woken up and gone out again in

147

the truck. A menace to himself and anyone else on the road. I don't s'pose you happened to think about that?'

Cliff, amazingly, managed to look pleased with himself. 'Matter of fact, I did. I looked around for the truck because it struck me as odd to see him in a car. I figured his truck must be in the shop. At any rate it wasn't at the house.'

Jacobsen gazed at him in silence. Dereliction of duty notwithstanding and through no fault of his own, Cliff had managed to be considerably helpful. On the other hand, he'd been considerably derelict. He deserved to sweat a little.

'Look,' Cliff said. 'I know I should have given him a DWI, but at least I made sure he couldn't drive any more. Heck, this is a small town, Olin. A lot of his buddies are my buddies. Besides, he wasn't such a bad ol' boy, at that.'

Jacobsen considered this plea.

'No,' he said finally, 'he wasn't such a bad ol' boy at all. But that's got nothing to do with this, Cliff, and you know it. The point is he was DWI and a menace. You should have booked him for DWI and locked him up for the night. You're here to enforce the law, Cliff, without fear or favour, and that means not making exceptions for guys you were buddies with in the seventh grade. It's about time you faced up to that.'

But it happened all the time, and until cops were replaced by robots, it would go on happening. And his own recent record of enforcing the law had not been exactly unblemished. So he let Cliff off with the reprimand. Cliff, in any case, had never been his primary target. Billy had. Or rather Billy's truck. For if Billy's truck had not been home that night, the chances were it had been in the wash. And at a time when Billy had been slumped in an armchair, dead to the world. So it hadn't been him driving the truck. And while the person who had could be almost anyone, there remained the fact that when Billy had parted with the truck he'd acquired another vehicle. So who better to ask what had happened to the truck than the registered owner of the Toyota Celica hatchback, licence plate AGH 7046?

25

The Golden Restaurant was on the outskirts of Buckskin, at the end of the long ribbon development which, for two miles or so, ornamented the highway between Buckskin and the neighbouring town of Miracle. At the east end, towards the centre of Buckskin, the road cut through a tropical forest of billboards and neon signs, but on the outskirts of the desert reasserted itself; development as confined to the immediate border of the highway and the buildings themselves became decently self-effacing: low, one-storey structures with modest signs, wood for the most part and weathered into a sort of harmony with their surroundings.

The restaurant was the next to last building on the left. It had plainly been conceived in a hunger of nostalgia for the Old West. In front of it, and looking out on the highway, was a long raised veranda where John Wayne or James Stewart could easily be imagined lounging, chairs tilted back and feet on the railing, slim, black cheroots in the corner of their mouths. There were also slatted bar doors at the main entrance, the sort you could hurl a drunk through or burst through with guns blazing, and next to them, nailed to the planking, a small wooden sign, clumsily hand painted:

THE GOLDEN I. MARK THOMAS, PROP. LIQUORS AND FINE VIT-
TLES. NO ROWDIES OR HOOKERS. NO GUNSLINGERS. CHECK ALL
HARDWARE.

It looked like the sort of place, Jacobsen thought, where Billy Dabbs might well have felt at home. But then again perhaps this was unkind. Billy's personality had been built on nostalgia, possibly, but there'd been nothing phony about it. His pickup had been used, fairly regularly, for hauling loads. His gun rack had held guns. You could imagine him, without too much effort, on a horse. The patrons of the Golden I, on the other hand – there were several of them lounging at the bar when

Jacobsen entered – were cowboys only to the extent of their boots and hats. There was also, of course, a belligerence in their manner – something loose and insolent in the way they turned their heads and stared, then looked away, the eyes casually appraising and dismissing – that they no doubt imagined to be cowboy but was not. It was just punk, Jacobsen thought, the old-fashioned variety with a small p.

'Hey, Sheriff.' The drawl belonged to the one closest, a red-faced, beefy-looking lout, with dirty-blond hair falling down to his shoulders. He spoke without looking up or turning, so that Jacobsen, had he answered, would have found himself talking to the back of a neck. 'You saw the sign. Check your hardware. Now ain't that a thirty-eight in that holster on your hip?'

Snuffles of laughter from the gallery. Jacobsen ignored them. He knew how the script went for this scene: answer and you laid yourself open to further wit. John Wayne, he thought wistfully, without so much as looking would have kicked the punk's stool from under him and sent him grovelling. Real life, however, called for underplaying. He spoke to the woman behind the bar.

'I'm looking for Mark Thomas. Is he around?'

She didn't answer but gestured with her head, her eyes flicking past him and over his shoulder. Though he had not been conscious of any movement, he saw in the counter mirror that there was now someone behind him.

'I'm Thomas, Sheriff. Some way I can help you?'

What Jacobsen registered first were good looks so extravagant they shouldn't properly, he thought, have belonged to a man: hair a red-gold so startling it looked almost dyed; eyes a brilliant blue-green; features classically regular and finely, almost delicately, chiselled. Second impressions, however, were slightly at odds with the first. On closer inspection the face seemed somehow empty, the gaze direct but unassertive, incurious. Meeting it, Jacobsen was reminded of a line of poetry he had run across in college, words which for some reason – perhaps because he'd never really understood them – had stayed with him: 'They are the lords and owners of their faces.'

Thomas, it struck him, was a lord and owner: reserved, self-possessed, wearing his good looks like a mask; suffering them, almost, but not belonging to them. The thought was startling but nonetheless apt because in context the good looks were a kind of cruel joke. Cruel because their owner, though perfectly proportioned, stood a good nine or ten inches shorter than Jacobsen's own six feet. He was a miniature, if not exactly a dwarf.

'Hey, Golden – ' The mutual scrutiny was interrupted by one of the cowboys. 'Don't you go messing with the sheriff now. The man is armed and dangerous.'

'Better hope he shoots you in the head then, Elroy. That way he won't hurt you at all.' Thomas kept his eyes on Jacobsen. 'Sorry, Sheriff, but you know how it is. They don't really mean any harm.' He jerked his head in the direction of the punks and shrugged. His voice was relaxed and pleasant.

'I'm not the sheriff.' A tab on Jacobsen's shirt pocket identified him clearly by name and rank, and he had seen Thomas glance at it. There were only two motives for making this kind of 'mistake'. Jacobsen liked neither of them.

'Lieutenant, sorry. Shall we sit?' Thomas led the way to a table. 'I'm not in any trouble, I trust?'

A faint smile accompanied this inquiry. Jacobsen responded to neither.

'You're registered as the owner of a beige Toyota hatchback, licence plate AGH 7046. Correct?'

'I own a beige hatchback. Tell the truth,' Thomas said, smiling again, 'I can never remember the number. Why?'

'Our records indicate that on the night of April 14, this year, it was in the possession of a Billy Dabbs. He was picked up in it and charged with dangerous driving. Would you know anything about that?'

'That he had the car?' Thomas shook his head. 'It's certainly possible. But I don't know about the date.'

'So he might have had it. He was a friend of yours then?'

'Billy?' Thomas nodded. The perfect features took on a look of vague regret. 'You could call him that, I guess. I expect he was drunk when you picked him up, wasn't he? He usually was by early evening. We stopped serving him in here, you know, but it didn't do any good. They can always get it from somewhere.'

'You were in the habit of lending him your car?' Jacobsen

deliberately made this sound like an accusation. Thomas frowned, looked for a moment as if he'd like to argue, then shrugged.

'I loaned it to him on a number of occasions. I can't give you dates, I'm afraid. But if your records show that he had it on April 14,' – another shrug – 'presumably he did.'

'You wouldn't happen to recall why he borrowed it?'

Silence. The eyes, which it seemed to Jacobsen had rested on him unblinking since the start of the conversation, narrowed a fraction.

'Since I don't recall the occasion, I'd hardly recall the reason.' Pause. 'Is there some problem about my lending him my car?'

'Not necessarily.' Jacobsen was making something of a production out of playing his cards close to his chest. It was his only strategy, he'd decided, since he didn't have many cards to play. 'I take it, then, that you own another vehicle?'

'A Jeep.' Thomas nodded. 'Why?'

Jacobsen thought for a moment. Since he'd thought it unlikely Thomas would volunteer anything, he'd expected to have to ask about the truck. What he hoped to suggest now was someone deliberately switching tactics, not someone forced back on the last of his resources.

'Matter of fact,' he said, 'it's not your vehicle we're concerned with here. It's Dabbs's. Since he was picked up in your car that day, it seems possible someone else was driving his truck. It occurs to us it might have been you. Was it?'

He was taking an unavoidable risk. If Thomas had borrowed the truck and had left it below Monument that night, this admission of police interest in it would put him on his guard. But even so, he wouldn't necessarily lie, not if he were smart, because he would realize that all his statements could be checked – and perhaps already had been – and a lie in that case could be more damaging than an admission. The best liars, Jacobsen knew, told as much truth as they safely could. The trick was to lure them into telling just a little bit more.

He studied Thomas. Thomas seemed to be searching his memory, though he could equally have been weighing his options. It struck Jacobsen that he'd already, though he wasn't quite sure when, decided to treat Thomas as a hostile witness. The punks were partly to blame, of course, but otherwise there

152

didn't seem to be much reason. Thomas had answered his questions with every appearance of candour, he had not seemed alarmed by this unheralded visit from a lieutenant of police, he had not even seemed all that curious. But that was it, wasn't it? He wasn't curious enough. He must know that even in Buckskin police lieutenants weren't normally employed on trivial errands. And Billy Dabbs was dead from a heroin overdose. But faced now with Jacobsen and a bunch of cagey questions about Billy's truck, Thomas was reacting as though no more were involved than an unpaid speeding ticket or a lapsed registration. Indeed it seemed to Jacobsen that he was not so much reacting as withholding his reaction, waiting to see, perhaps, what reaction was appropriate.

'Actually . . .' Thomas completed his memory search. 'Come to think of it, maybe I did borrow the truck. If I'm thinking of the right date, that is. Billy took the car because I wanted the truck, to pick up some fertilizer in Miracle, I think.' For a moment the blue-green eyes caught and held Jacobsen's. 'Would it be out of line to ask why the interest in Billy's truck?'

Indeed it wouldn't, Jacobsen thought. It would be very peculiar if you didn't. He wasn't going to answer, however. Not just yet.

'What time did you borrow it?'

'Early afternoon . . . One-thirty or thereabouts.'

'One-thirty that afternoon? The afternoon of the fourteenth?'

'The same day you picked Billy up in my car.' Thomas shrugged. 'Whatever day that was.'

'And when did you return it?'

Was it imagination, Jacobsen wondered, or was there, before the reply, just a hint of hesitation, the faintest suggestion that ideally Thomas would have liked time to think that one over? Perhaps it was imagination, because hesitation had been what he'd been looking for, and people, however much they tried to be objective, had a tendency to see what they wanted to see. In any event, the hesitation, if that was what it had been, was slight.

'I think it was next morning.'

'What time next morning?'

'Early. Between nine and ten, I think.'

'Can someone corroborate that?'

There was a pause. Thomas stared.

'Can someone what?'

'Corroborate. Back up your statement. Is there someone who can confirm what you've just told me.'

'I do know what it means.' For an instant Thomas let hostility surface, then he shrugged. 'Not offhand. Not now that Billy's dead. What I'm asking myself, though' – the stare now conveyed a definite challenge – 'is do I really need to?'

This was a question to which Jacobsen, before setting out, had devoted some thought. In theory, he supposed, he didn't have to reply. It was the police who asked the questions and the public who did the answering. But Thomas, clearly, was getting set to balk, and if he did there wasn't much Jacobsen could do about it. It would be much better to keep the man talking. So yes, he explained, allowing himself in the process to become just a shade deferential, it would certainly be helpful if Mr Thomas could produce support for his statement, because at 11:30 on the morning of the fifteenth there'd been a hit-and-run accident in Miracle involving a truck very similar to Billy's. A young girl had been seriously injured. No one had been able to describe the driver or remember the licence number exactly, but one witness thought it had been a New Mexico plate whose first three letters had been FHT. Subsequently the MVD computer had established that these letters were shared by the licence plates of several grey Ford pickups, among them Billy's.

Thomas heard all this in silence, his eyes not leaving Jacobsen's face.

'Miracle?' he queried, when Jacobsen had finished. 'This happened in Miracle? I don't recall reading about it in the paper.'

Jacobsen shrugged. What Thomas did or didn't recall reading in the paper, he conveyed, was Thomas's affair.

'So you're interested in the whereabouts of Billy's truck at eleven-thirty on the morning of the fifteenth? And whether I was driving it?'

Jacobsen nodded. 'When the computer turned up Dabbs's truck as one of the possibles he was already dead, so that seemed to be that. Recently, however, someone happened to notice the date of his citation. When we realized he was driving your car, we wondered if maybe you'd been driving his truck.'

154

'So you asked.' Thomas gave his faint smile. 'And lo and behold I was. Lucky guess, wasn't it?'

Jacobsen shrugged. 'Was it? You tell me.'

'Not if you think I was your hit-and-run driver,' Thomas said. 'I can't prove I returned the truck before ten o'clock, but I can prove I wasn't in Miracle at the time of the accident. I was here, in the restaurant, where I always am at eleven-thirty in the morning, helping with the lunchtime business. And any number of people can corroborate that.'

'Good.' Jacobsen smiled. 'Then we can cross you off. We're working through that list, you see. Any time we can eliminate someone, we're that much farther along.'

'Very conscientious . . .' Thomas paused. 'Especially when you consider the witness could have been wrong about the licence plate.'

'True,' Jacobsen agreed. 'But then that girl may die. So we're giving her our best shot. In my book, hit-and-run killing is not that much better than murder. And as you know, we'll go to any lengths over that.'

'That's good to know.'

Thomas turned and gestured to the woman behind the bar. 'Effie, could you spare us a minute?'

Effie was able to confirm Thomas's statement. She'd worked lunches every weekday for the last month, and Mr Thomas, to her confident recollection, hadn't missed a day. And the fifteenth had been a Monday, hadn't it? So yes, in that case she could certainly corroborate that, at 11:30 on the morning of the fifteenth, Mr Thomas had been at the restaurant.

On that note Jacobsen had taken his departure. He was not displeased with his efforts. The fact that Thomas had had Billy's truck on the night of Lisa's death might not in itself mean all that much – it was still far from proved, after all, that the truck in the wash had indeed been Billy's – but he'd nevertheless learned something that might mean a great deal. *Thomas hadn't believed him.* He hadn't been openly sceptical, but there'd been something in his manner as he'd watched Jacobsen question Effie, that suggested he felt himself to be part of a charade. Yet the charade hadn't been all *that* implausible, had it? Not inherently. Not unless one had another reason to doubt it. But what reason could Thomas have to doubt it? Why on earth suspect the police of lying, unless he knew of a more compelling reason for them to be interested in Billy's truck?

26

Mannequin – mannikin – miniman? Check
A perfect egg what the old geek said about foxes.
  Told B most beautiful man in world was Bowie because not hung up about manhood. B said, 'Hung up? Of course not. Bet he's not even hung.' Typical. Mamas don't let yr babies grow up to be cowboys . . .

Nolan contemplated the page in front of him. He hated being beaten, especially by puzzles. But this puzzle, at least for the time being, had him baffled. 'A perfect egg that old geek said about foxes'? 'A perfect egg' meant a perfect example, presumably, since elsewhere in the journal 'a perfect egg sample' had been used in that sense. But what was a perfect example? And what was it a perfect example of? And did it matter? Was this, the most enigmatic remark in the whole document, significant? Or was it just one of Lisa's many asides, interesting, but in context of the mystery of her death irrelevant? Nolan sighed. Perhaps he was getting too close to it. So close that he was missing the obvious. The contents he now had practically by heart, and the handwriting, so oddly neat and careful, with its steep rightwards slant and the circles instead of dots about the i's, was almost as familiar as his own. Perhaps he was getting too close. Perhaps what he needed was a fresh mind.

But you couldn't get too close, could you? To people, maybe. To problems. But not to documents. The trick with them was total immersion and patience. To the right mix of logic and inspiration most documents, in the end, would yield their secrets. But finding that mix took time. But there might not be much time. Lisa had been murdered, then Billy, and now a

156

dorm had been torched. Whatever was going on, there was no assurance that they'd seen the end of it.

'More wine?' Diana asked.

'Is there more?' He held out his glass. 'Then by all means let's drink it. I'm not a believer in pleasure deferred.'

She smiled. 'I've noticed.'

'What have you noticed?'

'Well for one thing, you've been guzzling the wine. And for another, you haven't been doing much grading. You've spent the past hour with your nose in that journal.'

This was true. She'd invited him for what she'd described as a working evening: drinks, accompanied by a little paper grading (the priorities here quite properly set, he thought), then dinner. But while she herself had followed this programme to the letter – sipping, reading, frowning, slashing away with her red pencil, sipping again – he had managed to yawn his way through barely a page of earnest misinformation on the Great Depression before pushing it aside in favour of the journal.

'This isn't pleasure. Actually it's rather hard work.'

'Oh sure.' She smiled. 'All that boring stuff about sex and drugs. Not nearly as fascinating as grading papers.'

'No, seriously. It's not titillating at all. Sex and drugs are mentioned, of course, but only in passing. There's no lingering over the details. Here.' He handed her the journal, open at the page following the one he'd been puzzling over. 'See for yourself.'

Perhaps she might be able to help, he thought. She was, he'd discovered, an acute, if intolerant, judge of character, and she'd been Lisa's teacher for the past two years. As a woman, also, she was presumably better able than he to fathom the workings of a young girl's mind. Enlisting her aid, of course, would involve taking her into his confidence, but she'd already proved her discretion in the matter of drugs. She could be trusted, he thought.

'Town trip,' she read aloud. 'Met Bronco, natch, at the Chateau, supposedly gardening, actually high as a kite thanks to a freebie from you know who. That man's generosity will be the death of somebody. We were making out, just hugging, on the back patio when the Slime materialized. Must have been peeping from the kitchen. He said, "I can offer the spare

bedroom, Bronco, if you can't resist the demands of your dick."
Then he went back inside. Never looked at me.

'He hates me. I'm still not sure why. He knows I'm trying to
get B to dry out, but that doesn't seem enough reason. I don't
know what he wants with B either. Power maybe. I don't think
he's gay. Sometimes when B's not around, I get these weird
vibes from him. Like he wants to jump me or something, but
doesn't quite have the balls. I've mentioned it to B, but he says
forget it, we need him. Which is true, in a way, so long as B has
his habit. I could force B to choose, I guess, but the habit he
kicked could well be me.

'You're right.' She made a face and handed the journal back.
'It isn't much of a turn on. Who is this Slime person, anyway?'

'That's the sixty-four-thousand-dollar question.' Nolan shook
his head. 'I know he lives in town and has a back patio you can
see from the kitchen, but beyond that, zip. She calls him "The
Slime" or "A" or sometimes "Ac", but she never gives details
that could help me identify him, probably because of his
involvement with the drugs. What's so frustrating is that he's
mentioned on every page. I know very well what he is, but
nothing about who.'

She frowned. 'He sounds like a real bastard.'

'I think you could say that. He's a heroin dealer. Also . . .'
He paused. 'Quite possibly a killer.'

'A killer?' At first the word seemed not to register fully. When
the implications struck her, she was suddenly still. 'Philip, you
don't mean . . . you can't mean . . . Lisa?'

He nodded. 'I'm afraid so. No one else here knows, not even
Sinclair, and it's vital for now that we keep it that way, but it
seems very possible that both she and her boyfriend – the one
she wrote that poem to – were murdered.'

'Oh my God.' She looked bewildered. The colour had drained
from her face. 'But the police . . . they said Lisa's death was an
accident. What happened to make them change their minds?'

He told her. She listened, mostly in silence, but interrupting
once or twice to ask questions. When he'd finished she said: 'So
you think this A must be the killer.'

'He fits.' Nolan nodded. 'Both because of that message and
because he was Bronco's connection. Bronco died of a heroin

overdose, which makes A the natural suspect for that one, don't you think?'

She nodded. 'But how will you find out who he is? The journal, you said, hides his identity on purpose. What else is there to go on?'

'It's got to be in here somewhere.' He tapped the journal. 'I'm sure of that. She may have meant to leave no clue, but inadvertently she must have. You can't mention someone as often as she did, without somewhere letting something slip. Sooner or later, I'm going to find it. For now I'm working on motive. If he killed Lisa, he must have had a reason. If I can figure it out, I'll have a lead to him.'

She stared. 'But surely the reason is obvious? Drugs.'

He shook his head. 'I don't think so. Not directly. In the three or four months she recorded her drug deals, the total take, so far as I can figure, was less than fifteen hundred dollars. That's peanuts. Not nearly enough to offer a motive for murder. I think the key was her relationship with Bronco.'

'With Bronco?' She looked sceptical. 'What kind of motive can you get out of that?'

'I don't know.' Nolan shrugged. 'A hated her, but she didn't know why. There was something weird going on between the three of them. It surfaces, for instance, in the passage you read. A kind of tug of war between her and A for Bronco.'

'Sexually, you mean?'

'I don't know. Not on the surface at least. On his side it was for control, I think. He used the heroin as a hook. Gave it to Bronco free at first, then later used it to bring him to heel. But what his motive was I don't really know. On her side I think it was love.'

'Love?' She looked dubious. 'Romance maybe. Infatuation plus a touch of "us against them". After all, she was only seventeen.'

'You think teenagers don't?'

She thought for a moment. 'Love? I wouldn't say not absolutely. They use the word a lot, but mostly I don't think they even know what it means.'

'Well in this case it wasn't romance or infatuation. Not on her side, at least. He was the romantic one, with notions of sharing a cottage and living on love. She was hardheaded. She knew

159

what she was taking on with him: an alcoholic, an incipient heroin addict. She knew how slim her chances were, but she went ahead anyway. She was one very tough young woman. Listen.' He flicked through the pages.

'Town trip. No B today. Snuck off instead to the Clinic to talk to the shrink. No names, of course, just the usual "got this friend" routine. I'm sure he thought it was me! At any rate he told me the only chance to get "my friend" clean was to get him cold turkey now and into rehab . . . Fat chance. B won't even admit to a problem – or not a drug problem – and he wouldn't be caught dead in rehab. "Some things a man's gotta deal with alone." Christ, sometimes he's such an incredible flake! . . . So it's Lisa who gets to soldier on alone . . . There is infinite hope . . . and screw you, Mr Kafka.' He stopped reading.

'Infinite hope?' Diana asked. 'What did she mean by that?'

'There is infinite hope, but not for us. It's a quote from Kafka. Kind of a favourite of hers. She uses it quite often. Not in despair, though, more as a kind of ironic battle cry. Whatever else she was, she was no quitter.'

'Whatever else she was,' Diana echoed doubtfully, 'we never really know, do we? I can see her now, in English 11, gazing out of the window while the rest of us discussed the moral complexity of "Daisy Miller". No wonder she looked bored.'

While you guys make noises like Plato's Academy, they're living lives out of an X-rated movie. An echo of Martin's comment returned to Nolan. And the waste here had been enormous. Lisa had had it all: brains, looks, honesty, and courage, and quite an exceptional capacity for caring. She had the makings of an extraordinary young woman, only someone had made sure she hadn't lived long enough. And that someone was going to pay, Nolan thought, that someone was going to pay in full.

'So it was Lisa versus the Slime.' Diana shivered. It was almost as if she'd been reading his thoughts. 'A battle for the future of Bronco. But if he wanted to control Bronco, what did he want to control him for?'

'That's what I can't figure out. The only practical consequence was that Lisa started to deal drugs at school to finance Bronco's growing habit. That was when the tug of war started. She didn't want Bronco to do drugs and she didn't want to deal, or at least not the kinds of drugs the two of them were forcing on

160

her. But A kept the pressure on through Bronco. But why he did it is beyond me. As I said, the money involved was negligible.'

'Then maybe he was just a psycho. From the sound of it, he had some kind of twisted sexual feeling for her. I think she was right about him. His sniping at her, the constant sexual innuendo, was a kind of rape it seems to me. He had these violent feelings because he felt threatened by her. So he makes that crack about Bronco not resisting the demands of his dick, for instance, yet can't quite manage to look at her when he says it.'

It made sense, Nolan thought, at least up to a point. And it squared with the rest of the journal, A's treating her always as if she were just a lump of flesh, a collection of appetites and functions, repellent but at the same time oddly fascinating. Those times at the creek, for instance, when she and Billy had skinny-dipped and A had sat on the bank, clothed, mouthing disgust yet unable, seemingly, to take his eyes off her. It made sense, up to a point, and yet . . .

'It's not enough. He detested her, clearly. Feared her. And maybe women in general. But it took something more specific, I think, to trigger the impulse to kill.'

'Specific? What, for instance?'

'I can't imagine.' He shrugged. 'But I know things came to a head in the couple of weeks before her death. She saw A alone, twice. And in the journal she starts talking about making some kind of deal to get Bronco off the hook. Then, in the last entry, she writes of having got him off. And after that, almost immediately, she was dead.'

'But no clue as to what the deal was?'

He shook his head. 'What she wrote was this: "The slime has made a proposition." That was about the beginning of April. Then for a while she wonders if she can risk Billy finding out about what she calls "a pact with the devil". But she never gives details. I can only imagine, though, that it had to do with getting A to quit pushing heroin on Billy. What her side was I've no idea.'

'I do,' Diana said. 'Or I can guess. It makes me sick.'

'Something sexual?' Nolan based his guess on the look on Diana's face. 'It's possible, I suppose, though it's hard to see how that would have led to his wanting to kill her. I have the

161

feeling, anyway, that if I knew what it was I'd be a whole lot closer to unravelling this mess.' He paused. 'And the hell of it is I just know those details are in here too, if I could only get at them.'

'Get at them?' She looked surprised. 'I thought you had it all sorted out. All ordered, dated, and put into English.'

'Oh I do. All the words, that is. All but a few elliptical one-liners that probably don't mean much, anyway. But there's still the passage in what looks like cipher. I've got nowhere with that.'

'And you think it has to do with the deal?'

He shrugged. 'It comes at the right point chronologically, just before the last couple of entries where she speaks of having Billy off the hook. I don't see what else it would be about.'

Diana thought about this.

'Well if it is cipher, I can't believe it would be very hard to crack. Not for an expert. I mean Lisa was smart, but she was only a high school kid. So why don't you send it to an expert? You must know someone at Harvard who does ciphers.'

'I do . . .' His look contained more than a hint of reproach. 'And I sent it to him. He took one look at it and decided it wasn't a cipher at all, but probably some kind of book code.'

'Book code?'

He nodded. 'Apparently much favoured by amateurs. Cumbersome but dead easy to work. You take a book, any book that has the words you want to use, and pick out the words of your message. Then, for each word, you substitute the page number, the line number, and the position it occupies on its line. The third word on the fourth line of the fifty-seventh page, for instance, would be 570403. The zeros are spacers. They're the giveaways, apparently. They, and the fact that the subgroups they separate are always less than three hundred and twenty, forty-five, and eighteen respectively. Lisa was using a book, in other words, of not much more than three hundred and twenty pages, with forty-five lines per page and not more than eighteen words per line.'

'He spotted all that straightaway?' Diana whistled in admiration. 'That's impressive.'

He nodded gloomily. 'Impressive but not much help. Book

codes are crude, but they have one shining virtue. Unless you know the book, they're virtually uncrackable.'

'And there's no hint of the book in the journal?'

'Not that I can find. There are lots of books mentioned. Writers too. But even knowing the title doesn't help. You have to know the edition. It looks hopeless.' He paused. 'Ironic, isn't it? She goes to all that trouble, and succeeds in protecting her killer.'

27

On the morning following his conversation with Diana, Nolan received a phone call from Jacobsen. It resulted in his paying a visit to the Golden I. He went late, hoping to avoid the lunchtime crowd, and took with him as camouflage Christie and her cousin, Marissa Devon, an eighteen-year-old with a friendly eye, a pretty face, and a truly sensational figure. It was vital, Jacobsen had stressed, that in striking up an acquaintance with Thomas he avoid doing anything to arouse suspicion. With companions like these, Nolan figured, he could strike up an acquaintance and not even be noticed.

But even assuming success in that venture, he was doubtful about his chances of achieving anything. In view of the discovery regarding Billy's truck, he could understand why Jacobsen felt Thomas would bear looking into. He could understand too that Jacobsen himself was pretty much disqualfied from doing the looking. What he didn't understand was what Jacobsen expected him to accomplish and how. What was Jacobsen suggesting exactly? That he trail Lisa's name in front of Thomas and watch him for guilty reactions? Or that he play things by ear and see what developed?

It looked unpromising in the restaurant. Though it was Thomas, unmistakable from Jacobsen's description, who greeted them, showed them their table, and came by later to ask if all was well; he did it with a vague, distant courtesy that discouraged conversation. Nolan did try, of course, when opportunity offered, but his efforts were met with monosyllables. He saw nothing especially sinister in this. It was not, he suspected, that Thomas was stonewalling, simply that he found them uninteresting. By the time coffee was served things were looking hopeless. Indeed, as Nolan later told Jacobsen, the lunch would have been a total bust had not one of the waiters, just as the check was about to be brought, come rushing in to announce that there was a rattlesnake in the parking lot.

'Mojave,' Thomas said. '*Crotalis Scutellatus.* Haemotoxic and neurotoxic. Nasty.'

It didn't strike Nolan as especially nasty, just a small rattler, alarmed at finding itself the centre of attention and announcing intermittently its willingness to defend itself. Nevertheless, he kept his distance. He wasn't particularly scared of snakes, but he wasn't fond of them either. And though rattlesnakes as a breed were not normally aggressive, there was no telling with individuals. Besides, this was Thomas's parking lot, therefore his rattler; let him take care of it.

'Kill it.' Marissa was keeping Nolan between herself and the snake and holding on tight to Nolan's arm.

'No, leave it,' Christie said. 'It's not bothering us; we're bothering it. It'll go away if we leave it in peace.'

'Don't bet on that.' Before leaving the restaurant Thomas had armed himself with what looked like a gardening tool, a long wooden handle with a small metal hook at the end. With this, he advanced on the rattler. It reacted by pressing back against the wall and buzzing frantically. The coils bunched and gathered, the head drew back, the lidless eyes watched, unwavering, hard and bright as onyx.

'Couldn't we just drive it into the boonies?' Nolan asked. He pointed to the wash behind the restaurant and the desert shimmering beyond. 'There must be a zillion of them out there. One more can't make any difference.'

There was more to this plea than conservationism. He was grateful to this rattlesnake. He wished it a long and peaceful life.

'I'm not planning to kill it.' Thomas advanced the hook towards the rattler. 'I'm more concerned to protect it, actually.

But these guys tend to hang around if you let them. If I just drive him off, the odds are he'll be back. Much better to catch him and take him where he'll be safe.'

'Good idea,' Nolan grinned. 'You catch; we'll watch.'

Thomas seemed to know what he was doing. Prodding the snake into flight, he pinned its neck to the ground with the metal part of the stick, then before it could work loose, he reached down and grabbed it just behind the head. It struggled for a moment, then hung limp as if dead. The jaws were open, though, the fangs extended.

'The trick is don't squeeze too hard.' Thomas spoke with a casual expertise. 'Snakes are actually very delicate. Squeeze too hard, you crush vertebrae. Go to the other extreme, of course, you end up with a fang in the thumb.'

'And have you, ever?' Christie seemed provoked by his manner. There was a note of scepticism in her inquiry, a suggestion that all this snake talk was basically bullshit. This might not be a bad approach to take, Nolan thought; hostility might work where friendliness hadn't. Christie, of course, had no idea of his interest in Thomas; he hoped she wouldn't overdo the hostility.

'Have I been bitten? Once.' Thomas nodded. 'Not handling, though. I was backpacking and stepped over the wrong log. But I was lucky, he only nicked me. My blue jeans got most of it.' He shrugged, dismissing the subject and with it Christie. He turned to Marissa. 'Do me a favour, would you? Run back inside and ask in the kitchen for one of the big pickle jars. Empty, of course, I need something to hold him in.' He gave her a film star smile, wrinkling his eyes at the corners and showing perfect teeth.

Marissa, charmed, nodded and set off. Bringing her had been smart, Nolan thought. Her friendliness offset Christie.

'What's haemotoxic?' Christie asked.

'Haemotoxins attack the blood, basically.' Thomas squatted down, taking the snake's body in his left hand while holding on to its head with the right. It seemed completely passive now, but the jaws were still open and the fangs extended. 'Neurotoxins hit the nervous system. Most species of rattler are only haemotoxic, but not this guy.' He inspected the snake with what looked like affection. 'This guy is bad news.'

'Neurotoxins are worse, then?'

'In general. It depends on the dose, really, but gram for gram they're worse. Take cobras for instance. A good jolt from one of them and your whole nervous system seizes up. Death comes from heart and respiratory failure. That's always assuming, of course, that you haven't already died of fright.'

'You seem to know a lot about it.' Christie reverted to disapproval. Such expertise, her tone implied, verged on the morbid.

'It's my hobby.' Thomas shrugged. 'Some people watch birds. I watch snakes.'

Christie considered.

'What's to watch?' she demanded. 'Birds at least fly and sing. Snakes don't do anything much. At least not the ones you see in zoos. They just lie around, looking bored.'

Thomas smiled. 'In zoos you never see them being fed. When they're hunting, they're not bored at all.' He paused. 'Not boring, either.'

Christie made a face. But her retort, to Nolan's relief, was pre-empted by the return of Marissa with the jar.

'Take the lid off and set it down there.' Thomas indicated a spot on the ground directly in front of him.

Marissa hesitated, unwilling to come that close to the snake. She set the jar down a good yard from where Thomas had indicated.

'Closer,' Thomas said.

Again Marissa hesitated.

'Don't worry,' Thomas said. 'I won't let it bite you.'

With her fingertips Marissa slid the jar closer, then quickly backed away. She was not remotely in danger, but Nolan knew how she felt. The mouth with its fangs was only feet away. Imagination was stronger than reason.

'Now,' Thomas said. 'I'm going to drop him in the jar. When I let go, clap the lid on. OK?'

Silence. Marissa looked panic-stricken. She shook her head.

'You can't be scared?' Thomas looked disbelieving. 'That's ridiculous. It won't strike, and anyway it can't nail you through the lid.'

Marissa said nothing. She gazed, in mute appeal, at Nolan.

'Give it to me, Marissa.' Christie's voice was gentle. She took the lid from Marissa and gave her a quick reassuring grin. She turned to Thomas. 'It isn't ridiculous. She doesn't like snakes. People don't, you know. Now,' she held the lid ready, close to the mouth of the jar, 'drop that thing in and take your hand away, fast. I'd hate it to get trapped in the jar.'

Silence. Thomas and Christie exchanged stares. For an instant there was open hostility between them, then Thomas smiled. It was almost the same smile he had given Marissa, only this time there was no warmth in it.

'Well, well,' Thomas said. 'We know who isn't scared.'

Christie shrugged. 'We all have our phobias. Mine is heights. What's yours?'

Thomas didn't answer. He held the snake at arm's length, grasping it now at both extremities, tail uppermost. Then he snatched his hand away from the head. The snake dangled, straining to get at him. He lowered it into the jar. When most of the body was in, he let go and took his hand away smartly.

There was a certain theatricality to all this, Nolan thought. Thomas had exaggerated the danger for the benefit of his audience. Christie evidently thought so too. When Thomas jerked his hand away, she paused a beat or two, perhaps as much as a second, before she very deliberately, without haste or hesitation, capped the jar and screwed the lid tight. As drama, her manner implied, the production had lacked a certain something.

Thomas let his eyes rest on her for a second. 'You're not afraid?'

'Not especially.' She shrugged. 'I wouldn't want to get bitten, of course.'

'Could you put your hand on the jar and keep it there while he took a cut at you?'

'Probably not. But that's a reflex, like blinking. It's got nothing to do with being scared.'

Again Thomas didn't reply. Instead he placed his hand on the jar. The snake, alarmed, rattled and struck, the movement so swift it was over before the eye could pick it up. It struck again, then a third time. Only then did Thomas remove his hand. The snake, Nolan saw, had a bead of blood on its nose.

For a second Thomas stared at Christie. Then he shrugged.

'You must have practised.' Christie wasn't impressed. 'Beats me why you would want to, though.'

'Well I couldn't do it.' Marissa rushed to conciliate. 'No matter how long I practised. You know it can't get at you through the glass, but your hand moves anyway.'

Thank God for Marissa, Nolan thought. Christie, though her reaction was understandable, could ruin things.

'Where will you take it?' he asked Thomas. 'How far do you need to go to make sure he won't come back?'

Thomas considered. 'A couple of miles. On second thought, though, I'm not going to let this one go. I don't have a Mojave.'

Marissa gasped. 'Have one? You mean you actually keep snakes? Live?'

Thomas smiled. 'What would I want with a dead snake?'

'What would you want with a live one?' This from Christie, sotto voce.

Thomas seemed not to hear.

'Poisonous snakes?' Marissa couldn't believe it. 'In the house?'

'A sight more poisonous than this one.' Thomas nodded. 'Apart from the rattlers, I've got puff adders, a boomslang, even a cobra. Enough venom, between them, to wipe out a regiment.' He paused. 'Want to see them?'

Marissa emphatically did. Christie, curiosity getting the better of her dislike, did too. Nolan, after a carefully judged show of reluctance, let himself be persuaded. He wasn't sure what had prompted the invitation, but things were working out well. This could push the acquaintance to the point where, without seeming overeager, he could pursue it. At the very least, it would get him a look at the inside of Thomas's house. Since Jacobsen felt Thomas might bear looking into, one might as well start, Nolan thought, by seeing if his kitchen overlooked the back patio.

168

28

Thomas's house was a few minutes' drive from the restaurant. It was more or less secluded, screened in front on either side by junipers and overlooked at the back by nothing but desert. Thomas offered no preliminary tour of the house but led them instead directly to what he referred to as the 'herpetarium'. It was therefore impossible to get an accurate picture of the topography, but Nolan did get a glimpse of French doors, next to the kitchen area, that led out to a Japanese garden – boulders and isolated cacti in a sea of whitish gravel – at whose centre was a circle paved in brick and furnished with ornamental cast-iron seats. At a pinch, he thought, you could call it a patio.

The room that housed the snakes was to the left of the hallway. Its walls were lined with long narrow tables stacked to shoulder height with glass-fronted cases. In these the thirty or forty members of the collection slithered or dozed.

Mostly they dozed, though dozing was hardly the word, Nolan thought, for their torpor. They seemed to be lost in some dim reptilian dream, sunk in an apathy more profound than sleep, indifferent even to the clatter of this invasion: rattlesnakes, half buried in the sand, still as the stones that littered their habitat; puff adders, like lurking diseases, loathsome in their bloated lethargy; the boomslang, recognizable because it looked like its name, long and oily green with bright obsidian eyes, looped round a dead branch like some lethal vine.

To all this inactivity there was, however, an exception. In the case next to the boomslang's was a small grotto of rocks, from which there had issued, at the first sound of intrusion, a large black snake. At the front of the case it reared up, head very close to the glass, and its neck flattened and spread into a hood. Its mouth opened to utter a fierce throaty hiss, easily audible through the vent holes in the glass, a sound like fabric tearing.

'Cobra,' Thomas said. '*Naja Naja Naja* . . . five and a half feet long, quick as a whiplash, wickedly neurotoxic, meaner than hell.' He spoke admiringly, as though these were all highly desirable qualities. And indeed, Nolan thought, the thing did have a sinister magnificence about it, an aura of darkness, like some lord of the night. He was conscious of holding his breath, and he let it out slowly, in a kind of sigh, glad of the quarter-inch plate glass that stood between him and this malevolence.

No one moved. Even Christie's flippancy had deserted her; her eyes were riveted on the snake. The cobra inspected the intruders with its glittering stare. It hissed relentlessly, made restless stabbing movements with its head.

'This one kills,' Thomas said. 'Those others, if you ran across them in the wild, would do their best to keep out of your way. This one attacks on sight. It's unusually aggressive, even for the species. Watch.'

He took a step towards the case. The cobra's head thudded against the glass. It thudded again. Thomas stepped back.

'It doesn't learn,' he said. 'Whenever I get within range, it attacks. I think it'd beat itself senseless just trying to get at me. It's a machine really, a venom-delivery system, with a great set of reflexes and a vicious disposition. What makes it worse is it's back-fanged; it has to chew the poison in. If it hits you, it's with you for a while, hanging on and chomping.' He turned to Christie. 'How does that grab you, Miss Not-Scared-Of-Snakes?'

Christie stared at him with the same look of slightly appalled fascination she'd just given the snake. 'It'd scare the hell out of me,' she said finally, 'if I spent as much time thinking about it as you apparently do.'

'It scares the hell out of me.' Marissa, once again, headed off the hostilities. 'It reminds me of our neighbour's Doberman, only worse. It just can't wait to get at you.'

'A bit unfair to Dobermans, don't you think?' Nolan, too, was anxious to keep the peace. 'They're trained, after all, to be guard dogs. You wouldn't want *that* in your backyard, prowling around in the dark.'

'Oh, these have been used as guards,' Thomas said. 'In Egypt they were used to discourage grave robbers. You go to steal the Pharaoh's treasure and instead you run across this guy in the dark. There's this tearing agony attached to your leg, and you ain't going home no more.' He paused. His smile was private and not altogether pleasant. Like a practical joker's smile –

170

Nolan was suddenly struck by the thought – it seemed somehow superior, smug with knowledge its owner had no plans to share. 'It's what I'd call the hard way of learning to mind your own business.'

'It hurts that badly?' Marissa asked. 'I thought being poisoned was meant to be peaceful, like being drugged and slipping into a coma.'

Thomas shook his head.

'Intense pain radiating from the site of the wound.' He was quoting, evidently, from some medical text. 'Dizziness and nausea. Respiratory failure. Incontinence and convulsions. Death. To summarize, you slowly suffocate. I imagine it's agony.'

Silence.

'Aren't we perhaps getting just a tiny bit morbid?' Christie asked. She turned to Thomas. 'You know, I keep having this feeling I've seen you before. Not here, but somewhere else. Were you ever in Taos, by any chance?'

Thomas shrugged.

'I've visited. But I don't recall meeting you. I'm sure I'd remember if I had.'

'We didn't meet. I just saw you somewhere. With my father, perhaps. You don't happen to know him, do you?'

'I don't know,' Thomas said. 'I'm afraid I've forgotten your name. What was it again?'

'Delafield. Christie Delafield. My father is Martin Delafield. He makes movies. You may have heard of him.'

Thomas thought for a minute, then shook his head. 'I'm afraid not.'

His tone suggested a lack of interest in the subject. Christie let it drop. The conversation, now that snakes were no longer its topic, flagged, and Thomas made no effort to revive it. He seemed bored with his guests, and he conveyed as much, not by hinting they should leave, but by offering no incentive to stay. As they left, he murmured an invitation to return, but in tones that noticeably lacked conviction.

So the visit, Nolan thought, could hardly be termed a success. They had learned nothing interesting about Thomas, unless you could count his strange passion for snakes, they had established no possible connection between him and Lisa, and had opened no avenue for further inquiry. Jacobsen would be disappointed.

'A creep,' Christie said. 'An overgrown version of the little boy who shoves spiders down little girls' necks. They squeal, so he feels like a stud. He was pissed at me because I wouldn't squeal.'

Nolan tended to agree. Thomas's fascination with snakes, though properly dressed up in jargon, was neither scientific nor, he'd have been willing to bet, aesthetic. There were only venomous snakes in Thomas's collection. What turned him on was deadliness.

'Well, I think he was kind of sexy,' Marissa said. 'It was cool how he handled that rattlesnake. You didn't like him because he didn't like you. And he didn't like you because you were a snot.'

'He liked you because you did squeal,' Christie retorted. 'And you liked him because you think with your hips.'

'So . . .' Marissa's grin acknowledged the truth of this judgement. 'You have to admit he was rather a fox.'

Christie shook her head. 'Even ignoring the personality, too small. Christ, I towered over him. Good features, maybe, if you go for the classical look, but too dinky to be a real fox. I like them more rugged, myself.' She looked sidelong at Nolan and catching his eye, fluttered her lashes theatrically. Marissa giggled.

The debate on sexual aesthetics engrossed the two of them most of the way home. Nolan paid little attention. He was more interested in Thomas's character. He hadn't liked him very much, though apart from the hint of sadism in his teasing of Marissa, there seemed nothing much about him to dislike. Nothing, at any rate, to justify the kind of loathing that Lisa, right from the start, had conceived for A. Indeed, beyond a certain coolness in Thomas, there seemed no likeness whatever between him and the monster described in the journal. Of course, he hadn't seen very much of Thomas, and the picture that emerged from the pages of the journal was less portrait than caricature, an image distorted by Lisa's hatred. It did seem, however, that with Thomas Jacobsen might be barking up the wrong tree. There was the matter of the truck, of course, but otherwise no grounds for suspicion beyond Jacobsen's intuition that Thomas hadn't swallowed his story about the hit-and-run accident. His own instinctive scepticism about that made Nolan smile. For people who relied on their own intuition so much, he thought, he and Jacobsen showed precious little faith in each other's.

'That's it!' These thoughts were interrupted by a sudden exclamation from Christie. 'The ranch. It's been bugging me since I first set eyes on him, and now it's come back.'

'We're so happy for you,' Marissa murmured. 'What's come back?'

'He was lying,' Christie said. 'That snakeman was lying. I knew I'd seen him somewhere. And I had.'

'At the ranch? You mean in Taos?'

Christie nodded emphatically. 'I remember it vividly. It was around Christmas, I think, or just after. He was coming out of the house as I was going in. We didn't speak, just sort of nodded to each other. He must have been going to see Martin, because no one else was there except me and the housekeeper.' She paused. 'I can understand him forgetting me – we only saw each other for an instant – but it's weird he wouldn't admit remembering Martin.'

'Wouldn't admit?' Marissa queried. 'Jesus, Christie, give the guy a break. He could have forgotten, couldn't he? Or you could be mistaken. Why assume he was lying? I mean, why would he?'

Christie thought for a moment then shrugged. 'I could be mistaken, I suppose. Only Christmas wasn't that long ago. I don't think I'm mistaken.'

'Of course you don't,' Marissa said. 'People never do.'

'Smartass.' Christie made a face. 'People don't quickly forget people as striking as he was, either.' She turned and appealed to Nolan. 'After all, that little snakeman is hardly your average face in the crowd, now is he?'

'Not exactly.' Nolan thought of the startling red gold hair, the cold, blue eyes, the perfect features. 'You could ask Martin, couldn't you? If he was at the ranch, Martin would probably remember.'

173

Christie looked puzzled. 'Why would I bother? Is it that important?'

Nolan shrugged. 'It isn't to me. But you've been arguing about it for the last few minutes. This seems an obvious way to resolve it.'

And I wouldn't mind having it resolved, he thought, because if Martin does remember him, that could give us a new slant on this Mr Thomas. And a new slant, at this point, is what we need.

But a new slant turned out to be only partly necessary. The trip to the Golden I was to pay an extraordinary dividend later that day when Nolan was browsing, once again, in the journal. Coming across the enigmatic series of comments that juxtaposed references to David Bowie, manikins, and foxes, he recalled, suddenly, what Christie had said to Marissa in the car. 'Good features, maybe, if you go for the classical look, but too dinky to be a real fox.' And with that recollection the reference to foxes, the most baffling in the entire journal, began to decipher itself.

'A perfect egg that old geek said about foxes.' 'Egg', as he'd learned elsewhere in the journal, was short for 'egg sample', or in other words 'example'. 'Old geek' was easy; the first quarter of the school's course on Western civilization was devoted to the study of what the students persisted in calling 'the ancient geeks'. Someone or something, therefore, was a perfect example of what some old Greek had said about foxes. Until now, however, the search for an old Greek who'd said something about foxes had led Nolan only to Aesop's fables, where much was said on the subject of foxes, none of it very enlightening. But Christie's remark now suggested another meaning of 'fox', and with it another interpretation. Someone or something was a perfect example of what an old Greek had said about good looks. That made more sense, but major problems remained: Who was the perfect example? Which old Greek was referred to? And what exactly had he said?

Inspiration is often no more than the process of freeing oneself from hindering assumptions. Nolan had always taken for granted that the puzzling entry omitted the verb and the subject, that A was the indefinite article, capitalized because it was also the first word. What he saw now, and with an intuitive certainty that made him want to kick himself to Albuquerque and back for having missed it before, was that what had been omitted was the verb and the indefinite article. A was the subject, capitalized because it stood for a name. It was Bronco's Svengali, in other words, Lisa's implacable enemy, the mystery man of the journal.

Only not so mysterious any more, because now Nolan remembered which old Greek had something to say about good looks. It was Aristotle, of course, who had something to say on everything under the sun. And what Aristotle had said was that good looks depended on size as well as form; no small man, however perfectly featured, could properly be regarded as good looking.

And now the whole page made sense, not only the 'foxes' remark but the references to 'miniman' and 'Bowie'. It was eerie, Nolan thought, like watching someone think; not a purposeful forward progression but a kind of decorated loop, the mind picking seemingly at random through a grab bag of separate ideas but stringing them like beads on the thread of a current obsession. The miniman remark reflected Lisa's pre-occupation with small men. The Bowie reference connected this, probably by unconscious association, to thoughts of red hair, green eyes, and perfectly chiselled features. Aristotle, with his theories about small men and good looks, had linked these reflections with Lisa's feelings about A. And what Lisa had written about A, Christie had subsequently echoed . . . about Thomas.

29

'Thomas?' Peters said. 'You don't mean "Golden" Thomas? Early thirties. Five-two or thereabouts. Red hair, green eyes. Also known as "Acapulco Gold"?'

'Sounds like him,' Jacobsen said. 'I wasn't aware of the alias, but the rest certainly fits.'

'Then sure I know him. Knew him, at least. A poisonous little bastard. What would you want with him?'

'Info,' Jacobsen said. 'Just background.'

'Suspected dealer.' Peters didn't ask what kind of info; if you came to him, it was about drugs. 'Coke mostly. And the pricier brands of pot. He was a part-timer, we think, never a pro. Worked the fringes of the yuppie market, people he met through the law firm he worked for.'

'Suspected dealer? That mean he doesn't have a record?'

'One arrest, no convictions.' Even long distance, the regret was clearly audible. 'It was case dismissed, as if you couldn't guess. The usual Fourth Amendment bullshit. Had him cold on the facts, but the arresting officer committed some legal no-no. So Thomas falls down and clutches his balls and yells "foul", and the judge swallows it. So technically, no, he doesn't have a record, but he was dealing and we knew it. And after the arrest he knew we knew, so he packed his bags and left town. Almost like a conviction, in a way.'

Almost, but not quite. And that, Jacobsen knew, was a piece of luck. For that small, crucial difference between a near miss and a bull's eye, which even now, three years later, brought a wistfulness to Peters' voice, would guarantee his assistance in a way that professional courtesy never would. It was not case dismissed with Peters; it was lingering animosity and a memory like an elephant's. Thank God for cops like this, Jacobsen thought.

'He ever deal any smack that you heard of?'

'Not his style,' Peters said. 'There are social distinctions to make here, you know. This is white-collar crime we're talking here. Respectable crime. See, yuppies dealing coke on the side to help pay for their Porsches is one thing. But smack? That's different. That's evil and dangerous. They leave that to the real criminals. They may do a bit, once in a while, but they draw the line at dealing the stuff. That way they get to be rich and hang on to their moral standards.' Beneath the irony his bitterness was manifest.

And understandable, Jacobsen thought, because if any job entitled you to be bitter, it was working narcotics in a big city. That was bailing the ship with a hole in your bucket. A handful of overworked, underpaid cops, swamped by a steady Niagara

176

of drugs, hampered by the courts, and abused by the public they existed to serve. No wonder they got bitter.

'You say he was just a part-timer? I'd have figured him to be bigger. When he moved here, at least, he did it in style. Bought a big fancy house and opened a restaurant. We're talking an investment of several hundred thousand, even if he did finance a piece of it. I wouldn't have thought you could make that kind of money in a couple of years of part-time dealing.'

'I doubt the dealing was the all of it,' Peters said. 'About the time we were ready to move on him he got canned by the law firm he worked for. They didn't prosecute, so I never got the details, but I heard it wasn't drugs. We figured he must have some other scam going.'

Another scam. Something like this was what Jacobsen had been fishing for. If Thomas were the killer, and if a case were ever to be built against him, they would need a motive – and one more substantial than nickel and dime deals with Lisa and Billy.

'You don't happen to recall the name of the law firm, do you?'

'Not offhand. I could have someone track it down, maybe, and call you back.' Peters paused. 'What's he been doing to merit your attention?'

'I don't know that he's done anything,' Jacobsen said. 'But we've had some bad drugs surface here recently. A kid OD'd on smack and died. And the name Thomas keeps cropping up. I wanted to know if he had a history.'

'Well he does. Not for smack, admittedly, but that may not mean much. It wasn't his style three years ago, but who knows? Maybe he changed. I'll have someone check on that law firm and call you.'

'I'd appreciate that. And thank you.'

'Don't thank me,' Peters said. 'Repay me. Repay me by nailing his mean little ass to the floor.'

'Dorrit, Waters and Riefenstahl? I've heard of them some-where.' Nolan thought a moment. 'Actually, come to think of it, they're Martin's lawyers. Martin Delafield, that is, Fremont's illustrious chairman of the board. There's Dorrit on the board

177

too, I recall. See, Martin's father, who at one time owned a sizable chunk of this part of the state, donated the land on which the school was built. Gave them some money too. So a Delafield and a Dorrit, Waters or Riefenstahl always sit on the board. Protecting their investment in education, you might say.'

'Do you know him?' Jacobsen had been tempted to tune out what had struck him as a rather gratuitous history lesson, but on hearing about Dorrit he perked up. 'Dorrit, that is.'

'I've met him.' Nolan nodded. 'I suppose I could ask him why Thomas was canned. I'll need to think of a damned good reason for asking, though. It's going to seem kind of impertinent, otherwise.'

'So think of something.' Jacobsen had no sympathy with social scruples. 'Because I'm getting convinced that Thomas is mixed up in all this. He used to be nicknamed "Acapulco" for one thing, which would square with those journal references to "A". She also mentioned an "Ac", remember.'

'Of course I remember,' Nolan said. 'But what would I be hoping to get from this Dorrit? I mean, I already knew that A was Thomas. Your conversation with Peters merely confirmed it. What can we expect Dorrit to add?'

'Motive,' Jacobsen said. 'We may have a murderer, but we've no clue at all why he did it. So if Thomas had a scam that got him canned from his job, it makes sense to me to find out what it was. It may turn out not to be any help, but we'll never know till we ask, now will we?'

'*We?*' Nolan said.

'I meant you,' Jacosbsen said. 'Fair division of labour. You know him, so you call him. Just like I called Peters.' He imagined Nolan interviewing Dorrit and found himself grinning. 'Now you know what it's like to be a cop.'

'Mark Thomas?' Ivan Dorrit said. 'I'm acquainted with him, certainly. Or should say was acquainted. He used to work for us at one time. But that was several years back.'

He sounded suddenly guarded, as if reviewing mentally the provisions of the statute against slander. The warmth with which he'd originally received Nolan's phone call had vanished.

'Pity,' Nolan said. 'I was hoping you could tell me about him.'

Pause.

'I see. Might I inquire into the nature of your interest in Mr Thomas?'

'I'm thinking of doing some business with him.' This had struck Nolan as the best pretext for the kind of inquiry he wanted to make. 'I'd like to get references.'

'Am I to understand . . .' Dorrit's tone was now freezing. Nolan could picture a faintly raised eyebrow, the thin curl of the mouth, cold blue eyes staring down a long, aristocratic nose. 'Am I to understand that Mr Thomas gave me as a reference?'

'No. I heard somewhere that he'd once worked for you, so I presumed a little on our acquaintance and took the liberty of calling.' Nolan despised himself for that 'took the liberty'. Jacobsen, he thought, you owe me for that.

'I see.' Dorrit seemed not much mollified. 'Well I can tell you this. My advice to anyone contemplating a business association with Mr Thomas is don't.'

'That so?' Nolan had expected some such response. His only option now was nosiness. He steeled himself for the snub it was likely to earn him and plunged ahead. 'I understand he left you under something of a cloud. Cocaine, wasn't it? He was indicted shortly afterwards.'

'That is true. He was indicted.' Dorrit paused. 'This may seem somewhat impertinent, but I find it strange that you would contemplate a business connection with someone who'd been indicted for selling cocaine.'

'Do you?' Nolan let some chill into *his* tone. It was impertinent; Dorrit had overstepped and must be made to feel it. He might try to atone, then, by being helpful. 'But he was acquitted, wasn't he? And therefore entitled to the benefit of the doubt, I should have thought.'

'The case was dismissed.' Dorrit's voice remained starchy. 'On Fourth Amendment grounds. If you know what *they* are?'

'I do, as a matter of fact.'

'Well in that case, enough said, don't you think?'

'Then it was the coke, I take it. No smoke without fire, I suppose? Even if the case was dismissed.'

Extended pause. Score one to me, Nolan thought.

'Mr Nolan, we do not dismiss employees on mere suspicion. It was not the cocaine.'

'What was it then?'

Outraged silence. You could, Nolan thought, almost *hear* Dorrit wanting to hang up.

'Look, Mr Dorrit, I know you think I'm prying, but what I'm actually doing is trying to be fair. I'd like to know if there's any question in your mind as to Thomas's integrity. If there isn't, I think he's entitled to have that stated.'

Another pause. Score two to Nolan. You could always, he thought, get to a lawyer by appealing to his sense of justice. Amazing, really, since a lawyer's sense of justice was a bit like a hooker's sense of romance.

'Mr Nolan . . .'

'Yes.'

'Do I understand you to say you're a friend of Martin Delafield?'

'Yes. We were at Exeter together, and Harvard.' Time for the Old Boy Network. 'It was at his suggestion that I came to Fremont.'

'I see. In that case I'm prepared to tell you, in general terms, why Mr Thomas left this firm. This information is in the strictest confidence, of course.'

'Of course.'

'Good. Mr Thomas was dismissed because we found that he'd used his knowledge of our clients' affairs for personal advantage.'

'I see.' Nolan was disappointed. A little insider trading, it sounded like. Thomas had worked on a merger, perhaps, and bought shares before he should've. Interesting to the SEC, of course, but not much help in suggesting a motive for murder. Unless, blackmail? That was a possibility. But even so, where was the connection to Lisa? Perhaps there was none. Perhaps this was one of those leads that led nowhere. In any case, one thing was utterly certain; he'd had all the information he was going to get from Dorrit.

'Mr Dorrit . . .' A little old-fashioned courtesy, at this point, might not come amiss. He owed it to Martin, since Dorrit, no doubt, would tell him of this call. 'I've trespassed enough on

180

your time and patience, and I much appreciate your help. You can be sure I'll hold what you've told me in the very strictest confidence.'

Except, he thought, I shall have to tell the police.

30

From her desk in the library Diana Pritchett gazed out of the window at the long sweep of valley beyond. She looked back at her desk. Her heart sank. Outside, the afternoon was a standing invitation to indolence, the kind that mocked the very notion of duty – cloudlessly perfect, with a suspicion of breeze to take the edge off the heat. But in here, in stacks on the desk, stood Duty objectified, the neglected paperwork of half a semester: books to be ordered, books to be catalogued, fines to be levied, delinquency notices to be sent out. And none of it could be put off any longer; otherwise the semester would be over and the students gone for the summer, with half the library in their suitcases. So here she was, and here, for the next several hours, she'd have to stay. Glumly, she reached for the list of books overdue.

The names on the list were tiresomely familiar. Fremont students, she had long ago decided, fell into two classes: those who didn't read, and those who didn't return their library books. Christie Delafield, for instance, had eight overdue, among them three volumes of the *Britannica* whose removal from the library premises was forbidden but which Christie, with typical insouciance, had signed out anyway. Most other students would have taken them and just not signed them out. But not La Delafield; that was not her style. La Delafield? . . . Diana detected, in her mental use of the phrase, a hostility that Christie, to be honest, had done nothing much to deserve, and this led, by a natural association of ideas, to Nolan. Christie and Nolan. Something, she suspected, was developing there. Or not so much developing, since the feeling between them went back years, as forcing on them, Nolan especially, the recognition of what that feeling had become. And it was something perhaps

181

more serious than the usual student-teacher romance. They were very alike, Diana thought, both brats. Spoiled, intelligent, intermittently charming, neither of them overburdened with respect for the conventions nor averse, particularly, to taking risks. One got the feeling sometimes, seeing them together, that they operated on a kind of private wavelength, that they formed, without being aware of it, a secret society of two. And while his sense of honour would undoubtedly keep her for the time being out of his bed, it was clear she had plans for that to change. Christie wanted him. And what Christie wanted more often than not she got. Which meant of course . . . it occurred to Diana that this line of thought was bringing her neither profit nor pleasure, so abandoning it, she went back to her list, consoling herself, as she passed to the next name, by zapping Christie a dollar each for her legitimate borrowings and an utterly vindictive five dollars apiece for the three illegal *Britannicas*.

The next name on the list was Lisa Bronowski. Her transgressions had been relatively minor. Only one volume was listed to her, the due date fairly recent. On April 2, twelve days before her death, she'd borrowed a copy of *Our Man in Havana*. She had never returned it.

Lost cause, Diana decided. It must have been packed and sent home with the rest of Lisa's stuff. It would be worse than tactless to pursue it. She made a note to order a replacement and moved on to the next name.

As she did, she was struck by a thought. This was the second time Lisa had borrowed that book. Like every student in Diana's class, she had been required to read and report on at least one book per semester that was not on the course reading list. *Our Man in Havana* had been one of her choices. But according to Diana's recollection, which a glance at the library card confirmed, it had been her choice for last semester. And she hadn't much liked it. She'd read it as a thriller, missed most of the humour, and found it decidedly wanting. Why on earth, then, had she decided to reread it?

The birth of an idea is always a little mysterious. Nolan had certainly been much in Diana's thoughts, and so to a lesser extent had Lisa. Somewhere in the basement of her memory, also, the plot of *Our Man in Havana* must still have lingered. But how these ingredients, like liquids which when combined miraculously form a crystal, transformed themselves into another book title – Lamb's *Tales from Shakespeare* – was never clear to Diana. What was clear, almost as soon as the title popped into her mind, was that Lamb's *Tales From Shakespeare* had been used, in the Graham Greene novel, as the key to a book code.

If Nolan's cipher expert had been right about Lisa's using a book code, *Our Man in Havana* – the thought struck Diana with the force of inspiration – was almost certainly the book she had used as the key.

31

'You were right,' Nolan said. 'And I was right. Here. Read it.'

He offered Diana some sheets of paper covered with type-script, single spaced. She glanced at them then back at him, dubious.

'Will it make me think worse of her? If it will, I don't want to read it.'

Nolan shook his head. 'I don't think so. She seems to have written it mostly as a kind of exorcism, to free herself from her feelings by putting them into words. She even writes at one point of wanting to have someone hear her confession.' He paused. 'I don't think she would have minded. She might even have welcomed it.'

'Welcomed it?' Diana stared. 'It took you, you say, most of the night to decipher it. It must have taken her five times as long to encrypt it. Why would she go to that trouble if she'd wanted us to read it?'

'When she went to that trouble, she didn't know she'd be murdered,' Nolan answered evenly. 'If anyone kills, I'd like him brought to justice.' He paused. 'If you thought we shouldn't read it, why did you tell me about the book?'

'It's not that I don't think anyone should read it; just that I'm not sure I want to . . .' She hesitated, anticipating comments about ostriches. 'Oh, what the hell . . .'

She took the pages from him and began to read.

Two days, and still I feel dirty. I can't avoid B much longer, but I can't go to him, make love to him, feeling like this. Maybe writing it down will help me get rid of it. Like whispering secrets to a hole in the ground, or spilling my guts to a shrink. I need to talk to someone and there isn't anyone. Besides, the one who needs to forgive me is me. So I am writing this down as my confession to myself. Coding it will be my act of contrition.

What I really need is a priest. But that won't work without belief. I thought at first I could absolve myself or that I wouldn't need to because I didn't do it for myself. I keep telling myself that – that the motive is all that's important – but it doesn't do any good. I don't believe in sin, yet I feel I've committed one. I don't believe in God, yet I need him to forgive me.

It made me feel sick. I tried to shut my mind off and just let it happen to my body, but that didn't work. You can't shut your mind off. In any case, it was my mind he was after; what he wanted was to have me betray B. I thought I could do what he wanted, strike my bargain, and be untouched by it because I was simply going through the motions, but he knew better. It seems there are motions you can't simply go through. Those who touch pitch will be defiled.

As far as sex goes there wasn't much to it. He made me shower first, as if maybe he'd catch something otherwise, then he had me lie on the bed fingering myself, like some porno movie. I waited for him to join in, but he just stood there staring. I said 'Let's get on with it, OK?' So he took off his clothes and came over to the bed.

I had to touch him, take him in my mouth. It didn't do anything for him. He told me to talk dirty, but that didn't work either. He said it would help if I showed some enthusiasm. I said that hadn't been part of the deal. He told me a whore should be able to fake it, at least. Then he started in calling me names.

So I said, 'What's your problem? Can't get it up?'

For a moment I thought he would cry. Then I thought he would kill me. He went white and his lip was trembling. I thought for sure he would hit me, but something held him back. He told me I didn't turn him on, he wouldn't touch me with a ten-foot pole, he'd done this to show me what I was.

So I said, 'Sure, nothing the matter with you. Nothing a course of hormones wouldn't fix, or a few thousand sessions with a shrink.' And I got my clothes. I told him I'd kept my side of it, and now he could keep his. No more smack for B. No more trying to get him to push it at school. No more drug dealing. Ever. And if he went back on his part of it, I'd tell all the boys at the restaurant, all his little hangers-on, what a fag they had for a buddy. He said I wouldn't dare. If B found out what I'd done, he'd kill me. But I told him B would kill him too, and I told him besides that if B stayed hooked I didn't have much to lose. I'd go to the cops if I had to, wreck myself, wreck B, wreck anything so long as I wrecked him too. I think he believed me, then, because he gave a kind of angry laugh and said it didn't matter anyway because B was probably hooked for good now, and if he didn't get smack from him, he'd get it someplace else. And he said too, with the same laugh, that for the rest of my life I'd never forget what I'd done, and he wouldn't forget it either. It would be our secret. Always.

Now I feel like filth. But I got what I wanted; he'll leave B alone. What baffles me is what he got out of it. He must have known what would happen – or what wouldn't. I guess he hoped it would be different this time, that if only he could make things ugly enough it would turn him on. Or maybe he's even sicker than that; maybe he just saw B and me caring about each other in a way he couldn't, and he wanted to spoil it. That would be like him. But I don't know. I think maybe even he doesn't know. If he weren't such a slime, I could almost feel sorry for him. But whenever I'm tempted, I remember what he was doing to B. I know how to put the needle into him, now, and he knows that I know and that I will. I think it's time for him to feel sorry.

Diana handed the pages back to Nolan. Some comment seemed called for but she couldn't find anything to say. She

185

was seized instead by an inarticulate anger, an urge to protest what she'd read, not in words but by smashing something. It was anger at herself for reading what Nolan had given her, and at him for having given it; it was anger at men for the things they did to women. But mostly it was anger at a world in which things like this could happen, where seventeen-year-olds, like Lisa, could be forced to learn so much, so soon.

'So,' Nolan said, 'we have a motive.'

They had a motive all right. Offer a psychopath that kind of threat to his ego, and you could almost guarantee the response would be murderous.

She nodded. 'You must be pleased with yourself.'

'Not at all.' He was too pleased to catch the irony. 'Most of the credit is yours for that intuition about *Our Man in Havana*. All I did was the donkey work. You'd make an excellent historian.'

Credit? . . . Who wanted it? Who'd want to be a historian, for that matter? All that consisted of, so far as she could see, was ferreting out men's dirty little secrets, the shady deals, the betrayals and backstabbings. Perhaps Nolan found these things interesting. She didn't.

'Well now you've got your motive, do something with it. Put him behind bars, or in an institution. Because I don't feel good about my part in this. I'd like to think we'd achieved something.'

'Not feeling good?' He stared. 'Why not?'

She shrugged. If he didn't understand already, explaining wouldn't help.

'Just nail him,' she said. 'Just nail the dirty little bastard.'

'We'll nail him.' Nolan nodded. 'We're getting there, but we're not there yet. We have a suspect and a motive, or part of one, but we still don't have the whole story.'

'The whole story. What whole story?'

'The story of why Lisa was killed,' Nolan said. 'Our evidence is mostly circumstantial so far, and there are too many gaps. We know she'd acquired a blackmailer's hold over Thomas, a hold that may very well have pushed him to kill her, but what we don't know is what he wanted with her – and Bronco – in the first place.'

'Does it matter?'

'I think so. See, I don't think the psychological motive is enough to convince a jury. You can't just say, "OK, jury, he did it because she'd found out he was impotent and was threatening to blackmail him with it." They would find it hard to buy that, if only because the mental processes of psychopaths don't generally make much sense to normal people. We need something harder, something a jury could relate to.'

'Like what?'

'Greed,' Nolan said. 'Everyone understands that. And it was present, I think. Greed enters into this somewhere. There's more to it than just the emotional turmoil of a weirdo. That wouldn't account, for instance, for the torching of that dorm, and I think that needs to be accounted for.' He paused. 'There was some kind of scam going on, and it centred in some way around the school. Thomas was involved, and Lisa and Bronco were caught up in it, probably without knowing. And we need to know what it was, because otherwise I don't think we've enough evidence for an indictment.'

She studied him for a moment. 'You know what I think?'

'What?'

'I think you're enjoying the hell out of this. I think you're having the time of your life, and I'm afraid I find that a little indecent. You can count me out here on in. I like to think of kids as kids. I want to remember Lisa as she was in my classroom. I'm through playing detective.'

He met this steadily. 'We want to know because we want to stop it. It's as simple as that.'

'I'd like to think so.' She continued to study him. 'But as you've said yourself, motives are seldom simple. You want to stop it, but you also can't resist a puzzle. You want to know because you want to know.'

32

'Got you!' Christie pounced. 'Now you're my prisoner. Don't even think of escape.'

Nolan wasn't. He'd heard her sneaking up on him as he sat

at the kitchen counter, thumbing through a review copy of some history text his publisher had sent him, but he'd let her think she was taking him by surprise. Now, with her arms around him, her face next to his, her chin resting lightly on his shoulder, he leaned back and allowed himself, for a moment, to be caught.

'Actually, this is rescue, not capture.' She kept hold of him. 'Don't bullshit me, you'd rather be reading that book. You were dying for me to disturb you, I could tell.'

He put the book down. Her statement was more or less accurate. It would have taken one hell of a history book to compete with her in interest. He was somewhat surprised by her visiting in the mid-afternoon, however. She usually didn't.

'Don't you mean *you* were dying to disturb *me*?'

'That too,' she agreed cheerfully. 'Otherwise I wouldn't be here.'

'Then since you don't want me to be reading my book, what do you want me to be doing?'

She hesitated for a moment, squeezed him a fraction tighter, then put her mouth to his ear.

'Making love to me.'

He was too startled to answer at once; all he was conscious of was her closeness, the warmth of her breath on his cheek, the heat and weight of her body against him, the sudden ache of his own desire. For an instant the feeling between them shed its remaining disguises; their bodies, ignoring the censorship of thought, exchanged messages as unambiguous as heartbeats. Then scruple reasserted itself. He took her arms and, disengaging them, turned to face her.

'That's nonsense, Christie. You mustn't say that, even in fun.'

She flushed slightly, but her gaze didn't falter. 'It wasn't in fun. I'm dead serious. I want to make love with you because I'm in love with you. Surely you realize that?'

He said nothing. He'd put off facing this situation. So long as things were left unstated, the possibilities remained open. But now she had forced the issue, there could only be one outcome. He hadn't wanted to be faced with it yet.

'Why can't we be lovers?' she demanded. 'Give me one good reason.'

One good reason? It seemed to him there were dozens. 'I'm your teacher, for Christ's sake. There's a little matter of professional ethics.'

'Professional ethics?' Her tone dismissed them. 'I'll be graduated – out of here – in thirty-two days. Who cares about thirty-two days?'

'It's not a question of thirty-two days, but of not violating a trust. And as to who cares about that.' He paused. 'I care.'

'Then I'll wait.' She placed her hands on his shoulders, met his gaze steadily. 'I guess I can spare you thirty-two days. I'm not just looking for some casual affair. I want you to know that, Philip. I'm talking about forever.'

She meant it. Or part of her did. And seeing in her the confident beautiful woman she would soon be he was pierced by a sudden sense of loss; an anger at circumstances which permitted their feeling yet placed this barrier of years between them.

'I'm too old.'

'Eighteen years . . .' She shrugged. 'It seems like a lot. But I don't notice it. In five years we won't even think of it. What you really mean is people might think you are too old. You're afraid of seeming some dirty old man, taking advantage of a schoolgirl crush.'

The bluntness made him wince, but she was partly right. He remembered something her mother had said, years before, when Christie was barely in her teens. 'She has a crush on you, of course. I suppose it was inevitable. But better you, my dear, who for all your faults have at least some sense of honour, than the sort of louse who would take advantage.' He was a prisoner of expectations. But they were his as much as anyone's.

'So big deal,' Christie said. 'Do you care what people think?'

'I do when it's what I think.' He paused. 'Look, Christie. This whole conversation is nonsense. We shouldn't be having it.'

'But we are,' she insisted. 'It's not fair, when your arguments are demolished, to retreat into teacher ethics and refuse to talk any more. After all, do you think it was easy to come right out and say it?'

That was true, he supposed. They'd taken this too far to back away now.

'OK, then. What I really mean is you're too young. You may

think you love me, but how can you know? You're eighteen years old. You haven't lived enough, seen enough, known enough – '

'Known enough men?' She cut him off. 'Jesus, Philip, I'm not buying a new car. I don't need to test drive other models. I know you, don't you see? I've known you forever, and I've seen all I need.' She paused. 'I love you. You're all I've ever wanted. *You*, Philip Nolan. It's that simple.'

'That simple?' God, how he wished it were.

'It can be. It is, if you'll let it.'

He shook his head. 'It's not.'

'Have it your way.' She shrugged. 'I guess finding hidden complexity in the apparently straightforward is the mark of the truly adult mind.' She rolled her eyes. 'God I can't wait to grow up.'

He let that one pass.

'I'm not giving up.' She seemed composed and oddly confident. In spite of the eighteen years, it struck him, it was she, not he, who controlled the situation. 'I'm not even close to giving up. You want to know why?'

He suspected he knew already.

'This really is simple,' she said. 'If someone propositions you and you want to shut her up, there's no problem, is there? If you really want to shut her up.'

She paused, inviting comment. He had none to offer.

'You say, "Thanks, but no thanks. Appreciate the offer, but no current interest." And if you say that, nothing else is needed.' She paused again. 'And if you don't say that, the odds are what you do say is bullshit. And you didn't say it.' Her smile was amused, full of ironic, affectionate, female knowledge. Not a schoolgirl's smile, but a woman's. 'You gave me all the bullshit, all that hidden complexity, but not the one thing that was guaranteed to stop me. So I'm not giving up. You can have your thirty-two days, if they're so desperately important, but then it's blitzkrieg, Philip, permanent open season on Nolan. I'm not giving up on the love of my life because he chooses, for now, to be a goon.'

She started to leave, hesitated, then leaned down swiftly and kissed him.

33

'April twenty-fourth,' Peters said. 'He entered at 5:35 PM and left twenty minutes later. It's your man, all right. I have the photos right here in front of me. No mistaking that pretty little face.'

April 24th, Jacobsen thought, would certainly fit. It was the day before Billy had taken his lethal overdose and a couple of days after Nolan had broken into his house. If Billy had mentioned that incident to Thomas – as given their shady business relationship he probably had – it must have made Thomas very nervous. Hence, possibly, Thomas's sudden need for extra-strength heroin and the dash down to Albuquerque to get it. A last freebie fix and no more threat from Billy. After the first time, people said, killing was easy.

'He bought smack?'

'Most likely,' Peters said. 'It's what they were mainly selling. But we weren't after him, you understand. We spread a net for other fish and he just wandered in.'

'A stakeout, you said?'

'Right. Pictures but no bugs. We needed a warrant to raid the house, so we were looking for probable cause – photos of known and suspected dealers going in and out like the place was a supermarket. I saw the photos shortly after you called, but it wasn't until after the raid that I remembered you'd said something about a kid who had OD'd on smack. That was when I started to put two and two together.'

'Because the raid turned up smack?'

'Close to a kilo and fifty per cent pure. Biggest single haul we've made in years. There was other stuff too, of course. A few ounces of coke, and a quantity of high-grade pot. But the smack was the main item.'

'Fifty per cent pure? Were they selling it that way?'

'They would have cut it to twenty per cent or maybe fifteen. They were wholesaling, you see. The guys they sold to would have cut it again, of course. They would have cut the shit out of it before letting it on to the street. When it gets to the user, it's only about two and a half per cent pure. But wholesalers don't tend to cut it much themselves. They'd need trucks to haul it around in if they did.'

'So Thomas would have bought it fifteen per cent or so pure?'

'I would guess . . .' In the pause that followed Peters found time to do some further guessing. 'You seem awful interested in this aspect of things. Don't tell me he was selling it that way?'

'I don't know how he was selling it.' Jacobsen hadn't wanted to get into that. He tried to cover up. 'I don't know that he was selling it at all.'

'But that wouldn't make any sense,' Peters said. 'Cutting's where the profit is. You slap on a normal markup, of course, a hundred, a hundred and fifty per cent, let's say. Then you multiply that times six by cutting. In any case, you have to cut. Put junk of that strength on the street, and sooner or later some poor ignorant bastard is sticking it into a vein. And that's not only bad business, it's murder.'

Exactly right. Jacobsen thought. Cold-blooded murder.

'Jesus! . . .' Somewhat belatedly things clicked for Peters. 'That kid who OD'd. Is that why you were asking?'

'I don't have much proof.' No point stonewalling now. 'I'm sort of playing it close to my chest, if you know what I mean.'

'I know what you mean.' Peters sounded as if he knew all too well. 'But I haven't been much help, in that case. The pictures don't prove anything.'

The pictures *don't prove anything*. The phrase was starting to sound overly familiar. But why else, for Chrissakes, would Thomas drive a hundred miles to see a big heroin dealer if not to buy heroin? It was only common sense. But common sense was not proof. Proof meant eliminating reasonable doubt. And that, when one was dealing with twelve good men and true, was like trying to rid fence posts of termites; there was always someone who believed the earth was flat. And there'd be someone in this case, no doubt, who'd believe Thomas had gone to Albuquerque to buy pot or cocaine (drugs which to Jacobsen's certain knowledge were readily available in Buckskin), or alternatively for twenty minutes of social chitchat. Common sense was not enough, especially in a case where so little was solid. The case needed nailing down. And what that would take, Jacobsen knew, was a witness.

'No chance of us making a deal, is there? With the wholesalers, I mean.' He knew that there was no chance, but he had to try, didn't he? 'You could bust every dealer in the state, by the sound of things, if those guys could ever be persuaded to talk.'

'You can forget that.' Peters tone was almost derisive. 'Talk, and they can start measuring life expectancy in days, and they know it. Besides, they never talk. They've got teams of expensive, Harvard-educated lawyers to do that. When we bust them, it's a phone call to their lawyers, and that's it. Next time they talk is the bail hearing, when they'll tell you their name and address, if you're lucky. They're not going to help me nail dealers or you nail Thomas. You're going to have to get him on your own.' He paused. 'I'm sorry if this hasn't been very much help, but at least now you know you've got the right guy.'

Jacobsen thanked him and hung up. He was after the right guy, but he'd known that before. And what consolation was it? He was no closer to nailing him.

34

'A hose is a hose is a hose,' Lewis Fairchild said. 'Only some of those hoses are shorter than they should be.' He peered at Nolan over his glasses. 'These familiar facts form the basis of our case.'

Robert Anderson frowned. 'For God's sake get to the point, Lewis. Stop trying to be clever.'

'You don't try to be clever.' Lewis transferred his gaze to Robert. 'You either are or you aren't. In your case, I have my dark suspicions.'

Nolan sighed. He had no classes that afternoon and had planned to spend it climbing. A new and intriguing route up the northwest face of Citadel had occurred to him in a US history class that morning and he was eager to try it. But Lewis had grabbed him at lunch and insisted on talking to him. He had new information, he'd said, about the fire. Since police investigations into the arson had stalled – the only suspects to date had had watertight alibis – Nolan had felt obliged to spare the time. Now Lewis was clowning and the afternoon was slipping away. Like many wits, Nolan thought, Lewis needed an editor.

'Summarize Lewis,' he said. 'What about the hose?'

'Well, we know someone cut a chunk out of one and used it to siphon the fire truck with, if you'll forgive the dangling prep.' Lewis, clearly, was not about to be rushed. 'And whoever did that must have done it between 5:30 PM Thursday, when I checked the gas, and 2:30 PM Friday, when the fire was discovered. That, I think you'll agree, is logic.'

'Impeccable,' Nolan said. 'But not new. Get on with it.'

'Most probably he did it when no one else would be hanging around the compound. Between the hours of, say, 11 PM Thursday and about 6:30 AM Friday when the maintenance staff get to work.' Lewis paused. 'Are you with me so far?'

'Hanging in there,' Nolan nodded. 'Sleep beckons, however. I assume this will eventually lead somewhere?'

'Certainly it will.' From the look Lewis gave him, Nolan thought, one could easily conclude that he, not Lewis, had been the one wasting time. 'So if someone, and especially someone whose business wouldn't normally take him there at all, were seen hanging around the compound at about 12:30 on Thursday night' – Lewis continued to build his case, inexorably, brick by brick – 'it would make him a prime suspect, wouldn't you say?'

'It would certainly give him some explaining to do.'

Lewis nodded. 'My sentiments exactly. Only this isn't someone you feel like asking for explanations.'

Nolan stared. 'You mean you saw someone?'

'Not me,' Lewis shook his head. 'If I had you'd have heard about it long before now.' He turned to Robert. 'Tell him, Robert.'

Robert hesitated. 'This is in confidence, right? I mean, last time I tried to be helpful I ended up confined to campus and attending six sessions with the shrink, discussing *my* chemical abuse problems, for Christ's sake.' He smiled faintly. 'Son of a bitch has a nose like a radish. Positively reeked of Jack Daniels.'

'It's in confidence.' Nolan nodded. 'As a matter of interest, however, what were you doing in the compound at that time of night?'

'I wasn't in it; I was going past it . . . on my way to the girls' dorm to catch up on my social life.' He gave Nolan a lop-sided grin. 'It was passing that risky stretch by the side entrance – there's a light there that's on all night – I heard footsteps inside, coming my way. I figured it was probably Sinclair, since he often cuts through there on the way to his office, so I ducked into the storage shed across from the kitchens and waited for him to pass. Only he didn't go towards the Admin Building, he came right by the shed. And it wasn't Sinclair either. It was Christie's dad, Mr Delafield.'

Martin? Nolan's initial shock was followed instantly by let down. It just didn't make any sense. It couldn't have been Martin who'd nobbled the fire truck. He was chairman of the board, son of the school's principal benefactor, father of one of the students. What could he possibly gain from burning down a dorm?

'You're absolutely sure?'

'Positive.' Robert nodded. 'He was right under the light. It was him. No question about it.'

'And the date?'

'The night before open house,' Robert said. 'The night before the fire.'

'Then how about the time? How come you can fix it at exactly 12:30?'

Robert grinned. 'You want to go out at night, you wait for the dorm head to hit the sack. Our guy, unfortunately, stays up late, but he's mostly snoring by midnight. I gave him an extra half hour, to be on the safe side, so it was around 12:30 by the time I set out. When I saw him it must have been 12:35, give or take a couple of minutes.'

'But anyway' – Lewis had now kept quiet for longer than he could bear – 'the point is it was way the hell after 11:00. And what was he doing there, in any case?'

'I don't know.' What Nolan did know was that Lewis would have to be headed off, now, before he created a scandal. 'Just how many people have you told about this?'

'Just you so far. Sinclair asked me to keep quiet about the hose because he didn't want people scared by talk of arson. So

195

I kept quiet. Only I did happen' – here Lewis had the grace to look sheepish – 'to mention it to Robert. In strict confidence, of course. And when I did, he remembered seeing Mr Delafield come out of the compound.'

'And of course it struck me as odd,' Robert said. 'Not to mention awkward, Mr Delafield being on the Board and also Christie's dad. So we thought we'd come to you. We figured you'd know how to handle it.'

'I see,' Nolan was relieved. This idea had been Robert's, of course. Lewis had brains and to spare, but no more tact than a baby rhinoceros. 'Well I can tell you what not to do, and that's take this thing public before we've got the facts. Otherwise feelings are going to be hurt. Christie's, for one. And her dad's. If you'll think about this for a second, you'll realize how highly unlikely it is that a board member and parent sabotaged that truck. There's bound to be some innocent explanation for Martin's presence in the compound that night. I seem to recall, for instance, that he went to dinner with the Sinclairs. Maybe he stayed late and took a short cut through the compound to the parking lot.'

'The parking lot?' Lewis wasn't buying. 'He wouldn't leave his car in the parking lot. He'd park at the Sinclairs', wouldn't he?'

'He might or he might not.' It was Robert who answered. 'We mustn't go leaping to conclusions.' He turned to Nolan. 'This needs to be handled discreetly, correct? So Lewis is disqualified right off the bat, and I'm not even meant to know about the fire truck. That leaves you. You know Mr Delafield, and you can talk to Sinclair. It'd be best for you to look into this, wouldn't it?'

'Yes,' Nolan said. 'It absolutely would.'

'And soon,' Lewis said. 'I see nothing the matter with now.'

'I do.' Nolan shook his head. 'I'm afraid I have other plans.'

'Other plans?' Robert inquired innocently. 'Don't tell me you're planning to grade some papers.'

'No, it's climbing.' Lewis looked utterly disgusted. 'There's a firebug on the rampage, the school is in jeopardy, the reputation of the fire department is in tatters, but all *he* can think of is playing spiderman. Jocks,' he rolled his eyes, 'God preserve us from bloody jocks!'

Nolan grinned. 'If you can't beat them, join them, Lewis.' He turned to Robert. 'Would you care to join me? There's a new route up Citadel I think I've found. It should be interesting.'

'I'd like to, but I'd better not.' Robert made a face. 'Not if you want that research paper on time. Though why you'd want it at all baffles me. It's forty pages already and spreading like a disease. I figure fifty at least before I'm through, and that's without footnotes.'

35

Sinclair put down the telephone and greeted Nolan with an attempt at a smile. He looked careworn, perhaps even defeated. His normal air of well-heeled rectitude, of leading an enterprise which, thanks to his management, was bound to prosper, had given way to an expression that was hunted, almost furtive. He looked, Nolan thought, like someone who expected the bailiffs at any moment.

'That was the Association,' Sinclair said.

'What association?'

'Of Independent Southwest Schools.' Sinclair sounded as if he wished he'd never heard of it. 'They give us accreditation, their seal of approval, so to speak. It's like a teaching certificate, meaningless really, but you can't be in business without it. No accreditation, no school.' He paused. 'They're threatening to withdraw it.'

'Why?'

'Inadequate fire safety precautions, improper supervision of students, pervasive influence on campus of alcohol and drugs . . .' Sinclair quoted bitterly. 'Basically, it's Lisa and the fire. Or rather the combination. One or the other would have been OK. But both? The Association thinks that's too much bad luck.' He threw up his hands and shrugged helplessly. 'It's hard to argue. If I didn't know better, I'd say heaven was out to get us.'

That's too much bad luck. Just because you're paranoid doesn't mean they're not out to get you. Nolan was reminded of his comments to Jacobsen after the fire. The school *had* had too much bad luck. He doubted, however, that heaven was to blame.

'You said they were threatening to withdraw our accreditation? That seems to imply alternatives. Are there any?'

'We could submit to an interim evaluation.' Sinclair nodded gloomily. 'We had our regular five-yearly one only last year and passed with flying colours; now they want to do it all again. I suppose you can't blame them. After all the publicity, all that garbage in the papers, they were almost forced to do something. But an interim evaluation is almost as bad as kicking us out. It's a public expression of doubt about the school.'

'Not if they give us a clean bill of health.'

'A clean bill of health? That's about as likely as their offering to rebuild the dorm.' Sinclair managed something of his normal asperity. 'They won't give us a clean bill of health. They can't. The Association is getting pressure from the State Board of Education and needs to look tough. The team they send will be under orders to find something to bitch about. Besides, by that time the damage will be done. Six kids have already withdrawn for next year; when the news of the evaluation gets out, there'll be a rush for the exits. It won't matter, then, that we've no money to rebuild the dorm; we'll have no one to put in it, anyway.'

Nolan nodded sympathetically. As Martin had foreseen, the insurance carrier, finding evidence of arson, was refusing to pay. The school had threatened to sue, but without much conviction. In all probability it faced a reconstruction cost of $350,000 and a close to zero chance of raising the money.

'Could you borrow from the endowment to rebuild the dorm? You could repay the fund later, when the school is back on its feet.'

'Maybe.' Sinclair looked unenthusiastic. 'There are probably legal obstacles. In any case, it would more or less clean out the fund. We need the income, even in the best of times, to help balance the budget. And the budget will take some balancing, next year, when we don't have the hundred thousand or so we normally make from donations. All in all,' Sinclair smiled bleakly, 'maybe it's as well you're going back to Harvard. There's a good chance, at this point, that the rest of us will be looking for work.'

'Then what about selling some land? There's far more out there than the school will ever use. You could sell fifty acres and never miss it. Rebuild the dorm and pocket a nice piece of change.'

'Can't.' Sinclair shook his head. 'There's some kind of restriction in the original deed of gift. For the first quarter century of the school's existence, we can't sell that land, trade it, or even borrow against it . . . What's really ironic,' Sinclair's smile was wan, 'is there are only two years to go. Had all this happened just two years later, we'd have weathered the storm without much trouble. As it is we're drowning, in sight of land.'

Drowning. Nolan was reminded, uncomfortably, of the assurance he had recently given Lewis. It seemed Fremont really was in jeopardy. Sinclair, at any rate, seemed to think so. Sinclair, in fact, was sounding downright defeatist, and that, perhaps more than economics, was the danger here. If Sinclair gave up, others would follow: more students would withdraw, faculty members would dust off their résumés, board members would find themselves overcomitted. The school would die, not because its wound was mortal, but because it had lost its will to live.

'Things are really that bad?'

'Maybe not.' Sinclair shrugged. 'Depends how many kids we lose, how we handle the evaluation. I'm hoping to persuade the Association to act as if it were our initiative. Perhaps if the school were perceived as actually requesting evaluation, it would be seen as confidence on our part. In any event, it's going to be nip and tuck. And I can tell you one thing: one more disaster, just one more, and that's it, we're dead.'

Disaster. The word reminded Nolan of what he had come for in the first place. 'About the fire . . .' he began.

'Inadequate fire safety precautions, my ass!' Sinclair, clearly, was still smarting about the phone call. 'We reviewed our safety precautions at the last board meeting, only a week before the fire. The Buildings and Grounds Committee made a thorough inspection – the alarms, the equipment, the works. They found everything in order. You can't protect yourself against sabotage and arson. They're beyond your control, like acts of God.'

Arson and sabotage were not acts of God, Nolan thought, they were acts of man. The question was, which man?

199

'I suppose the committee's inspection was thorough?' he ventured.

'Damn right it was.' Sinclair was recovering some of his starch. 'I was on it, for one. Dorrit, too. And Bill Aitchison. And Martin, of course. All businessmen and administrators, in other words, not mushheads like Karen Hopgood.'

Martin. It was a name Nolan hadn't much wanted to hear. In order to sabotage the school's fire safety system, you had to know how it worked. And outside the school's immediate family – staff, students, and faculty – few people did. But Martin knew – his membership on the Buildings and Grounds Committee confirmed the fact – and though this was far from proving anything, it formed, when taken together with certain other facts, a pattern that was rather disturbing. Martin had been the first to realize that the fire truck had been tampered with; it had been he who'd known about the insurance consequences of arson; he also knew how the fire safety system worked and therefore, presumably, how to sabotage it; and he'd been seen emerging, during the period when the sabotage was most likely to have taken place, from the compound where the fire truck was garaged. On the other hand, the suspicion was manifestly absurd, wasn't it? And badly reasoned. If each of the facts in itself had an innocent explanation, it was surely perverse to see, in their conjunction, a suggestion of guilt. Most probably Martin had been first to recognize the sabotage because he'd been thinking better than anyone else. The same went for the insurance. And though he'd been one of the few outsiders to know about the fire safety system, he was by no means the only one. The only remotely troublesome thing, indeed, was his presence in the compound that night. It was time, Nolan thought, to lay that doubt to rest.

'About the fire. You gave a dinner party for some of the parents that night, didn't you? There would have been strangers on campus late at night. Most of them, of course, wouldn't have known about the fire safety system, but I wonder was there anyone who would? Martin, for instance, was here for the open house and he was on your committee, but I think' – Nolan's smile acknowledged the absurdity of even entertaining the thought – 'we can safely eliminate him. I'm asking, I guess, was there anyone in the same position? . . . Bill Aitchison, for instance.'

It was meant to sound artless, but Sinclair wasn't fooled. 'What are you saying?' he demanded. 'That one of my board members burned down a dorm? I can't say I find that very likely.'

'Not one of the board members. Maybe someone at your dinner party. I'm not trying to accuse anyone. I just want to limit the possibilities.'

'I'm happy to hear that.' Sinclair didn't sound happy. 'But this doesn't strike me as a promising line of inquiry. I can't think of anyone offhand who'd be familiar with our system, but that doesn't mean anything. It's not exactly a closely guarded secret. Besides, all my dinner guests were gone by 11:00. I'd imagine anyone who wanted to tamper with the fire truck would do it later, when the rest of the campus was safely asleep.'

'That makes sense. Well,' Nolan shrugged, 'I guess we can strike that idea. If all your guests had left by eleven it makes sense to rule them out as suspects.'

'All of them,' Sinclair said firmly. 'Except Martin. He stayed about half an hour to discuss some business. But as you said yourself, we can rule him out for a number of reasons. Not the least being the absence, in his case, of any conceivable motive.'

So Martin had stayed. But if Sinclair were right about the time, he hadn't stayed late enough. Or had he? Robert had seen him at 12:30. What had he been doing for the previous hour? Would it have taken him all that time to drive off from Sinclair's, park his car somewhere, collect the hose, make his way back to the compound and drain the fire truck? How long did it take to drain a gas tank, anyway? But if not to drain the fire truck, why had he been in the compound?

There had to be some other explanation. It was really absurd to suspect Martin of burning down the dorm. He had no conceivable motive, for one thing, no connection whatsoever with Lisa Bronowski and Billy. And the fire and the murders were connected. Nolan was sure of it. So if Martin had been involved in starting the fire, something should link him to the murders. And nothing did. Nothing whatsoever, except . . . except that one morning around Christmas, Christie thought

201

she'd run into Mark Thomas, who almost certainly did have some connection to the murders. And, if Christie's recollection was accurate, Thomas had been coming out of Martin's house.

36

With a sigh, Christie heaved herself out of the armchair in which for the past fifteen minutes she'd been discontentedly lounging and started to drift around the room. Pausing first by one of the bookcases to study its contents, she mimed attitudes of exaggerated interest: knotting her brows and touching her forefinger to her lower lip, at one point bending almost double and peering under her armpit in order to read titles that were upside down. When she tired of this, she examined herself in the glass of a picture, profiling this way and that and striking extravagant, fashion-model poses. Finally, her wanderings having brought her as if by accident in front of the chair in which Nolan was sitting, she directed her attentions to the photograph of Robert E. Lee that hung over the mantel. For a while she made faces and blew kisses at it, then evidently despairing of her chances of capturing its, or Nolan's, interest by lesser measures, she pulled up her T-shirt and flashed for an instant small but shapely breasts. General Lee seemed unmoved by the vision, but Nolan, who'd been watching her antics from the corner of an eye while trying at the same time to read Robert Anderson's research paper, was not.

'Christie, would you please knock it off.'

This was, he instantly saw, a tactical blunder, the admission that he'd been watching her constituted a licence for further disturbance. She came and stood behind his chair.

'Incredible . . .' she breathed. 'An astonishing new concept. Nolan actually *reading* papers before he grades them. Next he'll start preparing his classes. Who knows where this could end?' She leaned over and blew in his ear.

'Dammit Christie!' He made a point of not looking at her. If he did, he would laugh and the battle would be lost. 'I said you could stay and have coffee, but only if you promised to shut up. Since you can't seem to manage it, you'll have to skedaddle. I've a stack of papers to read here. I need peace and quiet.'

'Why bother to read them? That's what baffles me.' Ignoring his previous statement, she settled into the ottoman at the foot of his chair. 'I mean, we know in advance what we're going to get: Lewis his usual B plus, Betsy and Michael both Cs, Robert an A or an A minus. And Christie . . . for Christie it's B minus, "Good idea; sloppy execution."' She pouted, pushing out her lower lip, then grinned. 'Ain't that she story of my life!'

He didn't reply. There was more than a grain of truth in what she'd said. Students, he'd found, tended to establish a level of performance with their first paper and to maintain it thereafter without much variation. The temptation to skim was almost overwhelming. But he was normally deterred by the remote but ever present possiblity that the odd student might actually learn from his comments.

Robert, however, was different. Nolan *wanted* to read his paper. Robert Anderson was made to be a historian; he had the imagination, the curiosity, the detachment. These gifts, and the willingness to use them, coincided, in Nolan's experience, very rarely. So if Robert chose to write fifty pages of text and another ten of footnotes on the subject of 'The Fremont School: Founding and Early History', then Nolan was going to read and comment on those pages, even if the process took up, as it was presently threatening to do, an afternoon that was perfect for climbing.

'Anyway,' Christie said, 'why the sudden burst of energy? I mean, who do *you* need to impress? You're not planning to come back.' She paused. 'From what I hear, there may be no school to come back to.'

'Where did you hear that?' Suddenly she had his attention.

'Around and about . . .' She thought for a moment then shrugged. 'I can't remember.'

'Martin, perhaps?'

'Martin?' She thought again. 'Maybe . . . I did phone him recently, but I don't recall we talked about the school. No, wait. I lie. We did mention it once. He asked if I'd heard of any students planning not to come back. It seems the board is worried. Could that have given me the idea?'

He shrugged. 'I don't know . . . maybe.'

203

'Anyway, why so concerned? You're going back to Harvard, aren't you? *You* won't be out of a job.'

'I'm going back.' He nodded. 'But you know, Christie, occasionally you overdo the cynicism a bit. I can sometimes manage to care about more than where my next meal is coming from.'

'And now you're caring about Fremont, the deprived young minds that may never get to be formed by it? First conscientious and now sentimental?'

'As a matter of fact, yes.' He caught her gaze and held it. 'I like this place. I think the students are happy here. I think it does a better job of raising them than their parents have. I think they even learn things. And I'd rather see a school in this valley than the housing development that would no doubt replace it. Call it sentimental, if you want, but I'd be sorry to see it fail through bad luck . . . or ill-considered gossip.'

At the hint of reproof in his voice she was serious. '*I* like it too. We all like it. But it's not entirely gossip, Philip. There are half a dozen kids not coming back, and a bunch of others talking about it.'

'All the more reason for you not to.'

'Point taken.' She paused. 'Can we maybe change the subject?'

'To what?'

'I don't know. Something upbeat.' She grinned. 'Us maybe?'

'Unpromising subject.' He kept his voice neutral.

'Depends where you sit.' She grinned again. 'Looks promising to me.'

'Taboo, anyway. Let's not discuss it.'

'Killjoy.' She made a sad face, but her eyes sparkled. It was the energy that got to him, Nolan thought, the way she turned life into a drama, light comedy mostly, in which one found oneself, like it or not, taking part. It invested her like an aura, this sense of her being someone around whom interesting things tended naturally to happen; at times, he thought, you could almost see it. 'What shall we talk about?'

'Nothing,' Nolan said. 'I shall sit here quietly and grade papers. You, on the other hand, will leave me in peace.'

'I'm on my way.' She made no move, however. 'You're going to have to watch it, Philip. This devotion to duty could make you very boring.' She paused. 'Did I tell you I asked Martin about Snakeman?'

'Thomas?'

'The one who owns that restaurant. With all those scary snakes. I don't know what his name is. Remember I was sure I'd met him at the ranch one time? Well I asked Martin and he said he didn't know anyone like that.' She frowned. 'It's been bugging me. I had such a clear recollection, yet Martin was positive. Oh my God!' She whirled on Nolan in mock panic. 'You can't get senile at my age, can you?'

He shook his head. 'But you can get beaten about the head and shoulders for bugging a man who wants to work.'

'Don't worry. I'm leaving. I only came because I had something of vital importance to tell you.'

'Oh? What was that?'

'I love you.' At the door she turned to face him, her eyes sparkling. 'And there are thirty days left to graduation.'

So Thomas hadn't met Martin. Or Christie, to be absolutely precise, hadn't been able to confirm that she'd seen him at Martin's house. So there was no connection, at least no demonstrable one, between Martin and the man who had probably killed Lisa and Billy. If Martin was telling the truth. But why wouldn't Martin tell the truth? He wouldn't, of course, if he happened to be involved in some scam with Thomas. But apart from the still unsolved mystery of his presence in the compound on the night the fire truck had been nobbled, there was no reason to believe that Martin was involved in any such scam. It was all so frustratingly circular, Nolan thought, and in this way so typical of the mystery as a whole: if Christie's memory were accurate and Martin had lied about knowing Thomas, then a sinister construction could be placed on his presence in the compound, but it was his presence in the compound, precisely, that underlay the suspicion that he'd lied.

So logically there was no reason to believe that he'd lied. And Nolan not only didn't want to believe it, he *didn't* believe it. One considered it at all, he thought, only because it was utterly grotesque; the thing was unimaginable, so of course one imagined it. Martin was a successful and wealthy man, he was

205

Fremont's chairman and Christie's father, a friend of Nolan since childhood. He had no motive for arson or murder, and in any case . . . in any case the problem would have to wait – reluctantly Nolan went back to Robert's paper – because 'The Fremont School: Founding and Early History' had a prior claim to his attention. And Theophilus Fremont, with his dream of refounding Plato's Academy in the wide open spaces and free, invigorating air of the American Southwest, was looking around for a suitable piece of land . . .

A suitable piece of land. For a while Nolan read with half a mind because his heart was not in it and the outlines of Robert's story were in any case familiar. Presently, however, his interest was recaptured, partly by the wealth of detail with which Robert had fleshed out his narrative, and partly by the sense of irony that lent spice to Robert's style. Theophilus Fremont had had a dream but no land and not much money. Anthony Delafield, on the other hand, had had an awful lot of land but not much education. And like many self-made men, Anthony Delafield had had a sneaking respect for education in the abstract, but no desire to make the effort to acquire it first hand. So he'd done the obvious; he'd bought it. Or rather he'd bought a share in Theophilus Fremont's dream. He'd deeded 300 acres near Buckskin, a parcel remote from his ranching operations and surplus to his needs, to Fremont's School – a gesture that had cost him, at the prevailing land values, about $3,000, and which had won for him and his heirs a permanent seat on Fremont's board and an enduring place in its history. Not a bad deal, Robert implied, and the gift had not come without strings. There were, for instance, certain restrictions.

Restrictions. The word struck a chord in Nolan's memory. Sinclair had mentioned restrictions. Something about deed restrictions preventing him borrowing on the land. But what were they, precisely? Note eight seemed to promise details. He turned to note eight.

The gift of land gave Delafield an irresistible opportunity to snipe at his political rival and arch-enemy, the then governor of New Mexico, Eugene Showalter. Informed that the school was a not-for-profit corporation whose assets, in the event of its dissolution, would by law revert to the state, Delafield inserted into the deed of gift a provision that, should the school fail before its twenty-fifth anniversary, the land would revert to the Delafield estate. When making this provision, he is said to have remarked that he didn't mind giving to a worthy cause, but if the cause died 'he was damned if he wanted that scrawny old buzzard, Gene Showalter, picking over the carcass.'

Three hundred acres outside Buckskin. Buckskin had been hardly a dot on the map then – a post office, perhaps, and a filling station. A $100 an acre had no doubt seemed high for what then had been just rather poor grazing. But times had changed. So had the demographics. Snowbirds had flown in, chasing the sun. Buckskin had grown and prospered. Anthony Delafield's gift was now worth $6 million. And Anthony Delafield's joke – the thought jolted Nolan like a kick in the stomach – conceivably had offered his son a motive for arson and murder.

37

After that it was digging. Just research, Nolan tried to tell himself, but it was accompanied now by guilt and foreboding. He'd heard it said that in the United States you could find out anything about anyone by making a couple of phone calls. He discovered that this was an exaggeration; in practice you had to make a lot of phone calls. You had to track down your sources: people who might know people who might know. Then, when you'd found the people who actually did know, you had to persuade them to share the information. This was not especially difficult. In practice, he found, your right to know was considered synonymous with your need to know, but the process could be time consuming, taxing to the imagination and, if you cared about truth at all, trying to the soul. He was forced to become, in pursuing his researches: Paul Ewing, of New Bedford, Mass., microchip manufacturer and would-be investor in the entertainment industry; Sinclair Pritchett of the Real Estate Investments and Mortgage Loan Division of the Wells Fargo

Bank; Lawrence Anderson of the International Revenue Service; and Everett Paisley Fairchild III, New York socialite coming west for a change of air and interested in leasing a Turbo Carrera from Hollywood Porsche Audi. And this was just the beginning. The knowledge acquired by these fictions had to be pieced together and analysed for consistency. The whole process, Nolan thought later, was like trying a jigsaw puzzle without most of the pieces. And all to establish a single fact.

But the US, after all, runs on credit. And credit relies on information. Almost every significant financial transaction leaves a mark somewhere, as an entry in a ledger or a number lodged in some computer's memory. It cost Nolan the better part of two days, a mountain of lies, and a phone bill which, he reflected bitterly, should have encouraged the phone company to declare an extraordinary dividend, but by the end he had his fact.

'Broke?' Jacobsen said. 'Did you get his D and B?'

'Hardly.' Nolan wasn't planning to burden Jacobsen with the full account of his labours – nothing, after all, was more boring than learning how hard someone else had worked – but he wasn't about to let this go by. 'I mean, when you're broke is the one time it doesn't pay to advertise. Besides, Dun & Bradstreet are no good for this kind of thing. The movies were all produced in private partnerships. His personal assets were kept separate.'

'Then how did you find out?'

Nolan shrugged. 'I asked around.' Surely, he thought, the understatement of the decade.

'D'you mean flat broke?'

'Getting there. Of course, broke for Martin is not like broke for you and me. For us it means we don't eat tomorrow. For Martin it means he's down to his last two or three hundred thousand.'

'His last two or three hundred thousand.' Jacobsen stared. 'Why can't I be that broke.'

'It's a matter of scale,' Nolan said. 'You have a steady job and a lifestyle it can comfortably support. Martin makes movies. If the movies do well, he's in fat city; if they don't his lifestyle eats him alive. And Martin's recent movies haven't done well. He had a couple of hits in the early seventies, but the money he got from them went into his last two, and they bombed. His lifestyle costs two or three hundred thousand a year, and he has to maintain it or he can't sustain his image. And if he can't sustain his image, he can't raise the cash to produce the hits at this point to get him out of the hole.'

'But he can't raise the cash anyway, because his last two movies bombed.' Jacobsen had no experience of finance, but he knew how the world worked. 'It's that old vicious circle, am I right? In order to succeed, you first have to be successful.'

Nolan nodded. 'The word I got on Martin is he's not considered bankable. And in the industry right now, if you're not considered bankable, you might as well have herpes.'

And for Martin, he thought, that was worse than being broke. The house in Bel Air (three mortgages resting on an equity base so thin you needed bifocals to see it); the Porsches and Mercedes (leased, and, to judge from the conversation with Hollywood Porsche Audi, constantly in arrears); the ranch outside Taos (sold off in discreet parcels until it consisted now of little more than the house and a couple of acres for the horses): these were nothing but the outward and visible signs. Losing them would hurt, not so much for the actual things, but for what their loss implied, a fall from grace. It would mean that Martin was no longer one of those magical people whose mere being commanded attention, whose involvement in a project ensured its success, whose gilded exterior hinted at virtues for which it – the whole shimmering fabric of cars, planes, houses, horses, servants – was only the fitting reward. It would mean he had failed. And for Martin that would be a kind of death.

'And what you're saying' – Jacobsen's voice cut in on these thoughts – 'is in order to save himself he's conspiring to wreck the school.'

Nolan nodded. 'If the school shuts its doors within the next two years, the land reverts to the Delafield estate, which in practice means Martin. And that land, right now, is worth twenty thousand an acre – six million dollars. Enough to get Martin out of the hole, and a motive any jury would understand.'

Jacobsen considered.

'It makes sense of the fire. But how about Lisa? How does she fit in?'

'Not too neatly,' Noland said. 'But I figure the key is the drugs. I see this as a kind of two-pronged attack. Foment a drug scandal – Thomas gets Billy hooked on heroin and Lisa dealing to finance Billy's habit. Then, when the school is reeling from the impact of that, finish it off with the fire. And, actually, that's about how it worked out in practice.'

'Except that Lisa was murdered.'

'Yes. She got out of hand. She became a threat to Thomas's ego and, more to the point perhaps, a danger to the scheme to wreck the school. She told Thomas, you'll remember, that unless he stopped supplying Billy she'd go to the cops about the drugs. I'm guessing that this, coupled with his almost psychotic hatred of her, was what finally prompted him to kill her. I can't believe murder was part of the original plan. It was risky, for one thing, so out of character for Martin . . .'

He broke off, shocked by what he'd heard himself say. Out of character for Martin? Murder was out of character? All this was out of character – wasn't it? – conspiracy and arson as much as the other. What had Martin ever done that his cousin and childhood friend should be so ready to accuse him? Nothing surely. But then why, the moment he'd read that note about the land, had suspicion of Martin sprung to mind? Because he'd already had grounds for suspicion, perhaps, but also because it really was in character. Because character, among other things, meant principles. And Martin's principles, in business, rested on a foundation of Clausewitz and Vince Lombardi . . . 'Business is war conducted by other means' . . . Martin was always saying that . . . 'Winning isn't everything, it's the *only* thing.' To Martin, with his back to the wall, the school would seem like just another business, a competitor in the cut throat battle for resources. Its destruction would be justified, he could hear Martin say it, by another of Martin's favourite maxims . . . 'In war there are always bound to be casualties.'

'This Delafield,' Jacobsen said gently, 'he was a friend of yours?'

Correct use of the past tense, Nolan noted sadly. But his friendship with Martin was really the least of it. The real casualty would be Christie.

210

When he'd realized what this would do to her, he'd almost dropped everything. When Martin was in the pillory, Christie would stand there with him. And along with the shame, which her pride would insist she endure to the fullest, would be the double heartbreak of knowing both that her father was a crook and that Nolan had helped to expose him. But he couldn't just drop it. Two kids had died in Martin's conspiracy, and they were owed something. So was the school. And Olin Jacobsen. And something abstract, but important, called justice. If Martin was guilty, Martin would have to pay. And along with Martin, Christie. And he himself, probably, would have to pay, because Christie, inevitably, wouldn't be able to forgive him.

'Yes, he was a friend.' With an effort Nolan returned to the present. 'Maybe that's why I want to believe he wasn't involved in the killing. Thomas had motives of his own, at any rate, that Martin had no part in. The journal clearly shows that.' He paused. 'I want to believe that Martin didn't know.'

Jacobsen shrugged. 'It's possible. Maybe even likely. Thomas was much more concerned, I would guess, with the threat to him personally than with any threat to their scheme. Lisa had nothing on Martin, probably, but she could bust Thomas for dealing heroin to Billy. Worse yet, she knew he was screwed up sexually, knew what a twisted, ugly, pathetic son of a bitch he really was. She had power over him, and she was planning to use it. For someone like him that could have been too hard to take.'

There was a long silence. Jacobsen looked out of the window. Presently, he picked up a paper knife and began to bounce the tip off the surface of his desk. After three or four taps, he realized what he was doing, and stopped. He felt invaded, suddenly, by the spririt of Sam Plunkett. He could hear all the objections of that eminently practical cop. It made sense, he supposed, it all hung together. But then all kinds of things made sense and hung together. It was so up in the air, that was the trouble. Almost no basis in what you'd care to call fact.

'Well?' Nolan demanded. 'What now?'

Jacobsen pushed back his chair and stood up.

'Now we come to the part I don't like,' he said. 'Now we get to go and talk to the sheriff.'

211

38

Plunkett looked from Jacobsen to Nolan and back again, his eyes resting bleakly on each, his face expressionless but conveying somehow its usual faint suggestion of resignation, a weary acceptance that the world was full of rogues and that he, Sam Plunkett, was fated to meet more than his share of them.

'Well, Sam,' Jacobsen asked. 'What do you think?

'Number one,' Plunkett growled, 'I oughta fire you and arrest Sherlock here,' – he jerked his head at Nolan – 'for housebreaking.'

'Couldn't blame you.' Jacobsen shrugged. He'd given the full, unexpurgated version of events, and so he was prepared for some bitching. This was mild compared to what he'd expected. 'What I mean is what do you think about the case?'

Pause.

'What case?' Plunkett said.

Silence.

'Tell you what.' Plunkett permitted himself a sardonic grin. 'It'd make a hell of a movie. They could get Redford and Newman for you guys and some old sourpuss for me. Be a bit of a problem with the ending, though, when you had it all figured but couldn't prove anything, but I guess you could solve that one by having the bad guys confess. You could lure them out climbing, let's say, dangle them over a big drop and threaten to cut the rope if they didn't talk. And then' – another grin – 'because forced confessions aren't evidence, you'd have to go ahead and cut anyway.'

'In other words,' Nolan said, 'you don't buy it?'

'Hell yes.' Plunkett sounded affronted. 'I buy it. Tell the truth, I think the pair of you did a damn fine job of detection. But I'm not the one you have to sell it to. No prosecutor would buy it. And that's because no jury would buy it. It's too goddamned complicated, for a start, and you just don't have the facts.'

212

'No facts?' Jacobsen stared. 'Seems to me we're knee-deep in them.'

'Maybe . . .' Plunkett looked dubious. 'But just how many of them do you think you can get into court?'

Silence.

'Let's take this step by step,' Plunkett said. 'If I have it right, we've got five, maybe six, separate charges here. Two counts of murder, arson, possession of heroin and dealing, all tied together by this conspiracy against the Fremont School. Far as I can see, though, there's a lot of vaguely supporting evidence, not a single damn one can be proved.'

He paused.

'Take this conspiracy, since it's basic to the whole thing. Thomas, you claim, runs across this deed restriction while working for Delafield's lawyer. He learns of Delafield's financial problems and dreams up this scheme to wreck the school, get the land back and split the profits. Sounds terrific, but what can you actually prove? That Thomas did work for the lawyer and so *might* have known about the deed restriction. That Thomas *may* have visited Delafield at his home in Taos on one occasion. *If* you can get the daughter to testify, that is. That Delafield is in financial trouble.

'That's it!' He looked at them. 'That's all you've got, and it doesn't prove shit. Oh I know you're going to remind me that Thomas was fired by his law firm for improper use of his knowledge of client affairs. But even if you can get the attorney who told you that to testify, which I doubt, what would it do for you? It suggests that Thomas is the kind of guy who, if he'd known about the deed restriction and found out Delafield was broke, might try and involve him in a conspiracy. But you've got to do a lot better than that. You've got to show that he did know about the deed restriction, did find out that Delafield was broke, did conspire.'

'You're forgetting the arson,' Nolan said. 'Delafield's involvement in that, surely, helps support the conspiracy charge.'

Plunkett shrugged. 'What involvement? All you've got is Delafield in the compound at an odd hour of the night. He might have been draining the fire truck, or he might have been taking a leak. We don't know. We don't even know what he'd say on the stand because nobody, so far as I can gather, has actually asked him.'

'We couldn't ask him,' Jacobsen said. 'We didn't want to spook him.'

Plunkett nodded. 'I see that. But what we're talking about is exactly how much you can prove.'

'But do we need to prove it point by point?' Nolan asked. 'I mean, take everything separately. You've got a bunch of circumstances that are just suspicious. Put it all together, it strikes me as fairly conclusive. Billy's murder, for instance. He shoots himself up with extra-strength heroin and dies with the needle in his arm. Suspicious circumstance, but maybe it was an accident. Now his buddy, the snakeman, who's been his connection for several months, is found to have paid a visit, just the day before Billy's death, to a known heroin dealer who's arrested not long after in possession of extra-strength heroin. Suspicious circumstance number two. This snakeman, moreover – suspicious circumstance number three – has a very strong motive for wanting Billy to OD. Now can't we just lay all this out for the jury and let them do the addition?'

Plunkett shook his head. 'For one thing, that whole journal is hearsay. Statements made out of court by someone not available for questioning. You can't use it. You've no evidence that Thomas was even Billy's connection. Besides, even if you could prove that Thomas bought heroin on that trip to Albuquerque, which right now you can't, you'd still have to prove he sold that particular lot to Billy. And if you did that you'd have him for dealing, but not for murder. To prove murder, you have to show that he deliberately misled Billy about the concentration. That would probably mean you'd have to show motive. And that in turn would involve proving the whole Lisa case, since Billy was killed, you claim, to stop him from pointing the finger at Thomas . . .' He shrugged. 'I could go on, but where's the point? This kind of case is like an arch. One stone can support another, but only if the first is solid. What you've got is a pile of stones in midair, none of them even close to touching the ground. You've got suggestion backed up by suggestion, but by itself suggestion is worth zero. And zero plus zero equals zero. In other words, no case.'

'No case?' Jacobsen asked.

'Nothing I see us going to the prosecutor with,' Plunkett said. 'Not until it's a lot stronger.'

'Stronger?' Nolan asked.

'Evidence,' Plunkett said. 'Evidence you could get into court. Get those heroin dealers, maybe, to admit supplying Thomas. Find someone to testify that Thomas sold to Billy. Dig up something solid to show that Thomas and Delafield did actually conspire . . .'

'Something solid?' Jacobsen's tone was bitter. 'Like an eye-witness? Or something in writing, perhaps? A contract to wreck the school, spelled out in words of one syllable, all nicely signed and notarized?'

'That'd help.' Plunkett grinned.

Jacobsen made a face. 'Your first idea was better.'

'My first idea?'

'Dangle them over a precipice and cut the rope. It's a lot more practical.'

'I know.' Plunkett's smile was sympathetic. 'Look. Don't get me wrong. I think you guys did a hell of a job. You've convinced *me*. What I'm saying is don't screw this thing up. Let's be patient, get the evidence, and *then* nail those bastards' feet to the floor. Let's not rush things, is what I'm saying.'

'That makes sense, I suppose,' Nolan said, 'except for one thing. Those guys are out to wreck the school. Two kids have died and a building's gone up in smoke, but the school's still there. And Martin Delafield still needs money desperately, and his partner is a killer and probably sick in the head. So what worries me is this: while we're patiently building a case and not rushing things, what are they going to be doing?'

'A contract,' Nolan said. 'A written agreement. You know, that may not be as goofy as it sounds.'

He and Jacobsen were in Jacobsen's office: Nolan had usurped the desk; Jacobsen was slouched in an armchair, gazing gloomily out of the window. An hour's discussion of how to go about strengthening their case had yielded nothing. Plunkett, ever practical, had gone to lunch.

'Not as goofy as it sounds?' Jacobsen made a face. 'Strikes me

215

it's goofier. Suppose they did have a contract and Delafield welched, what would Thomas do? Sue?'

'But that's my point,' Nolan insisted. 'Thomas needs to protect himself. If their scheme works, everything goes to Martin. Thomas gets paid only if Martin honours the agreement. But why would he? As any thief knows, there is no honour among thieves. Would you want to trust Martin?'

'But why a contract?' Jacobsen objected. 'I can see where Thomas needs leverage with Delafield. But why not blackmail?'

Nolan shook his head. 'That cuts both ways. Thomas spills the beans, he incriminates himself. He's a lawyer, remember, and Martin's a businessman. I think they'd naturally tend to go for something written. An agreement, let's say, that splits the profits but doesn't spell out the exact terms of the deal?'

'Would that be possible?'

'I don't see why not.' Nolan shrugged. 'For services rendered and provided Martin, on or by a certain day, owns or has owned a specified parcel of land, he agrees to pay Thomas x dollars. That sort of thing.'

'If you say so.' Jacobsen still sounded doubtful. 'But even assuming such a document exists, how are we to get our hands on it? It's not the sort of thing they'd leave lying around.'

'I guess you're right. Ah well,' Nolan sighed, 'another brilliant idea goes up in smoke. Martin would certainly keep his copy in a safe-deposit box. And Thomas . . .'

He broke off. Thomas was different. Thomas, according to his former employer, was a meddler in other people's business, a reader of documents he had no right to see. And, as someone who'd made a habit of exploiting others' secrets, he would tend to be paranoid about his own. Judging the world by himself, he would trust nobody, not even a bank. He would hide his secrets someplace only he knew, someplace only he could get at, someplace . . .

Afterwards Nolan would wonder what had made him so sure, what gave him such absolute faith in the intuition that flashed on him then, why it was that, at that precise moment, his head should suddenly be filled with an echo of Thomas's voice. 'These have been used as guards. In Egypt they were used to

216

discourage grave robbers . . . You go to steal the Pharaoh's treasure and instead you run across this guy in the dark. There's this tearing agony attached to your leg and you ain't going home no more . . . It's what I'd call learning the hard way to mind your own business.' But when he heard that echo he instantly was sure. He could see the look on Thomas's face as he'd said that – a secret smile, as if he were savouring some unpleasant private joke – and he knew, in a surge of conviction that excluded doubt completely, that there was a document and where Thomas kept it hidden.

But he didn't tell Jacobsen. He didn't believe Jacobsen would buy it. And even if Jacobsen did, he would probably insist, now that Plunkett was involved, in going by the book. But Nolan couldn't see anyone issuing a warrant to search Thomas's house on the strength of a wild hunch, and he couldn't see Plunkett or Jacobsen asking. Besides, he felt, people who had the wild hunches should be willing to act on them. He didn't want Jacobsen running his risks.

There would, he recognized, be risks.

Part 3

39

What bothered Nolan, or what bothered him most, was the prospect of a storm. Towards evening a bank of slate blue cumulus had piled up threateningly just beyond the rim. Now, as night fell, it was advancing, spilling over and rolling into the valley, its progress signalled, like the approach of battle, by lightning flashes and volleys of thunder.

He needed quiet. He needed a lot more than that – calm nerves, for instance, plus a good deal of luck – but most of all he needed quiet. It was odd, he thought, that the criminal aspect of this enterprise should be the one that most troubled him, more, probably, than the danger. An indication, perhaps, of how much he was conditioned by the culture. Death before dishonour for him, evidently. Or perhaps a better way to put it would be death before disgrace. Dying, at any rate, was at least respectable; going to jail for breaking and entering was not.

He needed quiet. The room with the snakes, he recalled, was at the back of the house. There was only one window, not visible from the driveway. He could therefore work with the light on (it was not an undertaking, indeed, that a sane man would contemplate by flashlight) and if he left the window open, he would have both an escape route and, he hoped, warning of any impending arrival. So long as the storm stayed where it was, everything would be fine. If it burst overhead, on the other hand, it would rob him of his warning.

But the storm was a good half hour to forty minutes away, he reckoned, and by now Thomas would have left for the restaurant. And it was either tonight or wait a week, because tonight was a Wednesday, the bartender's night off, the only night of the week Thomas could be counted on to be out late.

221

Besides, waiting another week wasn't really an option. There was the continued danger to the school; Thomas and Martin might very well try something else. Beyond that, there was the question of nerve.

He was psyched up for it. He had control of his fear. The adrenalin was working for him. Next week he might not be feeling the same. It was like climbing; if a move scared you, you psyched yourself up and did it *then*, before your imagination exaggerated the difficulty and danger. And if you didn't do it then, the odds were you wouldn't do it at all. Or your attempt would be halfhearted, and you would fall.

Imagination. It was always the enemy. It gnawed at your resolve and pilfered your courage, invented disaster, distorted and magnified risks. It took your mind away from what needed to be done and invited you to contemplate fictions, lurid scenarios that could paralyse the will. The ignominy of arrest, in this case, or the snake.

He tried not to think about the snake, but images of it kept haunting him, the glittering malevolent eyes, the spreading hood, the stabbing movements of the head, the hiss. He remembered what Thomas had said about it: 'It's a venom-delivery system, connected to a vicious disposition and a great set of reflexes . . . What's worse it's backed-fanged; it chews the poison in . . . What happens is you slowly suffocate. I imagine it's agony.'

He wasn't going to think about that for another whole week. It would have to be tonight.

There was no moon. The sky was darker now, half-blanketed by clouds. A few stars were still visible, however; enough, he figured, that he wouldn't need the flashlight until he got to the house. He drove past once to reconnoitre; then parked on a side street a block away. He was glad the streets in this neighbourhood were unlit; it meant less danger from curious neighbours. He just hoped no one would pass by before he was into the driveway. At this hour, and in a neighbourhood this isolated, a man on foot was inherently suspicious. The good citizens of Buckskin were not noted for minding their own business.

222

No one drove by. In the driveway the crunch of his footsteps on the gravel sounded to his ears excruciatingly noisy, but it seemed to disturb no one else. Nothing moved. Apart from his footsteps the only sounds were the swish of wind through the branches and in the distance the fitful rumble of thunder.

His first problem was getting in. He made a quick circle of the house, checking to see if Thomas had left anything open. He hadn't. It would have to be from the back, preferably through the French doors next to the kitchen. If the lock was simple, he would pick it; if not, he'd resort to the glass cutter. Ideally, he'd prefer to leave no trace of entry, but secrecy, though desirable, was not essential; speed, on the other hand, was. He didn't think there'd be an alarm system, he'd seen nothing in the house valuable enough to warrant one, but if there was, he counted on seeing it, or hearing it, in time. When the idea for this enterprise had first come to him, it had occurred to him that he could easily end up being arrested by Jacobsen. The irony, entertaining in theory, wasn't something he wished to encounter at first hand.

An inspection of the French doors ruled out any alarm system. The lock in the French doors was a mortise, way beyond his talents, and the doors themselves were unyielding, a fact that suggested they were bolted top and bottom. It would have to be the glass cutter. A kitchen window would be best, he decided.

Now for the first time he used the flashlight, quickly inspecting the window fastenings and scanning the frame inside for wires that might run to an alarm. There were no wires that he could spot, but the window proved, frustratingly, to be the type you opened by winding a handle. It was also secured by a latch on the side of the frame . . . Two holes – inwardly he cursed such thoughtless design – twice as much time and trouble, twice the potential for waking the neighbours.

With the diamond point of the glass cutter he scratched deep grooves in the windowpanes: complete half circles, roughly six inches in diameter, adjacent to the latch and the winding handle. These he crisscrossed with strips of the surgical tape he'd brought for this purpose, pressing down firmly to make sure it stuck to the glass. That done, he wrapped his folded handkerchief around the handle of the glass cutter and, using it as a mallet, tapped tentatively at the edges of the groove he'd made next to the latch. Nothing resulted except what struck him as an excessive amount of noise. He tapped again, harder. There was a sharp crack. The glass broke and gave. But the tape did its job; no pieces fell inside and shattered on the counter. When he peeled away the tape, the fragments stuck to it, leaving a neat hole through which he was able to reach in and undo the latch. A few taps later, the second half circle succumbed. Within seconds the window was open and he was scrambling through it.

As he did so the storm broke. Thunder crashed overhead, followed instantly by a gust of wind and the sudden patter of raindrops. Standing alone in the dark of the kitchen, he was seized by misgivings. What if his hunch was wrong? What if Thomas came back early? What if? Damn this storm, he thought, damn it for reaching here so far ahead of schedule! But there was nothing he could do now. He was committed.

Time to go deal with the snake.

It was there when he switched on the light, reared up at the front of the case, hood spread, hissing. It seemed larger than he recalled, more formidable, charged with a hostility no longer abstract but directed at him in person. When he moved, the hood swivelled, following his movements like a radar receiver; the eyes, bleak and unblinking as polished pebbles, never left him. In some corner of his mind he was conscious that the other snakes were also more active this time – it was the night, perhaps, or the storm had upset them – but he hardly gave them a glance; the cobra commanded his attention.

He didn't want to be fanciful. Imagination was his enemy. Since the reality was frightening enough, he needed above all to be businesslike, to hold on to fact. So doing his best to ignore the snake, he reviewed his plan of attack.

The trash barrel was where he remembered it, in the corner, next to it the snake hook. Step one was to place the barrel beneath the case. It was the thirty-gallon variety, heavy-duty vinyl, about three feet high. The cobra, he figured, was about five feet long; even with the wall of the barrel for support, it shouldn't be able to get more than half its length off the floor, so the trash barrel should safely contain it. Getting it into the barrel shouldn't be much problem – he'd just open the case and yank it in with the hook – but getting it back would be harder. Getting it back, in fact, might be something else altogether. But it had to be done because otherwise Thomas would know at once that someone had been after the Pharaoh's treasure. Nolan wanted a chance to confront Martin first. But what he wanted most of all – fear ambushed him then and almost overwhelmed him – was not to be doing any of this. He didn't *want* to manoeuvre the cobra back into the case. He didn't *want* to let it out. He wanted to have nothing to do with it. Perhaps this was all a waste of time. Perhaps there was no treasure. The thought had occurred to him often in the last few days, but never with so much cogency and force. Perhaps his trust in his hunch was absurdly misplaced, and he was about to risk his life, in this utterly unreal and grotesque manner, for a fantasy, a fiction about the mental workings of a madman.

As if to reinforce these promptings, a crack of thunder, louder than the rest, shook the valley. The light overhead flickered. Outside the rain came down in sheets, drowning all sound except the thunder. So much, he thought bitterly, for his early-warning system. Thomas could surprise him at any moment. An entire armoured division, with this racket going on, could surround the house without his even noticing. Or else . . . Enough! he told himself. Enough of this panicky bullshit. He was in it. Committed. Confident or not, he was going through with it. And no goddamned thunderstorm or snake was going to stop him.

The snake, however, had ideas of its own. When he put the barrel into position, it struck at the glass with such viciousness his resolve was all but shaken. It was as much as he could do to force his hand to undo the latch. When he did, the cobra surged out with a speed and determination that caught him off guard. It was almost out before he had time to react, pouring through the opening and twisting to the side in a sudden bid for freedom. It nearly succeeded, but at the last moment he managed to get the hook around it and jerk it back into the barrel. Moving the barrel, with the snake rearing and hissing with no distance at all, it seemed, between it and the rim of the barrel, was an exercise in pure will power. Reason might tell him it could neither jump nor fly, but imagination, faced with that unrelenting hostility, kept whispering otherwise. When it was done, the barrel safely away from the case, he found he was trembling and soaked with sweat.

Now for the Pharaoh's treasure. It was very hard, even wearing the gardening gloves he'd brought, to reach into the grotto of rocks that was the cobra's home. He kept expecting to grasp another coiled, sinewy body or feel his hand pierced suddenly by fangs. At first he found nothing, but probing the sand on the floor of the grotto, he came upon something parcel-shaped and squashy. A packet, he thought, or a pouch.

He drew it out. A pouch, wrapped in plastic and secured with a rubber band. Inside was a packet and what looked like a legal document. The packet contained a quantity of white powder – no prizes, he thought, for guessing what it was. The document entitled 'Option Agreement' consisted of two pages of text and an attachment. The attachment was a legal descrip-tion of a parcel of land. The signatures on the agreement belonged to Martin Delafield and Mark Thomas.

He'd been right. His relief was mixed with the fierce elation of backing a winning hunch. But there was no time to gloat, not even to read through the Option Agreement. He had to get out of there, and fast. But first he had to attend to the snake.

To psych himself up, he reminded himself of how Thomas had dealt with the rattlesnake. He'd simply hooked it around the middle, lifted it, and whisked it into the case. The trick seemed to be confidence. If you did it smoothly, without hesitation, the snake had no time to slide off the hook or wind itself around the pole. The rattlesnake had been totally passive, hanging limp from the hook and flopping meekly into the case, offering no more resistance than a ribbon of pasta.

But the cobra was another story. Much bigger than the rattlesnake, it was aggressive and angry. It refused to lie still and let itself be picked up. Instead it treated the hook like a mortal enemy, alternately striking and fleeing. At the first and second tries Nolan hooked it too close to the head, and it slid off when he came to lift it. The third time he hooked it too close to the tail. The fourth attempt was closer to success, but also closer to disaster; he had hooked it right and was lifting it clear of the barrel when somehow it wriggled free and landed half over the rim. Only a wild grab with the hook stopped it from slithering on to the floor.

Panting, Nolan paused to regroup. Outside the storm was at its height, rain hurtling down in unrelenting sheets to an almost continuous accompaniment of thunder. He himself was almost as agitated, sweating like a horse and trembling from tension. For Christ's sake calm down, he told himself. It's a snake, not a goddamned dragon. So what if it does get on to the floor? So long as you have the hook it can't get at you. Calm down and give this a couple more shots. If worst comes to worst you can leave it in the barrel.

A couple more shots. So long as you've got the hook it can't get at you. But there was also his unreasoning fear to contend with. It made his flesh crawl, his heart hammer. He had to force himself to slow down, go at it more deliberately, treat the whole operation as an exercise in mechanics. Ignore the head, he told himself; concentrate on hooking it in the middle. Fine. You've got it. Now, lift.

He almost did it. He had it clear of the barrel and half into the case when the neck, catching the edge, got purchase enough to slide the body forward. Gravity did the rest. Before he could stop it, five feet of angry cobra, missing the rim of the barrel, had slipped off the hook and landed in a pile on the floor.

At almost that moment a thunderclap exploded overhead. The lights dimmed, recovered, flickered, and went out.

Power failure. The thought hit him at the same instant as another. The flashlight! The cobra was between it and him! With that recollection, reason abdicated and instinct took over. He flung the hook in the general direction of the snake and blindly bolted.

He never knew how he made it out. Perhaps his body, more prescient than his mind, somehow anticipated and prepared for the disaster. Perhaps he just got lucky. At any rate he did it in what seemed at the time like a single, explosive movement. There was no sense of turning, running, reaching the door, grasping and twisting the handle, wrenching the door open, charging through and slamming it shut behind him. The whole sequence was achieved with one surge of adrenalin, compressed into a single terror-struck perception, no time lapse at all, it seemed, between flinging the hook and finding himself in the doorway, unharmed and savouring the purest relief he had ever felt in his life.

It was then he was blinded by the beam of a powerful flashlight. A voice – Thomas's – said:

'Don't move, I've got a gun. If you move, I'll kill you.'

40

Panic. For an instant his mind, slipping gears, raced but went nowhere. Conflicting instincts held him paralysed. Then, before he could decide whether to run or stay put, the power came back on and the choice was made for him. Thomas was holding a shotgun on him, pointing it at his stomach. But it wasn't just the gun that held him. Thomas wasn't alone. There was someone with him, staring at Nolan in astonishment and dismay.

Martin.

'So . . .' Thomas half turned. The muzzle of his shotgun, however, stayed where it was. 'Your friend, Mr Nolan, the schoolteacher. And breaking into my house. I wonder why?'

His voice was calm, conversational, just stating the terms of a not very interesting problem. He seemed neither alarmed nor surprised by this development. Martin, on the other hand, was shattered. His face had lost its colour, and his eyes, when he could force them to meet Nolan's, were dull and sick-looking. In them Nolan could read guilt, a tacit acknowledgement that Martin knew why he was here, admission that explanations were unnecessary. And besides guilt, there was fear. Martin was scared shitless.

In spite of it, he made an effort. 'Philip! What the hell are you doing?'

Nolan considered. Several answers came to mind but, none of them, apart from the truth, plausible. The truth, however, was what he couldn't tell. The truth would kill him.

He shrugged. 'Why do people normally break into houses?'

Thomas answered this. 'People normally don't.'

Score one to Thomas. Nolan said nothing.

'Burglary?' Thomas raised an eyebrow. 'You're claiming to be a burglar?'

Nolan, conscious of the pressure of Martin's gaze, shrugged again.

'A part-time burglar?' Thomas became derisive. 'That school not paying you enough?'

'Look,' Nolan said. 'This won't get us very far. You might as well call the cops. I don't see that there's much to discuss.'

It wasn't much of a chance, he knew, but he couldn't think of a better one. When Thomas took a look at the snakes, as sooner or later he was bound to, he'd know exactly why Nolan had come. And if the cops weren't on their way by then, they could save themselves the trouble. They'd be too late to do *him* any good. Unless Martin, of course . . .

'He *wants* us to call the cops.' Again Thomas turned to Martin. 'That's odd, don't you think? Most burglars would be on their knees begging us not to. Normal burglars, that is.'

'Look, Philip. Enough of this burglar bullshit.' Martin was recovering his self-possession. But he was still scared, Nolan thought; beneath the brisk, assertive tone was a note of appeal. 'What are you doing here?'

'He was after my silver.' Thomas smiled thinly. 'That incredibly valuable Japanese flatware and the priceless Cézanne reproductions.' He paused. 'And while he was at it, he couldn't resist a peek at my snakes.'

Nolan said nothing. It would have to come down to violence. At some point he'd have to take a shot at jumping Thomas. But the prospects weren't looking too bright. Thomas was watching him like a hawk. The muzzle of the shotgun hadn't wandered. He'd be cut down before he took a step. At this range there'd be a hole in him you could stick a fist through. The thought, lurid with his imagination's technicolor, made real what had up until then been only an abstraction. Thomas was a killer. He'd killed twice already. And Nolan was marked as the next victim. Unless Martin, of course . . .

Unless Martin what? His mind juggled with possibilities. Martin was not a killer. Martin, he was sure, had taken no part in the other murders, and perhaps knew nothing about them. Maybe he could drive a wedge between Martin and Thomas, persuade Martin that the game was up, convince him that his only chance of ducking a murder charge was to detach himself, now, from his partner. Maybe if . . .

'Lie down,' Thomas ordered. 'Facedown on the floor with your hands behind your back.'

Nolan hesitated, measured the space between him and Thomas. If he dived low and to the right, Thomas might miss with the first barrel.

Thomas shook his head. 'Don't even think of it. You'd be dead before you could move. Look,' he added, 'it's very simple. You broke into my house. I surprised you in the dark. You came at me, and in self-defence I shot you. Any cop would buy that. Especially since there'd be a witness, and no you around to contradict.'

'Do you go along with this?' Nolan appealed to Martin. The time for driving wedges was now. 'He's talking about shooting me, and you'll just stand there and let him? Accessory to murder? Is that what you want to be, Martin?'

'Just do as he says.' Martin wouldn't meet his eyes.

Nolan lay down. Martin would take some persuading. But Thomas, it now seemed, wasn't planning to shoot. Or not yet. It was hard to claim self-defence when you'd shot a man in the back.

'Turn out your pockets,' Thomas said. 'One at a time and slowly. The jacket first.'

He'd guessed. Slowly Nolan turned out the right pocket: glass cutter, Swiss Army knife, handkerchief.

'Now the other.'

This pocket held the pouch. When Thomas saw that he was dead. But there were also the surgical tape and the gloves. Perhaps – slowly he extracted the tape – there was no hope, but he hoped anyway. He extracted the gloves, then moved his hand to his left trouser pocket.

'You forgot something.' Thomas sounded bored. 'Maybe you should turn that one inside out.'

Nolan pulled out the pouch.

'Toss it over here.'

Nolan did so, flipping it backwards in the direction of the

voice, and noting that even now Thomas was remembering to keep his distance. His sense of hopelessness grew.

'Tie him up,' Thomas told Martin. 'Use the tape he brought with him. Do the feet first, then the hands behind him. Tape over his clothing. Make it tight enough to hold him for a bit, but not tight enough to cut off the circulation. And remember, stay out of my line of fire.'

Martin obeyed without comment. He seemed content to take orders from Thomas. That was strange, Nolan thought, because normally he liked to give them. There was something puzzling, too, about the orders. Apparently Thomas planned to keep him alive for a while; what was odd was the concern for his comfort.

'Sit him up and come back here.'

Martin did.

Thomas picked up the pouch.

'Presumably you know what this is?' He waved it at Nolan.

Nolan shrugged. 'Smack, I'd imagine.'

Thomas smiled faintly. 'But you didn't go to all this trouble for a couple of grams of smack.' He opened the pouch and removed the folded paper. 'He was after this.'

He showed it to Martin. Dismay crossed Martin's features.

'You know what that means, don't you?'

He cocked his head to one side and looked at Martin. Martin nodded. Thomas smiled. He was enjoying this, Nolan saw, playing the puppet master with both of them, taking pleasure from their distress.

'What puzzles me,' Thomas turned back to Nolan, 'is how you knew about this, and where to look.'

Nolan considered. No point now in feigning ignorance. His chances lay in the other direction: convincing them, and especially Martin, that he *and* Jacobsen knew, so there was nothing to gain by killing him, and everything to lose.

He ignored Thomas, focused instead on Martin.

'That agreement. That's the school's land you're fixing to sell there, isn't it, Martin? The land you hoped to get back when the school, with a little assistance from you guys, folded.' He paused. 'It wasn't hard to figure out. Not once we found out about the deed restriction and took a look at your finances. Once we found out you were broke, Martin, it all fell into place. The death of Lisa, the drug scandal, the newspaper article, the fire. They seemed like unrelated incidents at first, an extraordinary run of bad luck. But then we asked ourselves who stood to profit.' He paused again. 'We've got evidence to link you to the fire, Martin. Evidence to link Thomas to the drugs. And now that agreement links you and him in a deal to dispose of Fremont land. And that ices it, Martin. It binds the whole shabby conspiracy together.'

He kept his eyes on Martin. Martin started to say something, then faltered. He threw a look of appeal at Thomas.

'But how did you know about this?' Thomas waved the agreement at Nolan. 'And how did you know where to look?'

Nolan shrugged. 'Once I knew what you guys were up to it wasn't hard. I couldn't see either of you operating on trust, so there had to be an agreement. As to the where, you told me that yourself.'

'I did?' Thomas stared. 'How?'

'That crap about cobras and the Pharaoh's treasure,' Nolan sneered. 'The way you smirked when you said it. As if you knew something we didn't. Once I knew you had something to hide, it was easy to guess where you'd hide it.'

'Smart,' Thomas said nastily. 'Martin said you were smart. Now, since you're so good at reading my mind, tell me this. What do you see going through it right now? What am I thinking about doing with you?'

He smiled. Or rather his lips smiled. His eyes, however, didn't. They were dead, Nolan saw. Emotionally vacant. Empty of recognition that he, Philip Nolan, was anything more than in the way, a hindrance to be disposed of. What stared at him with that brilliant blue green gaze was solipsism, pure and simple, the clear, empty vision of the psychopath. There is only me, the eyes said. You are fantasy.

'What am I thinking?' Thomas insisted.

Nolan said nothing.

Thomas nodded.

'You've got it,' he said softly. 'I was sure you would. You're too smart for your own good. And you're getting in the way.'

'I'm getting in the way so of course I have to die.' Nolan tried to sound calm. 'That's always your solution, isn't it? First it was Lisa who got in the way. You pushed her off a cliff. Then Billy. For him it was an overdose of heroin. Now it's me . . .' He paused, turned to Martin. 'It was he who killed those two kids. Or didn't you know about that?'

Silence.

Martin had turned to stone. He was staring at Thomas, his face white, lips bloodless. There was shock on his face, but not disbelief, in its place a kind of sick certainty. Hope rekindled in Nolan. Martin hadn't known. He might have suspected the truth, but he hadn't let himself confront it. Now he knew, and it scared him to death.

'It's not panning out the way you expected, is it, Martin? What started out as a smooth piece of fraud turned into something messy. Now you're in line for accessory to murder. Those deaths were planned to look like accidents, but Mr Thomas here isn't as smart as he thinks. We managed to figure it out. And it's not a matter of guessing, either. We've got proof. So now what I want to know is this, Martin. Do you plan to sit by and let this psycho kill me?'

'That's bullshit!' For the first time, Nolan noted, Thomas had raised his voice. For the first time, too, he was arguing, appealing directly to Martin. 'Proof is what he doesn't have. It's what he's here for, don't you see? If they had proof, why did he break in? If they had proof, they'd have come in the front door, with warrants.'

'Of course,' Nolan nodded calmly. 'We don't have proof that'll stand up in court, but we've enough to convince us. If you think Olin Jacobsen will let this slide, or Sam Plunkett, you need your head examined. You can kill me and hide the agreement, but they'll keep after you. And sooner or later they'll nail you. You won't get the land, Martin. What you'll get is a cell on death row. Or you will if you keep on listening to this psycho.'

'Bluff,' Thomas said. 'It's clear what he's up to, isn't it? You're in this, Delafield, just as much as me. If I go down, we both do.'

'Not true,' Nolan said. 'The cops don't think you were in on the killings, Martin. The most they see charging you with is fraud, and maybe not even that. Agree to testify, and you could end up ducking everything. It's your buddy who has nothing to lose. You have plenty.'

'Don't listen to him.' Thomas had put the gun down. Now

233

he picked it up again, holding it casually, pistol fashion, the muzzle midway between Martin and Nolan. 'I can fix this, believe me. He broke in here, and there's all kinds of evidence to prove it. I can rig it so we're both in the clear.'

Silence. Martin's face was a study in warring emotions: hope and guilt, fear and greed. He was stretched, Nolan saw, on the rack of his own weakness. Led into crime by vanity and greed, he was deeper in than he had planned or dreamed of; deeper, probably, than he could tolerate. What he needed was the courage to pull himself out. The question was: did he have it?

'I can rig it,' Thomas repeated. 'You don't need to worry. Nobody even knows you're here. So go home. Drive back to LA and leave this to me. That way you don't run any risk.'

As he spoke, he swung the shotgun closer to Martin, so the muzzle was almost pointing at his midriff. Not quite a deliberate movement, it conveyed, nonetheless, a casual menace. A menace, Nolan saw, not lost on Martin.

For just a moment it seemed there was hope. Martin stood motionless, irresolute, suspended between possibilities. Then he glanced at Nolan, shrugged, and started for the door.

'Martin, wait,' Nolan said.

Martin turned, a message of appeal in his eyes. Help me, it said. Get me out of this mess. Do something. And if you can't help me, then for God's sake don't blame me.

'I want us to be clear about this, Martin.' Nolan kept his voice calm. 'When you walk out of that door, he's going to kill me. You know that, don't you?'

Silence. Martin looked at him like a sleepwalker. His face was still the colour of chalk, but his eyes had gone blank. He's written me off, Nolan thought. I'm not here any more. I'm history.

'You're letting him do it.' Instinct told him it was hopeless, but he kept talking. 'You're responsible, Martin. As surely as if you'd pulled the trigger.'

'What am I supposed to do?' Martin shrugged. He sounded petulant, like someone refusing a beggar. 'You want me to turn myself in? Hope to get off with a light sentence? It would kill me, Philip, prison would kill me. Besides,' he gestured help-lessly at Thomas, 'he's got the gun.'

Thomas nodded. 'You've got that right. And I'd use it, believe

234

me. As your teacher friend says, I'd have nothing to lose. So why not take yourself home and let me, as usual, do the dirty work. And remember, Delafield, if it crosses your chicken-shit mind to turn me in and throw yourself on the mercy of the law, I'll take you down with me. When I'm through confessing, they'll nail you to the wall.'

Martin nodded. 'Don't think I don't know that.'

He turned to Nolan.

'What can I say? I'm sorry, Philip.'

'*Sorry?*' Nolan stared in contempt. 'Spare me your mealy-mouthed regret, Martin. You're a murderer, just like your crazy little buddy. At least he has the guts to pull the trigger.'

Martin stiffened.

'OK,' he said. 'It's your own fault anyway. If you weren't such a smartass, you wouldn't have a problem. So certainly I'll spare you my mealymouthed regret. Fuck you, Philip. Fuck you and good night.'

He opened the front door and stepped into the dark.

Now they were down to it. Nolan found himself fighting off panic. It seemed to him he could feel his death coming – *physically feel it* – as if it were an actual presence, a kind of freezing mist, drawing steadily closer. Yet at the same time, it all seemed unreal; it had the quality of a monstrous illusion, something he could end by exercising willpower, by simply refusing to let it exist.

'This won't work.' He was pleased to find his voice steady. 'No accident you rig will foil Jacobsen. Blow me away and you'll get manslaughter at least. With a very good shot at first-degree murder.'

'But as you say . . .' Thomas was equally calm. He was smiling again, his thin, humourless smile, the eyes as empty as shotgun barrels. 'You have me cold for murder, anyway, so what do I have to lose? And who said anything about blowing you away? That's not what I have in mind at all.'

He started to walk towards the herpetarium.

'Don't go in there.' Without thinking Nolan blurted the warning. 'That snake is loose.'

His voice died in his throat. He knew what Thomas had in mind.

Thomas turned.

'Loose?' he asked softly. 'That saves me some trouble. Your prints are all over the case, I expect. That should help, too. You broke in, you see, and for reasons best known to yourself, started meddling with the snake. But you didn't know what you were doing, and it got loose and bit you. And with the shock and pain, you passed out and never came round. So it wasn't until later that I found you. And by then, of course, it was too late to do anything but call the police.'

'Jacobsen won't buy that,' Nolan sneered. 'He'll know – '

'He'll suspect,' Thomas cut him off. 'He suspects now. But what will he be able to prove? I'll have removed the tape, of course. There won't be a mark on you. Except for the fangs.'

He turned back to the herpetarium and opened the door a crack. Nothing happened. He opened it a little wider. No snake. Slowly he opened it all the way and cautiously peered round it. Still nothing. He closed it again.

'No sign of it,' he announced. 'But it's in there somewhere. Probably behind that stack of cases. It tends to head for cover when it gets loose. So what we'll do is turn down the thermostat a tad. Then, when it gets to feeling chilly, it'll come out looking for warmth . . . and it'll find you.' He paused and eyed Nolan appraisingly. 'Now, maybe you'll be able to lie still at that point, so maybe it won't strike you for a bit. But my guess is you won't. My guess is you'll cringe and try to get away, and that's just what'll provoke it. And then, Mr Smartass Mindreader Nolan, you're going to start screaming for your mother. And that'll scare it, so it'll hit you again.' He paused once more. 'It's not going to be quick, and it'll hurt like a bitch. So scream all you want. There's only me to hear. It won't bother me at all.'

He grabbed Nolan by the shoulders and hauled him like a sack to the herpetarium door. Then he pulled him to his feet and opened the door.

'Just like that, is it?' If this psycho expected him to whine and beg, Nolan resolved, this psycho was going to be disappointed. 'Lisa. Then Billy. Now me. They say it gets easier. Is that true?'

Thomas thought for a moment.

'I wouldn't know.' He shrugged. 'It wasn't hard the first time.'

He shoved Nolan in and slammed the door behind him.

41

Imagination was his enemy. He tried not to think about what was going to happen, but from the moment the door slammed behind him he knew, finally and beyond hope of reprieve, that nightmare had turned into reality. Imagination went to work on him, nudging him always towards an abyss of panic. Dying, now, was the least of his fears. That he had all but accepted. What terrified him, drove him close to the edge of hysteria, was an image of the face his death would be wearing. In his mind's eye he could see the cobra emerge from its hiding place and glide remorselessly towards him. He could see it rear up over him, hood spread and eyes glittering, deciding what part of him to fasten onto. He could feel the fangs in his flesh – the neck, perhaps, or the throat – and the venom invading his system, and it was all he could do to keep himself from screaming.

But he wasn't going to. What helped him, what kept him together, were pride and anger. The pride was a reflex with him, anyway, something his climbing, the years of practice at facing down his fears, had made second nature. You didn't flinch, and you didn't whimper. You did what the moment demanded, however much it might scare you, and if you hurt yourself, tough shit. And if what the moment demanded now was that you die, slowly, painfully and pointlessly, then you accepted that too and did it without flinching and whimpering, because flinching and whimpering weren't going to change things. It would be slow and painful and pointless whether you whimpered or not, but it didn't have to be abject. So there'd be no whining or begging, nothing – and here anger confirmed his pride's resolve – to give that bastard, Thomas, the slightest additional cause for satisfaction. He, Philip Nolan, was going to look that fucking snake in the eye and die without a sound and just hope that when that murderous, sadistic son of a bitch came in to investigate later the snake would do the world a favour and kill him too.

The cobra, however, seemed in no great hurry to kill anyone. When he looked around he could see no sign of it. Lying still and holding his breath, he couldn't detect any sound. The stacks of cases were on either side of him and on both sides of the doorway; behind one of them, presumably, the cobra was hidden, but there was no way of telling which one. All he could do was lie still and wait.

All he could do? It came to him suddenly that it was not quite all. Though his arms and legs were bound, he was not completely helpless. He could sit up, for instance; he could work his way across the floor. And if he could only haul himself to his feet, he could even manage to hop around a bit. Not that this would enable him to escape the cobra, of course, but anything was better than his present passivity.

The problem was that getting to his feet would require him to wedge himself against something, and the idea of pushing against glass cases containing rattlesnakes and puff adders was less than appealing. He'd have to get over to the wall behind him, where the window ledge would offer some purchase.

The window ledge. He'd forgotten the window. It gave him a whole new perspective. It offered a chance, didn't it? It was like the kitchen window, just a single pane of glass and no screen. And though he couldn't hope to open it, he could smash it. He'd cut himself up, of course, diving through it with nothing at all to protect his face. And the dive itself would be something of a trick – he'd have to go at it head first and hope for the best – but anything was better than waiting for the snake. And if he did manage to pull it off without cutting his throat, he could start yelling, couldn't he? The storm had died down a bit now; there was a chance some neighbour might hear him. And at the very least the attempt would foul up Thomas's story. A broken window and a lacerated corpse wouldn't fit very well in the snakebite scenario. Anything was better than waiting for the snake.

Step one was to get to the window. Thanking his stars for the hardwood floor and the sneakers he was wearing, he sat up and started to slide himself backwards, drawing his knees to his chest and then pushing with his legs like an oarsman. He did it slowly and as quietly as he could praying he wouldn't disturb the snake.

He got about halfway. Then, on top of the cases to the left of the door, he detected a movement. Inch by inch the cobra emerged, until all five feet of it were sprawled on the case. Then it spotted him and reared up, hissing angrily.

He froze, not daring to move a muscle or flicker an eyelid, terrified of his own heart thudding in the silence. The snake watched him, swaying restlessly from side to side while its head made little stabbing movements. He knew he wouldn't make it to the window. If he moved it would come down and attack him, and if he didn't move it would come down and attack him. The only uncertainty was when.

He would *not* scream. All that was left to him now was his resolve to deny Thomas that final satisfaction. No scream, and Thomas wouldn't know it was happening, would never see it, would miss the spectacle of his fear and agony.

The spectacle. But that was it, wasn't it? Thomas would be dying to watch. Thomas, who took pleasure in watching snakes kill and eat, would never be able to resist this spectacle. It would be like watching his own private snuff movie; to a psyche as warped and vicious as his, the ultimate turn-on. If he knew the cobra was attacking, he'd be in here like a shot. Now Nolan saw what he must do.

It might not work, it could easily backfire. He might succeed, merely, in hastening what he feared. These thoughts flashed through his mind, but he dismissed them. He had nothing to lose, and time was running out. Soon the chance would be gone for good.

He opened his mouth and screamed at the top of his lungs.

It was not entirely acting. To part of him, his imagination, the screams were real, a heartfelt release of the night's accumulated horror. What started as acting ended up, even to his own ears, sounding very like hysteria.

But whatever it was, it convinced Thomas. Within seconds he'd flung the door open and was standing in the doorway, oblivious to the proximity of the cobra, oblivious to everything except the figure of Nolan, writhing and screaming on the floor.

And the cobra, startled by this new and threatening intrusion, hit him square in the side of the neck.

Then Thomas was screaming, clawing at his neck where the snake was still fastened, flailing at it with his hands, grasping it, finally, to tear it off him. It struck again, twice that Nolan could see, before he broke its back with a sudden jerk of his wrists and flung it to the floor, where it twitched once or twice and was still.

'Bastard!' He turned on Nolan in a kind of incredulous fury, his face contorted with hate and terror, his voice issuing in strangulated sobs. 'Smartass, motherfucking bastard! I'll kill you!'

Clutching his neck, he staggered into the hallway.

Going for the shotgun. Nolan could follow his progress through the house, the sobs and curses punctuated by thuds and crashes when he banged into things or knocked over furniture. The poison would never work fast enough. Thomas would die all right – three jolts of cobra venom in the neck was not something from which you recovered – but he wouldn't die before he returned with the shotgun and gave Nolan both barrels at very close range. In a minute or so it would be all over.

And the truth was Nolan hardly cared. A curious lethargy had invaded his system. So many surges of adrenalin so close together had left him drained and physically exhausted. He hadn't the energy to feel afraid. He just lay back and listened, waiting for Thomas to return.

But the sounds had stopped. Thomas was resting perhaps, gathering his strength for the return. Seconds passed. Then a minute. Nolan waited, new hope gathering in the corners of his mind: venom didn't kill that quickly, but shock might. Another minute went by. Then two more. Then five. And by then he knew it was going to be all right. Thomas was dead. And *he* was not going to be. Not tonight.

Then it was just getting free and cleaning up. Ten minutes of chafing the tape at his wrists against the metal corner of the kitchen counter achieved the first of these objectives; the second took less time. Thomas was on the floor of the den, the shotgun next to him. The pouch containing the option and agreement and the heroin was on the desk. Nolan pocketed the pouch and placed the shotgun in the corner of the room, taking care to leave no fingerprints. He wanted nothing left that might lead the police to look beyond the obvious, and a shotgun lying beside the body would invite second thoughts. So would the kitchen window, of course, but there wasn't much he could do about that. What he could do, and did, was to knock out most of the rest of the glass and put the fragments in the trash, hoping it would look like an ordinary broken window, not a point of unauthorized entry. That done, he gathered up his belongings – gloves, flashlight, glass cutter, and what was left of the tape – turned out the lights and left.

Driving home, he was conscious, on and off, of a nagging suspicion that he had overlooked something important, but he couldn't think what it was. In any case he was too tired to care. He had saved his own life and contrived the death of a man. What he needed now was sleep.

Before he slept, however, he made one long-distance phone call.

42

He slept for thirteen hours and woke from the midst of a dream. He'd been at the altar of some large European cathedral, dressed in a morning coat, striped pants, and a pair of bright red sneakers. He'd been there to marry Abigail Delafield. The prospect of marrying her had been causing him only minor anxiety. What had troubled him much more was the prospect of marrying in sneakers. But release from this social nightmare brought none of the usual sense of returning sanity. On opening his eyes he saw Christie at the foot of the bed. She was crying.

'Christie.' He sat up abruptly. 'What's the matter?'

She didn't answer at once, just stood there, fighting tears.

'Martin . . .' she managed finally. 'He's dead.'

Sobbing, she flung herself on to the bed.

'He killed himself.' Her grief had spent itself and left her drained. She spoke without energy, tonelessly. 'The house-keeper found him in the small study. He'd shot himself . . . in the head.' She broke off, shutting her eyes and shaking her head as if hoping in that way to ward off the pain.

'Try not to picture it,' Nolan said.

He pictured it himself, though. He saw Martin as the house-keeper must have found him, slumped over his desk with half his head blown away. The image left him unmoved. It was messy in the immediate sense, but in the long run, cleaner. He thought of the message he'd left on the answering machine. He was instrumental, he supposed, but felt no guilt. Martin, as he had hoped he might, had taken the line of least resistance. But it had been his choice and his only. And if he'd spared them all the pain of a prosecution, that slow-grinding drama of sin and retribution in which the innocent, inevitably, suffered with the guilty, he'd also – and principally – spared himself. One could hope, of course, that he'd been somewhat moved by remorse, but knowing him, remembering the words with which he'd exited last night, Nolan tended to doubt it. And if putting a pistol to his head and squeezing the trigger had indeed been Martin's final judgement on his life, it was hard, Nolan felt, to disagree.

'But why?' Christie demanded. 'What could have made him do it? Do you know, Philip?'

Philip shook his head. If Martin, as it appeared, had chosen to go out in silence, so much the better. Christie would be spared the truth, and that was important. At this point, indeed, it was all that was important.

'He left no note?' Her question had suggested not, but it was best to make sure. 'Nothing at all in explanation?'

She shook her head. 'Mother thinks it was money, but then of course she would. Not that it matters now. He did it. It's too late to start asking why.'

Much too late, Nolan thought. He said nothing.

'All the same, I keep thinking about it.' She turned to face him. She was crying again now, not in the wrecked, abandoned way she'd cried before, but quietly, the tears overflowing her eyes and streaming down her cheeks. 'Not about why, exactly, but how he must have been feeling . . . so alone. So isolated and helpless.' She paused. 'I know what you thought of him. I

242

know that secretly you thought he was shallow and selfish, but it's worse – don't you see? – it's worse for people like him.'

'Worse?' Nolan recalled how he'd felt last night, when Martin had walked away and left him to die. It'd be hard, he thought, to feel more alone than that.

'Yes, worse,' she insisted. 'Because in spite of everything he was always scared. He had to look like a hotshot because he never really was. Maybe that was the reason he seemed selfish; it was hard for him to risk caring for other people, because he might not get it back, because in his heart he didn't think he deserved it.' She paused. 'That's what haunts me about him now. I knew that, and I never made allowances. I was so goddamn busy enjoying my grievance that I never let myself stop blaming him. I knew he was weak, and I wouldn't forgive him.' She paused again. 'I feel so . . . goddamn guilty.'

Guilty? A helpless anger came over Nolan. The parents screwed up, and the children inherited the guilt. Why was it always the same old pattern? And would they ever manage to change it?

'Look . . . Christie . . .' He let something of this feeling into his voice. 'You have to get this straight. Martin was responsible for what he was. Not you or anybody else. Just Martin.'

She frowned. 'Responsible for what he was? What do you mean by that? What are you saying he was, exactly?'

'I mean he chose his own life and he chose his own death.' It was best, he thought, to back off a little. Badmouthing Martin wouln't help her feel better. 'It's right to grieve, is what I'm saying, but not right at all to feel guilty.'

She shook her head. 'I didn't love him enough. He needed me, and I wasn't there.'

He put his arms around her. It was hard to agree with her way of looking at things – Martin's weakness, he felt, had been very much his own fault – but her charity struck him as amazing.

'It wasn't like that,' he said. 'You gave him love. You always did. He just wasn't willing to receive it.'

She turned to face him.

'What about you? Are you willing to receive it?'

'Me?' The unexpectedness caught him flatfooted.

'Yes . . .' Her eyes searched his face. 'I'm saying I love you.

243

I'm *always* saying I love you. I'm asking are you willing to receive it?'

'Of course I am. I love you too.' But it was too pat, he saw, too obviously meant to reassure. What had registered were the reservations.

'I mean really love. I mean going to bed with me and getting married and having babies kind of love. I can't take any more of that I'm-your-uncle-and-I-knew-you-as-a-baby routine. Not now. I guess what I see now is you can't afford to wait; unless you act on what you feel, when you feel it, you may lose it. So I'm asking you, are you willing to be loved?'

He almost was. In a way it would be easy. Easy to forget scruples and accept what she offered. To hell with scruples, he told himself. To hell with age. To hell, especially, with Martin. She loved him; that was the main thing, the important thing. And he loved her. And not with any parental kind of love, but the way she wanted. It would be so easy, he thought, and so wrong. She loved him now, perhaps, but how would she feel if she knew that he had helped to destroy her father? Would she love him then? Wasn't it more likely that she'd hate him? . . . He didn't know. Maybe she could manage to understand and forgive, but he couldn't be sure. And he couldn't ever ask her. For her present image of Martin – the tragic, lonely figure who for the relief of some private torment had chosen to take his own life – was an image she'd in time be able to accept. The truth, on the other hand, might blight her life.

'Are you telling me no?'

He continued to hesitate. It seemed such a small thing, such a moral technicality, that held him back. Was total honesty, after all, so vital? If I could just explain, he thought, if I could only tell her what happened and let her make the choice. But here he encountered the last, most bitter consequence of Martin: to shield her from one hurt he had to offer her another. He couldn't accept what she offered; he couldn't even explain why.

'I'm sorry,' he heard himself saying. 'I just can't.'

'I don't believe that.' Her eyes implored him to deny it. 'Last time, when I told you I wanted to make love, you wanted it too. It was in your eyes, in the way you were holding me. Don't tell me you didn't want it.'

He said nothing.

244

'You *can* accept it,' she said. 'You just won't. It's the same bullshit, still, about being too old. And it's unbelievably stupid . . . Look Philip, I need you. I need you now. I can't deal with this other stuff any more. Will you have me, or not?'

'I can't.'

'I see.' There was anger in her eyes. Tears too, but she struggled to check them. 'Then I guess you were right. You are too old. Too old and too scared.'

She stood up and started for the door.

'Look . . .' he said. 'We can be friends, can't we? Because I can't love you the way you want doesn't mean I don't love you.'

'Friends?' She didn't look round. 'Grandfather love? Who needs it?'

43

'So,' Plunkett said. 'Thomas gets nailed by his own snake and Delafield blows his brains out. Amazing, isn't it? Enough to make you believe in the workings of providence.' He gave Nolan a long, speculative stare.

Nolan shrugged. 'I guess you could see it that way.'

Plunkett waited, his look one of patience wearing a little thin. Jacobsen too, Nolan saw, was wearing an inquisitor's stare. The silence lengthened, grew heavy, hung over them, finally, like a pall. Nolan said nothing. He was here, in Plunkett's office, at Plunkett's wish; it was up to Plunkett to state his business. Stop by, he'd said, when you have a moment. In spite of the polite phrasing this had not been a request. Plunkett didn't believe in the workings of providence. He was looking for explanations.

He was entitled to explanations. But he was not, Nolan had resolved, going to get them. Plunkett was a servant of the law. So was Olin Jacobsen. And though justice, perhaps, had been served by what fate, and Philip Nolan, had ordained for Thomas and Martin Delafield, the law had certainly been flouted. Plunkett and Jacobsen wouldn't be happy about that. They might even feel impelled to do something. And that could involve public explanations, disclosure of the plot against the school and Martin's part in it. For Christie's sake this mustn't happen.

Nolan tried not to think about Christie. Remembering was like opening a wound. His parting from her, it was now clear, had been final. She'd left school early the next day to attend Martin's funeral, and she was not, he'd learned, coming back. He wouldn't see her again. By protecting her, he'd lost her, and he was only now realizing the extent of that loss. But this only made it the more vital the effort to shield her should succeed.

Plunkett picked up a penknife and started bouncing the blade on the top of his desk. A glance from Jacobsen made him stop. Nolan examined the sporting trophies on the wall. Ordeal by silence was a technique he employed on his students; he could sit here all day if necessary.

'Some funny things about that Thomas death, however.' Plunkett, finally, broke the silence.

'Funny?' Nolan said. 'How?'

'The kitchen window was broken, for one thing. From the outside, it looked like. At least, there was no glass on that side, but a bunch of it inside, in the trash.'

Nolan thought about the glass. He was sure he'd remembered to remove the strips of surgical tape from the fragments he'd dumped in the trash, but no doubt if someone examined them carefully, traces of adhesive would be found. He wondered if anyone had examined them carefully.

'What do you make of that?' he asked.

Plunkett shrugged. 'By itself, not much. It could have been broken earlier. Maybe Thomas broke it himself and hadn't got around to getting it fixed. It's just a small oddity, something that bothers me a little.' He paused. 'One thing among several.'

'Several?' It was reasonable, Nolan thought, to display some curiosity. 'There were others?'

Plunkett exchanged glances with Jacobsen.

'One or two,' he said, dryly.

'Such as?'

'How come he got it in the neck?' It was Jacobsen who answered. 'The way things were in that reptile house of his, we figure he was transferring the snake from its case to a trash barrel, or vice versa. Now it's possible, if he got careless, that he might have got zapped in the arm or the leg. But in the

246

neck?' Jacobsen shook his head. 'That doesn't make much sense.'

It would if you'd ever dealt with the particular snake yourself, Nolan thought. He said nothing.

'And why didn't he call for help?' Plunkett said. 'I mean, granted he'd taken three hefty jolts in the neck, but why would he just give up? Even cobra venom doesn't normally kill in minutes, and he couldn't have *known* he'd be having a heart attack. The phone was in the hall, for Christ's sake, right next door. But instead of calling a doctor, he goes wandering off to the other end of the house . . . Now why do you figure he'd do a thing like that?'

Nolan shrugged. 'Beats me. Maybe he was in shock.'

'Maybe,' Plunkett said. 'But then what was he doing loading his shotgun?'

'Loading his shotgun?' Nolan felt impelled to say something. Too little curiosity could be worse than too much.

'Another oddity.' Jacobsen took over again. 'The shotgun was in the room where we found him. Propped up in the corner. Loaded. And there was a box of shells, open, on the desk. Which suggested he loaded the gun not long before he died.'

'But not necessarily after the snake bit him,' Nolan said. 'He could just as easily have done it before.'

Jacobsen smiled. 'I knew we could rely on you for logic. But either way it poses an interesting question, don't you think? Why in God's name was he loading it at all? I mean, put the gun together with the window and it makes you wonder a bit, doesn't it? Especially . . .' he paused, 'in view of the lights.'

The lights? But he'd remembered to turn out the lights, hadn't he? He'd missed the box of shells, which was careless enough, but at least he'd not forgotten to turn out the lights. Nolan froze. The implications hit him with the force of revelation. You fool! he thought. You prize-winning dolt!

'See, that was what really bothered us,' Jacobsen continued. 'The rest of it – the window, the shotgun and so on – you could account for, at a pinch. But those lights baffled us. Because according to the pathologist, he died that night, between midnight and 3:00. When it was pitch dark, in other words. Yet when we found him, every light in the place was off.'

He looked at Nolan. Nolan said nothing.

247

'Think about it,' Jacobsen said. 'He gets bitten by a snake. Three times. In the neck. Then instead of calling a doctor, or poison control – instead of trying to save himself somehow – he goes around the house making sure the lights are off. He wants to die without wasting electricity. I mean, the man couldn't have been all bad, could he? He was evidently one very dedicated conservationist.'

Silence.

'Alternatively,' Jacobsen gave another faint smile, 'you have to ask if there might not have been someone else in the house that night. Giving providence a helping hand, so to speak. And that, of course, brings us to you.'

'Me?' The effort at incredulity, even to Nolan's ears, sounded less than convincing. But he'd exhausted, he felt, the defensive resources of silence.

'Yes, you.' Plunkett joined the attack. 'Because, apart from the mystery surrounding Thomas's death, there's also some mystery about Delafield's. The timing, for one thing. Why choose that particular morning to shoot himself, just hours after his partner kicked?'

Nolan shrugged. '*I'm* supposed to know about that?'

Plunkett gave him a long stare, eyes sceptical and chilly.

'It's like this,' he said. 'The only reason we can think of for Delafield shooting himself is he realized his scam was folding up. But he couldn't have known unless someone told him. And if someone told him, it had to be Thomas or you. Now I guess if you can believe that Thomas took the time to turn out the lights before he died, you can also believe he took an extra couple of minutes to put a long-distance call through to Delafield in LA. But for myself . . .' he shook his head, 'I don't seem to be able to manage it. I think the one who made that long-distance call was you.'

Dead silence.

Plunkett picked up a scrap of paper from his desk and waved it at Nolan. It contained some lines of typescript. 'This is the message you left on his answering machine. Just hours before he shot himself.'

He looked at Nolan. Nolan felt he should probably ask to see it. Or deny that he'd left it. Or at least act bewildered. He couldn't seem to summon the energy, however. Besides, as it

248

was fast becoming clear, there wasn't much to be gained by acting. He said nothing.

'I guess you thought the local cops wouldn't be able to trace it,' Plunkett said. 'And that we, here, wouldn't hear about it. But we read about Delafield's death in the papers. And it piqued our curiosity, you could say, coming so soon after Thomas's. So I got on the phone to Beverly Hills. Apparently they were short on ideas about motive – there was no note or anything – but one or two things did strike them as odd. He'd gone out of town the day before he died – he left before noon and returned after midnight – on a trip that put more than a thousand miles on his car. They knew that because his car had been serviced just the day before and his secretary kept records of the mileage. The other odd thing was this phone message someone had left him. An anonymous message.'

'Anonymous?' Nolan raised an eyebrow. 'Just now you said it was from me.'

'Well, anonymous in this sense,' Plunkett amended. 'The caller didn't leave his name, but from the content it's clear Delafield would have known who it was . . . Educated voice, apparently. And the message was left after 11:00 PM. We know that because it wasn't on the machine when Delafield's secretary called in at 11:00 to pick up his messages.'

Nolan smiled faintly. 'This secretary sounds like a treasure.'

'A real treasure.' Plunkett nodded. 'Anyway, all the other stuff was routine. Just business and social calls. Nothing you could connect with Delafield's sudden decision to shoot himself. But this anonymous message was different. Mysterious, for one thing, and a little vindictive. Would you like to hear it?'

'Sure.' Nolan shrugged.

'"This is your friend whom you left in the lurch,"' Plunkett read. '"But I made it, Martin, so you won't. I suggest you consider your options. Fuck you, Martin. Fuck you and good night."' He paused and considered Nolan for a moment. 'Now what does all that mean, exactly. The bit about considering options, for instance?'

'I'm supposed to know?' Martin had known, Nolan thought; that was the main thing.

'I think so,' Plunkett nodded. 'I mean, it all sounds like you. The phrasing. Even the grammar. I mean, let's face it, how many people, outside of college professors, would use "whom" correctly in a message like that?'

'Millions, one would hope.' Nolan gave a tired smile. 'As evidence, I must say, I don't find that up to your usual exacting standards. It may sound like me, but there's probably a million other people it sounds like.' He paused. 'It's not easy to be sure about voices on the phone.'

'You can do it with voice prints,' Plunkett said. 'But I doubt if we'll have to bother. My guess is we'll just have to look under "itemized calls" in your next phone bill. It was early hours, I imagine. I don't suppose you took the trouble to use a call box. Am I right?'

No response.

'You'd rather not say? I can understand that. But we've got you surrounded, my friend. If we want to, we can deliver you to the guys in Beverly Hills. You can do your talking, under oath, at the coroner's inquiry. But what I ask myself is this: do we really want to?'

There was a long silence. Finally Nolan said: 'Perhaps it would be better if you didn't.'

'Really?' Plunkett's blue eyes inspected him carefully. 'Better for you, or better for us?'

'Let's put it this way,' Nolan said. '*I* don't want innocent people to be hurt. And *you* don't want to compound a felony.'

For a while Plunkett didn't answer. His gaze wandered off into the middle distance. His brow furrowed a little.

'He wants us to trust him.' When he spoke it was to Jacobsen. 'He takes the law in his own hands, tries to make monkeys of us in the process, and now he wants us to trust him. I'll tell you this.' He gave a baleful stare at Nolan. 'He may not have the brains for a life of crime, but he sure does have the balls . . .'

Another silence. Nolan looked over at Jacobsen, who was looking out of the window.

'Thing is,' Plunkett pursued, 'I don't even know him very well. But you do, Olin. Or at least you damn well should. I figure you should decide. Shall we do what the man wants? Shall we trust him? Or shall we nail the son of a bitch?'

For a while Jacobsen didn't answer. He continued to look through the window at the town sprawled out below, his gaze travelling out, beyond it, past the outskirts where subdivisions and half-finished houses, billboards and realtors' shingles covered the landscape like a spreading blight, until his eye came to rest on the silent desert and the tall buttes surrounding the school. And his mind's eye travelled farther, to the cottage by the creek where Billy had struggled in his self-constructed prison, and the ledge where Lisa, for a moment, had dreamed of setting him free.

First Lisa's dead. Then Billy. Now Thomas and Martin Delafield. In a screwed up world, it was as close to justice as you could reasonably hope to come.

He looked at Plunkett then, with a crooked smile, at Nolan.

'I think we should buy the son of a bitch a beer.'

Epilogue

The speeches were over, the diplomas had been distributed, the choir had sung *Gaudeamus*. All over the quad, amid ragged lines of chairs and a litter of discarded programmes, scenes of parting were being enacted. Students and new graduates, attended by clusters of awkwardly hovering siblings, exchanged promises to keep in touch, fervent and tearful embraces. Fathers beamed and pointed cameras, mothers smiled bravely through tear-stained makeup. Here and there teachers, easy to spot in their ill-fitting suits, looked on with a mixture of relief and sadness. Another year was safely behind them.

Somewhat aloof from these proceedings, Nolan stood in the shade of a tree and waited for someone to bring him a drink. For the umpteenth time he wondered what he was doing back here, four years after he had left, and what on earth had possessed him, in the words of Sinclair's invitation, 'to assist in launching upon an unsuspecting world Fremont's twenty-seventh batch of only partly civilized seniors.' He'd always hated commencements. Even at Harvard, where the sense of booting fledglings from the nest was not so powerfully present, they struck him as being, in the main, pretexts for the utterance of some rather tired platitudes and occasions for the indulgence of some very bogus emotions. Worse, they made him feel old. As he looked over the throng of confident young faces, all about to embark on what one or other of the speakers unfailingly described as 'the next stage in life's journey', he had a sense of being left behind, of confronting a future that was slightly depleted of promise.

Sinclair came by with a glass of punch, predictably nonalcoholic, and promising to be back at once, was whisked away by a parent. Someone stopped to congratulate Nolan on his speech. A former colleague, on his way to the lunch line, waved. Nolan's melancholy deepened. He shouldn't have come. There was nobody he wanted to see here, nobody who wanted to see him. To the crowd he was just the commencement speaker, invited because he was vaguely connected with Fremont, and notable for some reason that one couldn't at the moment call to mind. He was well on his way towards full-scale depression when someone behind him called his name.

'Philip.'

It was Christie.

Though he'd thought of her more often than he'd have been willing to admit he hadn't set eyes on her for more than four years – not since the afternoon when she'd told him of Martin's death. At first he'd tried to contact her, but when she hadn't responded he'd given up. He'd concluded she was lost to him and had tried to make himself stop caring. Seeing her now he felt an awkwardness mingled with a rush of excitement. He was able to put a name to the regret that had most been oppressing him, and it was clear that a feeling he'd thought of as lost had been only in hiding.

'You haven't changed much.'

She had though. Not in externals – she was dressed as unconventionally as ever – but in ways more subtle and inward. It was is if she had found her balance. She still radiated energy and intelligence, but the energy seemed more contained, the intelligence more focused.

'You can knock off the careful scrutiny right now.' She was still the same Christie, however. 'A word of greeting might not come amiss. Or did the speech exhaust your powers of utterance? I thought it was good, by the way.'

He made a face. 'It had the virtue of not lasting very long.'

He paused. 'It's good to see you . . . after all this time.'

252

'Is it?' she studied him. 'I hoped it might be. Our parting was sticky, you'll recall.'

He shrugged. 'That was four years ago.'

'I know. But when I think about it, it seems like yesterday.' She paused. 'Have you thought about it ever?'

He nodded. 'But let's not talk about it. No point digging up the past.'

She looked at him quizzically. 'An odd statement for a historian.'

'I wasn't speaking as a historian.' He smiled. 'Historians study the Past with a capital P . . . with a small p, as in "personal", I think it's better let go.'

She considered this, her eyes resting on him gravely.

'I think so too. But to let it go I need to understand it.'

'Understand it?'

She looked at him for a while without speaking. It was a calm look, direct and candid. She wouldn't, she implied, waste words on evasions.

'I'm not here for the school,' she said. 'I'm here to see you. I heard you were giving the commencement address, and I came back to talk . . . about what happened.'

He started to interrupt, but she overrode him.

'I know something did. Something you never told me about. When Martin shot himself, things changed between us. Before that you were' – she hesitated, searching for words – 'open, at any rate, to the possibility of us. Afterwards you closed up completely. It was as if Martin had somehow prevented it. I didn't see that at the time, but I've thought about it since, and I can't come up with another explanation. Don't pretend there's nothing to understand. Don't lie to me, Philip. Don't treat me like a baby.'

What should he tell her? She was twenty-two. Was that old enough now to know the truth about her father? And was age even relevant? The question, surely, was what purpose would be served by her knowing?

'I know what you're thinking.' She continued to fix him with the same steady look. 'You want to shield me from something. But that's patronizing – don't you see? – because I don't want to be shielded. I don't need to be. Don't patronize me, Philip, you don't have the right.'

He considered this. Perhaps she had a point. Maybe he was patronizing. In his concern to protect her, maybe he was denying her right to grow up, to know who she was, to measure her strengths and capacities. In effect he was denying her right to be equal. In a sense, without consciously meaning to, perhaps he'd never had to risk his position with her, put it to the test of intimacy on an equal footing. And it was this, possibly – more than age, or position, or even what had happened to Martin – that had stood between them four years ago. And of course she was his equal. Facing her now, it was impossible to doubt it. Somewhere in the four years she'd become a woman, indeed a rather formidable one. At the very least, she was his equal.

Slowly he nodded.

'But not here,' he said. 'Not now . . . later.'

She shook her head. 'Cards on the table. I want you to take me to lunch. I want you to tell me about Martin, and why things changed between us. I want the whole story, nothing left out, nothing glossed over.'

'You won't like it,' he warned. 'You may not like me.'

She met this too. 'I'll take the risk. I haven't liked you in more than four years. That's far too long. As for the story,' she shrugged, 'I know I won't like it. I've known that a while now. All kinds of people have been shielding me. From things I wasn't meant to know about but sensed anyway, the way you do when everyone around you's on tiptoe. Grandmother Delafield holding meetings with Martin's lawyers, then selling chunks of stock. My trust fund mysteriously empty, then just as mysteriously not. It's been clear for some time that Martin was involved in something . . . discreditable.' She paused. 'I guess what I'm saying is this. Let's get this out of our way. Whatever you have to tell me, I can handle it, I think.'

Hearing her, he thought so too. He noticed that his depression had left him. It was not that the future offered guarantees – whose future ever did? – but it seemed, after all, to hold some promise.

He offered her his arm. 'Then let's go have some lunch.'